A Shed in a Cucumber Field

S. L. Russell

D1440203

Bright Pen

A Bright Pen Book

Text Copyright © S. L. Russell 2014

Cover design by © Naomi Russell

Scriptures and additional materials quoted are from the Good News Bible © 1994 published by the Bible Societies/Harper Collins Publishers Ltd UK, Good News Bible © American Bible Society 1996, 1971, 1976, 1992. Used with permission. www.biblesociety.org.uk

British Library Cataloguing Publication Data.
A catalogue record for this book is available from the British Library

ISBN 978-0-7552-1672-7

Authors OnLine Ltd
19 The Cinques
Gamlingay, Sandy
Bedfordshire SG19 3NU
England

This book is also available in e-book format, details of which are available at www.authorsonline.co.uk

AMDG

*With special thanks to Claire, who can always
see the wood for the trees*

'Jerusalem alone is left, a city under siege – as defenceless as a guard hut in a vineyard or a shed in a cucumber field.'
Isaiah 1 v.8

Vic

She knew something was different as soon as she opened her eyes. Even through the heavy winter curtains light leaked, a light that was nothing like the November dullness of every day for the past week. Groaning softly she threw back the covers and set her feet on the carpet. She leaned out and twitched the curtain aside.

The merciless brightness struck her eyes and she blinked. *What? It can't be.* She pulled herself up and opened the curtain wide. Her front garden was transformed, smoothed out, the small shrubs now rounded hummocks beneath a feathery six inches of snow. Beyond the gate lay the lane, in reality little more than a farm track, still virgin but for the spiky claw marks of foraging birds; then fields whose whiteness was punctured by stark black twigs and stumps, and in the hazy distance the huddled hills. Behind a thin layer of cloud the sun was struggling to emerge, casting an almost eerie light.

She stood and looked at it for a few moments, allowing rein to an upsurge of childish delight before realism frowned its way into her consciousness, and she saw beauty as a problem.

Then the phone rang at the bottom of the stairs. She dragged her dressing gown from its hook and padded barefoot down.

'It's Don. Have you seen the weather?'

'Just.'

'You'll never get your car out in this. I'll pick you up in mine.'

'Oh. All right, thanks. If it's not making your day difficult.'

She heard him clear his throat. 'You'll have to wait till I finish work, that's the only thing.'

'I've got plenty of marking to do. And there's nothing much to rush home for. Solomon can fend for himself.'

'See you about eight-fifteen, then. I'll honk my horn from the road. Better wear boots.'

She smiled. 'Thanks, Don.'

* * * *

She climbed up into the silver Landrover Discovery with an effort. 'Sorry – I seem to be getting snow all over the place.' The snow from her boots was melting into puddles on the immaculate rubber mats.

Don grunted as he shifted into first and pulled slowly out. 'It's only water.' He glanced over towards her. 'You all right?'

'Yes, thank you. This snow's a bit of a shock, though.'

'It wouldn't be if you ever watched the weather forecast.'

'I can't,' she reminded him. 'I don't have a TV.'

'Well, listened, then,' he said, turning away from her to look over his shoulder as they swung up onto the slip road. 'You listen to the radio, don't you?'

'Music. I ignore people talking. Or go and make a sandwich or coffee. The news is always bad, anyway.'

'That's true. But if you'd been listening to the news, you'd have heard there was a band of cold weather sweeping down from Greenland or somewhere.' He looked at her and a smile twitched his lips as he saw her shudder. 'It's only us getting it, not the coast. Cornwall is worse. There are people stranded there, up on the moors. I don't suppose it'll stay here for long.'

'Havoc on the roads, then, I suppose,' she said. 'We're always unprepared.'

'School half empty, d'you reckon?'

'I doubt it. Our privileged pupils have parents with cars for every situation. Including some like this one.'

Don's eyes crinkled but he said nothing.

They joined a flow of traffic moving slowly along the bypass. Almost without thinking she looked out, over the railing and down into the valley, indistinct now in the grey air, her eyes searching for the familiar roof. The shroud of snow made the old house look almost picturesque, hiding its decay. Then the sky darkened and the snow started to fall again, the rising wind driving it into whirling flurries, and with a conscious effort she looked away.

She spoke little for the rest of the twenty-minute journey. The gusting snow made visibility poor, and Don was concentrating. Later than usual, he turned the car into a tree-lined lane and the red-brick wall of the school appeared.

'Don, just drop me at the gates. I can manage the drive. Please, you

2

don't need to get me to the door. It's not far, and the wind's dropped.'

He frowned. 'Are you sure?'

'Of course. You get to work. And thanks for the lift. You were right: my little car would be stuck in a drift by now.' She turned to him and smiled, seeing the anxious puckering of his brows, the uncertainty in his pale blue eyes.

'I'll be back at six,' he said. 'Earlier maybe, if the weather sets in. I suppose I can ring the school office if I have to? It's a shame you're such a dinosaur. If you had a mobile phone it'd be so much easier.'

'I know. I am a terrible nuisance. Thanks again, Don. See you at six.'

She was sitting by one of the tall windows of the library when she saw his car turn into the school gates, a dull torpedo shadowy against the white of the snow. She had moved to the library, a bag full of books in her hand, after dismissing a recalcitrant pupil from the windowless detention room, deep inside the school buildings. The girl's habit of making random remarks had ruined Vic's concentration, and now she sat, the books still in her bag, gazing down to where the cleared drive ran like a black canal between snow-laden lawns. She stuffed her arms into her coat and tramped down the empty, echoing staircase.

Don had the engine running and the car was warm. 'Good day?' he said.

'Much as ever. I thought I'd do my marking while taking detention, but it didn't work out. The girl would talk.'

Don reversed carefully and picked up speed towards the gates. 'Is that allowed?'

'Not really. But she didn't talk that much. Just when I was getting stuck into a child's essay she'd ask me some personal question.'

Don's eyebrows twitched upwards. 'Do they do that?'

'All the time. I'm sure you wouldn't ever have thought of asking such things of your teachers when you were a schoolboy. Boys don't, I imagine; they probably don't think their teachers even have any kind of private life. But our girls love to quiz.'

'So how do you answer?'

'I try to be stern and deny everything. But whatever you say, they don't believe you. For example, she might ask me if the snow had held me up today. I might – though I didn't – tell her a friend had given me a lift. And from there she would weave some intrigue.'

Don's laugh sounded forced. 'Good heavens.'

'They all read such rubbishy magazines. And I suppose it's more interesting than maths or geography.'

'It's another world.'

'It is. Quite a nice world in its way, though far removed from most people's reality. How was your day?'

'Busy.'

'A good thing?'

'Good for business, certainly.'

They fell silent. The main road had been gritted, and cautious tyres rolled with a wet crunching. The snow, blackened from the passage of the traffic, was banked roughly at the roadside, and the harsh reflected street lights sucked all colour away. Vic shivered despite her winter coat, and thought of her small house, thick curtains closed, the sound of a bubbling kettle.

'Come in for a cup of tea, Don,' she said as they approached. 'You'll be safe enough parked by the fence. There won't be any traffic up here now.'

'All right. Thanks.' He locked the car and shuddered in the sudden chill. 'Someone's been about, by the looks of it.' He pointed to the deep, snow-filled footprints on her front path.

She frowned. 'Can't think who.' He followed her up the path, shoes softly crushing the creaking snow. She put her key in the lock and opened the door on to the darkened hallway. 'Oh. Must have been the postman.' She bent and picked up a small sheaf of letters. 'Come in, Don. I'll get a fire going.'

'I'll light the fire, if you like,' he said diffidently. 'While you make the tea.'

'All right. It's all clean and laid ready, there are logs in the basket and matches on the shelf.' As she opened the door into the kitchen she heard him say, 'Of course, you could have central heating. Then it'd be nice and warm when you came in.'

She smiled inwardly. 'I know. Maybe I will, one day.'

He grunted. 'Yes, when hens grow whiskers.'

Humming softly she poured boiling water into the teapot and put cups, milk and spoons on a tray. She shoved the living room door open with her foot. Don was kneeling by the hearth, feeding the fire with little logs.

'You have to admit,' she said, 'a proper fire's nice.'

'Yes. But labour-intensive, dirty and not efficient.' He got to his feet, dusting off his hands, and took a cup of tea from the tray. 'Thanks. Anything interesting in the post?'

'I'd be surprised if there was anything but bills, other than advertisements for things I'll never need. Like a conservatory, or a takeaway pizza.' She sank down on the lumpy old sofa and sipped her tea. 'See what I mean?' She dumped the mail on a low table.

He sat opposite her and stretched out his long legs. 'You might need a conservatory one day. For Solomon to sun himself in, when he gets old and full of rheumatism. And you might develop a taste for fast food.'

'You think? What was that about hens and whiskers? Hold on, there's a proper letter here. With writing I don't recognize. Would you pass me my handbag, please, Don? I'm going to need my glasses.' She took the bag from him and opened her spectacle case.

'Where is Solomon, anyway? Shouldn't he be indoors in this weather?'

'He's probably asleep on the end of my bed.' She put her glasses on and tore open the envelope in her hand.

'Shall I look?' he asked.

'If you like.'

He pulled himself up and turned to the door. Then he stopped, hearing her whisper, 'No. I don't believe it.'

'What don't you believe?' He turned to look at her, seeing her staring at the letter in her hand, a deep frown creasing her brows. 'Vic, what is it?' When she didn't answer, he squatted down beside her. 'Vic, speak to me. What's the matter? You've gone all peculiar. Is it bad news? Who's it from, anyway?'

She raised her eyes to his. 'I don't know what kind of news it is,' she said slowly, as if her thoughts had been stunned into immobility. 'The letter's from my sister, Isabel. Bel. The sister I haven't seen for twenty-eight years. She wants to come and stay.'

What did they call it in French? 'Une nuit blanche.' And tonight was a white night in another way. She sat at her bedroom window, staring out into the darkness that was illuminated by the snow, and her thoughts were like the landscape: ominously still after the chaos of the storm. The green glow of her bedside clock told her it was past three in the morning, but there was no sleep in her, though she had lain for hours with her eyes shut, breathing steadily, in the hope that oblivion would creep up on her and release her from this relentless battery of thoughts and memories, all, it seemed, at war with one another. Finally an uneasy peace had descended, not the peace of resolution, but the slump of exhaustion. Her head ached, her eyes stung, and sweat cooled on her skin.

She shivered and wrapped her dressing-gown more closely round her body. She had made a cup of tea, and now sat in her scratchy old wicker chair at the window, sipping slowly, staring at the desolate garden and the beautiful, empty world beyond.

Bel. My sister. Who is she now, anyway? What is she to me? Why does she want to come, after all these years? Do I dare to let her back into my life? Can I defend myself from her? Won't she destroy everything I have built around me? What is she like? Do I even want to know?

Don was the only person of whom she could ask these things, beside herself; and she knew that asking herself was useless and circular, full of pain and frustration. Don knew something of the past, and he could be depended on for pragmatism and charity, if not for imagination or any intuitive leap.

'What does she say?' he had asked that evening, when she had recovered her wits. 'Exactly?'

'She says she has nowhere to go. How can that be, Don? Surely everyone has someone. She wants to stay here, just for a few weeks, over Christmas and New Year. Three weeks, she says. Then she'll go back to London.'

'Why hasn't she got anywhere to go? Where is she living now?'

'Apparently the woman who owns the house where she lives, where other people rent rooms too, other theatrical people she knows, is going on a trip to America to visit someone, and she's having the place refurbished while she's away. Bel seems to have exhausted all her acquaintances, used up all the favours, imposed once too often. That doesn't surprise me, from the little I know of Bel. And she's broke. Which is also no surprise. She's probably borrowed money and can't pay it back. She says I'm her last hope. But why would she want to come here? We haven't spoken in all those years. I don't know her any more, and she certainly doesn't know me.' *And I don't want us to know each other any more, do I?* This fleeting moment of clarity she kept to herself. 'Don, what should I do? What would you do? You know, don't you, why I don't want to see her.'

Don frowned and rubbed his eyes. The armchair in which he stretched out was slippery and too small; he crossed and recrossed his ankles to avoid sliding off the seat. 'I only know what you told Ellen,' he said. 'And the few hints you've dropped since. You've never said much. As to what I'd do, how can I know? But isn't this an opportunity? God-given, even? To start building a bridge? Don't you want to be friends with your sister?'

She shuddered. 'I don't know if I do,' she said. 'I think what I want is to be left alone. By Bel, anyway. There's too much anguish and anger between us. I can't even look it in the eye.'

'Perhaps it's time,' Don said, looking across at her sombrely. She shook her head. 'All right, then, but if you say 'No,' how can you justify that? What decent reason is there to turn her down? Shouldn't you take her in out of sheer Christian charity?'

She had no answer. She stared at the carpet till its pattern swam out of focus.

'You're afraid,' Don said. 'That's obvious. But hiding away doesn't help. Some time you have to face it.'

Anger flared up within her. 'What do I have to face?'

'The past. Your parents. Your responsibility.'

'I thought you were on my side.' Humiliatingly, her voice choked.

'I am. I always will be, whatever you decide to do or not do. I'm just asking you to think. I mean, really think. What's the right thing?'

'Is it that black and white?' she said, her voice low.

'Yes, it is. Well, it is to me.' He pushed himself to his feet. 'I must go home – you'll have things to do. I'll ring you tomorrow.' He hesitated in the doorway. 'At least it's the weekend. They say the snow will have gone by Monday. I'll see you on Sunday. You'll be in church, won't you?'

'Yes. I'm down to read.' Her voice sounded strange in her own ears: dull and lifeless.

'I'll see you there, then. If not before.' He put on his coat, tucked his scarf in tidily, patted his pockets for his gloves. Still he did not go. Clearly the issue of Bel was still winding slowly round his brain. 'Ring me if you like.'

'Yes, perhaps. Goodnight, Don. Thanks for taking me to work.'

'Goodnight.' He lifted his hand as if to pat her shoulder as he passed, but hesitated and let it drop.

Long after the sound of the Landrover's engine had died away she sat staring at the fire. Bel's letter lay open on the low table beside her. She could not look at it.

Chilled, she went back to bed and drew the covers up under her chin. Something came back to her, something Don had said as he loomed in the doorway, seemingly reluctant to leave.

'When did you last see Bel, anyway?'

Remembering, she shivered. 'At our father's funeral. She came with that awful man in tow – Terry someone. He changed his name later, I think. For Hollywood. They came at the last minute in a honking taxi, dressed for a party, not a funeral. I suspect that's where they'd been the night before. Bel's eye makeup was smudged all down her face. And I swear they were still a bit drunk. I was furious: I'd done all the work and she turned up like that. I wonder if she's changed.'

'She was young and silly.'

'I suppose. She was twenty-one.'

'Hm. Would you recognize her now, do you think?'

'Yes, I'm sure I would. Didn't I tell you? Perhaps I never did. I saw her on television. In a soap.'

He looked up, astonished. 'But you don't have a TV. Even if you did, I can't see you as a soap addict.'

'No. But it was at your house.'

He frowned. 'I don't watch soaps!'

'It was ages ago. I was sitting with Ellen. You weren't even there.'

'Oh.' He paused, thinking, and a visible shadow passed momentarily across his face. 'Were you sure at the time it was her?'

'I remember clutching Ellen's arm and shrieking, "It's Bel!" Poor Ellen. Then afterwards I watched the credits, and I realized she was working under a stage name – Bella Morgan. Maybe she married that man, after all. Or at least took his name. He called himself Clive Morgan in America. Maybe you remember – he was a bit famous for a while. Well, I don't know what she did. But that was not long before –' She saw Don wince. 'Sorry. Before Ellen died. So it must be at least six years ago. Perhaps more.'

'What did she look like?'

'She'd put on weight. And dyed her hair, raven black.' She heard herself, the tinge of female malice. 'I guess I've changed too.'

Lying in bed, shivering slightly in the unheated room, she thought of herself as a child, Bel's sister, Bel's friend; as an adolescent, hopeful despite everything; then as a young woman in whom that hope had been so severely shaken, and saw in a moment of cold and devastating clarity how she had become the woman Victoria Colbourne was today. Tentatively, inwardly wincing, aware how easily prayer can change a life, afraid and driven, she prayed. *Lord, if it hadn't snowed, I'd have gone to work in my own car. Don wouldn't have been here when I opened Bel's letter. I could have torn it up and thrown it away, and that would've been the end of it. Is this what it is, an opportunity you have sent? Should I see it that way? Must I see my sister again, have her here in my house, my haven? Won't she tear everything apart, even if she doesn't intend it? Why have I become such a coward? No, I know why. And, of course, you know why. Lord, what shall I do?*

8

Bel

She sat on the edge of her rumpled bed, looking gloomily at a large, unruly pile of clothes and a small suitcase. A shadow passed by her open door and she looked up. 'Bertie! I need help.'

The shadow stepped back, almost silent on soft-soled shoes. Bertie Pellow inclined his sleek head gravely. 'What is it, Bella darling? I'm a little late, you know.'

'You're good at this sort of thing. I don't know what to pack.'

Bertie stepped into the room and surveyed the pile of garments. 'Why such a lot, Bella? It's only three weeks. Even I wouldn't take so much.'

Bel sighed. 'I don't know, Bertie. I feel useless, incompetent.'

'Of course you're not,' he soothed. Then, looking down at her, his head on one side, he said, 'So you're definitely going, then? To your sister?'

Bel turned away, feeling a sudden shiver ripple up and down her bare arms. 'Yes. She wrote me this letter. Take a look, Bertie.'

He came further into the room and threw his wide-brimmed hat on the bed. 'I don't have my glasses.'

'You'll be able to read it without,' Bel said. 'Her writing's thick and black. She must still write with a fountain pen.' She shook her head.

Bertie held the single sheet of paper between thumb and forefinger, at arm's length. 'It's very short.' For a minute he scanned the letter silently. 'Good heavens. She doesn't give much away. What's this about television and central heating?'

Bel laughed, but a tiny frown creased her brows. 'She doesn't have them. She's warning me. That's why I don't know what to take. You know me, Bertie – I hate to be cold. And no TV! I am beginning to wonder whether this was such a great idea.'

Bertie looked at her pleading face. 'Well, if it means that much, you can borrow my small one,' he said. 'If you really want to carry it on the train.' He paused. 'You look worried.'

'Oh, I know I'm silly. But I've got cold feet, Bertie. Look, I'm sorry, you're going out. I won't hold you up.' Her voice caught.

Bertie perched on the edge of the bed and patted her hand. 'No, no, it doesn't matter. Tell me what's bothering you.'

'Well, this letter, for a start. I don't know what I expected. Not this, though. "Dear Bel, By all means come and stay, if you want to. I should tell you, I live very simply. I don't have central heating so you might find my house chilly. Also I don't own a television. Let me know the time of your train, and I'll meet you at Stoke station. Vic." What does that tell me? Nothing. Am I making a big mistake, Bertie?'

He pursed his lips. 'It's only three weeks. Even if it's difficult, I dare say you can bear it. And then you'll be back here, and Josie will be home, and the place will be tarted up, and we'll all be together. Besides, darling, you said you didn't have anywhere else to go.'

'No. I wish I could come with you. But you said there won't be room.'

'I'm so sorry.' He released her hand, and his rings glinted in the lamplight. 'Anyway, perhaps it won't be so dreadful. Perhaps you can persuade your sister you're not such a bad lot.'

'There's a lot of history, Bertie. But you know some of that.'

'Yes. But it was a very long time ago, and maybe she's mellowed, grown more forgiving. Didn't you tell me she's rather religious?'

Bel nodded. 'We were still at school. She was eighteen, just on the point of leaving. She told me she'd become a Christian. I'm afraid I giggled. She didn't think much of that.'

'I'm not surprised. But she was young. Perhaps it all faded away. Perhaps it was a passing youthful enthusiasm.'

'No, she was still very much in with the church the last time I saw her, at our father's funeral. Things were very tense that day between us – did I tell you? And even before, when we were still at school, she seemed to become kind of distant, and quite stern. Judgmental, even. She certainly didn't approve of my associates at the AmDram. Said they were a bunch of shady posers.'

'That's our reputation, I'm afraid, Bella dear,' Bertie said, sighing. 'It's a horrible caricature, of course.'

Bel grinned suddenly. 'Actually, when it came to the West Stoke Players, she was probably right. Did I ever tell you how I got into that little Rep. company after I bunked off school?'

Bertie shuddered. 'Yes, you did, and very shocking it was. I hope you didn't tell your sister *that*.'

'No, but I might. Especially if she's turned into a stuffy old prude. Shall I, Bertie?'

Bertie got to his feet and picked up his hat with a flourish. 'For goodness' sake, Bella! Behave yourself. Remember, you need to keep on the right side of your sister, just for three little weeks. Surely even you can manage that.' He smiled. 'Now, darling, I really must get on. I'm meeting a very important man. Who knows what might come of it?' His eyebrows arched delicately up. 'Will I see you before you go?'

'Oh yes, I'm sure you will. I won't go till the last minute – just before the builders arrive.'

'Good. And you never know – there might be something from your agent in the new year. New year, new life – I'm always hopeful.'

'Ha! Now that would be something,' Bel said. 'Jason probably thinks I've sunk into oblivion. As far as he's concerned, I don't exist. Not trendy enough, I suppose.'

'Nonsense. He found you that part in the serial, didn't he? What was it called?'

'Oh, that. "A Cornish Life." I worked myself into the ground trying to get the accent, you know. But that finished months ago. I shall soon be destitute.'

'We've all been there, Bella. You've had better breaks than many.'

Bel shivered and wrapped her arms around herself. 'I know. But I have a very big, depressing birthday coming up next year. And there aren't that many parts for dried-up old hags.'

'Oh, Bel! "Hags," indeed! The way you carry on anyone would think you were a touch theatrical.'

'Ha, ha. Go on, Bertie. Off you go. Hope your meeting goes well, whatever it is. What is it, anyway? Work? Or one of your romances?'

Bertie smirked. 'I'll tell you when I find out myself. See you later, darling.'

Bel lay on her bed, eyes closed, stockinged feet resting on her bulging suitcase. She hadn't progressed very far. The room was warm, curtains closed against the night, the lamplight dim. Her stomach rumbled, and she remembered she hadn't eaten since that bowl of soup at lunchtime. She sighed and heaved herself up. Her handbag sat open on the floor, spilling its contents. She rummaged around and found her purse, greeting a few loose coins and a crumpled five-pound note with a grimace. *That won't get me much.* She padded along the corridor and down the winding staircase, her feet prickled by the threadbare carpet. She snapped on the kitchen light, opened the fridge and peered in. On her shelf lay a dried-up chunk of cheese and a withered apple. She scanned the worktops and saw that someone had left a fresh loaf. *I don't suppose they'll mind, whoever they are.* She helped herself to two slices and resealed the bag, then put everything on a plate and tiptoed back upstairs. There was half a bottle of red wine, turning to vinegar on her windowsill. She sat on the edge of the bed, chewing and sipping. *I hope Vic can cook.*

Her meagre meal finished, she sighed and lay back against her pillows. *I don't even know what Vic looks like these days. I wonder if she's changed much. I don't know anything about her, not really, not how she is now, not how she's been. I just remember the girl, my adored big sister, my friend and defender.* Tears stung her eyelids and she dashed them away impatiently. She pulled open the drawer of her bedside table and took out an envelope. Inside were a handful of photographs, all old, some faded with tattered edges. She riffled through them and took one out. There were two girls, one a chubby schoolgirl with a white ribbon in her bobbed hair, the other a tall and slender adolescent, brown hair in a ponytail, and they had their arms round each other's shoulders as they posed for the photograph. Vic was wearing her school's summer uniform, a dark blazer over a striped cotton dress, and Bel was in a short skirt, white socks, a cardigan and sandals. She remembered that day: it was the day they'd collected Vic from school, and one of her friends had a camera for her birthday and was trying it out. Some weeks later the girl sent Vic the print in the post. *Vic must have given it to me at some point. Or maybe I pinched it. We look happy.* She turned the snapshot over and saw the date, written in pencil on the back: 15 June, 1967. Bel shivered. *We had so little time. Just a few short weeks, and then everything fell apart.*

It took her a few days of bringing her thoughts to order before she was able to reply to Vic's letter. Even then, even after she'd posted it, she was full of misgivings. But something, some mysterious force, was driving her on, and anyway, she told herself, she was not spoilt for choice.

'Dear Vic,

Thanks for letting me come. I'll try not to be too much of a nuisance. I've got a bit of money coming so I can pay my way with the household bills.

If you don't mind I'm going to bring my friend's small TV. I can have it in my room so it won't bother you.

I'll come on December 14th. The builders are arriving on 15th so

Josie – that's my landlady – will want me out of the house by then. She's having major work done, so none of us can stay, apart from Josie herself. She's staying on to supervise for a while before she goes to America for Christmas.

I thought I should come by an evening train, in case you're at work during the day. I know so little about your life now. I hope the train that arrives at Stoke station at 7.25 pm will be convenient for you.

I'll assume these arrangements are OK unless I hear otherwise.

Love from Bel.'

Vic must have taken her at her word, as far as her last sentence went, because she did not reply to Bel's letter. As December ground on in dull grey cloud and gusting wind, Bel's heart grew heavier. She had far too much time to kill, and although she went through the motions of trying to find work, she knew it would most likely be fruitless. She went shopping, trying to find a Christmas present for Vic, but it served only to increase her sense of estrangement. What were Vic's tastes? What, if anything, did she lack? No, it would be better to wait till she had a clearer idea of who her sister had become.

When she wasn't in the public library, keeping warm at the local council's expense, or making a cup of milky coffee last an hour in the greasy spoon at the end of the road, she lay on her bed, a book open beside her, letting her thoughts roam at will, feeling that sense of loneliness, worry and sheer dislocation grow in her mind like a louring rain-cloud. *Perhaps I've been really stupid. Even when we were young, if I did something she didn't like, she certainly let me know it. Not that it happened often; she was very good to me most of the time, even when she went off to school and got new friends and left me behind. I remember how I used to love the holidays. I couldn't wait for Vic to come home, those three years before I joined her at Repley. But now – what now? The last time we met she was furious with me. Thinking about it after all these years, it seems there was more in her anger than just how I turned up to the funeral. I suppose she blames me for leaving her in the lurch. But if she is still angry (is that possible, after so many years?) why is she letting me come and stay?* A cold thought struck her, and she shuddered. *Maybe she wants to wipe the floor with me. Get some kind of revenge. But is she really like that? If she's still a Christian, oughtn't she to be trying to forgive? But if she had forgiven me, wouldn't she have tried to get in touch before? That cuts both ways, I know, and I haven't tried either. Till now. Sometimes I can't tell what I'm thinking myself, let alone decipher someone else's mind.* She rubbed her aching eyes. *I wish we could go back, back before everything went wrong. Vic and I were good sisters then. She was kind. I can't ever remember being scared of her, even though she could always out-talk me. And now look at me. I'm a grown woman – forty-nine, how awful. I've lived a life. And I'm dreading meeting my own flesh and blood. How stupid I am. I should have gone to old Hattie in Scotland. I could have done that, at a pinch. But Scotland! I could hardly afford the fare, for a start. And Hattie's place smells, what with all those cats.* She sat up, put her feet on the floor, and rested her elbows on her knees. *Come on, Isabel. Get a grip. Muster some guts. You've been in worse holes than this, far worse.*

But somehow her words sounded hollow in her own ears, and as 14 December approached her unease grew.

26 May 1963

Vic was woken by the familiar sound of her father's car coming to a halt with a soft crunching of gravel. She sat up, some unnamed fear making her shiver, though the night was warm. She had no idea what the time was, but she knew it was late, later than she had ever been awake before, except on those rare occasions when she'd been ill and then time seemed to have no meaning. She looked over to the other bed. Bel was asleep, her soft brown hair fallen over her face, her chubby fingers gripping her favourite doll, oddly named Betty Shakespeare, to her chest.

Vic slipped out of bed. She looked for her slippers, but couldn't find them. She heard the front door close with a thud, and froze. Then she heard her father's footsteps creaking on the wood floor of the hallway, and she tiptoed to the door, which was open a crack, as Bel insisted. As she opened the door wider she could hear the television in the lounge, and loud laughter: a teenager from the village, Heather Somebody, was babysitting. Standing motionless in the open doorway she heard the lounge door closing, and the noise from the TV was muted. Vic crept to the head of the stairs, a shadowy figure in her thin nightdress, and heard her father pick up the telephone on the hall table. His voice, when he spoke, sounded uncharacteristically loud, harsh and excited.

'Judge? Not too late, I hope?'

Vic felt a breath of air, and Bel crouched beside her, her eyes wide. Vic put a finger to her lips.

'We've done it, Judge, at last! A son, a healthy seven-pounder.'

The girls looked at each other solemnly.

'Of course, Judge, of course,' their father's voice came again. 'Another John Colbourne.' He glanced up then, and saw the two girls huddled together at the top of the stairs. Vic saw his wide, unfamiliar, unsettling smile fade a little. Then he looked away.

'Thank you, sir. I'll let you get back to bed.'

He put the phone down slowly, looked up the stairs again, and opened his mouth to speak, but the girls scampered away, back to their bedroom, and dived under the covers, breathless, hearts pounding.

A little later, Vic heard the door open and knew their father was standing there, a silhouette against the landing light. She kept her eyes closed and breathed evenly. She heard Bel say, in that hesitant babyish voice, 'Daddy?'

John Colbourne's voice was strange, not his usual quiet tone, but harsh and percussive. 'A brother for you, Isabel. Isn't that good news? A brother, at last.' As if this was the very thing the sisters had been waiting for all their short lives: but what did he know?

'Is Mummy all right? Will she be home soon?' Bel's voice was plaintive, and Vic felt a spurt of anger.

'Just tired. She has to rest for a while, then she'll be home, with baby John. Go back to sleep now.'

'Goodnight, Daddy.'

Vic's eyes remained steadfastly shut, but her ears were open, and in her inner ears, till sleep came to claim her, she could hear her father's voice, triumphant, exulting: 'A brother, at last.'

Bel

'Bertie? It's me, Bella. Of course I'm at Vic's. Yes, I'm OK, thanks. Vic's out – some church group or other. She said did I mind, and of course I told her she has to carry on as usual. She's putting herself out for me quite enough as it is. What do you mean, I don't sound like myself? What, I don't usually do charitable? Thanks, Bertie, you're a pal.

No, it's fine, actually. Vic has this really quaint little place, tiny, but nice, on the edge of the village, with fields all around. Used to be a farm worker's cottage way back, but then the last worker died or retired and the farmer, Dave someone, did it up and sold it. To Vic. It's very quiet. Oh yes, and really *cold*. Except right by the fire, or in the kitchen when the oven's on. She's got an enormous cat called Solomon, who rules the roost. And there's some bloke called Don, who she says is her friend. He may be a love interest for all I know, but Vic's playing it very cool. I haven't met him yet. I'll let you know what I think when I do. If I do. I think he's at this prayer meeting as well.

Has Vic changed? Well, yes, of course. She's older. Still in good shape though, not gone baggy round the edges like me. She eats the right food, I suppose. Yes, she's a pretty good cook, better than I've ever been, though that's not hard, as you know. The thing that really surprised me, Bertie, she's a teacher! Not only that, but she teaches at Repley, where we both went to school! Isn't that something? Apparently after our father died she went back to college and got qualified. She always was clever. She taught in a few other schools before she got the job at Repley. She said she always wanted to work there because she was so happy at school. Well, you know a bit about that, don't you? Home was pretty awful, especially after what happened. And we both found things we were good at. They encouraged us at Repley, made us feel we were someone... I don't know, Bertie, interesting, valuable. You went to school in a monastery, didn't you? You didn't? You see how ignorant I am. Oh, it was a Catholic school. OK.

Well, it was at Repley I first got into drama. No, the drama teacher

17

wasn't a handsome six-footer, she was tiny with red hair and a witchy laugh. I was in most of the school productions, a bit of a leading light, I'll have you know. That's why I joined the Stoke Players in the holidays.

Honestly, Bertie – your mind's a cesspit. Anyone would think I succeeded solely on the casting couch! No, that was the only time. The rest was native talent and lots of hard work. You've got such a cheek.

I was telling you about Vic. She's still religious, of course. Goes to church every Sunday. Reads her Bible every day. But she's been nice, I have to say, in a reserved sort of way. What? *Of course* we haven't had a row yet. I've been here barely twenty-four hours, for goodness' sake. Real life isn't anything like a soap. (Remember real life, Bertie? No, of course you don't.) I know we've had our rows, Vic and me. Not many, but horrible. The last one was at Mummy's funeral. We hardly spoke at Daddy's, except to make arrangements about the will. She was still angry with me then, more than a year later. She blamed me for not helping her when Mummy was ill. But I couldn't, could I? I was at Drama School, and lucky to get in. I wasn't going to let anything mess that up. And I had two jobs, just to pay my way. I worked in a nasty little cafe every evening and weekend and cleaned offices at night. It was foul. But I was determined to make a go of it, you know.

Vic said I could go along to one of her study groups if I wanted. She said the one she's going to this evening would be a bit of a party as well, because it's the last one before the Christmas break. She said it might be a good opportunity to meet a few people. But I didn't fancy reading Jeremiah, not on my second night here. I might go to church at Christmas, though. We always went to Sunday School when we were children. The old vicar was sweet to us, him and his wife. Of course that was years ago. There's a new vicar now, Vic says. Well, newish.

For heaven's sake, Bertie, anyone would think I am some kind of nympho, the way you carry on! No, the new vicar is not gorgeous and unattached, she's a young married woman, and a mother. She has a two year old child, Vic says, with another one on the way. So there. Anyway, in three short weeks I am not likely to be looking for that kind of diversion. Bertie, you really are dreadful. Just because *your* life resembles a perverted porn movie. You're such a tease.

Look, I must go. I'm running up Vic's phone bill, and I don't want to be in her bad books this soon. You've got the number here, haven't you? Ring me if you feel like a chat. I want to know what's going on while I'm out here in the sticks. All right, Bertie dear, behave yourself. Yes, I miss you too. Bye for now.'

Vic

Vic closed the scullery door with her elbow while precariously balancing a loaded tray on her other hand. Don, shirt sleeves rolled above the wrists, was already washing up. He turned and looked at her enquiringly when he heard the door click shut.

'Any more?'

'No, that's it, apart from the plates and glasses people are still using.' Vic took a tea towel from the drying-rack. 'Frankie looks shattered.'

'Small wonder. How long's she got, anyway?'

'I'm not sure. A couple of months, I suppose. Isn't the baby due in February? Or is it late January? Anyway, with a parish to run, a two-year-old to look after, and Rob away this week, it's not surprising she looks all in. I'm glad this study group's over for a while, anyway. She works hard preparing it, sometimes in the small hours, so she said.'

Don nodded. 'What did you think of tonight?'

'We didn't do much strict Jeremiah, did we? There are so many red herrings during the meetings I have to go home and do a recap in my own time. Sometimes I think Frankie should avoid inviting discussion at all.' She paused, a soapy glass in one hand, the tea towel in the other. 'Do you think we got anywhere, for example, with the question of why the wicked seem to prosper in this life?'

Don smiled. 'Of course not. I don't think we'll get a handle on that till we're good and dead.' His smile faded. 'But the passage we read tonight struck a chord with me. That bit where it says "... the people of Judah have as many gods as they have cities..." and then "...what right have they to be in my Temple?" I felt like saying something at that point. I do a lot of weddings and baptisms and funerals, as you know. And sometimes I find myself thinking, "What right do these people have to be in church?" All they want, most of them, as far as I can see, is a sort of pseudo-religious rubber stamp on their celebration, a nice warm glow, and then we never see them again. It's hypocritical, dishonest, dishonouring to God's house, cheapening of the sacraments – and we let it happen.'

'If you feel that strongly, why didn't you say something?'

Don shrugged. 'What's the point? The word these days is all about going with the flow, isn't it? People just mutter about making the church "relevant" and "inclusive," or they burble on with some tripe about the difficulty of achieving the right balance. Balance! It's all humbug. Bring back Jeremiah.' He tipped the dirty water down the deep sink with a splash.

Vic grinned and shook her head. 'I agree with you, on the whole. Except that there's always that chance we can't afford to miss, that someone in one of those heedless social congregations might hear God's voice.'

'So what's funny?'

'Nothing, really, except I wonder what people would make of their so-called mild-mannered organist and choirmaster if they ever heard you in this combative mood.' She dried the last of the plates and stacked them in an overhead cupboard.

Don folded his arms, leaning back against the draining-board. 'Well. I don't think you'll be revealing the real me to the members of our congregation. And everybody has a sore spot, even people who seem to be quiet and conservative.'

'Of course they do. And you do have a point. I was thinking, when we were looking at those verses where the sinners and idolaters were being condemned, what has really changed? These days sin and idolatry are covered up with the latest fashions, things like "new theology" and "new morality." Old immorality, more like. But we are getting very judgmental, Don. And I'm just as black a sinner as the next idolater.'

'I know, I know. Me too. And when I think these indignant thoughts, I remember that bit we read a few weeks ago.'

'Which bit?'

'Where Jeremiah complains that even the priests and prophets change the laws and cheat the people and tell them their wounds are scratches, or something. It reminds me of that parable about the faithful and unfaithful servants.'

Vic frowned. 'Sorry, you lost me. How does that connect with what we were just saying?'

'I'm just thinking about that quote, "Much is required of him to whom much is given…" I think that means us. So that means we should be more charitable, more forgiving, doesn't it?'

The door opened, and they both turned towards the sound. The

Reverend Frances Maynard stood in the doorway, leaning against the wall, one hand resting on her swollen belly. 'Hey, you two, that's where you got to. Aren't you angels! Thanks for clearing up.'

'You look worn out, Frankie. Has everybody gone? I'll get the last of the plates and glasses.'

'No, Vic, leave them. Mrs Weston can do them in the morning. How did you think tonight went?'

'Fine,' Vic said. 'But I'm glad we're taking a break. You'll have enough to do with Christmas coming up.'

Frankie groaned. 'Don't I know it.'

'We'll go now, won't we, Don? Give Frankie a chance to get some rest. Anyway, I should get home. I mustn't totally neglect my guest.'

'Oh? You've got someone staying?' Frankie said.

'My sister, Isabel.'

Frankie's eyebrows shot up. 'You're a dark horse, Vic. I didn't even know you had a sister.'

'Not many people do. Before she arrived yesterday we hadn't seen one another for twenty-eight years.'

'Wow.' She made as if to speak, then clearly thought better of it. Vic smiled inwardly. Not so long ago, when Frankie first came to St. Mark's, she'd have blurted something out about family feuds; she was, it seemed, learning a little tact.

Vic and Don passed her into the hallway and pulled down their coats from hooks on the wall.

'Your sister's welcome to any of our doings, Vic,' Frankie said. 'I hope we'll meet her.'

'I expect you will,' Vic said briskly. 'She's very sociable.' She turned to Don. 'You coming?'

Don nodded, and wrapped a scarf round his neck. 'I'll walk you home, if you like. 'Night, Frankie.'

'Goodnight, Don.' Frankie yawned. 'See you both soon.'

'I couldn't ask earlier,' Don said, as they trudged up the unlit track towards Vic's house. 'Not with everyone there. How's it going with Bel?'

Vic shrugged. 'All right, so far, but it's too soon to tell. We're both being terribly polite. She seems a bit nervous, as if she's afraid of annoying me or something. It was rather funny this morning, though. She looked out of the window and shrieked. I wondered what she could have seen in Dave Green's field that could be so startling. She gasped, "Vic! There's one of those wild cats in that field! Like a small panther!" So I went to look, and of course it was only Solly. I know he's big for a cat, but I feel she rather over-reacted. Must come from living in London. Anyway, she chats very brightly. Wants to know all about my life, and tells me stuff about hers. Superficial stuff mostly.'

'You did have a fairly major falling-out, though, didn't you?'

'Yes, indeed we did. But that was nearly thirty years ago.'

'In which time it hasn't been sorted, or even mentioned. Am I right?'

Vic sighed. 'Yes, you are. But I can't cope with a lecture on forgiveness, Don. Not tonight. Not even after your little reminder earlier.'

He stopped and smiled. 'I wasn't going to lecture you. You OK from here?'

'Of course. I can see my living room lights are on. And I've got my torch.'

'Right. See you on Sunday. Try and bring Bel.'

'I don't know. Maybe.' She patted his arm. 'Goodnight, Don. Go on, go home. You'll catch your death in this wind.'

When Vic opened her front door she could hear the tinny sound of Bel's borrowed television behind her closed bedroom door. 'Hello, I'm back!' she called up the stairs. She went into the kitchen and put the kettle on, and a moment later there were footsteps on the stairs and Bel appeared in the doorway.

'Hello,' she said. 'How was your meeting?'

'All right, thanks. Frankie says to bring you along to whatever you like. There'll be things going on over Christmas, not just churchy things. She wants to meet you.'

'That's nice. And I don't mind churchy things. Do you remember our old vicar when we were children? Reverend Alloway, and his wife? They were very kind.'

'Yes, they were. She was a great cake-maker, if I recall. Do you want some tea?'

'Lovely. I'll just pop up and turn the TV off. I hope it's not disturbing you.'

'No, it's fine. I'll take the tea into the living room.' She paused. 'Talking of the TV, Bel, we should get a licence for it.'

Bel made a face. 'That's very law-abiding of you.' She caught Vic's look. 'But I guess you don't want to be clapped in irons.'

'I think it would be more a case of a huge fine that neither of us could

22

afford,' Vic said. She spoke mildly enough, but Bel heard steel there and felt reproved.

'Right,' Bel said. 'I'll see to it.'

'So, tell me again, what's your group studying?' Bel asked as she sipped her tea.

'Jeremiah. We've been ploughing through it since September, and tonight we arrived at chapters eleven and twelve. But not much attention was paid to poor old Jeremiah. They were more interested in going off at tangents, and eating and drinking.'

'Who's "they"?'

'Oh, a random selection of the congregation. And Frankie, who does all the work. And Don.'

For a minute they drank their tea in silence, each with her own inscrutable thoughts, then Bel said, 'Vic, what happened to the old house in the end?'

'Angleby? It's still there. If it hadn't been dark when I drove you here from the station, you would have seen it. It's more or less under the bypass. Mouldering.'

'I thought you sold it to a developer.'

'I did. And he built a small and rather exclusive estate on a part of the land, and sold the houses. People moved in, and they're still there, of course, or people they subsequently sold to. I think the original plan was to refurbish the old house and turn it into a country club, or something similar. He had all sorts of ideas: parking, fishing, tennis courts. But he went bust, and then some years later the Thackham bypass was built. People living in Thackham itself thought it was a great idea, but the houses on our old land were rather blighted. So nothing was ever done to the big house, and now it's too late for refurbishing: it's only fit for demolition.'

Bel put her tea cup down carefully on a small table. 'I might go down there one day and take a look, if you tell me where to go.'

Vic shook her head. 'I don't know if you can get down there any more. There's a path leading from the housing estate, but the old house is fenced off. I imagine it's dangerous.'

'I wonder what will become of it,' Bel said wistfully.

'Oh, well, there are always rumours: someone's bought it for more housing, or it's going to be pulled down. But nothing's come of it so far.'

'What about the woods, and the river?'

'Taken up by the development, mostly. You can still walk by the

23

public part of the river, of course. There's a pretty bit down behind the churchyard, complete with a family of swans.'

'It sounds lovely.'

'A bit bleak at this time of the year, I'm afraid.' She stood up. 'I'm for bed. I'll call my panther, sorry, cat, and lock up, and say goodnight.'

Bel grinned. 'Well, he is big, you have to admit that.' She looked up at Vic. 'You look tired.'

'Yes, I am. It's the end of term. Lots to do, long hours, reports, school play, all those things – perhaps you remember.'

'I certainly remember the school productions. I loved them.'

'Of course. But then you were the star, not the already overworked and harassed teacher in charge of the costumes, or the sets, or whatever.'

Bel bristled. 'Acting is hard work, you know. Even for the so called *star*.'

'I don't doubt it. But teaching, especially these days, is a killer.'

Bel cocked her head. 'That bad?'

Vic sighed. 'Perhaps I exaggerate a bit. But even though I'm looking forward to the holidays, I know how much work I've got to do to catch up. There's always something: some new directive, some new target, some new ignorant threat from on high. By comparison even the task of encouraging a love of literature in teenage minds is a piece of cake.'

'I guess nothing is what it used to be,' Bel said.

'If only.' Vic smiled faintly. 'Goodnight, Bel. Perhaps I'll feel a bit more optimistic in the morning.'

Dear Victoria,

I regret having to write to you now when I am sure you are busy with your own life and career, though of course as things are I know little about either.

Unfortunately your mother has been enduring a long period of ill-health which she has attributed to 'nerves' and for which she has therefore refused to seek medical advice. However I am sorry to have to tell you that she has cancer, and is very unwell. She has been, of course, and still is being, treated, both by our local hospital's consultant oncologist and our family GP, Dr Paulson, whom no doubt you will remember. I have also offered to employ professional nurses to care for her, and this may yet happen, but so far she has refused to countenance such a move. In addition I am contemplating taking early retirement, but even if I do so I think it most unlikely that she would accept being cared for by me, though I would be willing, if not especially able, lacking experience of such things as I do.

Your mother increasingly asks after both you and Isabel. Of your sister I have had no news for some time and no record of her current address. In short, my dear Victoria, your mother regularly and with some urgency has been asking for you. Would you please consider at least visiting? Or even, if your own priorities permit, would you perhaps take the time to be a companion to her, as long as her painful and limited life lasts?

You realize, I hope, that I would not think of imposing on you at all were it not to ease what may be the last months of your mother's troubled life.

Yours somewhat anxiously,
John Colbourne

Vic

Vic had rarely before now had trouble sleeping, but the arrival of her sister in her life seemed to have stirred something up in the deep pond-bottom sludge of her psyche. After the conversation with Bel she got ready for bed in the usual way, and lay down yawning and heavy-lidded; but the mention of the old house had stimulated unwelcome memories. She had thrown away her father's letter long ago, but she had never forgotten its content and tone, nor the helpless fury she had felt when she received it: fury at her father for his buck-passing, at her mother for her illness, at Bel for being so conveniently unavailable, and at herself for what she perceived as her own weakness. As soon as she read John Colbourne's letter, she knew that she would, with bitter resentment, accede to his request. It was, she told herself, angrily and with no hint of resignation or genuine charity, her duty as a Christian, if not as a daughter. She felt not a shred of softness: for why should she now care for a woman who had never really, she believed, cared for her? And why should she help a father who had never for a moment valued her? The worst of it was that the letter had arrived when she was facing what seemed an intractable impasse in her own life. Humiliatingly, her attempts to escape had ignominiously failed, despite all her strenuous efforts, and at that moment to return to Angleby, unwelcome as it was, offered a way out, a means of survival. She wrote to her father, tersely and coldly; packed a meagre suitcase, and returned to her childhood home feeling more a disgraced sinner than a rescuing angel.

Now she turned over in bed, sighing. That part of her life she had long since consigned to oblivion, seeing it as full of her own shame and failure. But another memory surfaced, equally painful, and try as she might she could not blot it out. Don had referred to her quarrel with Bel at their mother's funeral, less than a year after Vic's return to Angleby, and now it came back to her almost verbatim, with distressing clarity.

In the face of Vic's resentment, unequivocally expressed, Bel had been defensive.

'Look,' she had said, brows furrowed under her heavy fringe. 'I couldn't come here even if I wanted to. Not permanently. Even when I did come to visit Mummy, I hardly saw Daddy at all and you were so horrible! I've got the possibility of a career I've dreamed about. I'm ambitious. Just being at Drama School is tough, but I was lucky to get in, and I'm not going to throw that away in a hurry. And I'm doing two pretty nasty jobs just to finance myself, pay the rent and my fees and all the other things. I'm not giving up on Terry either. Together we've got a life, and big plans. What have you got, except plenty of time? You don't have a career, or a boyfriend, or any ambitions at all, as far as I can see. Why shouldn't it be you?'

'I *had* a life,' Vic answered, her fists clenched tightly by her side as if to prevent herself from lashing out and knocking her sister to the ground. 'Yes, it was crumbling. I had a husband – and no, he wasn't up to much. But what do you know, or care, about my ambitions? Who are you to say my hopes weren't worth pursuing, weren't worth grieving for when I had to give them up – to do my duty? Yes, Bel, boring, isn't it, the very idea of sacrifice? What do you know about duty? All you seem to care about is yourself. How very like *them* you are!'

'Like who?'

'Like *our parents*, of course.'

'How can you talk about them like that,' Bel had said wildly, tears springing to her eyes, 'today of all days, with Mummy dead and Daddy grieving?'

Vic replied, her eyes narrow and her voice icy with contempt, 'If you knew anything, if you'd actually lived here the past ten months, even you wouldn't be so sentimental.'

'Well,' Bel said, looking exactly as she had as a sulky, stubborn child, '*I* don't plan to be any kind of martyr. And you'd better give it up too, all this high-flown stuff about sacrifice, or your life will be spoiled.'

'My life *is* spoiled,' Vic said. 'The rot started the minute I was born, it seems to me. Most of it was nothing to do with you. But when you could have helped, you turned your back on me. So don't bother to come back here. Live your selfish life, if you can.'

That hadn't, however, been the last time she'd seen Bel. The last time had been just over a year later, at John Colbourne's funeral; and then there had been little more than a stiff exchange between them, about Vic's plans for the house and land. Bel, despite her mascara-smudging tears, was apparently only interested in the value of her inheritance. She had written down her address and gone back to London.

Still sleepless in the dead hours of the morning, Vic tiptoed downstairs and made tea. She took the steaming mug quietly back to her room and sat up against her pillows, well wrapped against the cold in a huge ancient cardigan. What Don had said earlier wound round and round her brain, and in the end she opened her Bible and found the quotation from Luke 12: "Much is required from the person to whom much is given; much more is required from the person to whom much more is given." She frowned. How could Don think of himself as someone to whom much had been given, as he clearly did, when the thing dearest to him – his wife, Ellen – had been *taken away?*

Reluctantly and painfully she approached where she would so much rather not have gone, seeing herself also as one from whom much had been taken away, or never given – even though on the surface her life had been privileged; and the long-forbidden question came to her mind, why two perfectly nice, healthy, normal girls should be so little loved and esteemed, and how because of it her life – and Bel's too, most probably – had been damaged by decisions and actions based on starvation of love. She knew, though nowadays she rarely allowed herself to think about it, that her life had been blighted by anger, bitterness and blame, including self-blame; and she wondered, sitting up in bed, the cold pinching her nose, her hands warm around her mug of tea, how Bel really felt under her surface brightness. *All these years I've avoided finding out how Bel feels about anything. I didn't want to know, because it would have meant resurrecting the pain of that time. But is Don right? Is this a God-given opportunity? Come to that, has he dealt with all his own troubles? He doesn't often talk about Ellen, either the last few awful years, or even further back, when things were OK, before her illness.*

She finished her tea, and shuffled down in the bed with the covers up to her chin, and another thought struck her, a thought which gave her no comfort. *If I am a real Christian, why can I barely forgive my mother? Why have I not allowed God's grace to percolate down and make me less angry, more loving, more forgiving? Why have I not pitied Bel more all these years, when her offence was so small? I wonder if she has let the past blacken her life as I have. I suppose now I have the chance to find out; but have I the courage? Must I add cowardice to my list of moral failures? And do I even dare to pray? Who knows what might come of that?*

Bel

When she awoke Bel felt sluggish, as if she hadn't slept at all; and then she remembered waking in the night, and hearing the stairs creak, and knew that Vic too was awake and creeping about. She had curled herself into a tight ball and wrapped the covers round herself, feeling the chill in the air of the unheated house. *I could use a hot water bottle. An electric blanket. Even that damn' cat lying on my feet might help. But he's most definitely Vic's cat. Regards me with suspicion, by the look in those great green eyes. Boy, this house is cold.* As she drifted back to sleep the thought came to her that only a few centuries ago Vic might have been taken for a witch, living alone on the edge of the village with her black cat. She wondered if Vic had any warts, and smiled sleepily.

In the morning, looking at her watch, she realized with a jolt that in a week's time it would be the day before Christmas Eve. Small as her funds were, keen as she was to eke them out sufficiently not to be a financial burden on her sister, she wanted to buy Vic a present she would like. Yesterday Vic had told her that her friend Don would be coming for Christmas dinner, so Bel thought she had better buy something for him too. But what? They hadn't even met.

But Vic seemed disinclined to talk about Christmas at all, and Bel, assuming that her sister had already, in her quietly efficient way, bought everything she required, hesitated to mention her own needs. They spent a quiet morning, walking along the riverbank, doing a bit of housework, talking little. After lunch Bel said, 'Is there a shop in the village? Or a bus into Stoke? I need to do some Christmas shopping.'

'Oh,' Vic said, seeming nonplussed, as if it was the strangest request. 'Of course, I'm sorry, Bel, I should have thought. Look, it's a bit late now, and I can't go tomorrow, because I have to clean the church. Normally in the holidays I do it on a Friday, but the ladies will be arranging the flowers for the Carol Service tomorrow morning and there's no point in hoovering before they've finished – there'll be bits of stalks everywhere.

29

If you can wait that long, I'll drive you into Stoke on Monday. I doubt the village shop would have anything you'd want.'

'I don't want to put you out.'

'No, that's OK, there are things I need too. But meanwhile if you want some stamps or last-minute cards the village Post Office would probably do, and they're open now or tomorrow morning.'

Bel looked out of the window and shivered. 'Think I'll wait,' she said. 'It's getting dark already.'

Vic smiled. 'I'll fill up with logs. I think it's going to be a cold night.'

As they sat that evening, one on each side of the fire, hardly speaking, Bel felt the silence crowd in on her, as if it flowed up the garden from the lane in engulfing waves. 'It's so quiet here,' she said.

Vic looked up from her book. 'Yes. That's why I chose this house.'

'There's something I'd like to see on TV,' she said. 'Do you mind?'

'Not at all.'

'If there was anything you'd like to see, I could always bring it down,' Bel said.

Vic shook her head. 'Thank you, but I've gone without so long now I wouldn't even know what's on offer.'

'Sometimes there's stuff you might like, or at least I imagine you might,' Bel said with a feeling of desperation. 'The wildlife programmes, for instance.' A spark of inspiration flashed and glowed. 'And,' she said, 'sometimes even a Shakespeare play. Wouldn't you like that?'

Vic looked up at her over the rims of her glasses. 'Perhaps I would,' she said. 'But I'd rather see it in the theatre. And whatever gems I might be missing, I value peace more.'

'Oh.' *Well, that fell flat.*

Then Vic surprised her. 'I saw you on television once.'

'Really?' Bel said, astonished. 'When was that?'

'Oh, at least seven years ago,' Vic said. 'I was watching something at Don's, with Don's wife, Ellen. If I remember it was a series called "Cathedral Bells." It was the only time I saw it so it was quite a coincidence to have seen you.'

'Not really – I was in most of the episodes. I played the barmy housekeeper. But how did you know it was me?'

'I recognized you. And then I watched the credits, and realized what your stage name was.'

'Crikey,' Bel said thoughtfully. 'That seems ages ago. It ran for years, that programme. Then came the cuts, and out it went. Outran its popularity, I suppose.' She paused. 'What happened to Don's wife?'

'She had a horrible illness called poly – something. She'd been ill for years. They moved here because of it, for a more easily-adapted house in a quiet place. After a while she could do almost nothing for herself. All her muscles wasted, bit by bit. In the end she choked to death. I wasn't there. Don was always so vigilant, but he'd just gone into the garden to pull up a lettuce, or something. Poor Don.'

Bel grimaced, wishing she hadn't asked. 'How dreadful.'

'Yes, it was. Don was quite distraught. He'd looked after her single-handed half their married life. I only knew her for a couple of years, after they came to Thackham, but I was shattered too. She was a very dear friend.'

'Life can be very cruel,' Bel said. She saw Vic look at her sharply, and she shivered. 'I'll go upstairs, then, and leave you in peace. Let me know if the TV's too loud.'

Vic

On Saturday morning Bel decided she needed a few more Christmas cards. 'I know they won't arrive in time,' she said. 'But at least they'll know I thought of them, and maybe they'll blame the post.'

'I'll walk down with you,' Vic said. 'I wonder what changes you'll notice. When you live somewhere for a long time you forget how things used to be. Well, I do.'

Well wrapped against a biting easterly wind they trudged down the rutted track that ran between bare fields before turning into a made-up road. 'It's further than I thought,' Bel muttered.

'Don't you walk in London?' Vic asked mildly.

'Not if I can help it. I take the bus.'

'Here we are, anyway,' Vic said. 'The Post Office. The place to get your TV licence.' She raised her eyebrows meaningfully as Bel pushed open the door, and Bel made a face. 'The cards are over there. If there are any left. Oh, and there's Don.'

'The cards can wait,' Bel said with what could only be described as a smirk. 'Introduce me, please.'

Vic closed her eyes momentarily. 'All right.' And the thought came to her from somewhere unlooked for, and not even especially rational: *Bel, back off.* She sighed. However hard she tried, beneath the thin surface of her skin anger was ready to boil.

Don was turning away from the shop counter and saw them. 'Good morning,' he said, and Vic immediately registered the wariness beneath the civil greeting.

'Morning,' Vic said. 'Bel this is Don, Don, my sister Isabel.'

She watched them as they shook hands, Don bending down from his height like a ginger stork, Bel's eyes crinkling as she smiled.

'We're not a bit alike, are we?' Bel said.

'Apparently not,' Don answered gravely.

'We've come to buy a few last-minute cards,' Bel said. 'I know

I've left it far too late. You'll excuse me if I go and look, won't you?'

She went to the other side of the shop, and Don, a tiny frown appearing between his eyebrows, murmured, 'So, are you both surviving?'

'Just about. She's making a big effort, I think. I should too.'

Then Bel was back. 'There's absolutely nothing left,' she announced loudly. 'Only boxes of a dozen, and all I want is one or two.'

'We'll have to get some on Monday,' Vic said. 'Stoke has more choice.'

Don cleared his throat. 'I'm going to Stoke this afternoon. I have to pick up a few boxes from the warehouse and deliver them to the hospital so they are all right over the holiday period. I could give you a lift if you like, Mrs er...'

Bel laughed. 'Well, I suppose I'm still Mrs Morgan, or even Mrs Ilthwaite, depending on how you look at it. But just call me Bel, please. And thank you for the offer. That's most kind. I'm sure Vic was only going on Monday for my benefit. Now she won't have to.'

'I'll pick you up around two, then, if that suits you. I'll be a couple of hours, probably. Back around five?'

'Perfect.' Bel was beaming.

Leaving the church resplendent with flowers and greenery, candles ready for lighting, the brass gleaming, every wooden surface glowing with polish, and the dark blue carpet innocent of stalks and petals, Vic locked the heavy door, wrapped her scarf tightly round her neck and buttoned up her coat. Now that it was dark the wind seemed to be colder still. She shivered. *Straight from Siberia.*

She had been home barely ten minutes, and had just had time to draw the curtains, throw a few logs on the fire and feed a silently-appearing Solomon, when she saw headlights in the lane and heard the sound of an engine. She opened the front door as Bel climbed down from the car, several carrier bags over her arm. Vic walked down the path to the gate and Don opened his window.

'Tea?' she said. 'The kettle's on.'

'I won't, thanks,' Don said. 'A few things to see to.'

'But you'll come for lunch tomorrow?'

'Thank you. But I'll have to go early. I've arranged for an extra choir practice before the Carol Service.'

'No problem. We'll let you off the washing up this time.'

He smiled, released the brake and rolled away slowly over the ruts.

'Successful shop?' Vic asked Bel as they trudged up the front path.

33

'Yes, thanks. Quite an interesting afternoon, as it turned out. But let's get in out of this wind. I'm more than ready for a cup of tea.'

Once she had shed her coat and unwound her scarf, dropped her damp gloves and picked them up again, all the while talking about the changes she had noticed in the various streets and buildings of West Stoke, which she hadn't seen for more than two decades, Bel fell into a chair in the living room with a groan and settled her stockinged feet on a low stool. She wiggled her toes in front of the fire while Vic rearranged the logs, encouraging a steady upward-licking flame.

Vic made the tea and brought it in on a tray She handed a mug to Bel. 'So, tell me about your afternoon.'

Bel took a sip and leaned forward. 'I met someone I knew,' she said, her eyes bright. 'I certainly didn't expect that, not after all these years. Do you remember Connie Dawson? She's more or less my age, perhaps a few years older, but she looks a hundred! I wouldn't have recognized her, but she came bounding up to me. Her hair's like a blonde bird's nest, she had makeup on so thick you'd need a spade to scrape it off, and she was wearing teetering heels and a fake-fur coat. Talk about a caricature. Not only that, but she's such a luvvie, worse than my friend Bertie, and he's gay as well as an actor, so he feels he has to act camp. Anyway, up comes Connie, and behind her's a young chap I thought was her son, and he's carrying her bags. "Darling!" she shrieks at the top of her voice, and she always was a bit plummy. "It *is* Bella, isn't it?" At this she turns to the young chap, who's gone red as a ripe tomato, and says, "This is Bella Morgan, sweetie, one of the few from the Stoke Players who ever made it into the big time!" Well, of course I denied *that*, but she took no notice and introduced me to the young man who she said was her lodger, Gareth somebody. She's all full of tittering and winks and the poor boy's positively wilting. There was no holding her barrage of questions, and when she found out I was here for a few weeks she said, "Well, darling, in that case you absolutely *must* come to the Stoke Players' New Year's Eve party at the Headless Chicken. There might be a few of the old guard you'd know, and we can show off our celebrity to the younger members, who always think they know everything. Do come!" I hardly had a chance to get a word in.'

'Will you go?' Vic asked.

'I rather think I will. It'll be a hoot, and an excuse to get dressed up and wear my ridiculous red shoes. When she found I was staying with you, she said to invite you as well, but I told her it probably wasn't your kind of thing.'

'You were right about that,' Vic said with a slight smile. 'But if you want to go, I'll drive you there and collect you afterwards. There'll be no public transport on New Year's Eve.'

Bel frowned. 'Won't you be celebrating somewhere yourself?'

'I doubt it. Christmas is different, but New Year doesn't mean a lot to me. Lots of hysteria and false hope.'

'Well, in that case, thank you, I'll take you up on your kind offer.'

There was silence for a few moments, and then Bel hummed a little and a sly smile appeared on her face. 'And then,' she said, 'on the way home in the car, I had an interesting chat with Don.'

'Oh yes?' Vic's voice was calm, but something about her sister's tone made her feel slightly sick.

'You're a strange one, Vic. I was chatting to Don about his interests, you know, the music at church and so on, and I said something like, "I expect Vic's a member of your choir," and he laughed like the proverbial drain! He said, and these were his very words, "We're not that hard up!" I was very surprised and puzzled and I was going to protest but you know what? Something stopped me. I know I have a reputation for being tactless, but I must have improved. I figured if you don't sing in the church choir there must be a reason. But I'd like to know what it is.'

Vic's hands were shaking slightly, and she put her mug down with deliberate care. 'If I tell you,' she said, her voice low, 'I hope you'll say no more about it.'

Bel shrugged. 'All right.'

'I don't sing any more. I gave it up years ago. I always make out I have no voice, that it's like a bullfrog with laryngitis, that I'm tone-deaf. Whatever. When Don came to Thackham and became organist and choirmaster, that's what he thought, and I've never disabused him. That's how I want it to stay, so please, don't say anything.'

'Of course I won't if that's what you want, but why, Vic? It seems such a terrible waste. You had such a voice! Singing was your life – wasn't it? You wanted to make a career of it.'

Vic stared at Bel, but it seemed she hardly saw her. 'Yes, I did. But it was a long time ago. It didn't work out, like so many youthful ambitions. And now my lie has turned into truth, because my voice has gone.'

'How do you know that, if you never sing?'

'Leave it, Bel, please. It's how I want it, and that's good enough. Don't rock the boat.'

'I wouldn't dream of it,' Bel said, frowning.

Vic got up. 'Time for supper, I think,' she said briskly. 'Want to peel some potatoes?'

Bel followed Vic into the kitchen, but clearly she wasn't finished with her questions, and Vic's answers had, it seemed, served to stimulate rather than satisfy her curiosity. She stood at the sink, sleeves rolled up, her hands plunged into a bowl of water, and slowly peeled. 'Don seems a nice man,' she said.

She spoke without apparent guile, but Vic was instantly on her guard.

'Yes, he is,' she said.

'He was telling me about his business. It seems quite successful, even in these hard times.'

'I believe so,' Vic said. She closed the fridge door, a box of mushrooms in her hands. 'Medical equipment is quite specialised and always in demand, and a few years ago, before Don and Ellen came to Thackham, one of his technical staff developed some new form of tubing which was superior to anything else. Don patented that and it's allowed him to expand and take on a couple of new people, including a secretary. But it's still a small concern, which is how he likes it. He still does quite a bit of the delivering himself. Like today.'

'Hm. I suppose he is quite well off, then.'

'I really couldn't say.'

'No children.'

'No.'

Bel was silent for a few moments while she cut up the potatoes and put them into a saucepan of water. 'You could do worse, you know,' she said.

'What?'

'Well, you say Don's your friend, but wouldn't you like something more?' She caught the look on Vic's face and flushed. 'All right, tell me to mind my own business.'

'I think it would be better if you did!' Vic flared. There was a moment of hot silence, then she sighed. 'When Don and Ellen came here, about seven years ago, perhaps a bit longer, it was Ellen who was my friend. I helped Don so that he could go to work. When Ellen got really sick he had to employ people to take care of her so that he could keep the business afloat, but when I could I would keep her company. That was no hardship at all. She was a great friend and a wonderful person, and I still miss her.'

'She's been gone a long time, though.'

'Yes,' Vic said sadly. 'But Don was a devoted husband, and I don't think there'll ever be anyone else for him.'

'How can you be sure of that?' Bel said. 'And what about you? You're not dead yet, you know.'

'Look, Bel, can we change the subject? Things are as they are, and they're fine with me. When you've gone back to your life in London, life will jog along here the same as ever, I don't doubt. Let's just leave it at that.'

Bel had, indeed, dropped the subject, not without some reluctance and a small, knowing smirk that irritated Vic like a stinging fly. But later, when she was alone, trying to read, listening to Bel laughing upstairs at some hilarity on television, that peppery annoyance mutated into something altogether heavier. However hard she tried to control and banish them, her thoughts proved stubborn and intractable, and she recalled an afternoon in the school staff-room, sitting idly for a moment before a meeting, unwillingly listening to two colleagues talking about their private lives. One of them was youngish, married with two school-age children; she was harassed by the juggling of home and work, feeling that she rarely got the balance right, and whatever she did, exhaustion was its result. The other, a woman a few years younger than Vic, was describing, in a voice not quite low enough to be ignored, a recent weekend away with a new man. Vic wished she didn't have to listen. She told herself she didn't want to know. But the worst of it was her own sudden shameful spurt of envy, and thinking about it now redoubled her discomfort. She didn't want to think about it, not for a moment, because it was all pain in the past and fruitless in the present. What was the point of thinking about something you couldn't have?

Now she tried to concentrate on her reading, but the print swam and blurred, and she put the book down with a sigh, and leaned back in the chair, her eyes closed.

What do I really want? I hardly know. I thought I did, years ago, and for a while it all seemed right. But it didn't last, did it? It all went wrong, however hard I tried. And now, who would want me anyway, with all my baggage? I can't believe that anyone who got to know the real Vic wouldn't run away. There's only one man in this world I trust. But that has to be limited, or I shall lose him too.

Bel

Don poised the wine bottle over Bel's glass, an enquiring smile on his face.

'Oh, why not?' Bel said. 'Someone's got to do their duty, and you two are hardly drinking at all. It seems a shame to waste it.'

'Vic has to be careful,' Don said as he poured, 'with her digestion. And I can't afford to be too fuddled when I still have to play for the Carol Service.'

Bel took a large gulp, chuckled, and spluttered. 'Excuse me. No, well, we can't have that! You might play all the flats sharp or something.' She saw Vic look at Don with the slightest lifting of her brows, then turn back to Bel.

'You were telling us about your time with the theatre company,' Vic said. 'It sounds like something out of a play in itself.'

'Now there's a thought!' Bel sat up in her chair, then slumped again. 'A play about a travelling theatre! I should write it. But it's probably been done. Did I tell you about that ghastly woman in Doncaster?'

Vic shook her head. 'I don't think so.'

'We never had much money, you see. So we had to stay in some pretty awful places. We had favourite landladies dotted around the country, people who understood the way of life. Some of them were ex-actresses themselves, people who'd managed to scrape some cash together, or who'd married and had a family, or who'd just retired, and they'd open a boarding house for the likes of us, and usually it was just the sort of place we liked – not too many rules! But I remember on this occasion there was some problem with our usual digs – I think maybe the landlady was in hospital – and we had to go elsewhere. Oh, my dears! *What* a dump. Tepid bathwater I could cope with, even the odd cockroach. But this place was as cold as charity. It was February, the heating was measly, and we all had to sleep in our clothes. Who could blame us if we took to sneaking along the corridors at night? We bunked in together just to keep warm. Well, that was the excuse, but the old bat of a landlady was, to put it mildly, *most* put out. I remember her clearly: tight grey perm, pinched mouth, arms folded across her starched apron. "I'm not having that sort of thing in my house!" said she. "We're respectable people. I only took you in as a favour to Elsie Cantley. I can't think why she puts up with your goings-on. But *I* won't. You'll have to find somewhere else." This was when she found three or four of us in the same bed, fast asleep. I think Stefan was still in his blond wig, which probably didn't give a very good impression.'

Vic laughed. 'No, likely not. And did you find somewhere else?'

'We were going to move on anyway. The show hadn't done well, so we cut our losses and went south again. That was a pretty bad winter, I recall. People kept getting colds and flu and being laid up, and there were few enough of us anyway. Once or twice we had to take on extra people, and that was often a disaster in itself.'

'Why so?' Don asked.

Bel leaned forward. 'Well, they just didn't know our ways, you see. And some of them were *such* divas! We all muddled along. We didn't get too full of ourselves. You wouldn't be allowed to – the others would all take the mickey unmercifully. And when you've seen someone in their shabby old slippers, with their nose red and their eyes watering, or with their head down the loo puking, or tottering from the bathroom in their threadbare dressing gown, hung over after a heavy night, there's not much room for glamour. The glamour was for the punters, and went on with the makeup. New people didn't always seem to understand. I remember that winter there were so many of us off sick – not me, though, I never got ill for some reason – that Edna had to hire a leading man, and boy, did he fancy himself! What was his name?' Bel paused, frowning. 'Rudi something-or-other, a Russian-sounding name, I think. It wasn't his real name, of course – that was probably something quite pedestrian, like Ernest Brown, but he wouldn't tell *us*. He obviously thought we were the lowest of the low. Reckoned he was only taking the job as a stopgap. Nobody believed him, of course. We were all quite frightful to him, and he lasted about a week. He wasn't the only one. But somehow we battled through. Anything left in that bottle, Don?'

Don emptied the bottle into her glass. 'What about the audiences?' he said. 'Did you normally go down well? What sort of plays did you put on?'

Bel drank deeply, put down her glass with exaggerated care, and wiped her mouth on a napkin. 'Well, we had a stock repertoire, of course. What we did depended on the place we were in, and the time of year. And sometimes we'd have to learn something quite new. I liked that. But often the audiences were conservative. They didn't appreciate anything remotely intellectual or avant-garde. And if they didn't like something they would usually let you know, in no uncertain terms.'

'What, surely they didn't throw things?' Don said. His face was serious, but there was merriment in his eyes.

Bel nodded solemnly. 'Sometimes. And there might be boos and catcalls. You got used to it. But usually we went down all right, especially if it was some sentimental piece they all knew and liked. And sometimes it went down a bit *too* well.'

'What do you mean?' Vic said.

'Don't forget, I was young then,' Bel said. 'And not bad-looking, I suppose. It was the men at the stage door, after the show. They could get quite aggressive. I had to make sure I came out with some of our bigger chaps, for protection. It wasn't just my autograph they wanted, I'm afraid.' She giggled. 'Sometimes there was a nice young fellow there, looking for a bit of company; I didn't mind them. It was the beery louts, the ones after trouble, that could be difficult.' She looked sideways at Don under her eyelashes. 'I don't suppose *you* ever did that kind of thing in your youth, did you, Don?'

Don stifled a grin. 'No, I wasn't much of a theatre-goer,' he said. 'Perhaps I should have been – sounds like quite an education.'

'Well, it was certainly that, especially to a young girl like me. All the cold greasy breakfasts at unearthly hours of the morning, the chilly train journeys with all our stuff following in a lorry, and getting lost as often as not. But I remember the fun as well, the last-night parties, the drunken larks and giggles and creaking bed-springs.' She sighed, and looked up at Don coquettishly. 'I hope I'm not embarrassing you, Don. I'm sure you had a much more respectable life.'

Don shrugged. 'Well, yes, I suppose I did. I was working hard, married in my twenties, trying to save, and then build a business. Not a lot of room for drunken larks.'

'I can't believe you were *quite* as starchy as you are making out,' Bel said. She leaned over and laid her hand over his as it rested on the table. After a moment he removed it with an awkward jerk. Bel barely seemed to notice, but when she looked at Vic, even through the fuddled lens of almost a whole bottle of wine, she could not fail to notice the wide-eyed look of horror on her sister's face. 'Oops. Have I overdone it?' *Time to leave the stage, Bella old girl.* She pushed back her chair. 'Well now, enough of my heedless

40

youth. I'll get started on the washing-up, shall I?' She tottered a little and grabbed the back of the chair.

'Leave it, Bel,' Vic said, and to Bel's ears it sounded as if she was speaking through clenched teeth. 'Why don't you go and sit in the lounge? I'll make some coffee.'

'No coffee for me, thanks,' Bel said. 'If you're sure about the washing-up, I think I'll just go and lie down for half an hour. Got a bit of a headache. Do excuse me. Don't want to let the side down by puking, do I?'

Vic

Don had gone, off to meet his choir members for a last practice of their anthems. The dishes were draining.

Vic sat at the kitchen table. A blue folder lay before her, bulging with essays needing to be marked. They should be done now, ready to be handed back on Monday morning; the end of term was close, and this class had mock-exams in January. Vic opened the folder and extracted the first effort; it seemed depressingly thin, two pages stapled together. She read the child's name at the top, and sighed. Despite being decorated with hopeful floral swirls, the quality of the work was unlikely to be up to much. For this pupil Shakespeare was a tedious irrelevance, a necessary evil, and his language incomprehensible. For a moment, staring at the first page till the words went out of focus, Vic felt a surge of bitter anger. The burning in her gut suddenly worsened, and she heaved herself to her feet and took a pill with a glass of water, washing away the taste of acid bile. She leaned on the sink and groaned softly. Bel, it seemed, could drink like a fish and suffer nothing but mild embarrassment, while she, Vic, could be in agony from half a glass. Why was it that some people seemed able to sail along, shrugging off whatever life threw at them with a rueful laugh, while others endured tormenting doubt, a sense of defeat, whatever their efforts? But who was she angry with? With Bel, for making everything about Vic's life seem dismal, petty, grey? With God, for the sheer unfairness that seemed to underpin the created order? No, that was ridiculous. Certainly there was no equality in creation, but that didn't make it unjust. Perhaps she was angry with herself, simply for who she was, the way she reacted against her own interests. Why? She shook her head. There was no answer, none that satisfied. Why was she angry because Bel had been a bit drunk, and in her cups flirted with Don? – quite mildly, really, nothing outrageous or offensive at all. Hadn't she, Vic, told her sister she didn't see Don in that way, that he was a dear friend, but nothing else? Don was grown up, after all – surely he could deal with Bel and her ways quite easily without any help. There was no reason for anger; and yet here she was, unable to work, her stomach sour, her hands gripping the worktop, and misery threatening to swamp her. It was all so out of proportion, she knew that. And nobody was suffering from this non-problem but herself.

The medication began to work, and the pain receded. She wiped the sweat from her face with a towel, and sat down again at the table. *Lord, help me with this. I can't help myself. I scarcely know what the problem is, only that there is one. Help me to be nicer to my sister. She hasn't really done anything to warrant my disapproval, and you know I have no cause to sit in judgment, on her or anyone. I need to get these essays marked. I need to be calm. I need to be at peace.*

She sighed deeply, opened up the blue folder again, put on her glasses and took up her pen.

Bel

18 December 2005

Bel lay huddled in bed with the door closed, wrapped up to her neck in the bedclothes.

She could hear Vic and Don talking at the front door as Don took his leave. She couldn't hear what they were saying. She turned over onto her stomach and put the pillow over her head. A sense of discomfiture, almost of shame, wriggled behind her eyes. She knew she hadn't behaved particularly well, and it made her feel as if she were twelve again, gauche, loud, self-flaunting, embarrassing. Yes, she had drunk far too much of the bottle that Don had brought, and at first she was amusing, she thought, even a little shocking, with her stories. And Vic and Don, exchanging glances, had seemed to laugh with her. But then, of course, she had gone too far. She had forgotten for a moment that she was out of her normal milieu, and that she often became sentimental and flirtatious under the influence of alcohol. And Vic, who had seemed OK with it all till then, had suddenly looked appalled. But so what? Hadn't Vic as much as said she didn't see Don as any kind of mate for herself? Wasn't he fair game? Or was Vic just being a dog in the manger?

There was silence downstairs, and Bel rolled onto her back and sighed, pulling the quilt closer around her and shivering. Something in her sister's situation didn't ring true to her, even though she admitted to herself that there was a lot she didn't understand. If she was inclined to think of it as a scenario, that was hardly surprising. *If I was writing an episode for a soap, or even as the punter watching the programme, I'd know exactly what ought to come next. Vic obviously fancies Don but is too stiff-necked to admit it, even to herself. She's afraid of something – perhaps of losing her dignity. She certainly came over very frosty when I got a bit too friendly! Oops. But why? She said…well, people say things they don't mean. Could it be something to do with this singing thing? And as for Don, well, he's just a typical bloke. A very clever one in some ways, but blind, insensitive, just plain dumb in others. He's a nice man, trustworthy, kind, dependable; it's easy to see why Vic thinks so well of him. But he doesn't seem in touch with his own feelings or anyone else's.*

44

He plods through life taking things at face value, unaware of what he might be missing, or who he might be hurting. That's how it looks to me, anyway. What would it take to wake him up? What would it take to bust open Vic's precious shell? Trouble is, soaps aren't really anything like real life. Real people are a lot more complicated. They have pasts, hidden motives, secret thoughts, hurts they cover up.

She must have dozed, because the next thing she knew was her door quietly opening and Vic setting a mug of tea on her bedside table. She had changed into a dark blue dress, and put her hair up neatly – whoever wore their hair that way any more? Bel thought irritably. Then she remembered her own behaviour over lunch, and realised she was sprawling inelegantly, and her mouth tasted disgusting.

'I thought this might be welcome,' Vic said gently.

Bel felt a surge of embarrassment, a flood of heat rising up her neck, burning her ears, and she sat up, bumped her head painfully on the headboard, and swore. When she had recovered herself, rubbing her bruised head, Vic had withdrawn to the partially-open doorway and was watching her, a half-smile on her face.

'Vic, I'm sorry, I am such a fool, I really shouldn't drink.' Bel stretched out her hand, then let it fall. 'Please say I haven't made a complete fool of myself, or caused offence.'

'Forget it,' Vic said. 'It's fine. I just wondered if you still wanted to come to the Carol Service.'

'Oh, God – sorry, mustn't say that – is there still time? D'you think I should?'

'If you'd like to, of course. And there's plenty of time. Why don't you have your tea and then go and soak in a bath? It might make you feel a bit more human.'

Bel pouted. 'What do I look like now, then? An alien?'

Vic smiled, and a light of merriment, just tinged with malice, came into her eyes, a look that Bel hadn't seen for more than thirty years. 'No, more like a rumpled orang-utan.'

'Wow, thanks. But it's a good idea. Thanks for the tea. And Vic – thanks for not being po-faced.'

Vic

Vic watched her sister's face as they walked slowly behind a young family with a toddler through the heavy oak door of St. Mark's. It was barely six o'clock, but the pews were filling rapidly. The overhead heaters were on, but the ancient stone emitted its own chill, and people were still swathed in winter coats and scarves and hats. Babies in push chairs blocked the aisles, and a cluster of small children goggled up at the Christmas tree, resplendent with tinsel and stars, that stood twelve feet high at the side of the vestry door. A bowl of flowers had been set on every shelf and table, and at each pew-end stood candle-holders, each with four white candles ready to be lit. Against the darkness of the night the church glowed with festal light and colour, and mingled scents of flowers, pine branches and damp wool lay on the air.

Bel looked at Vic, her eyes wide, smiling delightedly. 'It's so beautiful, Vic!'

'Don't you remember the church?'

Bel shook her head. 'Not like this.'

'Well, people work hard to make it splendid for Christmas. This, and the music, is what they come for, I suppose, the ones we don't see for the rest of the year.'

'People like me, you mean.'

Vic smiled. 'Let's find a carol sheet and somewhere to sit while there's still room.'

At six-thirty the churchwarden closed the door. The church was packed. Against the murmur of voices the candles were lit and the lights switched off. Now the darkness crowded in, relieved only by the pulpit light, the candles, the red glow of the heaters, and the lamps in the choir stalls; it lent an air of mystery, and somewhere at the back of the church a small child whimpered and was hushed. Don was bringing the opening voluntary, an arrangement of 'For unto us a boy is born', to a close as the choir, in ill-matched blue robes, filed in. Behind them came Frankie, for once crisply-surpliced, her voluminous cassock hiding her belly but not her rolling pregnant gait. She was humming to the voluntary, and there was holly woven in her bright brown hair.

As she took her place at the lectern, looking round the full church with a satisfied expression, a shriek came from the front pew. 'Mummy!' and a small creature hurtled out and threw its arms round Frankie's knees.

Bel looked at Vic, her eyebrows raised.

'Rob and Frankie's son, Noah,' Vic said, her voice low.

'He's in a reindeer costume,' Bel whispered. 'Complete with red nose.'

Vic shrugged. 'It's not a conventional household. And he's only two and a half.'

They watched, with the rest of the grinning congregation, as Frankie bent, disentangled her son's arms, said something to him, then held his hand as she looked down the church and welcomed them all.

It was, by village-church standards, a glorious hour of praise and music. The readings told the familiar Christmas story, from creation to prophecy, from the birth of a baby and the heavenly portents to John's magisterial explanation, read in solemn tones by an elderly parishioner in a tweed suit. The choir did its best with 'In the bleak midwinter' and 'Noel nouvelet.' The carols were sung lustily, and Don accompanied them with his usual competence. Bel joined in with a lack of inhibition that Vic could only envy, but with a complete disregard for the appropriate key. Vic herself, as ever, mumbled and mouthed her way through the carols as if her teeth hurt. And then, with 'O come, all ye faithful,' it was over for another year, and some people, including the choirmaster and organist, sighed with relief. Don played them out with a ringing piece of Bach, then, as the bell ringers began their work, he gathered up his music and disappeared into the vestry with an airy flap of his robes.

Vic and Bel waited in their pew until most of the congregation had departed. 'Don's very good,' Bel said with what seemed genuine admiration. 'Not that I know diddlysquat about organ music.'

'He was a chorister himself as a boy,' Vic said. 'Learned the organ from the organist at his parish church, and just carried on.' She looked at Bel speculatively. 'Would you like to meet Frankie?'

'What, go backstage? Meet the leading lady who doesn't mind being upstaged by a two-year-old in a Rudolph costume? I can't wait.'

Vic led the way up the aisle, now empty but for the churchwarden who was making sure all the candles were completely extinguished. With the lights back on the atmosphere had dissipated. Vic pushed open the vestry door. A few choir members were there, talking to Don, who was putting piles of music into a cupboard. Frankie had divested herself of cassock and surplice and was now ready to go home, dressed in her usual elasticated jeans and enormous jumper. In the harsh light she looked tired, older than her thirty-two years.

'Frankie,' Vic said, 'I'd like you to meet my sister, Isabel. Bel, the Reverend Frances Maynard.'

They shook hands. 'Nice to meet you,' Bel said. 'What happened to Rudolph?'

'He went home asleep with Santa,' Frankie said. 'That's where I'm going too. I'm hoping Santa's got the kettle on. Nice to meet you too. Hope you enjoyed the service.'

'I loved it,' Bel said, so sincerely that it gave Vic a jolt. 'It made me think of when we were children.' Vic looked at Bel in undisguised disbelief for the tiny moment before she remembered herself, and to her dismay saw that Frankie was watching her and smiling. Somewhere in that small smile, Vic knew, was probing perceptiveness and sword-sharp sympathy.

'Well, we must let you get some rest, Frankie,' Vic said briskly. 'I could do with a cup of tea and a sandwich too. Let's go, shall we, Bel?'

'I'll walk with you to the gate,' Frankie said. 'You done here, Don?'

'Yes, I'm coming. Has everyone gone? I'll lock up.'

Outside the door Vic hung back, watching Frankie and Bel walk slowly down the church path, leaning together as if they'd known each other for years, talking about who knew what. But Vic knew this was one of Frankie's little-recognised skills; she had no doubt that Bel would be telling her all manner of things in that short walk that she had never intended to reveal. Vic herself needed all her own reserve to defend herself against this unspoken invitation that Frankie seemed to emanate. Normally Vic was fairly certain of safety in the bastion of her privacy. Now, the very presence of Bel seemed to be shaking that certainty.

She watched Don douse the lights and lock the door.

'Don.'

He looked at her enquiringly.

'I feel I need to apologise.'

'What for?'

'My rather dreadful sister.'

He laughed softly. 'It's not a problem,' he said. 'You can't be held responsible. And it didn't bother me. I was a bit startled, I have to admit. But I was amused more than anything. How have you two ended up so different?' He looked down at her, still smiling, and there was something in his expression which gave her pause, something akin to a tender concern she had never seen before. It made her shiver – with alarm, with unnamed longing, she hardly knew. She had hidden herself away for so long, and now, just because, it seemed, of the presence of Bel, both Frankie and Don were looking at her with new and troubling eyes.

Vic

Christmas Eve

The phone rang just as Vic was washing up the lunch things.

'I've shut up shop for the next few days,' Don said.

'I should think so,' Vic said. 'You work far too hard as it is.'

He ignored this. 'I'll pick you up later if you like,' he said. 'I'm taking a couple of other people from church as well. Four-thirty be OK?'

'Fine.'

'You all right? You sound a bit odd. How are things with Bel? Sorry I've been out of touch for the last few days – I've been trying to get things sewn up at work, finishing off orders and such.'

'Things with Bel are – I don't know, Don. Rather cool.'

'Is she there?'

'No, she took a walk down to the village.'

'So why cool?'

Vic took a deep breath. 'I'm beginning to think,' she said slowly, 'that Bel's memories of our joint past are completely different from mine. Why do you suppose that is?'

He was silent for a moment. Then he said, 'Well, everyone remembers things differently, don't they? The same event means different things to different people. And she's a bit younger than you. As a child that difference would have been greater. But what's brought this on? And why does it matter?'

'I don't know why it matters, except that it makes me doubt my own view of things, and then I feel unsteady somehow, as if the past is being rewritten.' She paused. 'I told her, last night, what we do on Christmas Eve, the Stoke soup kitchen at the Methodist church. How long have we been doing it, Don? Three, four years? And not just us, but a bunch of others too. And Bel reacted most queerly, went all sulky like a disappointed child. She talked about how Christmas Eve was always so special when we were children, and recited all the things we were supposed to have done, all the sweet family traditions, the treats and so on, and it was a shame I wasn't going to be at home with her, and I have to say I looked at her in utter disbelief. Which didn't go down well at all.'

'Did you actually challenge her?'

'Well, only in a very mild sort of way, but she lost her temper with me rather.'

'What did she say?'

Vic sighed and leaned against the wall. 'I made a remark about our grandfather, the Judge. As you know, I've always thought he was a horrible old man, with far too much influence over our father. In my memory he caused a lot of the trouble in the family just by his attitudes, in particular to us girls. Don, he acted as if we were of absolutely *no account*. But when I said as much to Bel she was shocked. She clearly thinks of him as a rather distant but kindly old fellow. She remembers, apparently, an occasion when he was visiting. She fell in a patch of nettles, he helped her out and was gruffly sympathetic and gave her a sweet. She thinks now I am just nasty and have distorted everything. She says I am bitter. Am I?'

'Mm. You are, sometimes,' Don said. 'But you have reason, I think. I wasn't there, so I can't say. Is she still annoyed with you?'

'Probably. But we haven't spoken much since then, except rather chilly civilities.'

'Should you say something?' Don asked.

Vic laughed shortly. 'I won't need to. Bel never would let anything go. I doubt she's changed.'

'Tomorrow is Christmas Day.'

'I hadn't forgotten, Don. Now you're going to say something about goodwill.'

'You've said it yourself. See you at four-thirty.'

Bel

Christmas Day

Bel woke on Christmas Day with a headache. It was mild enough but provided an excuse to avoid church. She felt conflicted: after the Carol Service, with all its memories of a happier time, she had been looking forward to church on Christmas Day, but Vic's attitude had soured it for her. Somehow, as soon as you scratched the surface, there was all Vic's black bile, her anger and contempt. *Am I included in that? I'm not sure, but it doesn't seem so. Except when I say something nice, however trivial, about our parents, or our childhood, or the Judge. Why does she loathe them all so much?* She poured herself a glass of water, took two painkillers and retired to her room.

Later, the headache receding, washed and dressed and a cup of coffee inside her, her good temper and easy-going nature resurfaced. *It's Christmas, Isabel. Be the better person.* She prepared the vegetables that Vic had left, and laid the table with festive napkins and a sprig or two of greenery that she found in the garden.

When Vic came in, followed by Don, her eyes widened. 'Oh, thank you, Bel,' she said. 'You've done it all. You've made the table look lovely.'

Impulsively Bel put her arms round her sister. 'Happy Christmas, Vic,' she said. 'Sorry if I flew off the handle yesterday.'

Vic disengaged herself gently. 'I'm sure it was my fault. Happy Christmas to you too. Come in, Don, don't hover in the doorway. There's an almighty draught.'

Lunch was festive in a quiet sort of way. Vic wasn't keen on paper hats and crackers, but they opened a bottle of wine and were cheerful, and the food was very good. Afterwards they went into the living room with coffee and exchanged presents. Bel, aware of the effects of alcohol, anxious not to make a fool of herself, tried her best to be civil to Don without any hint of coquetry, and was puzzled by the amused glances she intercepted between him and Vic. She was surprised, and touched, to find a small pile of gifts for herself under the tiny tree in the corner, one from Don, and two from Vic. Shyly she offered Vic her own presents. 'This is one I chose myself for you,' she said. 'I hope you like the colours. And this is one Don thought you would like. I guess he knows more about your tastes than I do, even if he is a man.'

Don laughed out loud. 'I realize that's a major disadvantage,' he said.

Bel blushed. 'Sorry, I didn't mean to be rude.'

'You're not at all.'

Vic opened her gifts, both colourfully wrapped. 'Bel, it's beautiful.' She held up a long, soft, fringed scarf. 'It'll go well with my dark coat. Thank you.' She unwrapped the second package, a small rectangle. 'I can see Don's insider knowledge,' she said. 'John Donne's sonnets. Marvellous. And what a beautiful binding. Wherever did you find it?'

'There were two. I liked the dark blue with the silver title.'

'An excellent choice. I shall read these later, quietly in bed. Some of the phrases are so lovely, so telling, they make me cry. So don't worry if you hear the odd sniffle.'

Bel looked at Vic in undisguised suspicion, and Vic laughed.

'Take no notice, Bel,' Don said. 'Your sister's a tease.'

'She always used to be,' Bel said. 'I never knew if she was joking. But I thought – '

'What? That she'd grown out of it? Got all crusty and tetchy?'

'Whatever do you mean, Don – crusty and tetchy?' Vic sounded indignant.

'Now *you're* in the soup, Don,' Bel said.

'Oh, I think I'll survive,' Don said. 'My hide's good and thick.' Then, to Bel's surprise, they were all laughing.

Vic

Christmas Day

It was a strange Christmas for Vic – so much the same as every recent year, but also profoundly different. Leaving Bel behind a resolutely closed door, nursing, so she said, a headache, Vic trudged down the lane to St Mark's for the 10 o'clock service. She didn't have to go; she'd been to the Midnight, and got home at almost one in the morning, and now she was up early enough to prepare Christmas food before going to church again. Partly it was simply that today was Christ's birthday, and she wanted her every action to declare it, that this was the point of it all, not the noise and the tinsel and the consumerist greed. Partly it was out of solidarity with Don, who had to be there.

Normally Vic could cope with late nights and early mornings, but today her legs felt leaden and her heart hardly less so. Fortunately the Christmas morning service rarely exceeded forty minutes. It was designed mainly for the children and their parents, and was as informal as it was brief.

After the service, having cheerfully said goodbye to the last of the families, Frankie turned to Vic in the vestry doorway, her eyes narrow. 'You look tired,' she said.

Vic shrugged. 'Four hours at the soup kitchen, on our feet,' she said. 'Lunch preparations. Midnight service. Up early, and now here. I suppose I am tired. Come to that, you look tired too.'

'I have very good reason,' Frankie said mildly. 'It's Christmas. Last night and this morning are the culmination of weeks of extra work. I am a pregnant vicar with a sometimes fractious toddler. No, Vic, you look more than tired – you look stressed. What is it – pressures at work? Or your sister giving you grief?'

Vic opened her mouth to speak, and stopped. She felt a pang that could only be identified as guilt, and no doubt Frankie had chosen her words for just this effect. 'No,' she said. 'Not really. It may be that I am the one giving grief.'

Frankie nodded. 'You know what, Vic, I really think we need to have a chat. I can't believe I have known you for three years and I never had any inkling you even had a sister. Something's adrift here, or I'm a chimpanzee. Tell me to mind my own business if you like, but I'm your pastor after all.'

Vic sighed. 'You've got eyes like gimlets, and I hate you,' she said, shaking her head. 'But you're away tomorrow, aren't you?'

Frankie nodded. 'First thing – me, Rob, Noah and Brutus. We're joining my parents at their cottage. I need a bit of down time before number two gets here.' She patted her belly. 'But when I get back, after New Year? I won't forget. And I'll bully you.'

Vic smiled. 'I know you will. All right, I surrender. But Frankie, forget work for a week. Put your feet up. Let other people look after you.'

'I don't have a problem with that. But with my job forgetting work's not so easy. Because it's about people – people I care about and feel a responsibility for. Like you.'

'I'll be fine. But I agree: we'll talk. Next year.'

Walking home with Don after the service, she said suddenly, 'I think I'm becoming someone else.'

'What?'

'I just admitted I need to talk to someone: specifically, Frankie.'

'Well, good. At last. There's a lot bubbling away inside that head of yours. No wonder your digestion is so bad.'

'That's an anatomical mixed metaphor. And anyway, my digestion is only bad sometimes. And I do talk – I talk to you. Don't I?' She turned to him, her stride faltering.

He shook his head. 'You talk to me on your own terms,' he said. 'That's not a criticism. I understand, or at least I think I do. But while we're being honest, you worry me. I think Frankie's right.'

To her astonished dismay, Vic felt her eyes well with tears. 'Why didn't you say so before?'

'I did. Sort of, anyway. You ignored me.'

'Did I? I'm sorry. What's going on, Don?'

'That's obvious, I would have thought. Your sister's here, under your roof. Your past is getting uncomfortably close. You're going to have to sort it out, you know.'

They arrived at Vic's front gate, and she pushed it open.

'God help me,' she murmured. 'God help us all.'

'Amen to that,' Don said briskly. 'Now I think it's high time for a festive pre-lunch drink. What have you got?'

55

* * * *

It's been a strange sort of Christmas. Just by being here Bel seems to be changing things – even things like my friendship with Don, and how Frankie is with me. I don't know how I feel about it. There's a certain rightness to it, in a way. But at the same time, it's very frightening. I'm not at all sure I can handle the fallout.

Vic lay in bed. The curtains were closed, but through the cracks in the window-frames she could still hear the gusting of the wind. She was warm enough, with the covers pulled up, her hairy old cardigan on and Solomon a gently-purring dead weight close against her side. She looked at the book, lying open in her hands. It was a beautiful artefact, its soft, silver-edged pages encased in its stiff cover, a modern thing, of course, but an improvement on the battered paperback of Donne's verse that had served her since her student days. She turned the pages carefully, looking for favourite lines, and it came to her, not for the first time, that reading these sonnets was very like praying, except that Donne was far better at it than she was. If she read the verses with a prayerful attitude, would that suffice? She found it chokingly difficult to articulate her own prayers, but some of the lines before her eyes expressed her feelings with uncanny verisimilitude.

"Batter my heart, three-person'd God, for you
As yet but knock, breathe, shine, and seek to mend;
That I may rise, and stand, o'erthrow me and bend
Your force, to break, blow, burn and make me new."

I guess that's what they're all saying I need, those few who care: that I need to be broken. Except that I already feel broken – patched, hardly holding together.

"...'Tis late to ask abundance of thy grace,
When we are there; here on this lowly ground,
Teach me how to repent; for that's as good
As if thou had'st sealed my pardon, with thy blood."

God has been very merciful to me, these last few years. Should I be asking him for something more bracing? Am I brave enough? Is that why Bel's here at all? According to Don, it's God's gentle hint.

"Oh might those sighs and tears return again
Into my breast and eyes, which I have spent,
That I might in this holy discontent
Mourn with some fruit, as I have mourned in vain..."

Vic lifted her swimming eyes from the page, and felt the familiar pain clench deep in her abdomen. She groaned softly. *Is that it? Is that what you are making me feel, "holy discontent?" Lord, I have no idea what to do, how to begin. I am afraid. I know how fragile my own strength is.*

She leaned over to her bedside table, pulled a tissue from the box, wiped her eyes and blew her nose. Before she closed the book her eyes fell on one last line, and it seemed like an answer tailored to her confusion. As she stared at it, reading it over and over, she felt for a moment as she imagined Job might have felt, when his misery was at its lowest depth and his so-called friends had failed – at once rebuked and encouraged.

"Thou hast made me, and shall thy work decay?"

No, how can it? What you have called into being, sustained, fed, called to yourself, given a unique destiny – that cannot fail, for it is of your making. I'm not going to fall apart, because I belong to you.

Vic

Bel stood by the lounge window, looking out at the driving rain. 'God, it looks horrible out there.' She turned to Vic, who was sitting in an armchair, reading. 'Don's gone back to work today, then?'

'He always does. This is as long as he allows himself at Christmas. Christmas Day and Boxing Day. And I've known him go to work on Boxing Day.'

'What about the people who work for him?'

'They get longer. I think they go back on 28th. Then they have New Year off as well.'

'So what does he find to do at work all alone?'

Vic pushed her glasses further up her nose and closed her book. 'He does a bit of stock-taking, I believe. Sorts out the storage area. Checks the books ready for the accountant. That sort of thing.'

Bel flopped into a chair beside the window. 'It's been a funny sort of Christmas. Quiet. Nice, but different.'

'So what would you normally be doing?'

Bel leaned forward, and her eyes gleamed. 'Partying. There's usually a few people left in London. We get together at someone's place and let our hair down. Even actors who can't afford to eat can usually come up with a bottle or two. Funny that, isn't it? It can get a bit uproarious – paper hats, silly games, lots of noise. We had a bash at our digs last year. Josie was out, luckily. All great fun, though I'm finding these days I can't cope with the hangovers quite as well as I used to. Then of course New Year comes on top, and nearly everybody who's been out of town comes back, and it starts all over again.'

'It sounds exhausting.'

'It wouldn't be your cup of tea.' Bel sighed. 'Oddly, as I've got older, although I enjoy all the nonsense, I find I'm missing something. Maybe it's the idea of having your family around you at Christmas. That's not something I've had for many a year. Not since we were children, really.'

'And not then either, if we're honest,' Vic murmured, opening her book again.

Bel frowned. 'We had family Christmases, I know we did. We had a tree, and decorations, and presents. Surely you remember.'

'Do you remember who put those decorations up?'

'Not when we were really small.' She looked up, and saw Vic looking at her intently. 'When we were a bit older, you did it, and I helped you. I remember quite distinctly you standing on a step-ladder with an armful of paper-chains.'

'Do you remember being read to as a child? Before you could read? At bed-time, for instance?' Vic pursued, her voice low.

'Yes, of course.'

'Do you remember who by?'

'What's this, Vic? An interrogation?' Bel leaned back in her chair and folded her arms. Vic said nothing. 'Well. You did it, I suppose.'

'When you came home from school, when you were five and six and seven, who heard you read every night?'

'You did.' Bel's voice was tight. 'But Daddy was too busy, and Mummy was so often ill. You remember that, don't you?'

'Oh yes,' Vic said grimly. 'Remind me one day to tell you about *Mummy's* illnesses.'

Bel seemed to shrink back in her chair. 'What do you mean?'

Vic shook her head. 'Never mind. Perhaps it's best left alone.'

'No, Vic. Obviously you've got something to say. So say it.'

'Look, Bel, I'm not trying to be unkind. But it seems clear to me that you don't have much idea what really went on when we were children. Perhaps you were too young to understand. But the bottom line is we were not wanted, and we were not loved. Except by each other.'

'No. I can't believe that. What mother doesn't love her own children?' Bel's voice sounded strangled.

Vic took a deep breath. 'A weak woman, dominated by her husband and her father-in-law. A woman worn out by repeated pregnancies. A woman in the grip of depression, crushed by a sense of failure, until the day she finally produced a son – that great prize. I would feel sorry for her if it weren't for her craven desertion of her two daughters. This isn't my imagination, Bel, nor just my nasty nature coming out. I nursed our mother for ten months before she died, and in those months she told me things I would much rather not have known. I'm sorry if this is upsetting for you, but perhaps it's time you had the facts.'

'What do you mean, "repeated pregnancies"?' Bel whispered. 'Not just you and me and Johnnie?'

'You really don't know? No, I suppose not: you were away from home as soon as you were old enough to have any real understanding. All those illnesses, all those trips to the hospital, all those weeks when she was shut away in her room and we weren't allowed to see her – remember all that? Either she was recovering from yet another miscarriage, or she was in a black depression. Or both.'

'Oh, my God,' Bel said. 'That's awful. Poor woman.'

'Yes. I pity anyone with depression too. It's a horrible illness. But our mother's was to a degree self-inflicted, Bel. She was so obsessed with producing an heir for our father and his family it took over her life. She came to see herself as nobody. She hadn't the mental strength or the self-belief to see what a wicked sham the whole thing was. She should have taken us and left. It was all they deserved, our father and that wretched Judge.'

'So,' Bel said slowly, her eyes narrow, 'what you're saying is Mummy wanted to please Daddy and Daddy wanted to please Judge? And when Johnnie came along everyone was happy?'

Vic laughed grimly. 'You make it sound so nice. It wasn't nice at all, it was insane. And among it all you and I fell into a crack and disappeared.'

'But, but,' Bel struggled, 'we weren't neglected or anything.'

Vic shook her head. 'Not in any obvious sense, no, we weren't. They fed and clothed us, took us to the doctor if we were ill, sent us to a good school. That was the best thing they ever did, even if they did it to get us out of the way. But Bel, think – can you remember any cuddles? Can you really remember any time when you chatted to either of them, and were listened to? Any praise? Except from me?'

Tears welled in Bel's eyes and dribbled down her cheeks. 'I do remember you being there all the time. I remember us playing. I remember you putting a plaster on my elbow when I fell out of that tree. I remember you being kind.'

'Well, I suppose that's something,' Vic said. She could hear the weariness in her own voice, the burden of the years. 'You remember someone being kind, even if it was only your sister, who was a child herself.'

Bel was weeping openly now. She pulled a tissue out of her pocket. 'God, I wish you hadn't told me any of this,' she said wildly. 'What's the point of it now? They're all dead. What difference does it make?'

'Yes, they're dead, but we're alive. I don't want a lie at the centre of my life. I'd rather live with a hard truth than a soft lie.'

Bel pushed herself up out of the chair. Her eyes were swollen and her hair fell in her face. 'Well, I'm different. I'd rather believe something good, even if it isn't a hundred per cent true. I expect you think that's cowardly.'

'Since you ask,' Vic said coldly, 'I do think so. It's the kind of weak attitude that our mother had, and look where that led. Perhaps you are content to be like her: feeble and deluded.'

'Perhaps I am,' Bel gulped. 'Not that you really know me now. I don't want to hear any more of this horrible story. I want to go on as I was, believing Mummy died of cancer and Daddy of a broken heart.'

'Oh, for goodness' sake! You don't really believe that, do you?' Vic said. 'Because it's sentimental claptrap. Yes, our mother died of cancer. But our father killed himself. He took his old rabbiting rifle, stuck it under his chin, and fired – standing in the shallows of the Angle. I should know: I heard the shot, and I found his body, face down in nine inches of water.'

'Do you have to be so bloody brutal?' Bel sobbed.

Vic shook her head. 'I'm sorry, truly. But you're not a little girl I have to defend, not any more. You're a grown woman who needs to face up to what really happened.' She paused, and frowned. 'But you knew he killed himself. I'm sure you did.'

Bel bit her lip. Her face was red and wet with tears. 'People said it was an accident,' she croaked.

Vic looked at her sister, and her face was sombre. 'Yes, they did say that. And the Coroner recorded an open verdict. Perhaps that was a mercy.' She sighed. 'Oh, Bel. Believe whatever you want to. But the river's a strange place to be cleaning a gun. And it seems quite a coincidence that it happened on the anniversary of Johnnie's death: ten years to the day. I dare say our father's heart was broken, as you say. But it was the gun that took his life.'

Bel took a deep shuddering breath and wrapped her arms round herself, still clutching the sodden tissue. 'I'll be gone soon,' she said, her voice rough. 'I plan to go back to London on 4th, if you can put up with me that long. Till then I'll keep out of your way, now that you've destroyed all my illusions.'

Vic shrugged. 'Do as you please.'

Bel

Bel lay in bed, shivering. She wanted to get up and fill a hot-water bottle, but she didn't want to bump into Vic: she wanted to hide. Tears bubbled up and spilled over as if from some deep spring. She knew her face was red and swollen, and her eyes and nose itched. She scrubbed at them with a wet tissue.

She wished she and Vic had never had that evening's conversation. She wished she had never come back to Thackham-by-Angle, the village of her childhood which, in memory, she had adorned with innocence and sunlight and roses-round-the-door. She knew it was false, of course she did; somewhere in the deep recesses of her mind lay examples of the truth that she had buried. But the present was not so great, nor the future so enticing, that she could afford to have a miserable past; and the shadow of her mother's depression, blown up by childish ignorance into something even more terrifying than it really was, lay ever-present like some kind of hellish incubus sucking the light from her eyes.

The trouble is, Vic is probably right. Not in every way, perhaps. But mostly. And she was older, and saw more, and understood more what she saw. What do I really remember? I suppose I wanted to think of us as a nice, normal family. But you've only got to look at what actually happened to see that's not true.

She sat up in bed suddenly as a thought struck her, and she felt an unusual clarity. *Is this what I really came for, even though I couldn't have expressed it, even to myself? Was I looking for the truth? Oh, but it's so cruel! Or did I come seeking my only family?*

She got out of bed, opened the door and stood on the landing, listening. She wanted to ask Vic if what she was thinking was right. But everything was quiet, and the lights were out. Vic had gone to bed.

Vic

27 December 2005

Have I done wrong? Should I have kept quiet? Or should I have said something, but not that? Or not so baldly? Poor Bel. But she's nearly fifty years old – she can't possibly believe everything was nice-as-pie in our charming family. All right, yes, when she was little, she wouldn't have understood. Children always think their own home is normal, until they get out in the world and do a little comparing. But Bel was fifteen, almost sixteen, when she left home for the last time. And she was a knowing young lady by then. Perhaps it's just what she wants to believe, to hang on to; but it seems like the worst of lost causes to me.

Oh, Bel. And now you're going, and unless something happens to prevent you you're going under a sort of joint cloud, and I don't suppose we'll see one another again. I do wonder if she has some kind of hidden agenda, hidden even from herself. I don't know what I feel: relief, I suppose, a bit, to have the house to myself again, to be quiet, not to have this sense of something about to erupt all the time. Guilty, too. Somehow I haven't behaved well even in a normal civilised-human way, let alone a Christian way. Frankie might help; but by the time I talk to Frankie, Bel will be gone. And, if I am honest – and I have to be, don't I, after being such a supporter of truth this evening – I am disappointed. Perhaps I was, after all, hoping for some cleansing, some resolution of the past. Having Bel here, even for so short a time, has made me creep a little way out of my shell; and now I find I don't want to go back in.

Did Bel come seeking her only family, even if she didn't really articulate it, even to herself? Is that what I was hoping for too?

Bel

The phone rang just after breakfast. Vic called up the stairs to where Bel
had retreated, as she had been doing the last few days: to her tiny bedroom,
or, if it wasn't raining, out for a walk. But since Christmas it seemed to
have been raining almost incessantly. The air itself felt damp in her lungs
when she ventured out, and it wasn't pleasant.

'Bel!' Vic called up, impatiently, for the second time. 'Phone, for you.
Someone called Bertie.'

'Coming.'

Bel caught Vic's look as she took the receiver from her. What was it
about Vic's silent expressions that could always make Bel feel she'd been
subtly wrong-footed? Vic went into the kitchen and closed the door with
a quiet click.

'Bertie? Is something wrong? Are you all right? Don't tell me, Jason's
looking for me. He's found me a fabulous part, a glamorous, well-dressed
older woman, a total bitch, a husband-stealer. No? Oh well, I didn't really
think so.' She listened for a moment, and her mouth dropped open. 'Oh,
God, Bertie, that's bad. What's the damage? Josie's going to go ballistic.
Builders are such idiots.' She shook her head slowly as Bertie spoke
again. 'How long? OK, Bertie, but you'll let me know, won't you? I mean,
immediately, as soon as you do? Thanks.' She paused. 'Actually, things
aren't going so well. But that's my problem. Look, Bertie, I can't talk now.
I'll have to ring you back another time. Bye, dear. Thanks for ringing.'

She replaced the receiver and stood for a while motionless in the
hallway, her thoughts galloping. *Oh God. What am I going to do now? I'm going
to have to be very nice to Vic. Where else can I go?*

The kitchen door opened. 'Coffee?' Vic said.

'Yes, thanks.' Bel followed Vic into the kitchen and sat down heavily
at the table.

Vic filled the kettle at the sink and set it to boil. She turned to Bel.
'Trouble?' she said gently.

To her amazement and horror, Bel felt her eyes well with tears. 'Oh, God, I'm sorry. I'm so bloody weepy, it's pathetic.' She pulled a tissue out of her sleeve and blew her nose. 'Sorry, I know you don't like swearing, or calling on God unless you mean it. I should watch my mouth.'

Vic said nothing. She poured boiling water into two mugs of coffee, added milk, and pushed one mug across the table to Bel. She sat down opposite, stretched across the table and took Bel's hand, still clutching the damp tissue. 'Never mind all that,' she said. 'I'm sorry you're weepy – I suspect it's my fault. I haven't been as kind as I should, have I? So what's the latest from London?'

Bel took a gulp of coffee and began to feel better. 'You remember I told you that Josie was having a lot of work done in the house? So much so that we all had to move out, all four of us? I think she must've come into money or something, because she decided to rip out both the bathrooms *and* the downstairs loo. They were a bit nasty, I have to say. All the bedrooms were going to be redecorated, and she was having fancy wardrobes put in her room. Then there was supposed to be a total revamp of the kitchen: new units, flooring, appliances, the lot. But before that there was something about renewing all the insulation and the wiring. Bertie wondered if she was doing it up to sell it. Then we'd all be on the street. It was supposed to take three weeks. I did think that was a bit optimistic. The workmen were coming back the day after Boxing Day and working flat out, apparently. Well, it turns out that one of the men left something flammable lying around, or threw a cigarette away carelessly. I don't know. But there's been a fire, Vic. The fire brigade was called by a nosy neighbour, probably old Mrs Feather – she's always gawking out of her window – thank goodness she was! Anyway, the house isn't burnt down, nothing like that, but there's a lot of smoke and water damage, and Bertie says Josie's been called back from America. She's going to be devastated. Now I suppose there'll be hassle with the insurance and the workmen and who knows when any of us can go home.' She looked up at Vic, and the tears started to drip down her cheek. 'I'm sorry, Vic,' she said miserably. 'I just don't have anywhere else to go.'

Vic shook her head and smiled faintly. 'Let's look at it as an opportunity, shall we? Start again? As for not having anywhere to go, don't even think about that. You can stay here as long as you need to.' A thought came to her. 'Was anything of yours damaged in the fire, Bel? Important things, papers, bank stuff, passport?'

Bel sniffed. 'No, I brought all that with me. There's not much in my room I value, just clothes and things, all replaceable. But I'm running out of money. I mean, Jason, that's my agent, though he's not been a lot of use lately, might come up with something in the New Year, but until then I'm not going to be able to make much of a contribution.'

'I'm not worried about that. I have enough for both of us – we won't be on bread and dripping just yet. And if you want to you can keep house when I go back to work. You might even learn how to cook.'

Bel's eyes widened. 'You're brave, aren't you? That's definitely not one of my skills. I did have a part once as a cook, though,' she said ruminatively. 'I can *act* a cook. Will that do?'

Vic smiled. 'I'm sure it would be very entertaining, just not too sustaining. I dare say we'll manage somehow. Perhaps I'll buy you a cookbook, and you can make it your New Year's resolution: "In 2006 I'll learn to cook." What do you think?'

Bel smiled feebly. 'More like, "In 2006 I'll poison my sister." Well, it's a thought. Apropos, when *do* you go back to work?'

'The staff go back on 9th, students on 10th.' She paused, thinking. 'If this Jason does find you work – '

'Ha! Some chance!' Bel snorted.

'Well, if he does, won't you have to go back to London?'

Bel sighed. 'I might. But it would depend exactly what was involved. I could travel up by train if necessary, but if I had to be there for several consecutive days I could probably bunk on someone's floor, if it wasn't for too long. But it won't happen. Jason's only interested in the under twenty-fives these days.'

The phone rang in the hall, a shrill interruption. Vic got up to answer it, and a moment later came back into the kitchen. 'It's for you – again,' she said. 'Somebody Dawson.'

'Connie!' Bel exclaimed. 'She's probably ringing to find out if I am still going to the AmDram party on Saturday. She's decided I am some kind of celebrity, and she wants to show me off.' She hesitated. 'Are you still happy to take me?'

'Of course,' Vic said. 'And bring you back. Promise me you won't get so drunk that you throw up in the car, though.'

Bel grinned and got up to answer the phone. 'Better bring a bucket, just in case.'

Vic

By the time Vic drove into West Stoke the rain had stopped. It had been raining all evening, a steady, cold rain that now lay in puddles, reflecting the street-lights, splashing the party-goers who stumbled along the pavements, giggling and shouting, tottering in foolish shoes. She had dropped Bel off at nine o'clock outside The Swan, and Bel had had to make a dash for it, swaying on her red heels, holding her handbag over her head, until she disappeared through the pub doors with a careless wave.

Now Vic cruised the High Street, looking for somewhere to park. She found a side street down from the pub, and slipped into a space beside three overflowing bins. She looked at her watch: it was a few minutes before midnight. She got out of the car, locked it, and turned up the collar of her coat. The scarf that Bel had given her for Christmas was folded snugly round her throat.

She walked round the corner to the front of the pub. There were lads leaning up against the wall, bottles in their hands. 'Happy New Year, Miss,' one of them said, his voice slurred, leaning unsteadily towards her. His companions lolled together and laughed.

'Same to you,' Vic muttered. She pushed open the pub door, and a wash of light met her eyes and for a moment blinded her. The bars were heaving with people, and the smell of beer was overpowering. She glanced towards the stairs. The West Stoke Players had taken over the upstairs room as they did, so Bel told her, every year. As she looked a roar came from above, and all around her people shrieked and embraced as the sound of Big Ben, chiming midnight, clanged out from the enormous television on the wall and fireworks exploded in violent light. She pushed through the throng and started up the stairs. A man came down them towards her, holding on to the handrail, a fez lop-sided on his head. 'Happy New Year, my love!' he shouted.

'You too,' Vic said and sidestepped past him. At the head of the stairs she undid her coat. The heat coming out of the function room was stifling, laden with the smell of alcohol, sweat and mingled perfumes. She put her head round the door. People were standing, sitting, hugging, leaning against each other. Everyone had a drink in his or her hand. Music sounded from somewhere, but it was almost drowned out by the roar of voices. A group was holding hands in a ragged circle, swaying, singing 'Auld Lang Syne.' Vic cringed back against the door-frame, her eyes searching the crowd for Bel. She finally saw her across the room, in the middle of a huddle of people. At that moment Bel saw her, and smiled. She beckoned her over.

Vic hesitated, and then gathered herself up and began to weave through the crowd. Her head swam with all the noise and fumes. As she came close to Bel's group she heard two obvious thespians talking very loudly, almost in her ear. She flinched away, but the pressing throng held her, for the moment, immobile.

A woman, probably somewhere in her forties, in a green silk dress that clung moistly to her generous, if flabby, curves, her lipstick smudged as if she'd been eating bread and jam rather too carelessly, leaned back, laughing, and the man talking to her, a younger man with shoulder-length curls, stooped over her, staring hungrily and shamelessly down her cleavage. Vic was almost sure she saw his fingers twitch.

'Omigod,' the woman squealed, 'if I was in that situation, I'd throw myself headlong – *headlong*, darling! – into the Angle. I would, truly!'

The man guffawed. 'But my love, the Angle's only about four inches deep!'

Someone else, another man, loomed into their conversation. 'Maybe that's just the point – she just wants to make a statement!'

'A wet statement!'

All three of them bent over, coughing with laughter.

'What kind of a statement would that be? An "I'm a complete prat" kind of statement?'

'Anyway,' the second man said, 'everyone knows you can drown in four inches of water.'

'Especially,' choked the woman, 'if you've just rolled out of the Headless Chicken!' She collapsed into the arms of the two men, who staggered back, and they hung onto each other, laughing helplessly.

Vic felt the world recede, as if she had gone suddenly deaf. A spasm of nausea clenched her stomach. In that split second she hoped wildly that she was not going to faint. She looked up, and saw Bel gazing back at her. Bel's face was drained white, her face an appalled mask. Nobody seemed to notice the sisters as they stood, staring at each other, the noise and hilarity rolling round them. Vic took a deep breath and mouthed, 'Let's go home.' She stretched out her hand. Bel patted a few people in the group, smiled and nodded. Then she took Vic's hand, and together they inched their way out of the room.

For a few minutes they sat in Vic's car, not speaking, just breathing.

Then Vic said, 'Tell me again, why do some people call the pub the Headless Chicken?'

'Oh, that,' Bel said shakily. 'It's the bloody thesps being pretentious again. A little nod in the direction of the Bard. Isn't the Black Swan in Stratford known as the Dirty Duck?'

'Ah. So it is.'

'But also, many years ago, so the local myth goes, some wag got a tall ladder and painted a moustache, hat and glasses on the swan, and the landlord had to have it painted over. So it was headless.'

'It seems all right now. Perhaps they got the sign done again.'

'Yes. But I guess there's also a sly reference to the AmDrammers running about like headless chickens, as they do, especially on opening night.'

'Hm. Shall we go home?'

'Yes, please. It's been a long evening.'

Vic started the engine and reversed out of the parking space. 'It seemed like quite a party.'

'Not so much for me. One glass of champagne.'

'Really?'

Bel yawned and leaned back in her seat, closing her eyes. 'It *was* quite nice being lionised for a while,' she said. 'And when someone bought champagne in my honour, I had to have a glass or seem rude and ungrateful. But I wasn't in the mood for getting wasted. And, as you know, when all the world is roaring drunk and oneself is sober, they all look such vulgar fools, laughing when nothing is funny.'

Vic concentrated on driving. As they left the outskirts of West Stoke the streetlights petered out, and the night was dark and starless. Bel seemed to doze. Then they were up on the bypass, and after a few miles took the slip road down to Thackham. Vic pulled up outside her house.

'Bel, wake up. We're here.' Bel opened her eyes. Her hands still on the steering wheel, Vic said, 'Bel, those people at the party, those drunk people —'

Bel laid a hand on Vic's arm. 'It doesn't matter. Forget it.'

69

Vic shook her head 'No, it's not that. People say things, stupid things in ignorance, and we have to live with it. It's not their problem, after all. But tonight, for the first time, I felt –' She ground to a halt.

Bel frowned. 'What?'

Vic turned to look at her. 'I felt, for a little while, not alone.'

Bel was silent for a long moment. Then she smiled faintly. 'Well, that's good. I'm glad.' She turned away, her hand on the door handle. Then she turned back, and her tired smile was warm. 'Happy New Year, Vic.'

Vic

1 January 2006

Vic lay and dozed, warm under the covers. She must have slept for a while, but was now awake at two o'clock and had no idea why. Solomon was curled up against her calf, pinning the duvet down, adding his own little pool of furry heat. Bel, she knew, was asleep: she could hear soft snoring from the next room. She thought about Bel, and smiled. *My sister is a treasure, after all. Even if she has been buried for so long.* She frowned. *I wonder if she feels the same. Alone. Perhaps not – perhaps she has told a friend, or a score of them, what happened to us when we were young; perhaps she was never alone with the secrets. I must find out. What do I really know of Bel's life after she left home? Precious little, and even less of how she thought about anything. But tonight I feel very thankful. Just seeing how she reacted to those stupid people was a kind of revelation, and I loved her for it. Why does that seem so strange? Perhaps it's because I am not used to love. Except, so many years ago, from this sister. How could I have forgotten?*

Vic closed her eyes, trying to still her puzzling thoughts. *I should pray. I should thank God for finding my sister again. Is this his doing? Was Don right after all? Have I wasted the years?* She took a deep breath, trying to still the urgency of her self-questioning. *Lord, I am not used to love, even though I acknowledge your love for me, and my timid and ignorant love for you. I am not used to praying, except in a conventional in-church formulaic kind of way, and that's shameful. I admit it. I want to thank you that I have a sister, and that she is here. Thank you that she, too, remembers. Remembers and cares. Help me to be kinder to her. If this is some opportunity you have sent, don't let me, in my blind pride and foolishness, throw it away.* She sighed deeply. *I must think about Frankie. She's bound to want to know things, and maybe I won't want to tell her, but she's very good at seeing beneath the surface, and going straight to where a person's real thoughts are. I've seen her do it.* Her eyes flew open. *Hold on, what am I saying? Isn't Frankie a true friend? Why am I already planning my escape? Lord, I thought I was ready to change, but it seems I can't do it. I can't do it alone, and I am too afraid to ask for help. What's to be done with me?*

71

Vic

Vic rang the Vicarage door bell.

'Come, in, it's not locked!' she heard Frankie shout from inside.

She pushed open the door. The broad, elegant hallway, lit by coloured lights over the front door, was strewn with toys, including a yellow-and-orange plastic tricycle, on its side.

'Come in, Vic, we're in the kitchen.'

Vic found Frankie, brilliant and huge in a red and black floor-length dress with a black shawl flung carelessly round her shoulders, sitting at the kitchen table on a teetering stool, munching on a piece of toast. Noah was beside her, kneeling perilously on a similar stool, each hand holding a ball of greyish dough. He smiled as Vic came in, and held out his hands.

'Thanks, Noah – I think I'll pass.'

'Sorry, we're terribly late this morning,' Frankie said. 'Rob flew out to work still buttoning his shirt. Coffee?'

'Please. Shall I make it?'

'No, that's fine, I must do something. Getting lazy and fat, can't imagine why.' She slid off the stool, grinning, and sailed towards the kitchen counter. Vic sat down opposite Noah and watched him pound the dough, singing quietly to himself.

'How was your week away, Frankie?' Vic said.

'Lovely. Bliss. My parents got Noah a trike for Christmas and Dad spent loads of time playing with him. Rob went to sleep every time he sat down, and Mum wouldn't let me do anything. She just kept saying,"Put your feet up, dear, while you can." She cooked, she made tea, she read bedtime stories to Noah. Mothers are wonderful, one of God's greatest creations.' She put two cups of steaming coffee on the table.

'Thanks.'

Frankie hitched herself back onto her stool and looked at Vic with narrowed eyes. 'So, what about you? How's it going with your sister? I thought she seemed nice. Not at all alike, are you? Not on the surface, anyway. I don't mean to say you're not nice, of course.'

Vic smiled. 'Oh, believe me, I'm not. But, oddly, after a few ups and downs, things are smoothing out a bit, I think.'

Frankie sipped her coffee. 'Caffeine, another gift from heaven. Actually, Vic, there was something I wanted to ask you.'

'Oh?'

'If it's not an impertinence. Or even if it is – you know me, leap in, hobnails and all. How did you first become a Christian?'

Now that I wasn't expecting.

'Oh. Mm. I have to cast my mind back a long, long way. I was still at school, at Repley, in my last year, exams looming. We had a very charismatic RE teacher – I mean that in its normal rather than technical sense.'

Frankie nodded. 'OK, so your teacher inspired you. Did she have this effect on other students?'

'I don't know. I don't think so. Well, maybe she did, but if she caused a revival I didn't notice it.'

'Did you tell anyone? Friends?'

Vic shook her head. 'My school friends weren't the sort of girls you'd confide in, not for that sort of thing. The fact that I never kept up with any of them might give you an idea why.' She paused. 'I told my sister.'

'Because she was closer than a friend? Because you trusted her?'

'Probably.'

'And what was her reaction? Sorry if this sounds like an interrogation, by the way.'

'She giggled.'

Frankie smiled ruefully. 'Oh, dear. Did you mind?'

'Not really. That was just Bel.'

'Was it only that, Vic? A great teacher?'

Vic shook her head. 'Frankie, I don't know anyone like you for asking the searching question! No, it wasn't just the teacher, and stop looking smug.'

Frankie raised one eyebrow, laid a hand on her chest and mouthed 'Moi?'

'This will sound odd, I know, but I believe I had a vision.'

Frankie's eyebrows shot through her hairline. 'Oh boy, am I glad I asked. A vision of what? Where were you? What were you doing?'

'I was in the school library,' Vic said reluctantly. 'One late afternoon in winter. I was doing some school work, and at the same time avoiding

73

a hockey match. I wasn't alone: a very young girl was sitting somewhere a few bookshelves down. I couldn't see her, but I could hear her, sighing. She'd probably been given extra work as a punishment and was sorry to be missing the hockey. Whatever. Miss Griffin, that's the RE teacher, had suggested I read some of the Epistles. I'd been breaking up my Shakespeare revision with 2 Corinthians, the bit where St Paul talks about all the troubles he has suffered. It was a revelation to me: at eighteen I thought I'd had plenty of troubles already. Not shipwreck, though, at least not literal shipwreck. Anyway, I looked up from my reading and there he was.'

'Who?'

'St Paul.'

'How did you know it was him?'

'I don't know. I don't remember ever reading a description of him, but I knew it was him, without a doubt. He was a short man, a bit bent in the back, with curly hair and beard, brown with grey streaks, and he was wearing a brown woollen garment that ended just below his knees, and sandals. And his feet were dusty.'

'How extraordinary. Did he say anything?'

'No. But he looked at me with the most piercing eyes I've ever seen, and I felt quite faint.'

Frankie shifted on her stool, and absent-mindedly moulded a lump of dough that Noah had put into her hand. 'Did it last long?'

'I don't think so,' Vic said. 'He sort of faded away, and I became aware of the other girl standing as it were behind him, looking at me open-mouthed. I must have been staring at nothing, from her point of view.'

'Was this the only time, Vic? Nothing at all before or since?'

'Nothing.'

Frankie was silent. Then she noticed that Noah was sliding off his stool. 'You need to wee, No? OK. Back in a minute, Vic. We're potty training, and at his age when you've got to go, you've got to go.'

While they were gone Vic got up, took her coffee cup and wandered over to the window. Someone, neither Rob nor Frankie, looked after the Vicarage garden, and even now in dark January it managed to look tidy and tended. A series of shrubs marched down a sloping lawn to a stout fence, beyond which lay a water-meadow and the winding Angle. To the right Vic could just see, beyond a prickly hedge, the furthest of the headstones in the churchyard, and the church itself, foursquare in the dull light. The only sounds were the harsh cries of circling rooks and the ticking of the

Maynards' kitchen clock. She shivered: something about the juxtaposition of the church, here in the twenty-first century, with her recollection of St. Paul, made her uneasy. What if the great Apostle returned, here to St. Mark's Vicarage? What would he think?

Then Frankie was back, with Noah holding on to her skirt.

'Success?' Vic asked.

'Yes, he's a very good lad, aren't you, sweetie?' Frankie heaved herself back onto her stool, pulled her son up after her, and finished her coffee in one gulp. 'Now, where were we, Vic?'

'St Paul. I was just wondering what he would think of us.'

Frankie grimaced. 'I think he would make us feel uncomfortable, don't you? So, how do you reckon this vision affected your Christian life subsequently?'

Vic sighed. 'For a while it sustained me. I walked on a cloud. I read a lot, even prayed. But, like most people I guess, it didn't last. Not at that intensity. I fell away. Life happened. I don't doubt what I saw, Frankie. And I suppose it was for some purpose. But I don't think that purpose has been realised.'

'*Yet*,' Frankie said. 'It's not over, Vic. Not till we stick you in a wooden box with flowers on top and I say nice things about you in church and your friends dab their eyes and think about all your good works.'

Vic laughed. 'Frankie, you're daft.'

'Maybe,' Frankie said. 'But I can't believe someone is vouchsafed a vision for nothing. I'd guess whatever God has in mind for you has yet to be fulfilled. You, or life, or whatever, have probably stood in its way. Am I right?'

'Very likely,' Vic murmured.

'So, what about your sister?' Frankie said, changing tack with unsettling suddenness. 'Why is this the first you've seen of each other in –what was it – twenty-eight years?'

'It's a long story, Frankie.'

'I'm not in a hurry. I'll get us some more coffee. I'll give Noah a drink and a biscuit and stick him in front of the TV. OK?'

Five minutes later she bustled back into the kitchen, replenished their coffee cups, and sat down again. She said nothing, just raised an enquiring eyebrow.

'I can spare you the details,' Vic said slowly. 'Something...something very bad happened in our family many years ago.' She hesitated. 'Bel and I had a brother. To say he was the apple of his parents' eye would be a massive understatement. They'd waited for him for a long time. My mother had many miscarriages, before me, between me and Bel, after Bel, all of them boys. Our brother came along when I was nine and Bel six. He was called John, like all the Colbournes before him, but he was always known as Johnnie. He was a dear little fellow, and Bel and I loved him too. I don't think we understood fully at the time, being children, just how much of a treasure he was to our parents, but as time went on the contrast between their attitude to him and to Bel and me became very clear. I never hated Johnnie for it, though. He wasn't responsible.' She came to a halt, feeling her voice dry up, and took several sips of coffee. Frankie said nothing, just waited patiently. Vic took a deep breath. 'One summer day, when Johnnie was four, our parents were having a big party. I can't remember why. They'd invited everyone they considered part of their set. This included my grandfather, who was a retired judge. That's what everyone called him, too: "Judge." I thought he was a horrible man, but maybe I am prejudiced, because Bel clearly has different memories.'

'What was so nasty about this Judge?' Frankie asked.

'I saw him as the root of it all,' Vic said bitterly. 'This adoration of the son, this insistence on having an heir. Anyone would think we were royalty, not the ordinary middle-class family of a country solicitor. I remember him coming on one of his rare state visits. It was just after Johnnie was born, and he had obviously come to inspect the baby. Of us he took absolutely no notice, even though we had to be there, silent and demure in our best dresses. It was all positively archaic. I saw my father under his thumb, and my mother under my father's thumb, and us girls left to get on with it as best we could.' She took a deep breath. 'Sorry, Frankie, I said I'd spare you the details, didn't I? I meant to. And my very nasty and unChristian resentment.'

Frankie shook her head. 'Who knows this stuff, Vic?'

'Well, the facts, Bel, of course, though I think she doesn't see it in quite the same way. She was a bit younger, of course. You didn't know Don's wife, Ellen, did you? She died before you came here. She was my friend, and I told her quite a lot. Don knows some of it too.'

'I'm sure there's more,' Frankie said quietly.

'Yes, I'm afraid so. You sure you want to hear it?'

'I want to hear it, and you need to tell it. Go on, Vic. Something about a party.'

Vic shuddered. 'Bel and I were given the job of looking after Johnnie and were told to keep out of the way while they got everything ready. We had a fine old time playing in the woods without too much supervision. You know, don't you, that we used to live in Angleby House, the old ruin under the bypass? It had five and a half acres then, including woods and a bit of the river. My father used to fish there sometimes. I was thirteen, and Bel was a month away from her eleventh birthday. She was due to join me at Repley that September.

'I think now we were too young to have the responsibility of a lively four-year-old, and perhaps it seems surprising that they let us. I don't know. Anyway, I had a plan of my own for that afternoon – I was making the most of our freedom. So for about an hour, perhaps a little less, I left Johnnie in Bel's charge. As she afterwards told it, the two of them were playing hide-and-seek in the woods and enjoying themselves hugely. Then Johnnie disappeared, and didn't respond to Bel's anxious shouts. When she finally found him he was lying face down in the shallows of the river. I was on my way back and heard her screams. I ran as fast as I could. Between us we dragged him from the water's edge. But we couldn't revive him.'

The silence stretched out, punctuated only by the sound of the TV in the next room.

'Oh, Vic,' Frankie whispered. 'What a tragedy. I'm so sorry. What can I say?'

'It's over. Nothing to be said or done.'

'Mm. But the effects go on. Your life was never the same again, I imagine, nor Bel's. Did they blame you, your parents?'

'Oh yes. They were quite restrained, but we were in no doubt. It was the beginning of the disintegration of our family. Of course the cracks were already there, but Johnnie held it all together. Without him, my parents fell apart. When Bel came to Repley we started to board; quite honestly I don't think my father could stand the sight of us any longer. But for us it was providential. We both thrived there, away from the atmosphere of home. Bel, for instance, discovered her talent for acting, and in the holidays she joined the West Stoke Players.'

'What about you?'

'When I couldn't wangle an invitation from one of my friends, when I had to be at home, I walked, or hid in my room. I did a vast amount of reading. When Bel wasn't with the AmDrammers, we spent most of our time together.'

'Did you talk about what happened?' Frankie asked.

'Not much, and then only obliquely.'

'So you were still friends? You didn't blame each other?'

'Not then, no. It brought us closer. I think we both realised that we were each other's only true friend. A tragedy like ours tends to keep people away; perhaps they think you're going to be talking about it all the time, or bursting into tears. But Bel and I didn't want to think about it. It was bad enough having to live with our parents. They were completely haunted.'

'So if you managed to stay friends then, what went wrong?'

'I'm not entirely sure. I think Bel gradually forged her own life with the acting crowd in Stoke, and started to have her own ambitions and to go about realising them in a very single-minded way. She left me behind. I had my own schemes too, but that's another story. Bit by bit we drifted apart. I think that was accentuated by my conversion, too. Bel didn't share it, though we were both well-grounded in Scripture, both at school and as small children at Sunday School. Looking back, I wonder if perhaps Bel felt the need to detach herself from that sense of guilt we both laboured under if she was ever to build a life for herself. Anyway, one day something was said that sparked an almighty row. That day she laid the responsibility for Johnnie's death, and for the family trauma that followed, squarely at my door. To some degree she was right, but even now I don't think it was all my fault, and at the time I saw it as a major betrayal.

'We didn't speak for weeks, despite the attempts by some of our teachers to reconcile us. Bel left school and home very suddenly, before she was even sixteen. She took off and joined a theatre group that travelled the country, at first in some very lowly position, sweeping the stage and making the tea, as far as I can tell. Our parents made no attempt to find her, nor to conceal the fact that they'd given up on us both. I took my exams and left school too. After that we saw each other again twice, at the funerals of each of our parents some years later – and then nothing. Silence.'

For a long moment Frankie stared out of the window. Then she heaved a sigh and turned back to Vic. She shook her head thoughtfully. 'You know what I'm wondering, Vic? Why Bel asked to come and stay with you, after all that happened. And why you agreed.'

Vic rubbed her eyes. 'I can't answer for Bel. Knowing her, if I still do, she probably forgot the row, or if not, just downplays it. It was a long time ago, we were both teenagers who'd been through traumatic times. She probably assumes I forgave her.'

'Well, did you?'

'Not for a long time. But something happened, Frankie, last Saturday, which made me realise that Bel too has been deeply affected by what happened to Johnnie, and to us. On the surface she seems to be in denial, but at some level she acknowledges the wounds. And I have to recognise that in this we still only have each other.'

'It won't be easy, though, Vic,' Frankie said sombrely. 'And I guess it would help if she remembered what she said and apologised.'

'Well, as to that, I probably need to be forgiven too. Yes, you're right. We have a long way to go, a lot to make up for.'

Frankie leaned over and patted Vic's hand. 'If there's any way I can help, I will. And in case you're worried, I will keep everything you've told me to myself.'

'Thanks, Frankie. I'm glad I told you – well, I think I am.'

Frankie chuckled. 'You're a funny one, Vic. But aren't we all.'

'I must go home. I'm sure you've got things to do.' Vic unwound her stiff legs from the stool.

'Child to feed, sermon to prepare, phone calls to make. Say hello to your sister from me.' Frankie slithered off her perch and followed Vic to the door. 'You know, Vic, if she's going to be staying for a while, we should get her involved with something. Would she come to the Bible study group? Or would Jeremiah be too much for her?'

'I don't know. I'll ask.' She hesitated. 'Thanks, Frankie. You've been a great help.'

'All part of the service.' She leaned on the door frame while Vic put on her coat. 'Your brother's not buried in the churchyard, is he? I noticed your parents there, but not him.'

'No. As far as I was able to work out, my father was concerned about my mother's mental state, never very robust, and he thought that if Johnnie was in the churchyard, headstone and all, my mother would be there all the time. It would become a sort of shrine, a focus for her obsession. So in his usual high-handed and unilateral way he had Johnnie cremated. I remember the time, even though we weren't allowed at the funeral itself. It was all very grim.'

'Who was the vicar then?'

'In 1967? It was dear old Reverend Alloway. Bel and I remember him very fondly, and his wife. He retired a few years later. Long gone now, both of them. He was succeeded by Ronald Cheeseman. I think he got to know my parents quite well, as well as anybody could, and he officiated at both their funerals. Nice man. After he moved on there was somebody called Anthony Welham, but he was often out of the parish, because he was the Bishop's chaplain, among other things. Bit of a high flyer. Then Richard Everard-Clowes. Then an interregnum. Then you.'

'Thanks for the potted history.'

'Which you probably knew anyway.'

Frankie grinned. 'Fount of all knowledge, that's me. See you, Vic. I want to know the rest of the story.'

Vic turned, frowning. 'How do you know there's more?'

Frankie threw her head back and laughed aloud. '*Of course* there's more.'

Bel

3 January 2006

'Do you have any drink in the house, Vic?' Bel said that evening while their supper was cooking, leaking delicious aromas out of the oven: tomatoes, peppers, basil.

Vic looked up from her book. 'There's some ancient sherry in the kitchen cupboard. Now you mention it, I should stock up.'

'What, now that your dipso sister's here?'

'If the cap fits. Pour me one while you're at it, please.'

'This tumbler do?'

'Steady on, Bel. You'll have me flat on my face.'

Bel handed Vic a glass and plumped down in an armchair. 'How was your meeting with the vicar?'

'Meeting? Oh, yes, fine, very useful. Actually that reminds me, something I wanted to ask you.'

Bel sipped her drink and made a face. 'You weren't kidding when you said this was ancient. So what did you want to know?'

'When you disappeared from the scene, from home and school, all those years ago, you told us you joined that theatre troupe, didn't you?'

Bel said guardedly, remembering her previous *faux pas*, 'Yes.'

'How did you get into it? A kid of not quite sixteen?'

Bel smirked. 'By my obvious and overpowering talent, of course! No, truthfully, it was through that old chap at the Stoke Players, Howie Malton. Someone he knew owed him a favour.'

'So,' Vic mused, 'in different ways, we each had a kind of Svengali figure. Except that I married mine. What a mistake that was!'

Bel hooted with laughter and almost tipped sherry over the upholstery. 'Well, I certainly didn't *marry* Howie! I was fifteen, he was forty-five if a day, and he was already spoken for. In fact his daughter Debbie was a friend of mine. Which made it all a bit incestuous. I suppose you'd call him a paedophile these days.'

Vic sat upright, a look of horror on her face. 'Bel! Please tell me you didn't sleep with Howie Malton!'

'Sleeping didn't come into it, dear. Oh, Vic, don't look so aghast! I was desperate to get away, and Howie promised me an introduction. To be fair to the old boy, he kept his word. Disgusting as it was, it was worth it.'

'Bel, it was illegal!'

'So? Are you going to hand me over to the law? Poor old Howie's dead, so you can't report *him*. I heard about his death on New Year's Eve at the Headless Chicken. Died of a heart attack at sixty, on the golf course, apparently.' She paused, and stared into her glass, suddenly serious. 'Anyway, there was more to it than that.'

'More to what?'

'My bit of casting-couch bravado with the middle-aged lecher.'

Vic frowned. 'I'm not sure what you're getting at.'

Bel sighed. 'I did it, I think, well, partly at least, to keep up with you.'

Vic shook her head in bewilderment. 'Keep up with me? But I was as ignorant as a baby! Eric took my virginity, even if we weren't *quite* married at the time. But that was later.'

Now it was Bel's turn to look baffled. 'What? What about that farm boy you were so determined to seduce? At the tender age of *thirteen*, Miss High and Mighty? You can't have forgotten him, Vic – it was the day our Johnnie drowned. What on earth was his name?'

Vic said faintly, 'Joe. Joe Crompton. Of course I haven't forgotten: either him or the day. I wish I could forget. But Bel, I lied. Joe stood me up. I hung around at the side of the lane, waiting, for half an hour or more before I realised, stupid little girl that I was, that he wasn't coming. I don't suppose he ever really meant to come. I heard months afterwards that he was busy running several village girls, and favoured a buxom sixteen-year-old called Julie who later got pregnant – by him or someone else I don't know. I should have known he wouldn't have wanted anything to do with a skinny kid like me, quite apart from the risk. He may have enjoyed having yet another girl throwing herself at him, but that was the sum of his interest, as it turned out.'

'But Vic, you came back with leaves in your hair and moss and mould all over your clothes!'

Vic smiled wanly, remembering the afternoon that had darkened both their lives. 'I did that myself. I was so humiliated. I wasn't going to admit to my little sister that the whole daring episode had been an embarrassing failure.'

Bel was silent for a long minute, blinking rapidly as tears welled. 'Oh, Vic,' she whispered. 'And while I thought you were rolling around in the woods in the lustful grip of a seventeen-year-old with a motor-bike, our poor little Johnnie died. Oh God, Vic. How bloody awful.'

Vic said nothing. Her eyes were shut tight so that all the lines around them were deeply etched. Then she opened them, raised her head and sniffed. 'We'd better eat. It smells just a little burnt.'

'You haven't drunk your sherry.'

'As you said, it wasn't wonderful. And perhaps with my digestion I'd be better off tipping it down the sink.'

Bel followed her into the kitchen and started to put cutlery on the table. 'We haven't seen much of Don the last few days,' she said.

'I expect he's busy at work,' Vic said, her voice muffled because her head was partly in the oven. She emerged red-faced with a bubbling dish in her gloved hands.

'Does he only come and eat on Sundays?'

'No, sometimes he rings and says his cupboard's bare so I tell him to come and share a crust.'

'Perhaps we should ring him now. There's enough for an army here.'

Vic slid into her seat, fanning herself with her napkin. 'Not tonight, I think. I want to hear more of your story.'

'You do?' Bel looked dubious.

'Talking to Frankie this afternoon made me realise how little I know about your life,' Vic said. She pushed the dish across the table to Bel, who helped herself.

Bel scooped up a steaming forkful and blew on it. 'Oh, so you were talking about me, were you?'

'Some of the time.' Vic looked up at her. 'Frankie wondered, as you're going to be here for a while, if you'd like to be a bit more involved in church things – she suggested Bible study.'

Bel made a face. 'A bit heavy at the moment for this dull old brain,' she said. 'But I would like to come to church on Sundays. It's an area of my life I've neglected, the spiritual side. I've been feeling the lack of it as I get older.'

'Fair enough.'

They ate in thoughtful silence for a while. Then Bel said, 'You say you want to hear more about my life. But it cuts both ways. I don't know much about yours.'

'More than I do of yours, I think. I've been here in Thackham most of it, looking after our mother, sorting out the property, studying, working. Not very interesting, really.'

'There's a blank, though, Vic: between leaving school and coming back here to nurse Mummy.'

'Ah. Another time, I think. You first – your doings were far more thrilling, I'm sure.' She took a last mouthful and laid down her knife and fork. 'I didn't quite run to dessert, I'm afraid. I'll make some coffee.'

Bel patted her stomach. 'Dessert I don't need. That was tasty in the extreme.'

Fifteen minutes later, the dishes draining and the coffee made, they took their cups back into the tiny living room. Vic threw two more logs on the fire and stood watching the flames take hold, licking mercilessly over the wood in tongues of orange and blue. Bel flopped down in her by-now favourite chair. 'You are a very good cook, you know,' she said. 'Whatever that concoction was, it was delicious. Where did you learn? I never did.'

'It was fish pie, and it was a case of having to,' Vic said, taking a sip of coffee as she sat down. 'We didn't have any opportunities as children, did we? And being a so-called high flyer I didn't do anything remotely domestic at Repley. I had a respectable bunch of A levels, but no practical knowledge whatsoever. Don't forget I was married a few months after leaving school, and Eric just assumed I'd shop and cook and clean and all those things. So I learned.'

'Whereas I lived on takeaways. Or didn't eat.'

'So, tell me a bit more about this theatre group you joined. You told us some of the more lurid stories, but I'd like to know more about how it all fitted in with your life. Fill in the blanks.'

Bel leaned back in her chair and stretched out her legs. 'It was an unusual little company,' she said. 'There weren't many of us, probably no more than a dozen, perhaps fifteen, and we all had to double up with jobs, because we couldn't often afford to pay for proper lighting people or anyone to make sets, and we recycled costumes all the time. At one point we got a grant which helped us to keep going. Most of the time we travelled. The director was a very small and rather fierce woman called Edna Beesley. She was in her seventies at least, and she wore a wasps' nest black wig and lots of makeup. The older members told me she'd been a successful actress in her time, and had great ambitions, but she'd contracted some disease which affected her vocal cords so she could only speak in a whisper. Obviously that meant the end of her career. But she couldn't give up the theatre, and I have to say she was a very good director – dictatorial, but she got results. And scary, too, especially with that whispery voice. When I first joined she worked me like a slave, and I didn't come anywhere near acting for quite some time. She was, I realise now, testing my resolve. Was I just another stage-struck kid, or did I have it in me to put up with the grind, pull my weight, generally be an asset? The odd thing was, though I was desperate to act, I loved all the other stuff, even the most menial of jobs, and I didn't mind at all being the company's little slavey. All the others were a lot older than me, except for spotty Dave. He was about twenty, I suppose, and he followed me about like a sad puppy till one day I got fed up and gave him what he wanted, up against the props room door. All over rather quickly, if I recall.'

Vic closed her eyes and winced. 'Oh, Bel.'

'Well, it was part of that world,' Bel said. 'It went on, and I accepted it. Apart from school, I hadn't had a huge amount of moral guidance, if you think about it. Anyway, the company became like my family. I loved them all, even spotty Dave and Edna. And they took care of me, in their own way. If I made hay with most of the men, well, that's just the way it was, and I didn't mind. In fact, I liked it. If it's done me harm, I've yet to find out how.' She fell silent for a moment, remembering. 'Anyway, after some considerable time a part came up for an ingénue and Edna made me audition for it even though there wasn't anyone else suitable. I must have done all right because I got the part, and I absolutely revelled in it. As time went on I got more and more meaty roles, and I like to think that by the end I was a useful member of the company. I owe them a huge debt – the experience, and the hard work – it's what's kept me from being dazzled by the hype and kept me working. I like to think I can turn my hand to most things.

'It was Edna who suggested, out of the blue, that I should go to Drama School. I'd been with the company for over two years by then, and we'd done the length and breadth of the country. I was flabbergasted. "Are you trying to get rid of me, Edna?" I asked. "Is it because I forgot my lines last week?" "No, dear," she said, and she was serious. "You've got real talent, and it would be selfish to keep you here with us when you should have the chance to spread your wings a bit. I want you to work something up, do a bit of practice. Get Arnold to coach you, especially with voice production. He's your man for that. I'll talk to someone I know. The rest is up to you.'

'I remember saying, "But it costs money, Edna! How am I going to afford it?" and Edna turning to me with that sombre look of hers and saying, "Well, dear, you'll have to work. You're no stranger to work, are you? And you needn't think the actor's life's an easy one. But if you've got what it takes to do it, then you will. All I can do is offer you a chance. Not everybody gets even that."

'Anyway, that's what happened. Arnold and I worked on voice production, in between the bouts of slap and tickle – he was a man of great energy, Arnold was.' She looked at Vic and grinned. 'You don't have to cringe quite so obviously, Vic. I was young and healthy, and it was all there for me on a plate, and in its way quite flattering. Anyway, Edna must've persuaded her contact, because I got my audition, and a few weeks later a letter arrived saying I'd got a place. Everyone was so pleased for me they threw an impromptu party. None of them ever seemed to have any money but various bottles appeared and someone went out for a takeaway and we were all eating chips and drinking wonderfully poisonous mixtures and were all completely plastered in no time. Quite a few people were crying – me included – and there was a great deal of hugging and kissing and protestations of always keeping in touch. It was all very soppy and over the top but in their own way they were sincere. And I *have* kept in touch with some of them: in fact, two of the original members of the company are among the people I live – lived – with in London. Which isn't bad going, considering how many years it's been.

'I woke up the next morning partly clothed in a Roman toga, with a headache from hell, in bed with two of the men, Arnold and Stefan, who were both wearing nothing but boots and snoring prodigiously. And I was due to begin at the college the next day!'

Vic shook her head. 'Are you sure you're not making all this up?'

Bel looked indignant. 'Certainly not! It's the plain unvarnished, with no embellishments. Well, not many. Haven't you had enough of this story of my rise to stardom?'

'No, I'd love to hear more, but I must refill my cup. How about you?'

'Yes, please. No, I'll do it.'

She picked up their cups and padded through to the kitchen, singing under her breath. A moment later she was back, and handed Vic her coffee. 'It might be a bit tepid by now.'

'It doesn't matter.'

Bel settled herself down again. 'I think I shall just tell you the next instalment,' she said. 'Not the whole story of my life. It's getting late.'

'All right. Just the bit at Drama School, then. Summarized.'

'I spent the first few weeks sleeping on the floor in a flat belonging to a cousin of Stefan's. He was extremely camp and had noisy parties.

I managed to find myself some work through this guy, washing up in a seedy little cafe round the corner from the flat. Then I met Terry. Well, no, we'd already met. But a few weeks after the start of term we got together. I didn't like him much at first, to be honest – all bragging and preening, and it didn't help that all the girls adored him, ninnies that they were. Compared to them I was already a hard-headed pro, so I should have had a tougher shell, but he *was* extremely good-looking, sulky and smouldering – you know the type. He came from Barnsley and he had an accent you could cut with a knife when he wasn't acting. But he also had an amazing ability to sound like pretty much anyone else. He could take off all the major film actors of the time.

'Against my better judgment, I fell for him hard. I fought it, but it was useless. You'd think I'd be immune to that sort of romantic thing after being with the company, but no, I was only eighteen, and as it turned out immune I wasn't. Long before the term was over I'd moved out of Stefan's cousin's and moved in with Terry, who had a grisly little flat on the ninth floor of a block with two lads who worked in a brewer's. Twins, they were. Hardly ever said anything, just grinned.

'Then money got to be a serious problem. I was still washing up in the cafe, and Terry had a job book-keeping, but it wasn't enough to pay the rent, especially because he drank like a man possessed. I've never known anyone who could drink like he could and still walk straight and sound sober. So I had to find another job. For a while I worked in a cinema, then I did a bit of cleaning. Somehow we scraped by.' She paused, reflecting. 'I suppose I could have got a grant. But that would have meant involving Daddy, because they based the grants on parental income. I wasn't going to go down *that* route.

'It was a pretty exhausting life – at college by day, rehearsing for productions, keeping up with our studies, at the same time doing two jobs, and in between parties and drunken revels and a lot of sex. Good job we were young and fit. I loved it all. Between us Terry and I scooped up a few of the prizes that were on offer, and by the end of it we were pretty pleased with ourselves and certain we were destined for great things. Terry was very ambitious – he was a competent actor, in a genre sort of way, but what he really wanted was to direct his own films. We had the ideas, the determination, the energy – all we lacked was the money. We were always terminally broke.'

'And then we come to the point where our lives touched again, if rather briefly,' Vic murmured. 'The point where our father's death provided you with funds and allowed you to chase your transatlantic dreams. Perhaps it's a good place to stop for tonight.'

Bel looked at her warily. 'I seem to remember we had a major falling-out,' she said softly. 'I'm sorry it happened, and I'm sorry for my part in it. Because that was the last time we saw each other, before now. What a stupid waste.'

Vic sat upright in her chair, and a red flush appeared on her cheekbones. 'It has been wasteful,' she said. 'But you can't just brush things off as if they never happened.'

Bel heaved herself to her feet. 'I know,' she said, gently touching Vic's shoulder with her finger-tips as she passed. 'Another time, OK? I'm for bed.' She yawned. 'Goodnight, Vic.'

Vic said, 'Bel, what happened to that theatre company? I can't believe it's still going.'

Bel paused at the door. 'No, it isn't. I don't think it could, not in today's world. Even then it was a bit of a relic, a hang-over from another age. There were other rep. companies around, but nothing like ours. It all folded when Edna died, in her eighties, a few years later. It turned out that she'd been supporting the company financially out of her own pocket. Nobody knew that while she was alive. It was her project, I suppose, and she wasn't going to let it die while she had breath in her body and a bean in the bank. There don't seem to be too many Ednas left these days, sadly. She certainly was a force to be reckoned with.'

The phone rang in the hall, and Bel jumped. 'I'll get it, shall I, as I'm on my feet?'

A moment later she put her head round the door. 'That was Frankie,' she said. 'She apologised for ringing late but said there was something she wanted you to read and ponder.' Bel looked down at the scrap of paper in her hand. 'Isaiah chapter one, verse 8. And Deuteronomy 32, verses 36 to 39. Mean anything to you?'

Vic shook her head. 'No, not at all. I'll have to look them up. Just like Frankie to be so mysterious. Thanks, Bel. Have you got everything you need?'

'I'll fill a hot-water bottle for my feet. They're always cold – I think my circulation's going to pot. Goodnight again.'

Vic

Vic lay in bed, her old cardigan round her shoulders. Solomon lay against her side, tightly curled, a paw over his eyes, as if he was protesting against the light from the bedside lamp.

Vic stroked him gently under his chin. 'I'm terribly sorry, Sol,' she said. 'Just let me read these few verses, then I'll switch off the light. I know you need your beauty sleep.' The cat stretched and yawned.

Vic took her Bible from the drawer of her bedside table and put her glasses on. The room was cold, and she could see her breath condensing. *Perhaps I should get central heating after all. I seem to be feeling the cold more. Maybe my blood is thinning as I get older.*

She opened the Bible and turned to Isaiah. 'Jerusalem alone is left,' she read, 'a city under siege – as defenceless as a guard's hut in a vineyard or a shed in a cucumber field.' She frowned. What on earth did Frankie mean? She shook her head and turned the pages back to the longer passage in Deuteronomy. 'The Lord will rescue his people when he sees that their strength is gone. He will have mercy on those who serve him, when he sees how helpless they are. Then the Lord will ask his people: "Where are those mighty gods you trusted?...I, and I alone, am God; no other god is real. I kill and I give life, I wound and heal, and no one can oppose what I do."' She read the verses again, and then closed the book. *Don't I know all this? What's Frankie saying? That I know it but don't act on it? And what's with the shed in a cucumber field? I never knew there was such a sentence in the Bible till now. Well, no doubt Frankie means me to quiz her, and so I shall.*

Vic

Screams awoke her, piercing, terrified, and she sat up abruptly, bedclothes tumbling, feeling her heart lurch erratically and sweat break out cold on her face. She gulped for breath, and as her whirling brain adjusted to a waking state she realised that the house was silent. Who had screamed?

Solomon, undisturbed, opened his eyes and yawned, and she knew that nobody had screamed unless it was herself. Then she remembered, and a cold shudder gripped her. Sucking in her breath she faced her fear before it faded, and in her nightmare saw herself as a child again. She looked down at thin legs, freckled knees, childish sandals treading a woodland path, and then, looking up, saw ahead of her a ramshackle hut, one wooden wall half-collapsed under the weight of a sagging roof heavy with wet leaves and moss. There was a door, hanging askew on rusty hinges, partly open, its rotting base tangled in rank grass and weeds, and from inside came something which she could neither see nor describe but which froze her to the ground in dread. Where was she? Why was she alone in the woods? What was in the abandoned hut that reeked of unspeakable horrors? Her arms stiff by her sides, her fingers clenched, the dream child Vic opened her mouth and screamed.

The wakeful adult shivered and shook her head. *What was all that about? I never dream, or if I do it's all gone by morning. Maybe it's Frankie's doing, giving me late-night texts about sheds. But why such fright? What was in that hut, anyway? Such nonsense.*

She reached for a tissue and wiped the sweat from her forehead and cheeks. Her heart slowed. She slithered back down into the bed and wrapped the quilt round her chilled body. Her clock showed twelve-fifteen: she had been asleep for less than an hour.

Now sleep eluded her, and the dream-images awakened her memory. Seeing those skinny, childish legs she remembered with a soft groan thirteen-year-old Vic the day that Johnnie drowned. For almost forty years, with rare exceptions, she had kept those memories away from her sight, burying them deep, never giving them the chance to overwhelm her. But tonight they were active and would not be governed; it was as if in her weakened state, shocked and vulnerable from her unaccustomed nightmare, they had flung open the prison door and come for her without mercy, without possibility of resistance, demanding to be seen and heard.

She remembered standing by the roadside, the road that bordered her own garden, separated from it by a thick belt of trees, half-hiding herself beside some bushes, a short way down from the bus stop. She was wearing a cotton dress, too short, she thought, too infantile, and the sandals were what Bel might wear, clumsy, unsophisticated. She looked at her watch for the fifth time. He was late.

Ears straining, she thought she caught the sound of a throaty engine, and her heart quickened. As it drew closer and louder, she moved behind the bushes and crouched down. But then it trundled past, and it was only a delivery van. She stood up, brushing the leaves from her hands, and looked at her watch again. He was fifteen minutes late. Cheryl had said he would be here on the hour. What had gone wrong?

She had told Bel she was meeting him. Of course she had: wasn't that the point? She told Bel that he had asked to meet her, that they were going for a walk in the woods, and Bel had stared, open-mouthed. 'But Vic, what if, supposing he, you know, he wants to…' Bel's face was flushed.

Vic, feeling her own falseness, had smirked and preened. 'That's the idea, silly. I dare say he will want to. Didn't you realise? See you later, Bel.' She had strutted off, deaf to Bel's protests, and to anyone but her sister the lie would have been clear. Joe had never done anything much more than wink at her suggestively as he held court, leaning on his motor bike in the square, surrounded by his admirers, both boys and girls. Always he had his arm round one of those girls, and his thick fingers would tangle in her hair or stray daringly down to her breast, and to Vic's eyes there seemed no reason why any particular one had his favour that day. But even as he fondled the favourite he would catch Vic's eye, and grin, and she would blush. Something about him drew her, with a fascination that was tinged with fear. He was huge, both tall and broad, with dark brows that met in the middle, and hands like shovels, and a darkly-bristling chin. Then one of the older girls, not the blonde one, Julie, but the small dark one, Cheryl, who wore makeup that made her look like a sick ghost, had sidled up to Vic, as she hung around on the edges of the group, pretending to herself and the world that she belonged, her eyes darting around, but always coming back, circling, magnetised, to Joe's heavy face with its slightly squinting look.

'What's your name, Victoria, isn't it?' Cheryl had demanded. Vic couldn't speak; she managed a nod. Cheryl looked at her, up and down, chewing gum which she shifted from cheek to cheek. At some level Vic knew this girl was corrupt, not to be trusted, but she didn't care. Cheryl was one of Joe's inner ring. How you came to that favoured place Vic had no idea, but she thought she would do anything – *anything* – to be there. To be a favourite of Joe's – to be envied by those scornful sophisticates, with their brazen, willing flesh – was worth almost any peril. 'He wants to meet up with you,' Cheryl said, tilting her head in Joe's direction.

'Me?' gasped Vic.

'Yeah. He says he wants to find out if you're really Little Miss Innocent.' She folded her arms, pushing up her breasts, challenging. 'So, you OK with that?'

'Of course I am,' Vic said, trying not to stutter.

'Be at the bus stop, then, tomorrow, three o'clock. The one on Palmer's Lane, by the woods. He'll pick you up on his bike.' She turned and stalked away, then looked back over her shoulder. 'Lucky you, love, if you can handle it.' And she had cackled with eldritch laughter.

That evening, for a heart-sinking moment that was nevertheless tinged with craven relief, she had thought her plans scuppered when her parents had given the two girls charge of Johnnie. But she had told Bel of the assignation, and sworn her to secrecy. 'Just for an hour, Bel. I'll make it up to you, I promise.'

'Well, all right,' Bel conceded. 'Just tell me everything afterwards. Everything, OK?'

Half-past three came. Two vehicles passed with a whoosh of tyres. Vic looked at her watch again, and knew it was no good. He wasn't coming, of course he wasn't. Had he ever meant to? How could she have thought for a moment that he could be interested in her, skinny babyish Vic, when he had knowing girls at his side, his for the taking, girls with dyed hair and black eyes and on-show curves? She crossed the road and stumbled back into the trees, her eyes stinging with tears of shame, furious, humiliated, miserable. She tormented herself with the knowledge that they would all know, all the others, Joe's hangers-on, and that she could never go back. Perhaps even now they were all laughing at her, poor gullible kid. She hurried on, deeper into the woods, barely seeing the familiar paths, scuffing the leaves up angrily with her bare toes. She rubbed her face with her hands, and stopped as the thought came to her that she wouldn't tell Bel – she couldn't. If the deception broke something between them, it couldn't be helped. She grabbed handfuls of leaves and leaf mould and scattered them over her hair and clothes.

Then she heard screaming, and her heart lurched sickeningly. This was no exciting game – in that scream she heard panic, and it was Bel's voice, on and on. Vic raced through the woods, sweating and panting, oblivious of brambles snatching and scratching. The screams and sobs got louder, and her own name was in them. She came to the river, and saw it all in a frozen tableau, her heart banging against her ribs with terrifying force: Bel up to her shins in the shallows of the Angle, her dress tucked into her knickers, her bare legs splashed with mud, her chest heaving, her face red and streaked with tears, and beside her in the mud, the limp sodden body of Johnnie.

I never wanted to remember that again. Not ever. Forty years on, Vic huddled under the bedclothes, and tears ran down her face. *What's the use of remembering? It happened. I can't change it. It's over. But it's never really over, is it? That's the trouble. It's with me, that scene, stamped on my brain, till the day I die. With everything that came afterwards, down the years. God help me, God help us. Because Bel must remember it too, just as clearly. She must have felt so helpless and abandoned. Lord, be merciful. We were just children, and it was too much for any child to bear.*

Vic

The phone rang again, early the next morning, while Vic was finishing a bowl of cereal. A stack of textbooks stood on the table beside her plate, reminding her of the imminence of school. She sighed and trudged through to the hall.

'Vic? It's Frankie. Yes, I know I keep odd hours. Sorry if it's rather early. I am a slave to my son, not to mention being kept awake by his brother or sister. Did you get a chance to read those texts I sent over for you?'

'I read them, Frankie,' Vic said. 'And I read them again. But I am not yet enlightened.'

Frankie chuckled. 'I thought you might be mystified. Well, we shall just have to continue our conversation and maybe I can shine a little light on your darkness.'

'That would be welcome,' Vic said.

'Actually, it's your sister I wanted to speak to,' Frankie said. 'Is she about?'

'Oh. Right.' Vic frowned. 'I last heard her splashing in the bathroom. I'll see if I can find her.'

She laid the phone down and called up the narrow staircase. 'Bel? Phone for you – yet again.'

Bel appeared at the top of the stairs, her head swathed in a towel, clutching her dressing gown round her middle. 'For me? Who is it? Not Jason?' She started down the stairs.

'No, it's Frankie.' Vic turned and went back to her breakfast. 'The phone never stops ringing these days,' she grumbled. 'And it's always for you.' She closed the kitchen door and sat down again at the table, resolutely not listening to Bel talking and laughing. What did she and Frankie have to laugh about?

Ten minutes later Bel appeared. 'Well, how extraordinary,' she said. 'Any tea going?' She flopped into a chair.

'What's extraordinary?' Vic poured tea into a mug, and pushed it across the table to Bel.

'Frankie says she's been thinking how to get me involved with the church while I'm here,' Bel said. 'She wants to use my professional skills, she says.'

'Frankie is full of blarney at times,' Vic said with some acidity.

Bel reddened. 'I do have some skills, you know.'

'Of course you do. So, what's her idea?'

'She wondered if I would help with the Sunday School. I thought, I don't really do kids, but she said there are already people running it.'

'Yes, two youngish mothers with the smaller children, Kate and Lesley I think they're called, and Jean takes the older ones. Generally, depending on the service, they come into church for the beginning, then go into the vicarage for their activities, and come back at the end. What does Frankie want you to do?'

Bel took a gulp of her tea and leaned forward. 'She thought I could read stories to the little ones, and do some drama with the older children. Apparently the ladies aren't too confident with that sort of thing, and Frankie thinks it's a shame, that it's something the kids would enjoy. She says it's a way of teaching them without them realising it. She said they could've done something at Christmas if there'd been someone to help them with it.'

'So? What did you think?' Vic took her crockery to the sink and started washing up. 'Don't you want some toast?'

'In a minute. I feel in a bit of a flap, having to make decisions this early in the morning. Well, I was a bit worried about muscling in on someone else's territory, but Frankie said the ladies would welcome it. She said she'd ring them later and set up a meeting so we could get to know each other and discuss some ideas. Then I could get started on Sunday.'

Vic shook her head and smiled despite herself. 'Frankie likes to get things done.'

'I expect she's in a hurry. Wants to put things in place, get people going, before she's out of action. You did say she was going to take some leave once the new baby arrives, didn't you?'

Vic turned to face Bel, leaning on the sink as she dried her hands. 'I think so, though I don't know the exact arrangements. So, after all that, did you agree?'

'Well, I had another possible objection.'

'Which was?'

'That I won't be here for the long haul. You know, to see it through. Eventually our place in London will be fixed up, and even before then Jason, bless his cottons, might – just might – come up with something. And then I'd have to leave them in the lurch. But Frankie had thought of that.'

'She would,' Vic murmured, half to herself.

'She said,' Bel continued, 'that whatever I could pass on, whatever ideas I could give them, even if it was only for a short time, would be useful. So yes, I'll go and meet them all and see what we can sort out. Apparently,' she said, clearing her throat, 'these ladies, Kate and whoever, are quite sold on the idea of having what they call a proper actor to do drama with their children. Amazingly they've all heard of me. Probably because I've been in quite a few soaps,' she added modestly.

Vic looked at her quizzically. 'I didn't realise you were quite so famous,' she said. 'But I guess I wouldn't, not being a soap fan.'

'I'm not famous,' Bel said, bristling. 'I've just been on TV a fair bit over the years. I have a face and a name that ordinary viewers know. I don't suppose you rate soaps much.'

'I'm hardly any kind of expert,' Vic said. 'It sounds as though you've done well in what must be a chancy profession. I always thought you had real talent, though.'

Bel looked up, her eyes wide and startled. 'You did? From when?'

'Don't you remember? I came to a couple of productions you were in with the Stoke Players. Before you disappeared.'

'Hm. I kind of remember that. I wonder what you saw.'

'Oh, one of them was something about a murder in a country house. I think you played a saucy maid.'

Bel grinned broadly. 'So I did! And wasn't Howie the Colonel with the roving eye? How very prophetic.'

'I think the other thing I came to was Shakespeare. One of the comedies – I can't remember which. You had to dress as a boy while looking alluringly female. So it was probably "Twelfth Night." You did it well, I thought. Even as a teenager you had presence.'

'Such praise! Thank you.' Bel bowed. 'And it was indeed "Twelfth Night." Great fun. I'd have liked to do more Shakespeare, but as it turned out I went where Terry led, and he went where stardom and money were beckoning. Or so he thought.'

'Where was that?'

'Oh, America, of course. Once my money came through – after Daddy died,' she added, blushing slightly, 'we went to the States. I told you Terry wanted to get into films.'

'Did it work out?' Vic asked.

'For a while. Can I have that toast now? Any more tea in the pot?'

'I'll make fresh.' Vic put the kettle on and dropped two slices of bread in the toaster. She slid into the chair opposite Bel. 'Well? Did he make films? Did you star in them? Would I have heard of any of them?'

'That depends.' Bel thought for a moment. 'Do you really want to hear all this?'

'Of course,' Vic said.

'Well, not to make too long a story of it, Terry did make some films. Some of them did quite well. Have you heard of a film called "Closer than your skin?" It was a sort of cult horror-movie. I was in that. Died quite spectacularly.'

'No, I can't say horror ever really appealed.'

The toast popped up and Bel got to her feet and went to retrieve it. 'It kind of made his name, that one. Oh, and by then he'd changed it, his name, I mean. He thought Terry Ilthwaite just wouldn't do, so he became Clive Morgan. His most famous film was probably "The Doors of Heaven". Does that ring any bells?'

'Yes, I think I might actually have seen it,' Vic said, surprised. 'I can't remember you being in it, though.'

'No, I wasn't,' Bel said. 'I was otherwise engaged at the time.'

Vic got up and poured boiling water into the teapot. 'Was he any good as a director? Terry?'

'Yes, he wasn't bad. He was a quick learner, which helped. And we were able to hire good people, always a wise move. It all went swimmingly for a while. What we lacked in experience we made up for with sheer self-confidence and bravado. After a year or so we even had a great frothy wedding. What we were doing was what everybody did, flaunting our wealth, cultivating people for what they could offer, all very tacky. The wedding cost the earth, and half the people who were anybody at the time were there.'

'But? It sounds as though there was a "but,"' Vic said. She brought the teapot to the table.

Bel sighed. 'Pass the marmalade, can you? Thanks. Yes, there was indeed a "but." We had a few years, seven or eight maybe, when we were riding high. Making money, living in a plush house, driving silly cars, all the glamorous nonsense, and we lapped it up. But we overstretched ourselves, and Terry got cocky, and there were newer, younger, cleverer people on the scene. We started to run up debts. I suppose we might have pulled through, drawn in our horns, I don't know. I'll never know.' She took a bite of her toast. Vic, watching her intently in the silence that followed, saw Bel's eyes mist over. She waited.

Bel drained her tea-cup, set it down, and rubbed her eyes. She took a deep breath. 'I'll never know, because Terry – I could never think of him as Clive – wrote off a car we didn't own one night, and wrote himself off at the same time.'

Vic's eyes widened. 'What? Not killed?'

Bel nodded. 'Wrapped himself round a tall pine, and that was it. Overnight I was a widow, and almost completely broke. That part of it was something I was used to. Being a widow definitely wasn't.'

'Oh, Bel. How horrible.' Vic stretched out and took her hand. 'How absolutely awful. How did you cope?'

Bel smiled, a dark smile full of memory. 'Badly. Luckily for me a very good friend, who also happened to be our accountant, got me out of a financial hole that I didn't know was there. Believe me, we hadn't spent our money wisely. I got work, some acting work, but not enough to pay my way, so, once again, I was waitressing and other such jobs, and some of them I'd really rather not remember in any detail, but they paid the rent. All our assets were sold to pay off creditors, and there were a horde of those, I can tell you. I had just enough for a one-bedroom flat in a run-down part of town. How are the mighty fallen, eh?'

'But you came back to Britain.'

Bel nodded. 'I survived for a few more years, but it was hard. Then I had a break. I got a call one day from someone we'd known way back, and he said if I was willing to relocate to the UK he had some work he could offer me. It was he who introduced me to Jason, as it happened. Jason has his faults, but I'm not going to get anyone better, not now. We're stuck with each other.' She smiled faintly. 'You know, I had no intention of telling you all this. Not today, anyway. It's all rather depressing.'

'But you've done all right here, from what I can gather. Better than many. You've had work, regular work. And not waitressing or cleaning offices or manning a call-centre.'

'Mm. I've done better than many, as you say. Considering the almighty cock-up we made of it, I've got off lightly.' She sighed deeply.

'What about Terry?'

'What about him?'

'Do you still miss him?'

Bel's laugh was more of a bark. 'Bless you, that was almost twenty years ago. Much water under the bridge, many men between the sheets, more hours filming, or rather standing around in costume in a draught with a paper cup of tepid tea, than I care to remember. One can't hang on to the past too long. I suppose,' she said thoughtfully, 'I suppose, at the time, he was the love of my life. But we all have many lives, I think, like cats.' She looked around the room. 'Where is that great panther of yours, anyway?'

'He crept in at five o'clock this morning, looking pleased with himself. I expect he'd had a good night's hunting. Now he's asleep on my bed.'

'Cats have a great deal of sense.' Bel pushed herself upright. 'I'd better go and dry my hair, or I'll look like a monkey-puzzle tree in a gale. Frankie could ring any time.'

'You think your meeting will be today?' Vic asked.

'You know Frankie,' Bel said. 'She won't be letting the grass grow.'

Frankie

From her seat in the choir stalls, standing, but leaning on the book-rest to take her weight, Frankie watched the Sunday School children and their leaders as they came through the little north door of the church during the penultimate hymn. She saw Vic, alone as usual towards the back of the church, glance round, and then, almost guiltily, turn back, head bent as if intent on her hymn book. Frankie looked at the children as they piled into the space behind the pews and scrambled onto two long benches set there for the purpose. She noted the faces of the Sunday School leaders, and particularly she studied Bel. She saw Bel's face alight with a quiet triumph, and she smiled to herself as she joined vigorously in the last verse.

'Well now,' she said when they were all seated again. 'Let's see what the Sunday School have been up to, shall we?' She lumbered to the front and leaned on the lectern. 'Who's going to show us what they've been learning about this morning?' A small blonde child jumped up and waved a crumpled sheet of paper. 'Come on, then, Melanie,' Frankie said. 'Come up here and tell me all about it.'

The little girl bounced up the nave with a broad grin. 'We been drawing pictures,' she said, and thrust the paper into Frankie's hand.

'This is very colourful,' Frankie said. 'I think you like red, Melanie.' She held up the blotched scrawl to the congregation, and the child beamed. 'So tell me, who's this?'

'It's Joseph,' the child said. 'That's his fancy new jacket what his daddy gave him.'

'It's very nice,' Frankie said.

'I had a new coat for Christmas,' the child said. 'But it wasn't stripey like Joseph's.' A subdued chuckle rippled round the assembled adults. 'It was green, and it had pockets.'

'It sounds great,' Frankie said. 'Thank you for showing us your drawing, Melanie. What about you older ones? Edward? Can you tell us what you've been doing?'

A dark-haired boy of about ten stood up, blushing and clearing his throat. 'We've been working on a play,' he said. 'We might do it one Sunday. Bella's been helping us. She's been on TV.'

'That sounds very exciting,' Frankie said. 'I look forward to seeing it when it's ready. Are you all in it?'

Edward nodded. 'Yes, because there's a crowd scene,' he said.

'Excellent. Well done, everybody. Now it's nearly time to end, so let's all stand up for the last hymn.'

Frankie trudged up the nave when everybody had gone home. She yawned and started to pull her surplice over her head as she pushed through the vestry door.

'Oh, hello, Don. I didn't know you were still here.'

'Just tidying up some music.' Don stood upright and dusted off his hands.

'What do you think of my idea, then?' Frankie said. She started to unbutton her cassock, now stretched to its limit round her swollen belly. 'Getting Bel involved with the Sunday School?'

'Yes, good,' muttered Don. 'She needed something to do, some purpose. But she'll need more than that, won't she? Especially as term starts again tomorrow. Vic won't be around in the day.'

'I'm thinking about it,' Frankie said. She hung up her robes and took her coat down from its peg. 'Don, you're a good mate of Vic's, aren't you?'

'I hope so,' Don said guardedly.

'How much do you know about her past? I'm not trying to be nosy, don't think that. It's just that she told me some things the other day, and I wondered who else knew.'

'I know about her brother that drowned, if that's what you mean,' Don said. 'And some things she told my late wife. But I think that was probably in confidence.'

'Of course. I don't want to pry. But Vic's been on my mind. More so, I think, since her sister's been here. She's more fragile than she wants us to believe.'

'Who is? Vic or Bel?'

Frankie looked up at Don, and saw suspicion. 'Both, I guess,' she said mildly. 'But it was Vic I meant. She's one of my flock, and Bel's only temporary.'

'What do you mean by "fragile?"' Don demanded.

Frankie patted his arm. 'No need to be fierce, Don,' she said. 'I'm just concerned for her, that's all. I've been praying for them both. Sometimes Vic strikes me like an over-full pan on a hob, about to boil over and make a nasty mess.'

'She's too controlled for that, I'd have thought,' Don said stiffly.

'The tighter the lid, the bigger the spill,' Frankie said. 'You'll keep an eye on her, won't you, Don? When I'm *hors de combat*.'

'I'll do my best,' Don said. He hesitated, then said in a rush, slightly stammering, 'It's what Ellen wanted. Ellen and Vic were close. Vic was very kind to her – to us both.'

Frankie nodded. 'We must keep praying, Don. For healing. Don't you think? There's a lot of damage been done to those sisters, and we don't know the half of it. One pretends it hasn't happened. The other looks at it in the eye, and I guess it's painful.'

Don shook his head and said nothing. He looked bemused.

Frankie smiled. 'You ready to go? I'll follow you and lock up.'

Outside, Frankie pulled the heavy door to and locked it. 'How about you, Don?' she said. 'How are you?'

Don frowned. 'I'm all right,' he muttered. 'No reason not to be.'

'Good. Well, I'm for home. Hoping there'll be a nice smell of cooking when I open my door. You having lunch with Vic as usual?'

Don looked at her under his sandy brows. 'Yes.'

'See you later, then.'

'Yes, of course. Bye.'

For a moment, still frowning, he watched her lumber down the path to the Vicarage. He was dimly aware that she had some agenda with all these innocent-seeming enquiries, but for now her thoughts were opaque to him. He shook his head and turned in the opposite direction, to his own front door.

Bel

'Frankie's a genius,' Bel said as she laid the table for three. 'I'm amazed how much fun it was this morning. Those kids aren't half as scary as I expected. Perhaps country kids are different.'

'They had a good time too, as far as I can gather,' Vic said. She lifted a saucepan lid and poked bubbling carrots with the point of a knife. 'What did you do with them in the end?'

'It's a closely-guarded secret,' Bel said, grinning. 'We're going to amaze everybody with our assembled talents once it's all rehearsed and ready.' She took plates from the shelf. 'Where's Don got to?'

'Talking to Frankie, probably,' Vic said.

'I was thinking,' Bel said. 'Sunday School's fine and dandy, and I'm going to meet up with Jean in the next day or two to plan this thing we're doing with the kids. But once you've gone back to work I'm going to need something else to fill the hours. I can do some housework, if you like.'

'Be my guest.'

'I suppose I should ring a few people too,' Bel said thoughtfully. 'Jason included. I don't want them to think I've dropped off the planet. You can get forgotten very easily in this business. Got to keep visible.'

'It sounds exhausting.' Vic looked up. 'There's the door – it'll be Don. I'll get it.'

Vic and Don spoke little during lunch, but Bel was restless, still full of her morning with what she ironically called her 'fan club.' She talked about it as they ate, summoning up the funny details, until in the end she withered and fell silent. Then, as she got up to clear the plates, scraping her chair back, she said suddenly, 'Don, could I come to work with you one day? I'd like to see your factory, or whatever you call it.'

One day, many years before, a director rehearsing a play she'd been in had demanded a 'small but significant silence.' Now, Bel understood exactly what he meant. Vic said nothing, just stared at the tablecloth.

Don's fair skin flushed and mottled. 'Well, of course, if you like,' he said finally. 'I can't imagine it'd be very interesting for you, though.'

'Oh, I'm interested in lots of things,' Bel said. 'But only if I wouldn't be causing any inconvenience.'

Don blinked rapidly. 'No, of course not. Um, what about Thursday?'

'It's a date,' Bel said, and then thought perhaps this wasn't the best choice of words. *Too late now.* 'Thanks.'

Vic

8 January 2006

I need to sleep. Tomorrow is the first day of a new term, even if it's all meetings and planning and no pupils. I can't be fuddled and gormless. Why can't I sleep? I never used to have this problem. It must be because of Bel, but I won't tell her she's brought insomnia with her. She's stirring up the sludge, I suppose, but it's my own fault for letting the sludge settle instead of clearing it out years ago. Oh Lord, I am so tired.

And, Lord, I'm not happy with myself. I should be glad that Bel's found herself something to do that gives her purpose, that helps someone else, that makes her feel useful, in a way that only she could do, not just any old thing. Don't we all need that? Of course I'm pleased for her, sort of, but that's a weak thing compared to this wriggling worm of envy that's winding and squirming around in my black heart. I shouldn't feel like this, should I? But it seems as if she's robbing me, slowly and innocently, of any tiny significance I may have built up for myself over these long years. In my own eyes, that is – I can't speak for how anyone else sees it. As if she is getting brighter, and I am fading.

I am so miserable, Lord. Always, it seems, on the verge of tears, or an angry outburst. Like something over-tightened, stretched, ready to snap. This is no way to start work – I should be rested. I know it's mostly my own fault. But is this your doing? I don't know. I'm so muddled these days.

Oh, Lord, tell me, why aren't I more like you?

Don

'Come into my office, Bel. I'll make some coffee.'

'Sure I'm not putting you out?'

'No, no. Sit down.' Don waved her to a hard-looking upright chair.

Bel looked round as he busied himself with the kettle. His office was clean and tidy. A row of filing-cabinets, gunmetal grey, stood against one wall. His desk was clear of papers, and there was only a small stack of letters in the wire in-tray. The waste-paper bin was empty. A flourishing white orchid graced the window-sill.

'My secretary,' Don said, seeing her looking. 'She's what people call a treasure. I imagine her house is just as spotless and organised.' He smiled.

'Not here today?' Bel asked.

'No, it's her day off. I shall make sure I mess things up a little, so she'll have something to tut about tomorrow.'

'Not, I take it, a blonde bombshell forever painting her nails.'

Don laughed and winced at the same time. 'Good heavens, no. Ann is on the other side of middle-age, like me. She's short, a little plump, well turned-out, married to a golf fanatic called Bill. She's very efficient, and has only one obvious failing: I haven't yet discovered that she has any sense of humour.' He poured boiling water into two china cups, added milk, and handed a cup to Bel.

'Thanks. These dainty cups, are they Ann's doing as well?'

'No, they're mine. My late wife liked china. I don't use them at home, so I brought them to the office.'

Bel sipped her coffee. 'Thanks for the tour, Don. It was nice of you to take the time. I thought it was very interesting.'

Don sat down on the other side of the desk. He raised an eyebrow. 'Really? I wouldn't have thought there was much to see. Do you want to go back to Thackham once you've had your coffee?'

Bel looked up, surprised. 'Certainly not, thanks all the same. I've taken up enough of your working day as it is, without using you as a chauffeur.

No, I'll do a bit of shopping now I'm here in the great metropolis, and then I'll get the bus home.'

'Oh, all right.' They drank in silence for a moment, then Don said, 'I'm sorry, there don't seem to be any biscuits.'

'Just as well,' Bel said. 'I would only eat them and regret it later.' She put her cup down carefully on the desk. 'There was something I wanted to talk to you about, though, as I'm here.' She looked up at him, and saw his brows contract in that defensive way of his. She took a deep breath. 'I'm worried about Vic: she's very pale, and ever since she went back to school on Monday she's seemed quite withdrawn, hardly says a word. She doesn't look well at all.'

Don stared at Bel and a welter of thoughts rushed through his brain, tumbling over each other. Was Bel acting? Was she ever not? Was it conscious, or just something she did instinctively? Did she even know herself? The thought came to him that he was used to sick women. He remembered Ellen's last weeks, and he felt himself start to sweat, though the room was cool. He knew that Vic had a problem, but was this something else? The thought of Vic ill made him feel uncomfortable, almost breathless, and he admitted to himself, fleetingly, that he too was worried.

He cleared his throat. 'Perhaps it's just the beginning of term. She's probably tired. There's always so much to get done.'

'Well, I hope you're right. I'll keep an eye on her. I bet she hardly ever goes to the doctor.' She pushed her chair back and stood up, resting her finger tips on the edge of the desk.

'Absolutely right,' Don said. He got up, crossed the room and opened the door for her. 'She says she doesn't have time to be ill. But if Solomon is off-colour he gets whisked to the vet before he has time to escape and hide. I'll show you out.'

When Bel had gone Don took time to wash up the cups, dry them and put them away. Normally he tried, as far as he could, not to think about the past, but sometimes the memories just presented themselves, and he had no choice but to face them till they faded. Now he thought of a conversation with Ellen, when she could still talk lucidly, a few months before her death. Vic had been there that afternoon, cheering Ellen up with an account of village doings, sometimes exaggerated for the sick woman's benefit, Don suspected. When Vic had gone home, Ellen, slumped in her wheelchair, had gripped Don's hand with surprising strength.

'Vic hasn't had an easy life, you know,' she said abruptly.

'I do know,' Don said. 'You told me some of it, didn't you?'

'Not the half. Don, love, when I'm gone, I want you to look after Vic. You will, won't you?'

He remembered saying to her, fierce in his misery, 'I don't want to talk about when you're gone.'

She had looked up at him, stretching her neck painfully. 'But we have to,' she whispered. 'We have to. Life is for the living. Isn't it?' A tear fell on the back of his hand. 'I've always loved you, you know that. Don't you?' He nodded, speechless. 'I love Vic too. She's been such a friend. She's had it tough, but she still gives out so much. Take care of her.'

He had told her – of course he had – that he would do his best. He hadn't known then, and he still didn't know now, what was really in her mind. He had an uneasy sense that he had somehow failed them both.

Bel

Bel sat on the slowly-chugging bus, staring out into the murk of the January afternoon. She had meant to be back in time at least to make Vic a cup of tea when she got home. But one thing after another had prevented her, and here she was now, impatient at almost half past four on a country bus that was in no hurry.

When she left Don she wandered about the streets of West Stoke, looking in shop windows, finding little to engage her attention, but ambling in a pleasant daze until hunger began to bite and she thought of going home, or perhaps of buying a sandwich to munch on the eight-mile journey back to Thackham. At this point she heard a loud banging next to her ear and looked up to see Connie Dawson rapping on the window from inside the Green Lion, a pub Bel remembered as sedate and respectable, unlike the Headless Chicken. Connie was with a clutch of people, some of whom Bel recognised from the New Year party, and she was gesturing, beckoning to Bel to come and join them. The smell of cooking wafting out of the pub door clinched it, and Bel went in.

She ate lunch with the AmDrammers, and drank several gins eagerly bought for her. Regaling them with soap and sit-com gossip, Bel felt herself at home, holding court and enjoying their rapt attention. The time sped by in a haze of alcohol and tobacco fumes, jokes and loud laughter, and she forgot her resolve.

Finally the bus lurched to a halt at the end of Thackham's main street. Now she stumbled up the track to Vic's, cursing her thin-soled boots, skin chilled by the freezing mist. When she arrived at the gate there were lights on upstairs, and Vic's car was parked by the fence. *Damn, damn, damn.*

She let herself in, and peered round the living-room door. The fire was laid but not lit, and the air was cold. The kitchen was in darkness, and the curtains were still open. Bel frowned and went to the bottom of the stairs. She was about to call out when she heard the sound of vomiting from the bathroom. *Oh my God, she really is ill.*

She kicked off her boots and padded up the stairs. She hesitated, then rapped softly on the bathroom door. 'Vic? Are you all right?' *Stupid question. Of course she's not all right.* There was silence, then a slight moan. 'Vic?'

Vic's voice was croaky. 'I'm all right, Bel. Don't worry. I'll be down in a moment. Make yourself some tea.'

'Never mind tea. What can I do to help?'

'Nothing. I won't be long.'

Bel went slowly back downstairs. She closed the curtains, switched on lights, and put the kettle on. She was kneeling by the fire, trying to induce it to light, when she heard a slight sound. She turned round. Vic was standing in the doorway, her old cardigan clutched round her.

Bel scrambled to her feet. 'Oh, Vic! You look terrible. Whatever is the matter?'

Vic waved her hand. 'It's really nothing. Probably something I ate. I've got a sensitive stomach, you know that.'

'You've not looked right all week. Shouldn't you see a doctor?'

Vic shook her head. 'I've seen doctors, and they all say there's nothing wrong with me. So please don't worry. It's probably stress.' She turned away, walked unsteadily down the hallway to the kitchen, and lowered herself into a chair, carefully like an old woman. Bel followed. 'Oh, good, you've boiled the kettle. I'll have a herbal tea. That usually settles my stomach.' She smiled, a pinched smile that spoke of heroic effort. 'How was your day?'

'It was good. But Vic, I meant to be home hours ago. I'm so sorry I wasn't here to make you tea and warm the place up. You've had to come back to a cold, dark house feeling ill. I'm very selfish.'

'You weren't to know. So tell me, what have you been doing?'

Bel poured boiling water onto a sachet of peppermint tea and stirred it. 'Here you are.' She put the mug on the table in front of Vic. 'Well, I had a tour of Don's business, and he made me a cup of coffee, then I did a bit of window-shopping, and then I bumped into Connie Dawson and a few of the Stoke Players and we had lunch in the Green Lion. They kept lining up the gins and I was enjoying a gossip and the time just...' she shrugged, '...flew. And then the bus was unbelievably slow. I swear it took a good hour with all the stops. Just to do eight piffling miles.'

Vic nodded and sipped slowly, her eyes half-closed, her hands wrapped round the steaming mug. 'This is very nice. Thank you.'

Bel hovered over her anxiously. 'Do you want to go to bed? I'll get you a hot-water bottle if you like.'

'No, really, I'm all right now. I don't feel much like eating, but you'll get yourself something, won't you? There's plenty in the fridge.'

Bel frowned. 'You're not going to work tomorrow, are you?'

'Good heavens, of course I am!' Vic said. 'It's the beginning of term. I've got countless things to do. Honestly, Bel, I've had this problem for years. It's not serious. Just a minor thing. I'll be fine.'

'What about just a small piece of toast? That's bland, isn't it? You shouldn't go all night on a completely empty stomach.'

Vic sighed. 'All right, if you like.'

Bel found bread in the bread bin, cut an uneven slice, and put it in the toaster. She leaned on the kitchen counter, her arms folded. 'I wouldn't have thought, as schools go,' she said, 'that Repley was a particularly stressful place. I'd have thought it was a nice place to work. But perhaps I'm just thinking of it from a pupil's point of view.' She took a plate from the cupboard and put it on the table.

'It *is* a nice place to work,' Vic said, her voice low. 'From the moment I decided to go to college I had my sights on a job at Repley, but it took eleven years of working in other schools before a vacancy came up in the English department. I'm happy there. The staff are nice, the girls are lovely on the whole, even the parents aren't too bad. But things are very different from when we were at school. There are targets to be met, lots of meetings, endless planning, mountains of paperwork. Parental expectations are high. Considering how steep the fees are, I think I'd have high expectations if I had a daughter at a school like Repley.'

Bel put the toast on Vic's plate, found her a knife and a jar of honey. 'Energy,' she said. 'You must have something.' She slid into the opposite chair.

Vic nibbled at the toast. 'What about you?'

'I'm not hungry,' Bel said. 'I had a huge lunch in the Green Lion, courtesy of Connie Dawson. Maybe later.' She smoothed out the table-cloth, thinking. 'Do you ever wish you did have a daughter at Repley?'

She heard Vic suck in her breath. 'What do you mean? Do I wish I were that well-off? No, I don't. That ambitious? No. Which is why I didn't apply to be Head of Department when it fell vacant eighteen months ago. I didn't want that much bureaucratic responsibility added to my workload. That's why I now work under someone who's fifteen years younger than me. But she's good, very good, and we get on well. No, wealth and ambition don't interest me.'

Bel said nothing, looking at Vic's face. A few moments ago it had been spectral, white and shadowed. Now a red flush stained her forehead and cheeks.

'But if you mean,' Vic said slowly, 'do I wish I had a daughter, yes, I do. Or,' her voice choked, 'or, indeed, a son.'

Bel caught the intensity of her sister's tone, and frowned. 'Eric didn't want children, then?' she said. She saw Vic's eyes close, as if in pain, and fly open again; she saw her lips clench in a sudden spasm, and she realised – *too late, as usual* – that she was walking on shards of glass. 'I'm sorry, Vic – it's none of my business.'

Vic took a deep breath, closing her eyes again as if Bel had not spoken. 'Let me tell you what happened after you and I parted company, after that stupid quarrel at school.'

'You don't have to.' Bel's voice teetered on the edge of panic.

'No,' Vic said, her voice a monotone. 'It's probably time you knew.' She paused. Bel watched her, seeing her eyes glaze as if they were no longer registering anything in the outside world, but scanning a life long gone. Vic sighed and focused on the present again. 'I married Eric in November, a few months after we finished at Repley. You remember the big fuss he made of my singing, and how he wanted me to go on with it and make something of it, with him as my mentor and my agent. I was nineteen, and my silly head was turned. Well, I married him. That was part of the deal: I'd become a Christian that year, and my standards of virtue were high, or so I thought. No living in sin for me, or at least, not for long.' She shook her head. 'I didn't even care that he didn't share my beliefs. In my innocent arrogance, I thought I could draw him in somehow, by the power of my example.' She gave a bitter little laugh. 'Well, we got married. My wedding was the very reverse of yours, from what you've told me. It took place in a Registry Office, with the desk clerk and the father of one of Eric's pupils as witnesses. I did buy a new dress, but I wore it afterwards many times.' She paused, and smiled slightly as if at her own thoughts. 'I adored Eric. I thought he was the most wonderful man on the planet: funny, wise, attractive, sophisticated, knowledgeable, and by some miracle, mine. I believed that he wanted to nurture me, turn me into a great singer. I was very naive.

'But you know, oddly enough, things did go well for a few years. Eric continued to teach me, just as he had while I was still at school and he was a peripatetic music teacher. I did a number of public recitals – just local things, but I thought they were stepping-stones to something altogether more ambitious and glamorous. I went down especially well, I remember, at a concert at the Town Hall – we didn't live here, of course, we moved north, to Cheshire, where Eric lived as a boy.' For a moment Vic fell silent, picking at the edges of the table-cloth. Then she said softly, 'It was a recital of French song cycles: Poulenc, Debussy, Ravel. Eric accompanied me. He looked very handsome in his penguin suit, and he played with fire and panache. I wore a long dress in apple-green satin, and matching slippers. It was an extraordinary evening. I can still remember how it felt, all that applause, people standing up and calling out. Afterwards we went out for supper. We drank champagne! Someone must have bought it for us, because we couldn't have afforded it. I felt light as an angel's wing.' She paused again. Bel watched her, and saw that she was reliving her moment of triumph, and she understood, because she too had had such moments. 'I wish I'd been there,' she said quietly.

Vic smiled. 'Eric was very pleased and proud, and I think I fell in love with him all over again. There was a lot of hero-worship in my feelings for Eric – he was twice my age, and seemed to me to be terribly experienced and worldly-wise. We went back to our cramped little flat, and nobody got much sleep that night.' She looked at Bel with an eyebrow raised. 'I probably can't compete with your life of pleasure, but I didn't go completely without. Eric at his best was everything I had ever wanted – or thought I did.'

'But?' Bel said. 'To quote you, it sounds as if there's a "but" coming.'

Vic paused, as if bringing painful thoughts to order. 'Eric drank,' she said sombrely. 'At first it didn't amount to much. But life wasn't easy. We never had much money, so I got a job in an office to help things along, and at the same time we were practising and working for my supposed career. But, bit by bit, so that at first I didn't really notice it, he drank more and taught less, and as his drinking got heavier so his pupils began to fall away, and he did unpleasant and awkward things. I got angry with him for spending money on drink when we had so little, and I had to take another job in the evenings so that I had no time for singing practice and no energy. What hurt most was that Eric didn't seem to care, and I gradually came to realise that all he wanted me for was sex and skivvying. That was a bad moment for me. But I wasn't going to give up: I was a Christian, he was my husband, I had made promises and I was determined to hold to them. Poor, deluded, high-minded little fool.' She looked up at Bel. 'Could I have some more of that peppermint tea?'

'Of course.' Bel got to her feet and put the kettle on. 'I'll have some tea too now, I think. Nice, normal, Indian, brown. How are you feeling?'

'Better, thank you. At least physically. But the worst part of this nasty story is yet to come.'

Bel made the tea and brought it to the table. 'Do you want to save it for another day, when you feel stronger?' she said gently.

'No,' Vic said. 'I've got this far – I must plough on, or I shall lose all my courage.'

'Well, I'm listening.'

'Things were bad, but just about bearable. Unfortunately, accidents happen. No, Eric didn't want children, and I certainly didn't want any then, although I'm sure I thought I'd be able to persuade him later, perhaps when my career was more firmly established. My career – what a joke. I discovered I was pregnant, and after the initial shock I accepted it and was happy. In my youthful optimism I believed we would manage somehow. But Eric was furious. Anyone would have thought he'd had nothing to do with it, that it was all my heedless doing. He wanted me to have an abortion. I think of all the things he did and said, that shocked me the most. It was such a clear message to me, that his so-called love was a sham. I was devastated.

'When I think of my foolish young self, what followed is the only thing that gives me any sense of pride. I refused to get rid of my child, and I told him the marriage was over. We were still living in the same cramped little house – neither of us could afford anything else. I was working, two jobs, and when I looked at Eric I couldn't fail to see he was deteriorating. I don't know how he survived. It came to the point that he was hardly teaching at all.

'My baby was due in June. That hope was all I had, and all I lived for. I worked ridiculously hard, very long hours. Although I had no idea what I was going to do in the long term, I saved what money I could. It wasn't an easy time, but I had purpose, at least.'

She fell silent again, staring at the table cloth, her hands gripped tightly together. Bel held her breath. Then Vic looked up at her, and her eyes spoke of despair that had never healed.

'I went into labour one chilly night in March,' she said. 'Ten weeks early. I was shopping at the time, and I was carrying two heavy bags of groceries. I managed to get to the hospital in a taxi which I couldn't afford. The taxi driver helped me through the doors and wouldn't let me pay him. I wish I could meet that man again and thank him.

'My baby was born at one o'clock in the morning. He weighed just over three pounds, and he lived for an hour and a half. I called him James.'

Bel looked at her sister, her mouth agape, her eyes wide. Abruptly she pushed her chair back and jumped up, came round to the other side of the table and put her arms round Vic, hugging her tightly, as tears ran down her cheeks. Vic sat unresisting, unmoving as a stone. 'Oh, Vic! How awful, how desperately sad. You poor, poor thing.' She gulped back her tears. 'After everything that went on at home, after losing Johnnie, that this had to happen to you. I can hardly believe it.' She let Vic go, took a handkerchief from her sleeve, and blew her nose. She squeezed Vic's shoulder, and went back to her seat. Vic still sat, dry-eyed, pale. After a moment, Bel said, 'Who knows about this, Vic?'

Vic shrugged. 'The hospital staff who attended me, though I'm sure they've forgotten. It was thirty years ago, after all. Eric knew, because I told him.'

'What did he say?'

'He didn't say anything. He didn't know what to say. He looked stricken, even a little guilty. I didn't really give him a chance, because I didn't think he deserved any pity. I was merciless. After that, once I'd recovered my strength, I worked, and ignored him. I tried to plan, but I was a mess – I'd rested all my hopes on my child, and I had nothing left. I felt very close to ending my own life, oh yes, very close several times, but at some level my faith kept me alive, even though I railed at God. So when I got our father's letter, asking me to come back to Angleby, it was a way out, a way of escape. Of course I didn't want to come back. It seemed such a backward step. I was very, very bitter for a long time.'

'Did you ever tell anyone else? Did anyone ever help you?'

'I told Ellen, and she cried. She and Don never had children, and that was a great sadness for them, so she felt able to understand just a little. She may have told Don. I didn't actually ask her not to. He's never said anything about it, but then, I guess he wouldn't.'

Bel leaned across the table and took Vic's hand. 'I am so, so sorry,' she said, her eyes brimming. 'You didn't deserve such a horrible thing.' She paused, thinking. 'Your James would be thirty, almost thirty-one. You might even have been a grandmother by now.'

Vic nodded. 'Yes. I might have had a family, maybe made up for the one I didn't have as a child.' She patted Bel's hand as she withdrew her own. 'But now you're here,' she said, her voice husky. 'And I'm thankful that we have found one another again, whatever happens in the future.'

Bel caught her tone, and frowned. 'Are you worried about the future?

Do you suspect you might have something really wrong with you, even though you swear it's all something and nothing? Please, don't leave me out of this.'

Vic shook her head. 'No, it's not that. What I said is true. I *have* seen doctors, and they all say the same: they can't find anything wrong with me, but my digestion is weak and I react badly to stress. Which is where we started.' She sighed. 'Today at school I heard a rumour. People who should know were whispering. Repley is in financial difficulty, it seems. I didn't know any of this. There are worries among the staff that people may be laid off, that contracts may not be renewed. Some of us, and that includes me, may be out of a job by the end of term. It came to me that if I don't have my work, there won't be much left for me, at least in a worldly sense. So I guess if anything made me sick, it was that.' She hesitated, frowning. 'I wonder if that's what Frankie meant,' she murmured, more to herself than to Bel.

'What Frankie meant by what?' Bel said.

'You know she sent those texts for me last week? Hold on a minute – I'll get my Bible and read them to you.'

She left the room and walked heavily up the stairs. A few minutes later she was back, riffling through the pages of her Bible. She cleared her throat. 'Deuteronomy 32, verse 36: "The Lord will rescue his people when he sees that their strength is gone. He will have mercy on those who serve him, when he sees how helpless they are." There's more, but what do you think? Is it something about needing to be at rock bottom before you call for help? That God is waiting to help me, but I haven't asked? How did Frankie know, anyway?'

Bel held up her hands. 'Vic, don't ask me. I don't know much about praying and all that. Frankie's pretty canny, though. She's probably just a good guesser. Maybe you should talk to her one day.'

Vic closed the Bible and looked at Bel, smiling wanly, and Bel saw affection there as well as sadness. 'Well, perhaps I will. One day.' She pushed her chair back and stood up. 'I'm going to rest for a while, if you don't mind me abandoning you.'

'Of course I don't. If you're insisting on going to work tomorrow, rest is the best thing for you. Bang on the floor if you need anything.'

'I will. Thank you.' She moved towards the door.

'Vic, what happened to Eric?'

Vic stood still, her hand on the door handle. 'I have no idea. If he didn't drink himself to death, then I suppose he's still around. But I don't know. After I came back here I divorced him, as quickly as the law of the land allows.'

'I wonder,' Bel mused, 'what he thinks about all that now. Does he have regrets, do you think?'

Vic wrapped her cardigan round herself more tightly. 'I neither know nor care to know,' she said dully. 'I've spent years trying to forgive our parents. Eric is at the bottom of the list.'

'Why are you bringing *them* up again?' Bel said.

Vic's face set hard. 'If you bring a child into the world, you should be prepared to love it and do your best for it. Don't you agree? And they failed, not in every way perhaps, but in most of the important ways. I hope, I like to think, that I would have been a better parent to my son. Sadly, I never had the chance. And of course I don't blame Eric for James's death. I do blame him for his neglect of me, his cold, shallow vanity. I look back and I see a trail of disasters. Betrayal of responsibility. Broken promises. Lack of love. They're hard to swallow.' She turned away. 'Anyway, I'm going to bed. If I feel better I might get up later. Otherwise I guess I'll see you in the morning.'

Bel tiptoed into her bedroom. She could feel her heart thudding painfully, and she realised she'd forgotten to breathe. She closed the door soundlessly and collapsed onto her bed. She let out her breath and sucked it in again with a gasp. *Oh my God, what am I going to do now?*

A headache began to drum somewhere behind her ears. She pulled open the drawer of her bedside table and pulled out a torn-open envelope. With clumsy fingers she extracted from it a Christmas card, showing a conventional scene: a robin in the foreground, perched on a snowy gatepost; a group of people in Victorian costume trudging through the snow to a church, a golden glow of light pouring from its open door; and in one corner a random sprig of holly. She opened the card. On the left hand side, in his sprawling writing, an address: 75, Waterfield Road, Barnsley, South Yorkshire. On the right-hand page, under the faded genteel verse, simply, "Happy Christmas, Mum. Love from Matt."

She put the card back in the drawer, and held her head in her hands. A sheaf of Christmas cards had arrived a few days before. Now that the London house was off-limits, she had asked for post to be sent to her agent, Jason Korba, who had agreed to post it on to Thackham. Some Christmas mail had taken a long time to arrive – having sat, Bel suspected, on Jason's disordered desk until he had finally remembered it. She had looked cursorily at the others and recycled them. But this one was different. Not only had he sent her a card, he had included his address. She hadn't heard a word from him in two years, and now this. What could it mean, except that he wanted things to be better between them? Giving her his address must surely be an invitation to get in touch, mustn't it? So far she had done nothing, said nothing, in an agony of indecision.

And now, this revelation of Vic's. Of course it changed everything. What could she, Bel, possibly say? 'Oh, by the way, Vic, forgot to mention, Terry and I had a son, Matthew. I was a lousy parent, according to him. I didn't see a lot of him even when we were living in the same house, and I haven't seen or heard of him at all in the last two years.'

She looked again at the address. Barnsley: Terry's home town. Was Matthew there looking for his father's family? He'd be unlucky. Terry was the product of a fling between two teenagers, one a soldier, killed by a stray bullet in Korea a few weeks before Terry was born, the other a streetwise hardnosed girl who had given birth to her baby, then left him with her mother one morning when he was barely three months old, and disappeared. A month later a postcard arrived, a picture of Big Ben and a London bobby. 'Living in the smoke now. You can have the kid.' All efforts to trace her had failed, and Terry was raised by two women, his grandmother and his great-grandmother. It was just possible, Bel thought, doing some rapid arithmetic, that Terry's grandmother, Pat, was still alive, but she'd be in her eighties if she was. Terry's mother, the teenage runaway, would be sixty-eight by now, but she hadn't been heard of since that one enigmatic postcard.

Bel heaved a sigh. Whatever Matthew was doing in Barnsley, that wasn't the issue now. What was she, Bel, going to do? How could she tell Vic about her son? But how could she not?

She got up, and padded onto the landing. Gingerly she opened Vic's bedroom door. She couldn't see much in the darkness, but Vic's breathing was regular and she seemed to be asleep. Bel closed the door quietly, took her shoes in her hand and tiptoed down the stairs. She picked up the phone, dialled, and waited, holding the receiver close to her ear as if to stop any sound escaping.

'Frankie?' she said when the phone was answered. 'It's Bel. Isabel, Vic's sister. I hope I'm not disturbing you. Oh, good. Look, would it be OK if I came down to see you? Yes, now, if it wouldn't be too inconvenient. Of course I don't mind – you've got to see to your little boy. All right, thank you. I'll be there in about half an hour.'

Vic

Vic woke from a muddled kaleidoscope of a dream in which Eric had figured in varied guises. She didn't want to think about Eric, but talking to Bel had revived his image in her mind, and memories that were sweet in themselves but soured by hindsight came on a march-past uninvited, as if for her inspection.

At fifteen Vic had been, she supposed, 'discovered.' A new Head of Music came to Repley, and heard Vic sing with the school choir. One day this lady kept Vic behind when all the other girls had been dismissed.

'That's quite a voice you have there, Victoria.'

'Thank you,' Vic replied, blushing.

'You could develop it, you know. Ever thought of having singing lessons?'

Vic had stared open-mouthed; afterwards she had cringed with embarrassment: the teacher must have thought her stupid. 'No, I haven't,' she stuttered.

'Would your parents consider it? We have some excellent peripatetic teachers here, you know. Mr Whitley might teach you. I could have a word.'

'I don't know.' Vic hung her head. The idea of writing to her father, when they hardly spoke, was unthinkable.

Perhaps the teacher had heard something of the Colbournes' family tragedy; perhaps her heart was softened. 'Would you like me to write to your parents and suggest it? That's if you yourself like the idea.'

Vic nodded vigorously, colour and heat flooding her cheeks, foolish tears stinging her eyes. 'Yes, yes please. That would be wonderful.'

It all took a while: the singing teacher had to rearrange his schedule, and then Vic had exams, but in the autumn term as she entered the sixth form Vic had her first lesson with Eric Whitley, and she remembered it with a vividness that even now made her flinch.

What had she expected? Certainly not a good-looking man in the prime of life, tanned from a holiday in Greece (so he told her), thick black hair flopping over his forehead, dark eyes full of humour; certainly not someone who played the piano standing up, a cigarette stuck to his bottom lip; who, as soon as the door was closed, tore off his regulation tie and unbuttoned his shirt, so that black curling hair was discomfitingly visible, or who shouted at her when she got something wrong, or when her singing was 'too feeble.' Not someone who winked at her if they passed in the corridor on a day when she was not due for a lesson, making her burn with sudden heat, but who could wipe her out with a stinging phrase if her singing lacked passion or power, or if clearly she had not practised well.

For a few months she suffered in silence. She had no words to name the thoughts she had about him, apart from a sense that they were shameful; but one day his name came up among a group of her more sophisticated friends, and she realised from their casual smutty talk that what she felt for Eric Whitley was overpowering desire. Night after night she lay in bed in her cell of a study-room at school, surrounded by her books and music, and dreamed of his arms around her, the smell of masculine sweat, his mouth teasing her skin, and she shivered with terrified longing. But it was safe enough, all the same. There was nothing she could do about her feelings. She was sixteen, he was thirty-five. For all she knew he had a wife and children or a string of girlfriends. The thought of him with some other woman made her want to howl, but at the same time she acknowledged her own folly.

She spoke to no one, of course; but canny little Bel somehow suspected what was going on in her sister's mind. She was lounging on Vic's bed one Sunday afternoon, escaping from Games while Vic battled with a history essay. 'You like Mr Whitley, don't you, Vic?' she said, all innocence.

Vic looked up. 'What? Oh, he's all right.' But the bloom of sudden blood in her cheeks gave her away, however much she affected indifference.

Bel chuckled. 'Don't worry, darling sister, I won't tell.' Bel, now thirteen, had recently discovered that she could act, and she did it all the time, to the enormous frustration of her teachers.

Vic cuffed Bel with an exercise book. 'Don't be ridiculous, infant. He's as old as the hills.'

'Maybe he's Methuselah, but you still fancy him, Viccy. You might as well admit it.'

'I admit nothing.'

She barely admitted it even to herself, so hopeless, so clichéd it seemed, and the months went by, and every week she looked forward to her singing lesson in a fever of agitation, and when the lesson was over, or if for one reason or another he didn't come, she fell into dejection. How had no one noticed? Perhaps they did. Perhaps they thought it was all hormonal. *Which it was, in spades.* And all the while, inevitably, the bright, pretty, awkward child Victoria was becoming the woman Vic, growing in confidence, even sometimes daring a little cheek. Of course she practised her singing assiduously, and Eric was pleased, and then she floated on a cloud all day. And she thought this was how it would end: she'd take her A levels and leave school, and he'd say how well she'd done, and she'd never see him again.

As the girls grew older the school allowed them greater liberty, a privilege which they routinely, but discreetly, abused. They wandered about the streets of West Stoke in a chattering gaggle, and boys from neighbouring schools, doing much the same thing, hung around like bees in honeysuckle. Some of them openly admired Vic, who at seventeen was tall and slim, but filling out appropriately. Her light brown hair fell to her shoulders in waves that shone with natural highlights in the summer. Her skin was clear, her eyes a greenish-brown. She looked fresh, young, innocent. No one would have suspected the turbulent and highly-charged imagination that lay behind the smooth brow. She did her best to fit, to like boys, but found them uniformly fatuous, loud and vain. Her passion for her older man blinded her to a knowledge she would one day bitterly gain, that he too could be all those things, without the excuse of youth.

Then, as she had told Frankie, things changed for Vic with the force of total revolution. Her vision in the library, her subsequent researches, her prayer of commitment, added a potent ingredient to her mental and spiritual chemistry. The odd thing was that her conversion, her alliance with God, didn't alter the strength of her feelings for Eric Whitley. As she imperceptibly grew up, she began to understand the power she had, and one day she told herself that she could have and love both Eric and Jesus. It was a moment that replaced longing with determination. She wouldn't do anything wrong – on the contrary, she would behave impeccably – but she would go for what she wanted, with God on her side.

Vic passed her eighteenth birthday soon after the beginning of her last year at Repley. By this time she had got to know Eric Whitley well: she had the motivation, and he was not a careful man. She knew he was not married, for instance. He lived locally, and taught at several schools. She also knew that she was his star pupil, his protégée. He wanted her to prepare a recital to be sung in the school hall at Easter, before the need for serious revision arose. She worked very hard, and the recital was a great success. *For the first time in my life, I felt like somebody.*

Vic turned over in bed and smiled to herself, remembering her daring. At her next singing lesson, after the recital, Eric came into the music room frowning ominously.

'Why are you looking so grumpy?' Vic asked. 'Didn't I do well on Saturday?'

He looked surprised. 'You did very well. I told you so at the time.'

'Yes. I even got a hug. Lucky me!' She spoke lightly, but felt a flash of heat at the memory of it: his arms around her, the scent of him. 'So? Why the beetling brow?'

He smiled despite himself. 'You've got very forward all of a sudden, Miss Colbourne. If you must know, I am having a lot of trouble with some of the students at St Mary's, none of whom like to work.' He studied her with something, she thought, of a new look, and it made her stomach lurch.

She took a deep breath and gathered her courage. 'You know what, I don't feel like singing today.' He stepped back in feigned shock. 'It's a beautiful day, and I have a free afternoon. I happen to know your only other pupil has a bad cold and nasty sore throat. So how about we go into town and you can buy me a cup of tea and a sticky cake?'

For a moment he was speechless. Then a grin spread across his face. 'Am I being propositioned here, young lady?'

'Yes,' said Vic, 'and please, just call me Vic.'

'All right, and how are we to organise this escapade?'

'I shall tell Miss Forsyth you have been called away and have cancelled my lesson, so I am going into town for a few things I need. You will drive your car out of the school and I will be waiting by the gate. OK?'

'Your cheek is irresistible. Do you realise, if anyone should see us, I will lose my job?'

'It's worth the risk,' Vic said firmly, marvelling at herself.

He laughed aloud. 'I do believe it is. But you will forgive me if I am careful. If we see anyone who knows either of us, we take evasive action. For your sake, as well as mine. You don't want to be expelled just before your A levels.'

'I suppose not.'

That afternoon, talking and laughing in a tea shop, not in West Stoke where they were likely to be seen and recognised, but in the next town, Vic took what she knew to be another huge risk. He had paid the bill, and they strolled along the pavement in the spring sunshine, side by side but not quite touching, to where he had parked his car – a pale blue sports car, with many scuffs and dents. 'I must get you back to school,' he said. 'I think we pulled off this mad outing, but we shouldn't push our luck.'

'Eric,' she said, stopping suddenly, 'I want to tell you something.'

He was startled by her use of his name, and for a moment he stood blinking and frowning. 'What?' he said uncertainly.

'I think you should know I've been in love with you for almost two years.'

He opened his mouth to protest, but something stopped him. Long afterwards, laughing at her extraordinary boldness, he remembered seeing her at that moment in a completely new light, as if a switch had been thrown: not as a pretty and promising pupil, but as a desirable woman. 'You stood there, squinting in the sunlight, gorgeous even in that school uniform, and you looked, I don't know, *unstoppable*. I was lost.'

'You struggled a bit, but not much.'

'And some time after that, I forget when, you told me that you were a Christian, that you weren't interested in grubby affairs, and if sex was on my agenda – which it undoubtedly was, every painful waking hour – I had to marry you. I'd avoided matrimony for thirty-seven years, but I just caved in. Astonishing.' He shook his head, then grinned wickedly. 'But you didn't get it all your own way. You didn't quite make it to the altar pure and virginal.'

'We got married in a Registry Office – there was no altar,' Vic said. 'And who says I didn't get my own way?'

He laughed and swatted her backside. 'Minx.'

Lying in bed feeling seedy, more than thirty years later, Vic felt a knot forming in her chest, tight under her ribs. She breathed in and out, carefully and slowly, till the pain eased. Tears leaked under her closed eyelids. *Oh, you fool, you fool. Just remember, he threw everything in your face. He treated you like rubbish. He showed no kindness or remorse, even when your baby – his baby, too – died. He drank till he was disgusting. If he's still alive, he's in his seventies now. There's no room for regret, not for Eric Whitley.*

She heard a tap, and the door opened, letting in light from the landing. 'You OK?' Bel whispered. 'Need anything? Cup of tea?'

'What's the time?'

'Just after nine. You've been asleep.'

'Tea sounds good. But I'll come down. I'm feeling a lot better.'

'All right. I'll get the kettle on. I've got a fire going.'

When Bel had gone, Vic closed her eyes again and breathed deeply, trying to still the turmoil of her thoughts. *Lord, I am in a mess. I have shored up this ruin, but my repairs are failing. Thinking about what Bel told me the other night, and now, remembering my time with Eric, I can see what we have both been doing, and it's no surprise. In our own separate ways we looked for love in all the wrong places. Well, I looked for it in the right place too, and I'm thankful for that. I hope Bel will look in the right place one day. But for me, because it all went wrong, because of the hurt, I'm not even searching any more, but fleeing — yes, even from you. Lord, I need courage. I have become closed in, because of fear. But in my feeble way I do trust you. Help me to rest my weight on you, trusting you won't let me fall.*

Bel

Bel had arrived at the Vicarage, cold and out of breath, soon after six. 'Door's open!' she heard Frankie call from somewhere upstairs in answer to her knock. She kicked off her shoes and stood uncertainly in the hall. Then Frankie appeared at the top of the stairs, resplendent in a bright orange floor-length towelling robe. 'I'm just going to put Noah in his bath,' she said. 'Come on up.'

Bel hesitated. 'Perhaps this really isn't the best time,' she said. 'I'm intruding.'

'No, it's fine, isn't it, No? We don't mind.' A tiny naked figure materialised beside his mother.

Bel began to climb the stairs. Then she looked back. 'Oh, brother. What is that?'

'What is what?'

'That enormous black creature emerging from the kitchen.'

Frankie laughed. 'That's only Brutus. He's harmless. Just a big black softie.'

'I'll take your word for it. He looks sinister to me. What is he?'

'He's a Bouvier de Flandres, a cattle dog. Never been cute, even as a pup, but we're fond of the old fellow, aren't we, No?'

Noah pointed and chuckled. 'Boots.'

'He can't quite say Brutus,' Frankie said. 'Anyway, let's get this cherub into the tub.'

'Doesn't it bother him to have a stranger in his house?'

Frankie took her son's hand and led him back to the bathroom. The door was open, and great billows of steam were swirling out onto the landing. 'He's used to all manner of people traipsing in and out at all times of day.' Frankie shrugged. 'He thinks it's normal. OK, sweetie pie, let's see if this water's too hot. You want to turn on the cold tap?'

She lifted the child into the bath and waved Bel onto a tiny bathroom stool, where she crouched, knees drawn up. Frankie knelt by the side of the tub and began to lather the little boy's hair. She looked up at Bel, and was surprised to see tears in her eyes.

'You all right?'

Bel shook her head. 'Yes, I'm fine. Your little fellow reminded me just then of my son at the same age. He was like a shrimp on speed.'

Frankie laughed. 'I know exactly what you mean.' Then her expression sobered, and she said, 'I didn't know you had a son.'

'Nor does Vic. That's the trouble.'

Noah was waving his arms about and whining.

'What? Oh, I forgot your ducks. Your mummy's very forgetful these days. Here you are.' Against a sound of splashing and tuneless childish singing she said to Bel quietly, 'Why would your having a son be a problem with Vic?'

'Did you know that Vic was married, a long time ago?'

'No, I didn't,' Frankie said as she soaped her son's slippery body. 'I assumed she was single as she uses your family name.'

'She was married for about four years, in her early twenties,' Bel said. 'She had a baby, James. He was very premature and died soon after birth. I only found this out tonight. Poor Vic. Her marriage crumbled after that. And, getting back to the present, she isn't at all well. She's got possible trouble at work, and it's making her sick. She doesn't want to eat, so I left her sleeping. How can I tell her about my boy, Frankie? After what happened to her baby. It just feels cruel.'

Noah, unobserved, brought his two palms down on the surface of the bath water, splashing up onto Frankie, soaking the bathrobe, her arms, her neck.

'Oh, Noah, you monkey!' She took a plastic bucket, filled it with water and emptied it over his head. The little boy spluttered and giggled. 'Vengeance is mine.' She heaved herself to her feet, bent over, and picked him up. 'You're clean enough.' She sat him in her lap and rubbed him all over with a towel till his fine dark hair stuck up in spikes. 'Come on, stinker, let's get your nappy on and your PJs. This way, Bel.' The child scampered down the hallway and disappeared through a door. Frankie lumbered after him and Bel hesitantly followed. She found Frankie kneeling on the floor of the boy's bedroom, securing his nappy, and blowing bubbles on his bare skin, making him squeal.

'Come in, don't be shy,' Frankie said. 'It's a mess, but it's home, eh, No?' She slid the wriggling child into a blue sleepsuit with elephants parading round it.

'Won't your husband be home soon? I don't want to be in the way.'

'Rob? No, he's away on business, with his dad. Family firm,' she added, seeing Bel's puzzled frown. 'Look, you're great at story-telling, I know. The Sunday School ladies were full of your praises. Would you read to Noah while I get out of this wet gear? Then we can go downstairs and be proper grown-ups. Maybe I can give some thought to your dilemma.'

'Won't he mind it isn't you?' Bel said.

'I doubt it. A story's a story, whoever does it. He'll choose the book. Into bed now, Noah my lad.'

Ten minutes later Bel joined Frankie in the kitchen. 'He liked the story, but his last word was "Mummy."'

'OK, I'll go and do his prayers with him and say goodnight. I thought you might like a coffee, so I put the kettle on.'

Prayers? With a two-year-old? I suppose you have to start early.

Bel scratched around, found coffee, a spoon and two cleanish mugs. She was stirring when Frankie reappeared. 'You're an angel,' Frankie said, settling herself on a stool with a groan of effort. 'So, you're wondering how to tell Vic about your son. Why hasn't he been mentioned before?'

'It just hasn't arisen,' Bel mumbled. She caught Frankie's look. 'And I haven't seen him, oh, I don't know, at least a couple of years.'

Frankie frowned. 'That's quite a while.'

'When they're little,' Bel said, 'like your adorable Noah, you never for a moment think there'll be a time when you don't know where they are or what they're doing. Then they grow up.'

'How old is he?'

'Twenty-four. The thing is, I do know where he is. After all this time. He sent me a Christmas card with an address in it.'

'And you want to get in touch.'

Bel nodded. 'Of course I do. But the last thing I want to do is hurt Vic.'

Frankie thought for a moment, savouring her coffee. 'This is great,' she said. 'I only allow myself two cups of caffeine every day. It was agony at first. You don't realise how dependent you get.' She sighed. 'You know what, I don't think you should worry too much about Vic. Just go and tell her. She'll probably be annoyed with you because you've lost touch with your son – what's his name?'

'Matthew.'

'Ah. Good Biblical name. But as to her little one, she's probably learned to cope. Thirty years is a long time, and she's had to see plenty of people with babies and live with that sadness. It isn't your fault your son lived and hers didn't, and Vic's a reasonable woman, I think. Once she's vented her disgust at you, if she does, she might even feel glad to have a nephew. Your family's not a big one, I think.'

'No. Most of them are dead.'

For a few moments they drank in silence, each deep in her own thoughts. Then Frankie said abruptly, 'So, what about you, Bel? How do you feel about God?'

Bel gaped. 'Uh, I'm not sure,' she stammered. For a moment she hesitated, marshalling her errant thoughts. 'Well, we were always sent to Sunday School when we were children, and dear old Reverend Alloway and his wife kind of took us under their wing. Maybe they suspected that beneath the respectable exterior we were babes in the wood, Vic and me. Then at Repley we had RE, of course. I remember Miss Griffin, the one who had such an effect on Vic. She was lovely. So I'm not exactly totally ignorant. Just a bit of an outsider.'

'Is that your choice? Keeping God at arm's length?'

'I don't think so. I just assumed, when I thought about it at all, that he wouldn't really want to know me. My life hasn't exactly been sinless.'

Frankie smiled. 'Whose has? Doesn't sound like you're an atheist, though.'

'No, I don't suppose I am. More of a lost cause.'

Frankie put her empty cup down and laid her hand briefly on Bel's arm. 'In God's eyes there's no such thing,' she said gently. 'The question is, do you want to be found?'

'That's a tough one, Frankie. I suppose I'm a bit scared too. Of having to change too much.'

'Well, at least you're honest. He can work with that. '

Bel thought for a moment. 'I just wonder, you know, how having faith in God really helps. Vic said it got her through some terrible times, but she still had to go through them.'

'That's a very big subject,' Frankie said. 'We need more time than we've got. But if you really want to explore this stuff, I'll happily run alongside. Well, plod, perhaps.'

'But won't you be taking some time off, when your baby comes?'

'Yes, I will. When Noah was born I took him along everywhere – parish visiting, school assemblies, whatever. He used to snooze in his car seat, or I'd just jiggle him on my hip. But with two it won't be so easy. I'm going to back off for a few months, maybe get Noah into pre-school, before I get back to full-on work. But I'll still be in overall charge. I'll be here for anyone who needs me.' She looked at Bel narrow-eyed. 'Don't think me presumptuous,' she said, 'but you were asking how Vic's faith has helped her. So what are your supports?'

Bel shrugged and pulled a face. 'I just muddled through, I suppose, with whoever was around at the time. Went along with whatever was going on. Line of least resistance.'

'Probably the commonest route to hell, that,' Frankie said. 'Nothing too major, no murders, nothing spectacular, just slithering down the slippery slope, barely awake.'

'What?' Bel said, astonished. 'You don't actually believe in hell, do you?'

'I believe in eternal punishment, because it's in the Bible,' Frankie said calmly, her eyes never leaving Bel's face.

'And do you think I'm in danger?' Bel said, half-sceptical, half-horrified.

'That's between you and God,' Frankie said. 'But although I don't know Vic all that well, and you hardly at all, it seems to me you could learn a lot from each other. Sounds like God at work. His style, if you get me.'

The phone on the wall shrilled, and Frankie slithered off the stool to answer it.

'Look, I must go,' Bel said. 'Leave you in peace. Thanks for talking to me.'

'We must talk again, Bel,' Frankie said, picking up the receiver. 'Soon. Till then I'll keep praying for you both.'

But what for, Frankie? What will you be praying for?

Don

14 January 2006

As he came out of the bathroom that Saturday morning, a towel round his neck to catch the drips, Don caught sight of his living room through the open door and realised that he had the same thought each time he looked: that it was a room without character, and rather cheerless. Normally he dismissed the thought as soon as it arrived and did nothing about it. Today, he stood for a while, taking in the clean, dull carpet, the sparse and functional furnishings, the uncluttered surfaces. It seemed to him that if a burglar broke in one day and looked around, he would conclude that no one lived here.

When he and Ellen had moved to Thackham-by-Angle something more than seven years ago they had chosen the bungalow simply on the basis of Ellen's needs. Then, although she had a wheelchair for longer outings, she could still get around the house with a stick. On the mantel, above the gas fire, stood a solitary framed photograph of Ellen, already beginning the decline that led to her increasing disability, but still able to walk after a fashion, to prop herself up against the kitchen counter and peel potatoes or spread butter on bread. In the photograph she was supporting herself against the promenade railings at a seaside resort, on the last holiday that they had taken. Her eyes were screwed up against the sun, her short cap of dark hair shone, and she was smiling broadly. Beside her, her two sticks leaned up against the railing to which she clung. Without the sticks, to someone who wasn't looking too hard, she looked like anyone else, enjoying a sunny seaside break. But Don, who knew better, saw the tight grip of Ellen's hand on the railing, the awkwardness of her pose, the slightly sagging knees. A moment after the picture was taken, he remembered, she had buckled and cried out, and he had to support her under her arms, put her sticks in her hands, and guide her to a bench while he went to fetch the car.

Vic had commented one day that only two rooms in the bungalow reflected the man who lived there. One was Don's study, converted from the smallest bedroom, where he kept his computer, his telescope and his binoculars, and where one wall was devoted to bookshelves. Here he stored records of his business, trade magazines, and books about birds. The other was the little utility room that divided the kitchen from the back garden. Here, though it was never untidy, were the signs of Don the man at leisure: well-worn walking boots, a waxed jacket, a small backpack hanging on a hook.

Registering an uncomfortable chill round his bare legs, Don padded into the bedroom and dressed. He rubbed his hair dry and threw the towel into the laundry basket. Then, as he did every day, he sat on the edge of his bed and bowed his head. After a moment of silence, stilling his thoughts, he thanked God for the life that he had been given, his good health, the modest success of his business, his continued ability to pursue his interests, his friends at church. He prayed that whatever happened during the day his words and actions would bring honour to the God he served, and not disgrace. He asked that some opportunity might be given to him to witness to his faith by some kind act or generous word.

Usually his communion with his Saviour left Don feeling at least calm and purposeful, if not always full of joy. Today, however, some shadow seemed to press down over his thoughts, some undefined barely perceptible worry plucking at the outer edges of his consciousness. He shrugged. There was nothing to be done with such nebulous feelings, and activity sometimes cleared them away. Downstairs, he opened the front door and looked out on a dull, damp day with a chill that would soon eat into your bones if you stood still too long. He took a coat down from a hook in the hall, shuffled off his slippers and stuffed his feet into the boots that he kept on a rack under the hooks. He patted his pockets to make sure he had money and keys, then stepped out on to the front path and closed the door behind him.

The bungalow was set back from the road, and stood opposite the church. Heading for the village shop for his newspaper, Don took a short cut across the churchyard, where the gravestones stood hard and grey among the sad winter grass. Some of them had small metal pots beneath, with expensive shop-bought flowers in various stages of wilting. Don strode out along the path, the gravel crunching beneath his feet.

On the far side of the church, facing the road in which the shop stood, he saw with a jolt of surprise someone kneeling beside a grave, arranging sprigs of greenery in a vase. A moment later he knew that it was Vic, and that the grave was Ellen's.

Something of his earlier anxiety resurfaced, and as he stood there for a moment, looking at Vic's back, he realised that it was Vic herself who was its cause. It wasn't unheard of for her to put flowers on Ellen's grave, or even, in the spring and summer, to trim the grass round it and pull up the weeds. He had never commented on this, or remonstrated with her, saying that it was his job to keep the site tidy; he knew that Vic almost certainly missed Ellen more than he did himself, though he had never voiced this thought aloud. Now, however, something in her hunched pose have him pause, and he came up behind her making enough noise to alert her to his presence.

'Hello,' he said. 'You're about early.'

She turned round abruptly, almost losing her balance, and her face as she looked up at him filled Don with sudden alarm. She looked exhausted, grey-tinged, lined, older than her fifty-two years. Her eyes were red, whether from weeping or sleeplessness he could not tell. He squatted down beside her. 'Are you all right? You don't look well.'

He was dismayed when, instead of answering, she made a choking sound and blinked away tears. He stood up and stretched out his hand to her. 'Come on, it's freezing out here. Come over to my place and get warm. I'll make you a cup of coffee.'

She took his hand and stood up with a slight stagger. 'Aren't you going for your paper?' Her voice was husky.

'That doesn't matter.' He looked down at her, and she averted her eyes from his concern. 'Your hands are icy. Come along, I insist. You're not getting away.'

She smiled slightly. 'Bully.'

'Guilty as charged. A good thing too. Where are your gloves?' She pulled them out of her coat pocket and put them on. Tucking her unresisting hand in the crook of his elbow he turned back towards his front door, and she followed, for once speechless.

Don closed the front door behind them and turned up the heating at the thermostat in the hall. 'Park yourself somewhere,' he ordered, 'and I'll get the kettle on.'

Vic shed her coat but not her gloves, and trailed after him into the kitchen. With the kettle filled and set to boil he turned and looked at her as she sat at the table, his face grave. 'What's the idea, lurking in the churchyard on a miserable morning like this?'

She shrugged and stared at her gloved hands. 'Don't ask me,' she said. 'I hardly know myself. I got up this morning and thought, I must go and see my friend.'

132

Don sighed and poured boiling water into two mugs. 'Vic, Ellen *was* your friend, just as she *was* my wife,' he said with utmost gentleness. 'But she isn't any more. You have living friends now, myself included, I hope, who can be more help to you. Tell me what's eating you up. Is it that dear sister of yours?'

Vic looked up, visibly startled. 'Bel? No, Bel's OK. She's been kind. Bit of an issue at work, though.' Don handed her a mug of steaming coffee. 'Thanks. There's a chance some of us will be out of a job at the end of term, or at the end of the school year. Repley's in financial straits, apparently. I didn't know any of this. What will I do without my work?' He saw her eyes well with tears again and frowned. *This isn't the Vic I know.*

'Well,' he said cautiously, 'you don't know that you will be without it. If someone has to go, why should it be you? You've been there a good many years, I think. What is it, twelve?' She nodded, and scrubbed at her face with her hands. 'And suppose the worst happened. Suppose you had to go, would you be begging on the streets?'

Vic took a sip of coffee. 'No, I could retire. Or,' she shuddered, 'do some supply work. But I don't want to. Repley's a big chunk of my purpose in life. I think I'd feel useless without it.'

He slid into the seat opposite her. 'Sometimes what feels like utter loss turns out to be just a turning-point,' he said, passing her the milk. 'I know that very well. God hasn't finished with you yet.'

'That's what Frankie said.'

'And she's right. She often is.'

Vic smiled faintly. 'Annoyingly so.' For a moment she seemed sunk in thought. Then she said, 'I had a rough night. I guess it's anxiety about the future, and it's always worse in the early hours. My stomach was giving me grief. Whatever the reason, I woke up feeling fairly grim. Bel was fast asleep and snoring heartily in the next room, and I just felt totally alone.' She sighed deeply. 'Oh, Don. I miss Ellen. She had a great gift for empathy, didn't she? But how stupid I am: you must miss her even more.'

Don shook his head. 'Of course I do, sometimes. Of course I wish she had never got ill. But she did, and I'd never wish her back to suffer. Those last months were horrible, for her to go though, for me to look on, feeling so helpless. In those circumstances, I'm glad she's free. It's been six years, Vic. I'm not grieving now, not really.'

Vic looked him in amazement. 'Not?'

He said nothing for a moment, watching her struggle with her thoughts. 'No, not any more,' he said finally. 'I've taken a deep breath and got on with my life. With God's help, and good people's prayers. I know everybody's different, and so are their experiences and how they cope with them. But isn't it time you did the same? Shouldn't you give yourself a break? Leave the past where it belongs?'

She shivered and took a gulp of coffee. 'There are things,' she stumbled, 'things that even you don't know. I never even told Ellen. Things nobody knows, except me. I've tried not to think about them for more than thirty years, and mostly I've succeeded. But now I'm thinking about them, and it makes me shrivel up with shame. I suppose because my sister's reappeared in my life, it's stirred it all up again, and it's destroying my peace.'

Don drummed his long fingers on the edge of his coffee cup. 'Do you want to tell me now? Would it help?'

'I don't know. It might. But if anyone's to be told, it should be Bel. It's her business as much as mine, but she has no idea. And that's my dilemma: should I tell her everything, or leave her in ignorance? There's not much to be gained from her knowing.'

'Except to share a burden, perhaps.'

'But then, think how she's reacted to my telling her much more innocuous things. She seems to be accepting reality a bit more now, but at first you'd think, to hear her, that our parents were saints and our grandfather a dear sweet old man.' She closed her eyes momentarily. 'Sometimes,' she said slowly, 'sometimes my family reminds me of Isaac and Rebecca and Jacob and Esau. Not in the details, of course. But in the overall picture – wrong thinking, bad decisions, sinfulness, sowing seeds of trouble for generations to come.'

'Unpack that for me.'

'Well, you remember, Isaac and Rebecca waited twenty years for those boys. And then we are told that Isaac favoured Esau, and Rebecca preferred Jacob – and for what seems the stupidest reasons. When I read that, I shudder. Because what followed? Deceit and cheating, murderous thoughts, twin brothers at loggerheads, exile. All because two grown-up people who should have known better couldn't treat their sons the same. The boys grew up with rivalry instead of brotherly love. They took their parents' example, and thought it was OK to lie and swindle to get what they wanted.'

'But Jacob got his come-uppance. And in the end the brothers were reconciled. God had his way. So he will with you, and all your past, if you let him.'

'You said Bel coming was his doing,' Vic said, her voice scarcely above a whisper. 'Do you still think so?'

'Certainly. I think she's an answer to prayer. In a funny kind of way, but then, he does work in mysterious ways.' He smiled.

Vic frowned suddenly. 'An answer to yours?' she said sharply.

'What?'

'Well, all this worming her way in, coming to work with you, all that. She's only been here five minutes!'

'Oh, Vic. This isn't you speaking. I was just being polite. You could come and see my boring place of work any time. I wish you would. But you never said you wanted to.'

A tear slid down Vic's cheek and she closed her eyes and breathed deeply. 'I don't really. I'm just being an idiot. I feel I've bungled pretty much everything. Brought it on myself. Trying to do the right thing. Doesn't work, does it?'

Don reached out and took her hand, still in its glove, wrapping it in both his hands. 'Of course you've got to go on trying to do the right thing, as far as you can. But you need help. We all do.'

'You seem to have it sorted, though. Getting on with your life.'

'I can't change what's happened. And yes, I'm all right, as good as the next man, I suppose. A bit lonely sometimes, but mostly OK. What else can you do but get on with it?'

Vic's lips twitched. 'Collapse in a crumpled heap?'

Don released her hand. 'Not an option,' he said firmly. 'And at the risk of being shot down, perhaps you should think about going back to the doctor. If you aren't well you can't think straight. You know that.'

Vic glowered. 'I've seen doctors. There's nothing wrong with me.'

'That was then. Perhaps things have changed. How can you say there's nothing wrong when you look like death?'

'Thanks for that – I feel better already. Oh, all right, maybe I will, just to shut you up.' She pushed herself to her feet. 'I've gobbled up quite enough of your morning. Go and get your paper.'

He followed her to the front door and watched her button her coat. He pressed on. 'And another thing.'

'What?'

'Go and talk to Frankie, while she's still around and not swamped with two babies.'

'Talk about what?'

'Don't be obtuse. It might help you to decide what to tell Bel. If anything. How to rid yourself of the burden, whatever it is.' He paused. 'We've prayed for you, you know.'

Vic frowned. 'Who? You and Frankie?'

'Yes, and others. Don't you pray for people?'

'Of course.' She stood still, her hand on the door-handle. Then she smiled, turned towards him, put her hands on his shoulders, stretched up and kissed his cheek. 'Thanks for the coffee. And the sympathy. I'll try not to make a habit of it.'

When she had gone, he stood in the hallway for several moments. Somehow, despite his calm and sensible words, he felt his composure had left him. What was going on? He shook his head and went back into the kitchen.

Matthew

6 January 2006

'What did you want to bring all those books for? Term doesn't even start for another week.' He pushed the door to.

Jessica pulled her bag off her shoulder and lowered it to the floor with a grateful sigh. 'Hey, that was heavy. Because I'm getting ahead of the game, that's why. Didn't you get any work to do over Christmas?' She unzipped her jacket.

Matthew slid his hands round her waist, under her sweater, feeling her skin warm through the thin cotton of her shirt. 'Work? Not that I remember.'

'Ugh, you're hopeless. Anyway, I've only got a few months to go before finals, so can't be slacking.'

He pulled her close and nuzzled her neck, getting a mouthful of fine blonde hair. 'Did I ever tell you I love your accent? It's so brass tacks.'

'Frequently,' she said, shoving him off. 'How about asking me if I'd like a nice cup of tea?'

'Sex first, tea after.'

'Don't beat about the bush, will you? And they say romance is dead!'

He slumped in a chair, tilted it perilously on two legs, balancing its rickety back against the wall, and folded his arms across his chest. His T shirt needed a wash. 'It's what you came for, isn't it?'

'You watch too many films. Why would I want anything to do with a slob like you?' She threw her jacket on the end of his bed and pulled her sweater over her head. Her shirt came with it, and he gazed at her bare stomach in unashamed appreciation. 'You *have* showered recently, haven't you?'

He looked at the ceiling. 'Mm, let me see... last Wednesday fortnight, if I remember correctly. That recent enough?'

'Good job I don't believe you.' She unzipped her jeans and wriggled them down over her hips, grinning back at him with eyebrows provocatively raised. Then her eyes narrowed. 'You can get rid of that stubble,' she said sternly. 'If I go home with chin rash, my nasty little brother will never let me live it down. Go on, you disgusting tramp, do it now.'

Matthew groaned, flopped the chair forward with a crash and got to his feet. 'You're such a tyrant,' he muttered. He shambled out of the door and down the corridor to the bathroom.

When he got back she was sitting up in bed, the covers modestly tucked under her armpits, her hair tied back, her glasses on the end of her nose and her laptop balanced on her knees.

'You're not *working!*' he said in disgust.

She stared at the screen. 'Might as well, you took so long.'

He peeled off his T shirt and jeans. 'Nothing's sacred in this dump,' he complained. 'Someone's nicked my razor. Had to use one that was lying around. So blunt I cut myself.' He dabbed at his chin with his fingers, and looked pathetically at the tiny smear of blood.

'Oh, Matthew,' she said tenderly. 'You're such a failure of a human being.'

He slid into bed beside her, took the laptop and put it on the floor. 'It's because I was neglected as a child.' He removed her glasses and put them on the laptop. 'But I make up for it with my skills as a lover.'

Jessica sighed and put her arm round his neck, drawing him down. 'Says you.'

Darkness came early on a January afternoon, and from where he lay Matthew could see that the streetlights were coming on. 'Did you bring my post?' he mumbled sleepily.

'Yes, but there's nothing there of any interest,' Jessica said. 'It's all bills and stuff from the Uni.' She was sitting up again, her jacket slung round her bare shoulders, tapping on her keyboard.

'She won't reply,' Matthew said. 'It probably didn't even get there.'

Jessica stopped typing and looked down at him. 'Don't be so defeatist. You're pretty sure she's still got the same agent, aren't you?'

Matthew stretched and yawned. 'Jason, yes, I think so. Last time I saw her he still was, and I can't see why she'd want to change, even if she could get someone else. But did he ever send stuff on? I wish I knew where she moved to, after I left and she gave up our flat. I don't know if I can trust Jason. Maybe he chucked all the mail in the bin and flew off to Greece for Christmas.'

'And maybe,' Jess said firmly, 'he readdressed everything and put it in

a post box like a responsible person. Letters get delayed this time of year.'
She shut down her computer. 'Matthew.'

'Mm?'

'What do you say we watch an episode of "Cathedral Bells" in a minute?'

He opened one eye. 'What for?'

'I want to see what your mum looks like. Do you take after her?'

'No, I'm heart-stoppingly handsome, like my dad. Anyway, you know what she looks like. I showed you that photo.'

'But I want to see her in action.'

'Why? So you can laugh?'

Jessica brushed his hair off his forehead. 'Don't be so sensitive. It *is* quite funny in a retro sort of way, I admit. And you've been known to laugh at *my* mother.'

'Maybe later.' He closed his eyes.

'Matt, don't go back to sleep. Mum wants to know if you're coming for lunch on Sunday. She misses you.'

Matthew didn't open his eyes. 'Tell her I'd love to. I miss her too. Especially her cooking.'

'She also said, come early so you can come to church with us.'

'Hm. Maybe a step too far.'

'Whatever. If you're not there I can ogle that good-looking drummer. Or his brother.' Matthew stretched out a snaky hand and pinched a soft fold of skin. 'Ouch! That hurt!'

'So do my feelings,' Matthew said in mock-sulk. 'You're such a tart, leering at the musicians, when you're supposed to be such a devout Baptist and all.'

'Don't.' Jessica shuddered. 'If Mum and Dad knew what I was up to right now they'd have a fit. They think I'm in the library.'

'You're studying in the Library of Love,' Matthew mumbled into the pillow, his arm still round her, his hand stroking her hip. He rolled onto his side and propped himself up on one elbow. 'Anyway, they'll be OK when we're married.'

'Please, don't mention the m-word. Not to them. I'm much too young. Trouble is, they got hitched when they were nineteen or something.'

'Your dad probably thought it was the only way he was going to get his sweaty hands on your mum.'

'Or vice versa.'

'Like mother, like daughter?'

Jessica giggled. 'Cheeky.'

'Have you heard from Jack?'

Not lately.' Jess sighed. 'I try not to think about Jack. Me worrying won't keep him out of danger.'

'Praying will though, according to you.'

She shivered. 'I hope it will.'

'And Grandma? Is she OK? Still enjoying her stay in *my* bedroom?'

'It's not yours, idiot.' Jessica punched him lightly. 'It's Jack's. And you can hardly blame Dad for wanting his mother to stay after she fell over and busted her arm.'

'I know. It was nice of them to take me in like that when I had nowhere to go. Especially as I was already sneakily feeling up their innocent lamb.' He was silent for a few moments. 'I wish I had a big family like yours.'

'It's not all sunshine, you know. I had to share a room with Josie till she got married and moved out. Gran's always making rude comments about my clothes. And as for my horrible spotty loud-mouthed teenager brother, you can have him and welcome.' She closed the laptop and slid it onto the floor, then turned on her side, facing him, and walked her fingers idly down his chest. 'But I know what you mean. Things other people have got always look better from the outside. And I guess you had hopes of finding some of your family when you came up here.'

'It was probably a stupid thing to do. But I'd just had that huge row with Mum and stormed out like some diva, and I didn't know where to go.' He paused, and heaved a deep sigh. 'God, Jess, I was really foul to Mum. Some of the things I said. She didn't deserve that. Even if she does get my card, she probably won't want anything to do with me.'

'Rubbish. My mum says no normal mother would reject her son or daughter for ever. You'll hear from her. She's forgiven you already. Bet you a tenner.'

'You haven't got a tenner.' He looked at her hopefully. 'Have you?'

Jessica laughed. 'As if I'd tell you! You'd have it off me before I could blink.'

'So, my beautiful and sweet-natured woman, how do you fancy popping round to the chippy with that tenner you haven't got? I'm starving.'

'Not a chance.'

'Please? I promise to pay you in the only currency I have handy.'

'Which is?'

He lowered his face to within inches of hers and whispered throatily, 'Lurve. I'll send you to heaven.'

'Big talk.'

'You're a hard woman.'

'Someone needs some sense around here. OK, I tell you what. You can have a fiver, but you can be the one to get dressed and go to the chippy, and don't eat everything on the way back. That way I get to do some more work while you've gone.'

'Done.' Matthew scrambled out of bed. 'There might even be some beers in the fridge. They're Billy's, but he won't mind.' He pulled on his jeans and T shirt and shoved his feet into greasy trainers. 'OK, doll, give us the cash.'

'In my bag, side pocket.'

Matthew scrabbled in her bag and waved the note triumphantly. 'I'm rich! At last, a wealthy woman to keep me in beer and chips.' He sat on the side of the bed and leaned over her. 'Jess.'

'What?'

'I adore you.'

'Go on, you big fool. Don't forget your jacket. It's freezing out there.'

Matthew turned off the TV with a flick of the remote.

'You know what, Matt,' Jess said thoughtfully, watching the credits roll, 'your mum's really good. She manages to portray an eccentric old bat without turning her into a caricature. Most actors, especially in a popular soap like this, would be tempted to overdo it.'

'Yeah, she's OK.'

'Be honest with me – do you really think you were neglected? I mean, was that what you and your mum fell out about?'

Matthew groaned. 'Oh, I was a mouthy opinionated kid, no denying that, thought I knew everything. I sort of remember Mum moaning about something – maybe me spending too much money, or living like a pig, or spitting chewing-gum down the toilet –'

'Ugh, Matt, you didn't!'

'– or maybe she was trying to get me to do something and I was resisting, like going to the dentist, I don't know. Whatever, I thought it was all beneath my dignity, wanted to be treated like an adult, etc. The usual things. Well, I *was* twenty-two, but I'd never had a proper job, and we weren't rich but I drank a fair bit. No, let's be accurate, a lot. It's like you said, love. Mum was working, any crap job she could get, and I was a useless sponging layabout, and to rub salt into the wound I idolised my dad.'

Jessica shrugged. 'You hardly knew him if he died when you were seven.'

'That's just the point. The better you know someone, the more reality bites. There was Mum, warts, bad temper, bathroom-hogging and all. Whereas all I had of Dad were vague memories of childhood treats, photos of a glamorous film director who was hardly ever there. I'd kind of edited out the failed-and-broke bit.' He smiled crookedly. 'Anyway, you set me right a long time ago, didn't you? The problems of being a single parent and all that. I was a brat, but I hope I've grown up a bit.' He shivered suddenly.

'What's up?'

'I was thinking about some rather horrible people I was left with when I was about eleven. I threw that in Mum's face as well. She was mortified, but what was she to do? Someone had to look after me when she was working, and I never told her at the time what was happening, at least, not in so many words.'

Jessica frowned. 'So it wasn't entirely made up, the neglect thing?'

'No. There were some…unpleasant experiences. I was a skinny, undersized, washed-out specimen, not very appealing, but I had a gob on me and I was prone to posturing. Not so surprising, I suppose, considering both my heredity and early environment. But it didn't make me at all popular with child-minders or teachers.'

'Clever, though.'

'Lazy.'

'Not much change, then.'

He turned to her and pinched her ear. 'You'll see. I'll get my degree next year, and you'll say all amazed, "But Matthew, I never saw you do a stroke of work! You must be a genius!" And then you'll be sorry for the insults you've piled on my long-suffering head.'

'Yeah, yeah, that's exactly what I'll say. I'll faint out of sheer admiration. I'll have to take my turn in a queue of adoring naked women. Blah, blah.'

Matthew smirked. 'Now you're talking.'

'Your mum will be surprised, though, when you get to see her.'

'If.'

'*When*. When she finds you're a student, doing quite nicely on no work, supporting yourself after a fashion, *and* with a wonderful girlfriend.'

Matthew looked around the room. 'I have a wonderful girlfriend? Where is she?'

Jessica gave him a withering look. 'Watch it, Matthew. Your genes are showing.' She rolled over and scrabbled myopically on the bedside table. 'Where's my watch?'

'Where are your glasses, you mean.' He picked them up and planted them on her nose. She found the watch and shrieked.

'Matthew, it's twenty past six! My bus goes at quarter to seven.' She threw back the covers and stumbled out of bed, collecting her clothes from where they lay strewn across the floor. Matthew followed, pulling on jeans and T shirt and forcing bare feet into trainers.

'Don't you have any socks?'

'I think they're all under the bed.' He thrust his arms into his jacket. 'Ready. I'll walk you to the bus stop.'

She looked at him and shook her head. 'Promise me you'll look less like a tramp when you come over on Sunday.'

'Scout's honour.'

'You were never a Scout.'

'True. You got everything?'

She scooped up laptop, notebooks, textbooks and dropped them in her bag. 'I think so. Let's go.'

They hurried along the dark, damp street. 'I wouldn't bust a gut,' Matthew wheezed. 'The bus is always late.'

'You can bet it'll be on time tonight,' Jessica shouted back over her shoulder. 'Come on, grandpa, keep up.'

'We're not all cycling, running, tennis-playing athletes like you.'

'You're not kidding. That's what comes of a diet of beer and chips. You're a wreck.'

By the time they arrived at the bus stop Matthew was gasping for breath. 'Jess,' he said between gulps, 'text me if a handwritten letter comes, OK?'

Jessica frowned. 'OK, but you need to stop worrying. You've cast your bread on the waters by sending her your address. Now you just have to wait, hope and trust.'

'I've done what?'

'I'll explain on Sunday. Here's the bus, Matt. Told you it'd be on time.'

The brightly-lit bus appeared at the end of the street and trundled towards them. Matthew pulled her into his arms and kissed her. A group of lads on the other side of the road wolf-whistled and shouted, 'Hey, mate! Get a room!' Matthew ignored them.

Jessica pulled away as the bus ground to a halt, but she held his gaze. 'Trust in God, Matt. If you can.' He pulled a face. The bus doors creaked open and she climbed on. 'See you Sunday.'

'Yeah,' he muttered. 'Sunday.'

Vic

Frankie said the final blessing and swept off towards the vestry in a flurry of outsize robes. Don began the closing voluntary, and the congregation settled on knees and backsides according to their habit. After a respectful pause, Vic whispered, 'Bel, can you and Don see if lunch is cooking OK? I want to talk to Frankie for a minute before she dashes off. No knowing how much longer she'll be available.'

Bel nodded. 'Sure. She does look enormous, doesn't she? Still, she probably looks bigger because she's short. When's she actually due?'

'I'm not certain. I'll ask her. See you back at home. I won't be long.'

She threaded her way up the nave, against the flow of people going out, smiling, greeting, nodding. Frankie was in the vestry, invisible beneath the white expanse of surplice that she was pulling over her head. She emerged, her face flushed.

'Oh, hi, Vic. You OK?'

'I'm all right, thanks. How about you?'

'As well as can be expected is what the medics usually say, isn't it? I guess you want to quiz me about those rather cryptic verses I sent you.'

'Yes. Though I have my suspicions.'

'Of course you do.' Suddenly Frankie's open, smiling face contorted in a grimace, and the blood drained from her cheeks.

'Frankie? What's the matter?'

'Nothing, nothing,' Frankie said. 'Pull that chair over, can you?'

Vic dragged the chair from under the table and Frankie sank into it. 'Don't look so alarmed, Vic,' Frankie said. 'It's just those queer practice contractions – I get them all the time. Only sometimes, like now, they make me feel a bit faint. Probably a drop in blood pressure or something.' She smiled bravely. 'Don't panic – I'm not in labour. Your midwifery skills won't be called on.'

'Just as well,' Vic said, 'since I don't have any. You sure you're all right?'

'Positive,' Frankie said firmly. 'Now, what about those verses?'

Vic had her Bible in her hand, and she opened it at Isaiah. She glanced at Frankie. 'You ready for this?' '"Jerusalem alone is left, a city under siege – as defenceless as a guard's hut in a vineyard or a shed in a cucumber field." I'm sure I've read Isaiah more than once all through, but I don't remember ever before reading about cucumber fields.'

Frankie smiled. 'I find new things all the time. I'm sure we're directed to the things we need to know. They leap out at us from the page, and we say to ourselves, "I've never noticed that before." The Bible's quite amazing like that.'

'I suppose the key word here is "defenceless,"' Vic said.

Frankie nodded slowly. 'Of course. Not one of us has resources of his or her own. If we think we have, we are deluded. Even a dictator with a huge army and an arsenal of modern weapons at his disposal is as vulnerable as the barefoot beggar in the street. God in his mercy maintains us in existence. It's all there, scattered around in these pages: he breathes life into us, or he takes our breath away and we return to the dust. Without God we are defenceless. Man-made provision is useless if God has decided otherwise.'

Vic thought for a moment. 'Do you think this applies to me in particular?'

'No more than anyone else, I dare say, but you're the one I was thinking about at the time. I hope I'm not speaking out of turn, but I think you've been building up a stony citadel of your own for years, something to make you feel safe. But it won't do, you know.' She spoke with great gentleness, and her smile was kind. 'It won't do, because it doesn't work. And if I'm not mistaken it's beginning to crumble even now.'

Vic stared at the vestry carpet as if some wisdom was written there, something to illuminate all her dilemmas. Frankie was silent, waiting for Vic to speak. Eventually Vic said, 'What about the quote from Deuteronomy?'

Frankie closed her eyes. 'Let's see if I can remember it. "The Lord will rescue his people when he sees that their strength is gone. He will have mercy on those who serve him, when he sees how helpless they are." Did I get it right?'

'Spot on.'

'Sometimes,' Frankie said, 'we have to abandon all our pretences. All the things that make us feel vulnerable in the face of other people. It's no use pretending with God – he knows every frailty, every weakness, every grubby little temptation, every unworthy thought.'

'When you stop relying on your own resources, which you would say

145

are illusory anyway, God can get to work in you. Is that what you're saying?'

'Yes, that's about it. But you have to admit it to him and to yourself first.'

'Well, I don't need to ask if that applies to me. I constantly rely on myself, right or wrong. So what do I do, Frankie?'

'Let's pray together, shall we?' Frankie said. 'Don't worry, I'll provide the words. But remember, if you say "Amen" to my prayer, it's your prayer as well. No backsliding. Agreed?'

'Yes, OK.'

There was silence for a few moments. Frankie shifted in her chair, adjusting her bulk to its shape. She took a deep breath. 'Gracious Lord, look on your servants with mercy, forgiving their sins and failures which are so countless. Look especially today on your servant Vic. Where she is anxious, grant her peace. Where she is fearful, help her to be courageous. Above all, teach her to have complete trust in you for everything, every day, to the end of her life. And be with her, Lord, giving her your strength. In Jesus' name I ask. Amen.'

And Vic echoed, 'Amen,' sensing with a thrill of terror the step she was taking, out into a void where human sight was blindness and human wisdom counted for nothing.

'I've got another couple of verses for you.' Frankie's voice broke in. 'Have a look when you get home. Ephesians 2, 20 to 22. Great challenge, but also great encouragement.'

'Thank you,' Vic said faintly. 'Now I must let you get home and rest. How long have you got to go now?'

'Officially,' Frankie said, heaving herself up from the chair, 'four weeks. But it's not an exact science. I have a feeling this one might come early. I'm sure the head's dropped, because I can feel it banging on a very sensitive place.' She grinned. 'Sorry – too much information.'

They walked together to the door. 'Don't forget to look it up, will you?' Frankie said.

'I won't. Thanks, Frankie.'

'No problem.'

Don

When they left the made-up road and entered the track, to his surprise, Bel took his arm. She was shorter than her sister, and her weight dragged on him, but he made no comment.

'You don't mind, do you?' Bel said, looking up at him and smiling. 'This surface is so uneven, and my boots have stupid heels.' He shook his head. 'When we get in, I'll put the vegetables on while you lay the table. OK?'

'Fine.'

They walked in silence for a few minutes as Don tried to adjust his long stride to her more teetering gait. Then she said, looking at the ground, 'I don't know about you, Don, but I'm getting quite concerned about Vic. I thought things might be getting better, but I'm sure they're not.'

He registered a moment of alarm. 'In what way?'

'She's definitely not well. She doesn't admit to anything, of course. But it's not just that: there's something on her mind. She's worried about work, I know, but would that make her sick?'

'Sick?'

'Yes. I heard her throwing up the other day. She brushed it off, said she's got a dodgy stomach, that it was a reaction to stress, because of the school situation.'

Don frowned. 'Well, since you mention it, she has seemed a bit strange lately, not her usual self, but I don't know if I'd be breaking a confidence.'

'You're very loyal, Don. But I'm her sister. Did she ask you not to say anything to me?'

'No, not exactly. And I don't know what's really bothering her anyway.' He thought for a moment. 'She seemed – I don't know – not so in control as usual when I saw her yesterday.'

Bel looked up at him. 'You saw her yesterday? She didn't say.'

'I went out for my paper early,' Don said. 'She was in the churchyard, at Ellen's grave. That's not unheard-of, but it was a chilly morning for that sort of thing. I persuaded her to come home with me and made her a cup of coffee to warm her up. She didn't really tell me anything, but she seemed upset.'

'There's something weighing on her, something she's not telling, I'm sure of it.'

They came to Vic's gate and Bel released Don's arm. They walked up to the door. Solomon appeared round the corner of the house and began to weave in and out of their ankles as Bel fished in her pocket for the key. 'Hey, cat!' she complained. 'You'll have me over! Use your cat-flap!'

She opened the door and Solomon streaked in before them. Don took off his coat and hung it over the end of the stair-rail. Bel unbuttoned her coat and turned her back on him, and Don realised she was expecting him to help her off with it. As he fumbled with the coat, trying to hang it up, he muttered, 'That's just what she said.'

'What?'

'That there were things nobody knew except her. Things that she's tried not to think about for thirty years, because she's ashamed. What on earth has she got to be ashamed of?' He shook his head in puzzlement.

Bel went through to the kitchen, and he followed her. He watched her as she bent over and pulled saucepans out of the cupboard. She took an apron from a hook on the wall and tied it round her waist, at the same time looking up at him and biting her lip. 'I'm sure I don't know. She's told me things, but they weren't something she'd done wrong. It was about our parents, and she seemed angry and bitter, but not ashamed. Whatever is she talking about?'

'That's just it. I asked her if she wanted to tell me about it, and she said if anyone should know it should be you.'

'So it must be something to do with our family, rather than something she's done herself. Apart from that, we're none the wiser, are we? But what are we going to do, Don?'

'I've no idea. Look, I'd better lay the table. She'll be back in a minute.' He opened a drawer and took out cutlery.

Bel found vegetables in the fridge and started to peel and wash them. 'The thing is, Don, there's something I should tell Vic, but I'm not sure how to go about it.' Her face was flushed.

He raised his eyebrows in enquiry.

'I need to know, you see,' she stammered, 'how much she's told you about her past. Like you, I don't want to blunder into telling her secrets.'

'Vic has told me hardly anything,' Don said. He opened a wall cupboard and took out salt and pepper. 'But she told Ellen things, and she didn't say they were secrets, so Ellen told me. I'm sure Vic knows I know, but it's never been mentioned. There didn't seem to be any need.'

'You know she was married once, a long time ago?' He nodded. 'And –'

'I know about the baby she lost, if that's what you're getting at,' Don said. 'Ellen wanted children, but it didn't happen. I think she and Vic felt it was something they had in common. It's not something you can share with just anyone, I suppose.'

'I didn't know anything about it till Vic told me the other day,' Bel said. 'Poor Vic. Her marriage ended and her baby died. It's terribly sad. She must have felt her whole life was over. But it makes it all the more difficult for me, Don.' She stumbled to a halt, pressing her lips together. He said nothing, just stood with his fingertips resting on the edge of the table. 'You see, I have a son. Matthew. Grown up now, of course. I hadn't got round to telling Vic – I thought she would criticise me, because I lost touch with Matthew two years ago. Then she told me about her baby, and now I don't know what to say to her. But I have to say something. It isn't right not to, and anyway, I heard from him just a few days ago. He sent me a Christmas card with his address in it.' She looked at him beseechingly. 'What do you think I should do?'

Don pulled out a chair and sat down. He stared at her, frowning. 'It's a pity you didn't tell her before. But there it is. Of course you have to say something, and the sooner the better. This afternoon. Let's have lunch first, then you decide if you want me to be here or if you want to tell her when you're alone. The way she is, I think she'll take it badly. So of course I'll stay if you need a referee. Just remember I have to be at Evensong later.'

'Right,' Bel said, her voice low and shaky. 'Now I'd better get these potatoes on.'

When Vic got back from church she seemed distracted. She went through the motions of getting lunch on the table, but had little to say. Don and Bel made desultory conversation, watching Vic covertly. Don felt strange: for the first time it was almost as if he was afraid of her, or, if not quite that, then that he didn't know her as well as he had thought. The women were at the sink, finishing off the dishes, and Don was clearing the table, when Bel said to Vic in a tone that was too bright to be authentic, 'So, how long has Frankie got? Did you ask her?'

'Four weeks, apparently,' Vic said. 'But Frankie herself thinks it might be sooner.'

'Oh.'

Watching them, Don wondered if the whole subject of babies should be avoided. But then, the tragedy of little James was so long ago; surely Vic, in all that time, must have found some strategies for coping. After all, babies were being born all the time. Then, with an inward shudder, he remembered what Bel had to tell her sister.

Vic turned to them. Her face was pale and drawn. 'Would you mind very much if I leave you to your own devices? I feel quite worn out.'

Don murmured that he would go home and leave them in peace.

Then Bel said in a rush, 'Wait a moment, please, Vic. There's something I need to tell you.'

Vic looked at her, a slight frown creasing her brows. She was drying her hands on a kitchen towel. 'What?'

Bel gripped her hands tightly together. 'I should have told you this long ago, but somehow I…just didn't. And when, you know, the other day, you told me about your baby, I felt I couldn't. But you see, now I know where he is, and –' Her voice cracked and faded.

'Whatever are you talking about?' Vic said. 'You know where who is?' There was a pause. 'Bel?'

'My son. Matthew,' Bel whispered. She had been staring down at her hands; now she looked up at her sister's face, and her eyes were wide.

Vic shook her head. She looked utterly bewildered, and at that moment Don felt an extraordinary urge to gather both of them up in his arms and murmur soothing words, as if to hurting children.

'You have a son?' Vic said. Bel nodded. 'Why didn't you say so? Why wasn't he mentioned weeks ago? I don't understand.' She felt for the table as if in a daze, and sat down heavily on a kitchen chair.

'Because,' Bel said, 'I haven't seen him for two years. I haven't even spoken to him. I didn't know where he was until a few days ago. You remember I had that bundle of Christmas cards? Sent on by Jason? There was one there from Matthew, with an address in Barnsley.'

'*Barnsley*?'

'I don't know why. It's where his father came from. Perhaps he was looking for someone.'

'But why? Why didn't you know where he was? Why hadn't you seen him?'

Bel sighed deeply, and sat down in the chair opposite her sister. 'We had a row. It wasn't unusual. We were living in a flat in London then, together. Not a nice area. I was working all hours. Matthew didn't seem to be making much effort. Anyway, whatever the reason, we argued. He threw a lot of accusations at me. What a lousy parent I'd been, what a rubbish childhood he'd had. And then he stormed out. I've no idea where he went after that. I was angry and hurt, but I also felt he might have had a point. I don't think I was much of a mother, not really. Matthew idolised his father, but Terry wasn't a great parent either. Too busy making money, too busy making contacts, just too busy. Poor Matthew. But I figured that he was twenty-two and old enough to look after himself. I moved not long after that, to the place I live now. It was cheaper and more central and I was with people I knew. And then the other day you were talking about our parents, and I felt even more of a failure. I'm sorry, Vic, truly. I didn't want to add to your troubles, so I kept quiet. I wish I'd said something sooner.'

Vic said nothing for a long moment. To Don, leaning on the kitchen door frame, his eyes fixed on her face, she looked almost as if she was made of marble: milky-white, cold, hard, unmoving. Suddenly she pushed her chair back and stood up. 'I'm going upstairs,' she said abruptly. 'I need to think. Make yourself some coffee if you like.' She brushed past Don, her arms folded tightly across her chest. 'Please excuse me, Don. I think I'll give church a miss this evening.'

Don stood aside, and listened to her footsteps heavy on the stairs, and the door of her bedroom closing.

'Oh, Don,' Bel said. 'I feel I've given Vic one more thing to make her sad.'

Don shook his head. 'She'll work it out for herself, eventually. Surely knowing she has a nephew is a good thing. She'll come to that conclusion herself, I shouldn't wonder.'

'I hope so, Don, I really do.' She got up. 'I'm going for a walk, see if I can clear my head. What about you?'

'I think I'll just go home. I've got a bit of paperwork to do. What are you going to do about Matthew?'

Bel shrugged. 'I know what I want to do, but it's not just about what I want, not while I'm living here with Vic. Of course I want to see Matthew. I want to sort things out with him. Whatever he's done, whatever he thinks of me, he's my son. When he sent me that card with his address in it, I was so happy and relieved I cried. I expect you'll think I'm stupid.'

Don shook his head. 'No, I don't think that. I hope it comes out all right. For you, for Matthew, for Vic too. I'll pray for you.'

Bel's eyebrows shot up. 'You too?'

'Of course. What did you think? That I play the church organ just because I like music?'

Bel laughed softly. 'I don't know what I think. I've never met so many praying people before.'

'It works in ways you can't imagine. Ways we don't expect. I only hope Vic remembers that. If anyone needs to pray it's her.'

Vic

Vic lay on her bed, her eyes closed. She heard Don's and Bel's voices downstairs, talking quietly. She thought it likely they were talking about her, and she wished it were not so. Not for the first time in her life, she wished she could simply disappear, not only from the sight of others, but from her own: to be nothing, to feel nothing, to have no thoughts.

She heard Bel saying goodbye to Don and the front door closing. She heard Don's retreating footsteps, and something about the sound made her groan softly. She wondered if her behaviour over the past days would make Don retreat from her in some permanent way. How could such a man as he was value a friend who was so erratic, so unpredictable? Over the years since Ellen's death their friendship had grown in quiet trust and mutual appreciation − she felt sure of that much; but how far could he cope with someone feeble, volatile, disorganised? Or was she doing him a disservice? Clearly he was capable of self-sacrifice and devotion − but that had been for Ellen, and she could not imagine it might ever apply to anyone else, certainly not to herself. He could hardly be blamed if he had had enough of weakness.

A short while later she heard the door close again, and now it was Bel's footsteps she heard on the path under her window. The sound faded, and she was alone. For the first time something like peace washed over her weary brain.

She woke, cold and stiff, but rested. It was already dark. She pushed herself up, closed the curtains and switched on the bedside lamp. Her glance fell on her Bible, and she picked it up and held it in her hand, unopened, feeling its weight, the weight of all the wisdom within. And finally, tentatively, perched on the edge of her rumpled bed, she remembered to pray.

Lord, what has gone wrong? I have lived badly, even though I have walked in your light. I have become a sour, envious, life-denying, angry coward. My sister, for all her faults, is kind, generous-spirited, human. She shames me. Who is your true disciple here, me or her? Lord, I have tried too hard, but I am still a failure. I ask your forgiveness, and your help. I want to go back to the place where I took a wrong turning. With your help, perhaps I can find it. Perhaps I can undo the knots I've tied. Please, help me.

She came out from her prayer like someone surfacing from a deep dive, shaking the water from her eyes, blinking in the sudden sunlight. She got to her feet and opened her door quietly. Bel's bedroom door was closed, but there was light beneath it. Vic crept down the stairs and into the kitchen. She put the kettle on and waited for it to boil. The cat flap clacked and Solomon appeared, tail aloft, purring mightily. Vic picked him up and held him close, breathing in the fresh-air scent of his fur. He protested and she set him down. She made two mugs of tea and put food in Solomon's bowl. Then she took the tea upstairs. For a moment she paused outside Bel's door, drawing breath. She knocked softly. 'Bel?'

Bel opened the door, her eyes wide and wary. 'Oh, Vic, you're awake. I was going to make tea for you. I didn't hear you go down.'

'Can I come in?'

'Of course.'

Vic gave Bel her tea and sat on the edge of the bed. The TV was on, the sound barely audible. 'Sorry, were you watching something?'

'It doesn't matter.' Bel flicked the remote and the picture died. 'Are you feeling any better? You look better. I'm sorry – I gave you a shock.'

'Please, Bel, don't apologise. It's for me to be sorry. I've been behaving like an idiot, and I'm not pleased with myself. Who am I to judge anyone else? I don't know anything about your life with Matthew.' She reached over and took Bel's hand. 'You are going to write to him, aren't you? I hope you are.'

'If I do, he might want to meet up, maybe even come here. Would that be OK?'

Vic smiled. 'I can't wait to meet him.' A thought struck her. 'Does he even know about me? That he has an aunt?'

'Of course he does.'

Vic wrapped her arms round herself. 'What is he like?'

Bel hesitated. 'He's like Terry. Dark-haired, blue-eyed, very good-looking. Clever, articulate, lazy and stroppy. Can be extremely charming if he wants to be. Yes, just like his dad.' She laughed. 'I've got a photo somewhere.' She opened the drawer of the bedside table and pulled out the tattered envelope. 'Here's one of all three of us, when Matthew was about six.' She handed it to Vic. 'And here's one when he was a teenager. See the sulky expression, the attempt at a moustache?'

Vic looked at the pictures intently. 'You were a beautiful family,' she said quietly. 'You look happy.'

'That was the year before Terry died. Yes, I suppose we were happy.'

They fell silent for a few moments. Then Vic said, 'What other photos have you got in there? I have nothing to speak of.'

'They're just a random collection, ones I rifled from the old house. Are you sure you want to see them? It won't upset you?'

'You don't have to treat me like an invalid, you know. I'm tough.'

'No, you're not. You're not at all. But look at them if you like.' Bel shook the photos onto the bed and spread them out.

Vic took each one in her hands and scrutinised them. There was one of their parents, John and Margaret, formally posed and smiling stiffly, on their wedding day; and one of their grandfather, the judge, in his robes. Vic's expression was unreadable. There was one of Vic and Bel aged thirteen and ten, Vic in the Repley school uniform. 'How young we were,' Vic said, almost to herself. She turned the photo over, saw the date and shivered. 'Just before Johnnie drowned.'

'Here's one of Johnnie. I love this one,' Bel said, picking up a small picture of a blond barefoot cherub in blue dungarees.

Vic studied it and smiled sadly. 'He was a beautiful child, our little brother.'

'What about this one?' Bel said with an air of triumph. 'Us at school, your last year. You were such a stunner. No wonder Eric was smitten.'

'Good grief,' Vic said. 'And there's you – what were you, fifteen? My goodness, what on earth had you done with your hair? I don't remember it being like that. It looks a bit like a haystack.'

'Doesn't it just,' Bel said, laughing. 'But do you see who else is there? Apart from the whole school, that is?'

'I see Miss Griffin. She was a big influence on me.'

'No, there on the far edge. It *is* him, isn't it? Your not-so-beloved ex?'

Vic peered. 'So it is. This is extraordinary, Bel. I haven't thought about this photo for years.'

'I didn't get to pinch that many. But there must have been lots at the old house. What did you do with them? Surely you didn't throw them away?'

Vic shook her head. 'I just left everything,' she said quietly. 'The photo albums are probably still there, mouldering with the rest of the house. I never wanted to be reminded. I'm glad you kept these, though.' She got up and walked to the window. Fingering the curtain aside she looked out onto the dark farmland beyond the garden. For a moment she was silent, trying to collect her whirling thoughts, her conflicting memories. She turned back to her sister and spoke with increasing urgency. 'Bel, please, write to Matthew tonight. Post it in the morning. Invite him to come and see us. We mustn't let the poison of the past trickle down to another generation. We've got to try to live like normal people, a kind family that gets on with each other, for Matthew's sake, and for any children he might one day have.'

Bel heard Vic's intensity, the way she talked of the past, with a shiver of discomfort. But she mastered herself and spoke calmly. 'Thank you, Vic, I will, very gladly.'

'Don't forget to give him the phone number.'

'Of course.' She paused. 'I've upset your apple-cart, haven't I? Turning up on you like this, invading your space, bringing back things you'd probably much rather forget, and now springing Matthew on you, a nephew you never knew you had. You must wish you'd written to me and said, Thanks, but no thanks.'

Vic smiled. 'No, I really don't.'

'You know, Vic, changing the subject entirely, and risking having my head bitten off – while we're thinking about trying to change things – I reckon you should have your hair cut. All off, short.'

'My hair? Really?'

Bel nodded. 'I think it would suit you. And think how speedy it would be – in and out of the shower, a quick brush, no fuss. It would make you look ten years younger.'

'Ha! Now you're having me on.'

'All right, five.'

'You think I should?'

'I think you should.'

'Then I will. I'll make an appointment tomorrow.' She threw back her head and laughed aloud at Bel's undisguised gape of amazement. 'We'll think of it as symbolic. Chop off something that's weighing me down, travel light. Freedom, yes? That's what we'll go for. You write to your son, and I'll get a haircut.' Her grin faded. 'Look, Bel, I have to get ready for tomorrow. Have a bath, wash my hair.' Her smile was bleak. 'That awkward mass of hair, for the last time, perhaps. You're right, it takes ages to dry. Then I have some work to finish. Something tells me that this week will be a bit of a turning point at Repley. There've been so many rumours flying about – someone will have to make some kind of announcement soon. Everyone's unsettled, and it's percolating down to the girls. We'll have a sandwich later, shall we?' She bent and kissed Bel's cheek. 'Thanks for bearing with me.'

Later Vic sat in front of her bedroom mirror, wrapped in a warm dressing gown, passing a hair dryer over and over through her abundant hair, its vibrant brown now dulled with many strands of grey. *Yes, Bel, you're right. It's high time I stopped playing the part of a respectable and deadly dull middle-aged middle-class teacher of privileged young ladies. I wonder what those young ladies will make of it when they see me shorn? But if that's a part I'm playing, where is the real person? Who is Victoria Colbourne, anyway? Does she even exist?*

She sighed. It had been a strange day. And now Bel had heard from her lost son, and with Vic's blessing she would contact him – perhaps even now she was writing a letter – and then, with any luck, he'd get in touch and they'd be reunited. In a few short weeks both sister and son had been restored to Bel, and for her sake Vic was thankful.

But the serpent of envy wasn't dead, though he should have been, for she had fought him often. Sometimes it was like a physical feeling, that coiling and coiling deep within, and a sudden biting of sharp teeth. If she were to tell Bel all she knew, would it be charity that prompted her, or envy? Should she, Vic, tell Bel everything in the name of truth and clarity, in the belief that knowledge is freedom and power to choose, thus destroying her sister's last illusions? Or should she keep it to herself, as she had done for so many years, until it ate her away?

Her hair was dry enough. She twisted it into a manageable hank and tied it back. She stared at herself in the mirror, and was not encouraged. *I look so old.*

Suddenly she remembered Frankie, and their conversation after church, and she realised that she hadn't yet read the text that Frankie had given her: Ephesians 2, 20 to 22.

She picked up her Bible and put her glasses on. She found Ephesians, tracked down the page with her finger, and read. "You, too, are built upon the foundation laid by the apostles and prophets, the cornerstone being Christ Jesus himself. He is the one who holds the whole building together and makes it grow into a sacred temple dedicated to the Lord. In union with him you too are being built together with all the others into a place where God lives through his Spirit."

She put the Bible down on the bed. Somehow, although she knew that Frankie had chosen these words to encourage her, reading them made

Vic feel worse. The contrast between her present circumstances, her own fallen condition, and the promises of God was too stark to bear long contemplation.

She was no further forward, it seemed. What to do? *Lord, what to do? What did charity demand?* She had no answers. Then a phrase from the reading dropped into her mind. It didn't even have a verb: "In union with him you too..." What did it mean? Surely, that she was included in whatever plan God had; but that plan could not come to fruition without his help and her own obedience.

I will make Bel a sandwich, and be a kind and loving sister for once. Then I will go to bed, and like anyone else with a clean conscience and a good digestion – though I have neither! – I will wait on God's guidance.

Bel

It was a tense week.

On Monday Vic came back from school with news that a meeting had been arranged for Friday afternoon, once lessons were over, and the day girls had gone home, and the boarders were busy and supervised. Then the Head would tell them what was happening: the current situation, the options that were available.

Now Friday had come. It was half past three and already getting dark. The day had been cold and blustery, with sharp showers. Bel was restless. She wandered round the house which she had already cleaned within an inch of its life, searching for things to do, unable to concentrate on reading, finding the TV's daytime offerings inane. Despite the weather and her normal inclinations she longed to go for a walk, just to get out of the house; but the thought that Matthew might ring kept her indoors, a caged beast pacing. She had written to him and posted the letter on Monday morning with a first-class stamp. If he wanted to get in touch, what was holding him up?

And she was worried about Vic. She looked increasingly ill and drawn, and Bel was sure she was in pain, though she denied it. Was it anxiety because of the uncertainty at the school? Bel understood that Repley wasn't just a place of work that Vic happened to like. It was the one place where she'd been happy as a child, and as a teenager; where she had felt valued, discovered her voice, fallen in love: a potent mix. It was the place on which she'd set her sights for years, finally getting a job there after less satisfactory schools. Yes, it was somewhere that held significance for Vic far beyond the desire for fulfilling work or the need to pay the bills. Bel understood this instinctively, because she too had been happy there, and she realised that for her also, though she had not really articulated it to herself at the time, it had been a haven away from the atmosphere of home. But Bel was sure there was something else eating away at Vic from the inside, something that made her look haunted.

159

She drew the curtains against the dreary darkness outside, and switched on the lights. Soon she would light a fire. Vic would be late home after the meeting, and perhaps the news would be bad. A warm, welcoming house, perhaps even a smell of cooking, might help a little. Bel's heart sank: she had learnt a lot about cooking in her weeks here, but didn't trust herself to produce anything edible completely unaided.

She thought about her sister, about Don, and Frankie, what made them tick, and the mystery of their faith-driven lives; and she wondered what it would be like to have that trust herself, and what difference it would make to her life. She suspected that even to search might take more courage than she possessed. She had few illusions about her own character, beyond the ability to survive, and a general goodwill.

The shrill of the phone made her flinch. She raced into the hall and grabbed the handset. 'Hello?' she said breathlessly.

'Mrs. Ilthwaite?'

Bel felt a spasm of nausea. It wasn't Matthew, just some man whose voice she didn't recognise. She gulped. 'Speaking.'

'My name's Malcolm Josephs. I'm ringing from Repley College on behalf of your sister, Miss Colbourne. Please don't worry unduly, but I'm afraid she's been taken to hospital this afternoon.'

'Oh, my God! I knew it, I knew she was ill! What happened?'

'She collapsed in the staffroom, after lunch. She came round quite quickly, and said she was all right and that we weren't to worry, but we thought it best to call the paramedics. She was taken to West Stoke General in an ambulance. I'm sorry it's taken me this long to let you know – there've been a few problems with pupils that demanded my attention. The thing is, your sister's car is still here at the school. It'll be all right, I'm sure, but she can't easily get home, of course.'

Bel took a few deep breaths. 'I can handle that, I think. Thank you, Mr er, Josephs. I'll get over to the hospital as soon as I can. You don't think, then, that it was too bad?'

'I don't know, of course. But she was lucid and calm when they put her in the ambulance.'

'Right. Thank you for letting me know. I'll keep you posted.'

Bel put down the phone and thought for a few moments. A notebook lay on the table with phone numbers in it. She riffled through till she found Don's number at work, and dialled. A woman answered. 'Stoke Medical Supplies. Can I help you?'

'Could I speak to Don, please? Mr Fincham, that is.'

'He's not in the office at the moment,' the woman answered. 'You might catch him on his mobile, but if he's driving you'll have to leave a message and get him to call you back. May I ask who's calling?'

'Oh, yes, I'm sorry. My name's Isabel Ilthwaite. My sister, Victoria Colbourne, is Mr Fincham's friend, and she's in hospital.'

'I see. Do you have his mobile number?'

Bel looked at the notebook. 'Yes, it's here. I'll ring him now. Thank you.'

She tapped in the number, but her hands were trembling and she misdialled. Cursing under her breath she started again. The phone rang several times, and when Don answered her relief was enormous. 'Don? It's Bel. Can you speak?'

'Hold on a minute.' She heard him mutter something, and someone else's voice, then footsteps and a door closing. 'All right, Bel, I can talk now. What's up?'

'I've just had a phone call from the school, Don. From Repley. Vic collapsed this afternoon. The man who called said she seemed OK, but they took her off to hospital, and her car's at the school of course, and I've got no transport –'

'All right,' Don interrupted. 'Don't worry, Bel. I'm finished here anyway. I'll come and pick you up, and we'll go and find her. Where is she, Stoke General?'

'Yes.'

'Did they say what was the matter?'

'They didn't know. Perhaps it was nothing, but they were being cautious. I'm certain she isn't well, Don. I just hope whatever it is the hospital have found it and can sort it out.'

'Yes, of course. Well, I'm not too far away, as it happens. Should be with you in about twenty minutes.'

'Thanks, Don. I'll be ready. You didn't mind me calling, did you?'

'Of course not!' Don sounded shocked. 'I'll see you soon.'

Bel had her coat and boots on and her handbag in her hand when she heard Don sounding his horn in the lane outside. She locked the back door, checked she had a key, and hurried down the path. She was out of breath by the time she pulled herself up into his car. The heater was on; it felt warm and enclosed, and she began to breathe more easily.

Don took his hand off the steering wheel and patted her arm. 'Don't worry,' he said gently. 'It may even be a good thing this has happened.

Maybe we can find out what's really going on.' Bel smiled and nodded as she clicked her seatbelt on. She felt absurdly tearful. Don pulled away, down the lane, onto the approach road and then the bypass. 'I heard something today,' he said, 'about your old house, Angleby.'

Bel glanced at him. 'Oh?'

'Just a rumour, perhaps. Someone I know vaguely said he'd heard the land had been sold again. Perhaps a new developer, someone with funds. He said he'd heard it in the pub, so you might have to take it with a pinch of salt. On the other hand, these things are usually not completely without foundation.'

'Who'd want to live under the bypass?'

Don shook his head. 'It may not be housing they're planning. It may be facilities for the folk who already live on the estate. I've no idea.' He looked at her enquiringly. 'Didn't Vic say something about the original developer wanting to build some kind of country club, with all the works – fitness centre, tennis, swimming and so on? Perhaps that's what they have in mind.'

Bel was silent for a few moments. 'They'll pull the old house down, won't they? Vic says that's all it's fit for now.'

'Will you mind?' Don said.

'I don't know,' Bel answered. 'But I can't do anything about it anyway, can I? Oh, Don, I'm really worried about Vic.'

'We're almost there.'

A few minutes later he swung into the hospital and drove round to the back. 'I deliver here frequently,' he said. 'I can use a space they keep for me. Saves the hassle of parking.'

He locked the car and led her through a back entrance and via several busy corridors until they came to A and E. 'I guess this is where they brought her,' he said. 'Go and ask at the desk. You'll get more joy as you're a relative.'

After a few minutes' queuing Bel spoke to a nurse manning a computer, then she came back to Don. 'Someone'll come and call us.'

'Probably in about six hours, as this is A and E,' Don said, smiling.

Bel shuddered. 'I hope not. Anyway, we might as well sit down.' She sank onto a hard plastic chair. 'Did I interrupt anything important, Don?'

'No, I was pretty much done for the day. People don't like being held up on Friday afternoons, on the whole.'

Ten minutes later a nurse appeared. 'Mrs Ilthwaite?'

Bel sat up. 'Yes. That's me.'

'Come this way, please.'

'You too, Don,' Bel murmured. 'I need moral support.'

They followed the nurse down another corridor, round a corner and into a small ward that was almost deserted. 'Your sister's here, Miss Colbourne,' the nurse said cheerfully. She turned to Bel. 'I'll leave you to it.'

Vic was sitting, fully dressed, in an upright armchair next to a neatly-made bed. She looked flushed and cross.

Bel hurried over and gave her a hug. 'Vic, are you OK? You've given us quite a fright.'

'I'm perfectly fine,' Vic said, disengaging herself, at the same time squeezing Bel's arm. 'It was all a fuss over nothing and a stupid waste of people's time. An ambulance, for heaven's sake!' She looked up. 'Oh, Don, hello. You've been dragged out too.'

'Nobody dragged me,' Don said quietly. 'And Bel needed transport.'

'Of course, and my car's still at school. Will you take me there so I can collect it?'

'Yes, but not today.'

'What?' Vic frowned.

'When you're well enough to go back to work, I'll drive you,' Don said. 'And then you can bring the car home yourself.'

'I'm fine now.'

'So you say, but I want to hear it from the medics first.'

'Vic, what happened?' Bel interrupted, sensing a disagreement brewing.

'It was all silly and unnecessary,' Vic said. 'I went to the staff room after lunch. I had a sharp pain, here.' She indicated the side of her stomach. 'I'm sure it would have gone away in time. I've had it before. The staff room was terribly hot and stuffy. I expect I'd run up the stairs too quickly. Anyway, I fainted, that's all. And I felt no end of a fool when I came to and was told they'd called the paramedics.'

'Have you been seen here?' Bel asked. 'Have you had an X-ray or something?'

'I've been seen, quizzed and examined,' Vic said. 'They think I have a gastric ulcer. I may have to have an endoscopy at some point. I have to make an appointment with my GP. What a nuisance! Anyway, they don't think I'm about to expire, so there's no need to look so tragic, Bel. I can go home just as soon as someone comes with some pills beginning with O. I've no idea why it's taking so long.'

They were interrupted by another nurse. 'Here we are,' she said. 'Your prescription. Take these for two weeks according to the instructions, and then make an appointment with your GP and tell him how you're feeling. We'll be writing to him, of course. What happens after that depends on how you respond to the medication.'

'When can I go back to work?' Vic said, getting up and taking the pills from the nurse with a murmur of thanks.

'Take at least a week off,' the nurse said. 'You're a teacher, aren't you? So you have a pretty stressful job. Go home, put your feet up, and take it easy.'

'Small chance of that,' Bel muttered.

'Got everything?' Don said. 'Here, I'll take that.' He picked up Vic's briefcase. They left the hospital by the main entrance, pausing in A and E for Vic to thank the staff. Then they found their way to the back of the building and climbed into Don's car.

'You were lucky,' Bel said. 'You didn't have too long a wait.'

Vic nodded. 'Fortunately it wasn't too busy this afternoon. No drunks. No prisoners handcuffed to policemen. But some pretty harrowing cases all the same.' Don glanced at her as he pulled out onto the main road. 'When you're in a cubicle,' Vic said, 'waiting to be seen, and all that divides you from the next bay is a curtain, you can't help hearing what some other poor soul is suffering. The man next to me collapsed this morning, while sitting on the toilet, apparently. When he came round he was in a twisted heap on the bathroom floor and he'd broken his ankle in three places. I heard the doctor going through the options.' She shuddered. 'One involved pins in his bones. And the situation was complicated by his heart condition. It sounded like he was almost completely dependent on his wife. Then a little while later there was a sudden panic, doctors and nurses homing in on A and E in droves, asking what cupboard certain drugs were in, and a little wail, and a kindly voice saying, "You all right, Mum?" I couldn't actually see what was going on from behind my curtain, but I gathered it was a one-year-old with a seizure.'

'Oh! Did you hear what happened?' Bel said.

'Yes. He was all right after their ministrations, thankfully. All these really sick people made me feel fraudulent.'

Don left the High Street and took the exit from the roundabout that led up onto the ring road. 'Will someone tell you what happened at the meeting? The one you missed?' he asked quietly.

Vic turned to him, shaking her head. 'It never happened. The Head was called away on some important and unavoidable business, and the meeting was postponed – till when, I don't know. So we are still in the dark.'

'That's frustrating,' Don said. 'To be still on tenterhooks.'

As the car gathered speed along the ring road Bel leaned forward from the back seat. 'Don's heard some news about our old house, Vic.'

'A rumour, no more,' Don corrected. He looked sideways at Vic and smiled slightly. 'You know how it is in a place like Thackham. A man in a pub tells you something hinted at by his friend who knows a builder… and so it goes. But my informant was Eddie Chilham, who usually has his ear to the ground.'

'Apparently someone's bought up the piece of land and the house,' Bel said. 'How would we find out if it was true, Don?'

Don considered. 'I suppose you could check it out with the Council's planning department. Or visit the Council web site.'

'If I had a computer.'

'Vic's got one,' Don said. He indicated her briefcase with a jerk of his head. 'In there, I imagine.'

'Really?' Bel's eyebrows raised. 'I've never seen it.'

'I know you think I am an unregenerate dinosaur,' Vic said acidly. 'And I certainly don't surf the internet or play time-consuming games. But I need a computer for school – for record-keeping, entering exam results on the school database, and so on. Most of the time I keep it in a locked cupboard in the staff room. I suppose you think I am some kind of Luddite because I don't have TV or a mobile phone.'

'Kind of.' Bel paused. 'So we could look it up later, could we?'

'Be my guest.'

'Thanks, I will. I'm afraid I didn't have time to prepare any dinner, Vic.'

Vic smiled. 'I would have fainted again if you had. I daresay there's something in the freezer I can heat up. You'll join us, won't you, Don?'

'If I won't be in the way.'

'You're never in the way. And you can do the washing up while I play the feeble invalid.'

'Gladly.'

For the last few miles they were silent. Then Don took the Thackham exit and swung down the curving ramp onto the approach road to the village. As he bumped up the track to Vic's house the car's headlights swayed about in all directions. He came to a halt by Vic's fence. 'Here we are,' he said. 'Better hurry – it seems to be drizzling again.'

'I laid the fire,' Bel said. 'It just needs a match.'

Vic stepped out of the car and stretched. 'It's good to be home. Just think, Bel – if I'd been kept in hospital overnight, I'd have missed my appointment at the hairdresser's.'

Bel grinned. 'So you would. And we can't have that.'

With three of them huddled in front of the fire, Vic's tiny living room seemed crowded. They sat with coffee cups at their elbows, warm, replete, somnolent.

Don yawned. 'I should be going,' he said, not moving. Then he sat up and hunched forward. 'So what's significant about the hairdresser's appointment?' he said to Vic. 'Can't it wait till you're a hundred per cent?'

Vic exchanged a look with Bel. 'No, if I don't go tomorrow I might chicken out.'

Don frowned. 'Am I missing something here? Since when was a haircut such an adventure?'

Bel said, without opening her eyes, 'Because tomorrow is the beginning of the new Vic. She's getting it all cut off.'

'What? Why?'

Vic shook her head. 'Bel persuaded me. She said it would make me look younger, as well as being easier to handle.'

'What do you think, Don?' Bel said. 'Good idea?'

'I hardly know,' Don mumbled. 'I guess I've got used to Vic as she is.'

'Just like you're used to your old sofa?' Bel said slyly.

'No, not like that,' Don protested. Then he saw they were both grinning. 'I give up. I'm going home.' As he got to his feet the phone rang. 'I'm on my feet – I'll get it if you like.' He left the room and closed the door. A moment later they heard him speaking. Then he came back in. 'Bel, it's for you.'

Bel pressed her hand to her heart. 'Me?' Her voice came out as a squeak. 'Is it –'

'Matthew.'

'Oh!' She pushed herself up out of the low armchair and hurtled into the hall, banging the door shut after her.

'I think you'd better sit down again, Don,' Vic said. 'Leave her to it.'

Don sank back into his chair and stretched out his stork-like legs. 'So what's all this about a haircut?'

'I think Bel feels I need to join the world.'

'Aren't you in it already?'

'Probably not, according to her. She sees me as an anachronistic hermit, mired in the past.'

'Oh. Well, I don't know about the first bit, but she may have a point with the second.'

'You think so? Well, perhaps you're right. In a way it will be a relief to get rid of my hair. We're thinking of it as symbolic, you see – shedding dead weight. Easier to visit the hairdresser, though, than to delete one's memories.'

Don cleared his throat and stared at the floor. 'Some people hang on to the past because they haven't got much going on in the present. But that's not you, is it?'

'And some,' Vic said softly, ignoring his question, 'because they don't see much of a future. Is that me?'

Don's sandy brows knitted together. 'It shouldn't be, should it? You should be confident of an eternal future.'

Vic sighed. 'I know. It's the bit between that's difficult. What to do with the rest of one's life. Perhaps getting my hair cut off is a way of saying that if I can change myself, I can change my circumstances.'

'You know what? I think you read too many books.'

Vic laughed. 'Impossible.'

They both looked up as the door opened. Bel's face was flushed, her eyes bright.

'He wants to come down here,' she said. 'This weekend. I said I didn't know, what with Vic unwell. And where would we put him? He'd have to stay over. It'd be a bit of a rush, coming from Huddersfield just for a day.'

'Is he still on the phone?' Vic demanded.

'No – I said I'd talk to you and then ring him back. He has to come at the weekends, you see. He has lectures on Monday. Can you believe it, Vic – Matthew's a student! He's in his second year at Huddersfield University, doing Business Studies! I'm astonished.'

'You said he was clever, Bel.'

'Yes, he is, and he got good A levels on minimal work, but he didn't seem in the slightest bit interested in further education. Or getting a job, come to that.'

'Bel, he must come. Ring him back now. We'll manage somehow.'

'Vic's right, Bel,' Don broke in. 'You don't want to lose the opportunity. He can stay overnight at my place. I've got plenty of room.'

'Oh, Don! That's really kind of you. Are you sure it's not a great imposition?'

'Of course it isn't. Tell him to come. Find out when his train gets in, and I'll pick him up from the station.'

'We'll all go,' Vic said firmly. 'It'll be like meeting visiting royalty.'

Something woke Bel around two in the morning; but when she came fully awake and listened, there was nothing to hear. There was no sound of wind in the trees, no splashing of rain, no water dripping from the eaves. Reluctantly she got up, opened her door carefully and padded to the bathroom. Back in her bedroom she pulled the curtains aside a foot or two and peered out.

The rain had indeed stopped, and the wind had blown away the weight of cloud, leaving only a ragged darker wrack against a clear indigo sky. Stars were out in myriads, but they were smudged by the wetness of the window pane, and on an impulse Bel opened the window and leaned out. At once the cold struck her, making her gasp, a clean unforgiving cold stinging her cheeks and lips. In the still air the stars shone with a crisp brightness, hard and unwinking, and as she continued to look more stars became visible, and behind them a dim wraith-like light. She looked down at the ground, deep in shadow, and saw the first frost forming. Something moved in the lumpy shrubbery, and Bel's eyes followed a shape that detached itself from a bush, a shape that loped close to the ground, something with a long, bushy tail. She smiled, then shivered. Gooseflesh stippled the bare skin of her arms. She closed the window, and for a few moments continued to stare out, her eyes wide, feeling somewhere in the pit of her stomach the beauty, the cruelty and mystery of the world as it seemed to her then, untouchable, incomprehensible in its reality. As she crossed the room again to get back into the warmth of the bed she sensed something brush against her – or perhaps she only thought she did – something light and insubstantial, like the wing of a passing angel. She shook her head, scornful of her nocturnal fancies, climbed into bed and pulled the duvet up under her chin, still shuddering from cold.

She thought of the evening's events, and a smile spread unchecked across her face. Matthew was coming tomorrow. *My maddening, wonderful son.* Her mind peopled itself with images of Matthew through the years: the perfect newborn with his tuft of dark hair, the clinging toddler, the rather serious child, the morose adolescent, the often insufferable adult. He had the ability, perhaps alone among every other being on the planet, to deal her joy and misery with unthinking ease. Somehow against him she had few defences. But now he was coming to visit, and whatever he had to say hardly mattered. She would see him again: her child.

A warmth of gratitude swept over her, upwards from chest height into her eyes, making her blink. She realised that it had no object, that in her godless state she had no one to thank for the apprehensive happiness she felt. Of course she was thankful to Vic for her unreserved welcome, and to Don for his offer of hospitality, and in an odd way she was grateful to Matthew himself for his relenting. But this sensation was somehow more universal, almost inspiring awe. She blushed and squirmed at her own foolishness, but something impelled her to mutter under her breath, 'Thank you, God. If you are there. If you even exist. If you care. If this is your doing, thank you.'

Vic

21 January 2006

'Oh, Vic, did you hear?' Bel looked up from her bowl of cereal. 'There was a whale swimming up the Thames yesterday.'

'Really? It's not April 1st, is it?'

'No, it really happened. It was on the news. A female Northern Bottle-nosed whale, sixteen feet long. And lost.'

'Poor thing. Where should it have been?'

'Scotland, Ireland, the Arctic. With her buddies somewhere nice and cold.'

'Is she still there?'

'Mm. According to the news this morning they're trying to rescue her, get her back out to sea. Vic, don't you think reality's very odd?'

Vic, sitting on the other side of the table, looked at her sister over her glasses, a small frown bunching her brows. 'That's a strange remark in itself. As a matter of fact I do think it's very odd. But I'm surprised to hear it from you.'

'Oh? Why?'

Vic shrugged. 'You seem, I don't know, grounded somehow. Connected to the here-and-now. Pragmatic.'

Bel grinned. 'I'm not at all sure that's a compliment, coming from you, but I'll take it as one. Don't want to spoil the day so early.'

'I can't believe anything I say could spoil this particular day for you. Did you know you've been competing with the Cheshire Cat ever since Matthew phoned?' She looked up at the clock. 'Heavens, I must get going! Can't be late for my appointment.' She pushed her chair back, got to her feet and put her breakfast dishes in the sink.

'Leave those – I'll do them,' Bel said.

'Thanks. What time did you say Matthew was arriving?'

'Four-ten. If he gets up in time for the London train.' She looked at Vic sideways. 'I must say you don't seem in the least perturbed by the imminent loss of your hair. I'm surprised. Thought you might back out.'

'It's only hair.'

'Yes. But part of you.'

'I've lost a few parts of me over the years, and survived. Well, after a fashion. And hair's a replaceable part of me.' She caught Bel's look. 'Not, I imagine, that I will want to replace it. Now I must go and get ready.'

Little more than an hour later she sat in the hairdresser's chair, a floral nylon robe tied backwards round her neck. Saturday was a busy day, and the small room was full of women under hot-air dryers. It was noisy and uncomfortably warm.

'There you are, then, Miss Colbourne, all done.' Bleached-blonde Natalie picked up a hand-mirror and showed Vic the back of her head, the hair now neatly tapered into her neck. Round the chair, as yet unswept, curls and hanks and tendrils lay, brown and grey, looking somehow forlorn. 'What do you think?'

Vic looked in the mirror, and saw someone she barely recognised. Her head felt cold and vulnerable, but light and free. *I look like every other woman.* 'It's fine, thank you, Natalie. You've done a good job as usual. Maybe I'll get used to it in a hundred years or so.' She smiled.

Natalie looked at Vic critically, turning her own head from side to side. 'I like it,' she pronounced. 'Takes years off you. What do you think, Mrs Drake?' She turned to one of the women under the dryers, an old lady with regimented rows of curlers in her wispy white hair.

'Turn round and let me see,' Mrs Drake said. Feeling self-conscious, Vic obliged. 'Very nice, my dear. Now we can see more of your pretty face.'

'Thank you,' Vic muttered. She saw the row of women, mostly elderly, looking back at her, smiling encouragingly as if they understood the small revolution that had taken place there that morning. Suddenly she found she was no longer embarrassed. She smiled back at them. *Bel was right. I think I am beginning to rejoin the human race. Here I am, at the hairdresser's on a Saturday morning, a woman among women. I wonder if their visit is as momentous.*

Don arrived at three thirty and sounded his horn from the lane.

'I'm relieved to see you, Don,' Vic said as she climbed into his car. 'I think if I'd had to put up with Bel's incessant fidgeting much longer I might have had to lock her in the shed.'

Don turned to look at her, his hands resting on the steering-wheel. 'Take your hat off,' he said. 'I don't think I've ever seen you in a hat.'

171

'It's cold,' Vic said. She kept a straight face, but a grin was cracking open around her eyes.

Bel climbed into the back seat and shut the door. 'Boy, that's chilly out there! I think you'd better get it over with, Vic. Be brave.'

'It's Don that needs courage. He's naturally conservative.'

'You have such a nerve!' Bel spluttered. 'You're not conservative, I suppose.'

Vic buckled her seat belt on. 'Not any more,' she said calmly. 'Please note who's the one who had all her hair chopped off.' She pulled off the hat. For a moment a charged silence reigned in the car. Vic looked unblinking at Don, whose face seemed oddly flushed.

Even Bel was quiet – but not for long. 'Well?' she demanded. 'What do you think, Don?'

Don shook his head. 'You look so…different.'

'Good or bad?' Bel pursued.

'Good, I think. Yes, definitely.' He smiled. 'You look friendlier. Not that you looked unfriendly before, of course.'

Vic smiled back, and her eyes never left his face. 'Friendly is good. And I feel different. So, world, watch out.' She settled back in her seat. 'Hadn't we better get to the station? We don't want Matthew catching his death on a freezing platform.'

They stood together at the barrier, waiting for the train. A chill wind blew from behind them, and Vic put her hat back on. Her neck felt unfamiliarly exposed. She looked at Bel. Her gloved hands were gripping the railing, and her face was pale. Vic found she couldn't imagine just what was going on her sister's mind: it was at that moment another country, inadequately mapped. She put an arm round Bel's shoulder and briefly squeezed.

The train appeared round the bend with a noisy rumble of rails, and screeched to a slow stop. Doors clanged open, and people began to alight, their breath condensing in the cold air, and then a dozen or more hurried towards them, their faces intent, purposeful, mysterious.

'There he is,' Bel said, clutching Vic's arm.

Vic saw a dark figure standing on the platform. He seemed uncertain. The train pulled out with a great noise, drowning all possibility of speech, but Bel was waving. 'Matt! Over here!'

At last he saw her and began to walk towards them. Vic saw a slim young man, dressed in black jeans and a jacket with a big collar. He was bare-headed and carried a small backpack. As he approached, she noted his dark, wavy hair curling around his neck, his smile, his bright blue eyes. Bel slipped around the barrier, and Matthew dropped his backpack.

'Mum.'

'Oh, Matthew.' Bel threw her arms around him and he hugged her back. He was a head taller, and after a moment he looked up at Vic and Don and smiled. 'Come on, Mum. This station's freezing.'

Bel, her face alight, tucked her hand in Matthew's elbow. 'This, obviously, is your Aunt Vic,' she said.

Matthew took Vic's proffered hand, and then, in an almost courtly gesture, bent and kissed her cheek. 'It's good to meet you,' he said. His voice was soft. 'Despite my million relations dotted around Yorkshire, you're my one and only aunt.'

Vic smiled. 'As you're my one and only nephew. This is our friend, Don. Kindly provider of transport, among other things.'

Matthew shook Don's hand. 'Nice to meet you, too. Thanks for coming to get me.'

They sat around the table in Vic's kitchen, a pot of tea and a half-eaten cake before them.

Matthew demolished his second slice. 'For a moment there, Mum, I thought you might have learned how to cook.'

'Hah!' Bel snorted. 'Not a chance. I have learned a few things, though, haven't I, Vic? Just nothing this clever. Your aunt's a dab hand.'

'She certainly is.'

Vic hefted the teapot. 'Top-up, Matthew?'

'Please.' He passed his cup over and looked around. 'This is such a nice little house. Have you been here for years?'

'Ever since I sold the old place. Angleby.'

'Mum's told me a bit about it. Is it still there?'

'Yes, but not, possibly, for much longer.' Vic told Matthew what Don had reported earlier.

Matthew nodded thoughtfully. 'Maybe, if there's time, I'll take a stroll up and look down on it.'

Bel broke in. 'You were going to tell us what you've been doing the last couple of years, Matt.'

Matthew glanced at Don. 'It's not all that interesting to anyone else, Mum. Don't want to be a bore.'

Don smiled. 'Go ahead.'

Matthew leaned back in his chair and stretched out his legs. Vic, watching him, could see what Bel meant: his resemblance to his father, down to the lazy charm, the self-mocking humour – everything but the Yorkshire accent.

'Well,' he said after a thought-gathering pause, 'after a week or so dossing on friends' floors, I decided to go north. We're talking two years ago, right? I thought maybe I could trace some of Dad's original family. I guess I was feeling pretty rootless then, out on a limb. I hitched several rides and wound up in Barnsley. I don't know what I thought I was going to do, how I was going to find them. Bit naïve really. To cut it short, I found a grim little bedsit I could just about afford, and after a day or two touting round I managed to get a part-time job in a fish and chip shop. It wasn't much, but it kept my head above water for the time being. In my spare time I had nothing to do, and I was in a strange town, so I wandered round, asking questions in pubs, looking things up in the local library. I found some of my relations too, much to my surprise.'

'Really?' Bel said, leaning forward in her chair. 'Which ones?'

'Well, you know the story of my errant grandma, don't you?' Matthew said.

'Yes, but Vic and Don don't.'

'Briefly, my grandma, Frances Ilthwaite, known as Franny, daughter of Pat and Jack, was a bit of a wild child, especially for those days. Remember it was the fifties. At sixteen she got involved with a young squaddie called Robbie Telfer, and lo and behold, he knocked her up. The family went berserk, but hard-nosed Franny didn't care. She had the baby – my dad, of course – and when he was a couple of months old I guess she got sick of all the Shame-and-Disgrace and did a bunk. Wrote a note to her mother from London, and basically disappeared. Nobody I spoke to had heard of her since. Poor Robbie got killed in Korea a month before Dad was born. So Dad was raised by Pat and her mother, Ivy Ebbs.'

'I remember your dad mentioning the Ebbses,' Bel said.

'Well, I'll spare you the family tree details,' Matthew said. 'I worked it out for myself one idle evening and what struck me was how young they all seemed to be when they got married and had kids – eighteen, nineteen, that sort of thing. Maybe that's how it was done there in those days. Anyway there are a fair few Ilthwaites, Ebbses, Pitts, Stanleys, Willses, etcetera all living in the Barnsley area. Franny had an older brother, David, and he had three children, and they had children, and so on. I met one of them for a drink, one of the few close to me in age, Paul Wills. I suppose he was a sort of distant cousin. He was a nice enough bloke, but we didn't have much in common. I'd hoped to find some of the older ones, but Ivy was dead, of course, and Pat was in her eighties and in a home and not all there, they said. I went to see her one Sunday afternoon, but she didn't have a clue who I was. It was funny: when I mentioned the name Terry she seemed to sit up, and her eyes went wide, but then she sort of clouded over again and was back in her own little world. It was sad to see.

'So I knew of their existence, and they knew of mine, at least some of them did, but we were worlds apart. I went on working in the chippy, but after a while I began to ask myself what the hell I was doing, in this strange place where I didn't belong. I didn't really know what to do – it was depressing, to say the least. And that's when I met Jess.'

'Jess?'

Matthew smiled. 'Any chance of another cup, Aunt Vic?'

'Of course. I'll make a fresh pot. Go on, Matthew – I'm all agog.'

'One evening there I was, in my greasy apron, smelling of old fat, and in came this beautiful girl: tall, as tall as me, willowy but womanly, if you get me, with this cloud of blonde hair, and I just... goggled. Totally smitten, life-changing moment, etcetera.

'Well, there's no point in giving you a blow-by-blow account. We went out, we got on, she's my girlfriend now. It was she who persuaded me to apply to Uni, and she who got me out of that revolting dingy dump and offered me her brother's room while he was away. Jack's in the army,' he explained. 'Poor bastard's in Iraq at the moment. Not funny.

'Jess is coming up for her finals, and I'm a year behind her. Her grandma broke her arm so she's in Jack's room for the time being, and I'm living in a student flat in Huddersfield with three other blokes. Jess lives at home with her family in Barnsley because it's cheaper. She travels into Huddersfield on the bus, to use the library, or go to lectures, or to see me. It was her family's address I sent you. Jess brings me my post. Quite often I go back to her house for meals. Her mum's a great cook, and the family kind of adopted this poor waif and stray. They've been very good to me. They're staunch Baptists, and keep trying to get me to church. So far I've resisted, but if I marry Jess one day, if she'll have me, I expect I'll end up toeing the line.' He grinned, and Vic saw that the prospect was not altogether a disagreeable one for him. Clearly Jess's charms far outweighed any theological doubts he might have had.

'Vic and Don go to church here, you know,' Bel said. 'In fact, Don's a very important part of the operation: he's the organist and choirmaster.

I go now as well. I wouldn't call myself a believer exactly. But you should meet their vicar. She's a one-off.'

'She?'

'Frankie. Young, pregnant and feisty.'

Vic put the teapot back on the table. 'Keep going, Matthew, I'm listening. But I must get some dinner for us all.'

Matthew sighed. 'You know what, Aunt Vic, I love you.'

'And anyone else who feeds you, I imagine,' Vic said. 'You look as if you need feeding up.'

'I'm naturally skinny,' Matthew said with a broad grin. 'Very handy. People take pity on me. In fact, I eat like the proverbial horse.'

'You'll stay, won't you, Don?'

'If you're sure there's enough and I won't be imposing.'

'Imposing, indeed!' Bel snorted. 'What nonsense. You're another one that looks like he needs fattening up. And you practically live here anyway.' She turned to Matthew, and so missed Don's wince. 'Tell us more about Jess, Matt. If she's going to be my daughter-in-law I need to be forearmed.'

Matthew laughed. 'Even if she says yes, Mum, it won't be for ages. She swears she'd never marry a bum like me. But I'm working on her. I'll wear her down in the end. What's she like? I've told you she's tall and blonde. Her hair flies in all directions, untameable. She's very athletic, unlike me – plays tennis, runs, swims, cycles. She's studying Nutrition and Public Health, and works ridiculously hard. She's very short-sighted. What else do you want to know? Oh yes, I've told you she comes from a Baptist family. She has an older sister, Josie, married to Wes, with a baby, Poppy. She has a younger brother, Jacob. He's a gobby lout of fourteen and drives her mad. He'll be OK in a few years. The Burbages seem to regard me as another son, which makes me feel a bit incestuous. Sorry, perhaps I shouldn't have said that.' For a moment he looked worried. 'Wouldn't want to offend you, Aunt Vic, not when I've only just found you.'

'I'm a teacher, Matthew. Not easily shocked.'

'Right. So, there you go, Mum. Potted history. Not much else to tell you. I wanted to bring Jess down with me, but she said no, not this time. But it's she who said I should send you my address when I was humming and hahing whether I should. I thought you wouldn't want anything to do with me. She said that was rubbish. And, luckily for me, as usual, she was right.' He paused, stretched across the table, and took Bel by the wrist. 'Mum, I'm really sorry for all the horrible things I said. They weren't true, and you didn't deserve them. I was an arrogant little prick, but I think, I hope, I've grown up a bit. Jess said you'd forgive me. Was she right?'

'Of course, you fool,' Bel said. Her eyes were teary. 'I'm your mother.' She turned to Vic. 'Have we got any alcohol in the house, Vic? Apart from that rather mouldy sherry? I think we should celebrate.'

'I'm sorry, I never got round to buying any,' Vic said.

'I've got a bottle or two at my house,' Don said. 'I'll go and get them, Vic, if I've got time.'

Vic looked at the clock. 'Dinner will be ready in about forty minutes. So you've got plenty of time. Thank you, Don.'

'I'll leave the car at home and walk back,' Don said. 'Then I can have a drink too. And *we* will do the washing up.' He turned to Matthew. 'Your aunt was in hospital yesterday. She's supposed to be taking it easy.'

'Fuss, fuss, fuss,' Vic said, pretending to scowl. 'Go and get the wine.'

The meal was eaten in record time, and the two bottles of wine disappeared as if a spell had been cast on them. Matthew and Bel talked and laughed, and Vic put in the odd comment, glad to see her sister happy. Don said little, watching them all with a smile. Vic felt his eyes on her especially, watchful and protective.

'You know,' she said quietly, turning to him, 'I really am all right. Don't worry.' To her surprise he took her hand briefly and squeezed it.

'So, Matthew, what are your plans now?' Don asked him as they stacked the plates.

Matthew paused and considered. Then he said, 'To get my degree, to find some work, to make some money, to find a better place to live. To persuade the delicious Jessica Burbage to marry me.' He turned to Bel and winked. 'And to bask in the reflected glory of having a famous mother.'

Don

By the time Don and Matthew left it was nearing midnight. Don had brought his torch for the unlit track, but Matthew, well-oiled by the wine and wearing flimsy shoes, stumbled and staggered over the ruts and half-frozen tyre-tracks, to his own vast amusement.

'Steady on, there,' Don said. 'We don't want you in A and E. Had enough of that for the time being.'

They managed to reach the end of the village street without injury, though Matthew's shoes were soaked through and covered in mud. 'They'll dry off by morning,' he said philosophically. 'So, Don, you're the organist and choirmaster here at the church. Been doing that long?'

'Since we came to Thackham, eight years ago,' Don said quietly, then, catching Matthew's enquiring look, 'I came here with my wife, Ellen.'

'Oh, I'm sorry, I didn't realise you were married.'

'Widowed.'

'Oh. I hope I haven't put my foot in it.'

'Of course not. You weren't to know. It's this way.' He led Matthew down the main street, deserted now, towards the black bulk of St. Mark's.

'This the church?' Matthew asked.

'Yes. I'll be there tomorrow morning, and so will your aunt. Maybe your mother too. She's been helping out with the Sunday School – did you know that?'

'No, I didn't.' He hesitated. 'You're a good friend of Aunt Vic's, I think.'

'Yes. She and my late wife were friends.'

'She's an interesting lady, my aunt. And not a bit like Mum.'

Don looked amused. 'You could say that. Here we are.'

He led the way down the path to his bungalow and unlocked the door.

'I'll take these wet shoes off,' Matthew said. He looked around appreciatively. 'It's nice and warm in here. Why doesn't Aunt Vic get central heating?'

Don closed his eyes briefly. 'Heaven knows.'

Matthew chuckled. 'You've tried to persuade her?'

'Many times. But I've given up. Would you like some coffee?'

'Yes, please.'

Matthew followed Don into the kitchen. 'So I suppose Aunt Vic is a leading light in your church choir, is she?'

Don was filling the kettle, and for a few seconds he found he couldn't move. The moment passed, and he set the kettle to boil. He turned to Matthew, perplexed. 'That's very strange,' he said.

'What is?'

'Your mother asked me that same question several weeks ago, as if it was something quite obvious.'

Matthew shrugged. 'Well, it is, I suppose. I mean, I've never heard Aunt Vic sing, of course. Not in the flesh. I only met her today. But – '

'Wait, Matthew,' Don interrupted. 'There's a mystery here. In all the years I've known her, Vic has claimed she can't carry a tune, that she's tone deaf, that she sounds like a frog. In church she sits in the pew and mumbles.'

Matthew frowned. 'Mum told me lots of stories about herself and Aunt Vic when they were growing up. How she, Mum that is, found out about acting while she was at school – near here, isn't it? And how Aunt Vic discovered her voice. Mum said it was terrific, that she gave a public concert in her last year at school. She even married her singing teacher. Apparently she was all set for a great career.' He paused. 'I'm sorry if I'm speaking out of turn, Don. Didn't you know this stuff? Have I accidentally let a secret out?'

'Let me make this coffee,' Don said. 'I must think.' Matthew sat down at the table. A minute later Don handed him a steaming mug and sat opposite him. 'I knew your aunt was married briefly in her twenties,' he said. 'But not about the singing teacher, or the voice, or the concert. Nothing. Could your mother have been exaggerating? I don't mean to suggest she's a fantasist or anything like that,' he added hastily.

Matthew shook his head. 'There was a recording made at that concert. I've no idea if Aunt Vic kept a copy, but Mum definitely had one. I don't know if she's got it with her, or if it's still in her room in London, or even if she's lost it. But she played it to me when I was a kid, and even though I was a total philistine like most kids, I could tell it was something special. Mum was so proud! And you're telling me Aunt Vic's never said anything to you?'

'No. Nothing. She's let me believe she can't sing at all. Why do you suppose that is?'

Matthew sighed and took a gulp of coffee. 'Maybe when it all went wrong it was the only way she knew to handle the disappointment. I can't really guess. Like I said, I only met her today. You know her better than I do.'

Don rested his head in his hands. 'Well, after what you've told me, I'm beginning to doubt that.' For a moment he was silent, his coffee untouched beside him.

'Would you like me to ask Mum if she's still got that tape?' Matthew asked.

Don looked at him. 'I would very much like to hear it. But I wouldn't do it behind Vic's back. If she doesn't want me to know, then that's her prerogative.'

'Fair enough,' Matthew said. 'But I can still ask Mum if she has it, I suppose.' He finished his coffee and yawned. 'Mind if I go to bed now, Don? Feeling a bit knackered.'

'Yes, of course. I'll show you where the spare room is, and the bathroom.'

Don had the habits, at times, of an owl. Frequently he found himself restless at a time when most people, especially those who had to get up for work the next day, would have had enough. Then he would power up his computer and surf the internet for hours, until staring at a screen made his eyes tired and he was ready for bed. Once there, he rarely suffered from insomnia and never remembered his dreams.

But on the night after Matthew innocently dropped his bombshell, Don knew he would lie awake. Once he had heard Matthew finish in the bathroom and the house was quiet, he padded along to his study. He turned on the computer, cleared his e mails and visited some favoured sites; but everything seemed hollow and pointless to him, and he slumped in an easy chair with a bird book in his hands and closed his eyes.

Don was a practical man, thoughtful enough, his opinions mulled over and tested; but he was not much given to soul-searching. Tonight, though, he was confused, painfully aware that something was askew in his ordered life. *I feel winded, as if someone just punched me in the stomach. Why? Why should it matter to me that Vic never told me about her singing? It was years ago, and it's not strictly my business. Obviously she never told Ellen either, or Ellen would have told me. Unless Vic did tell Ellen, and swore her to secrecy, just because I have an interest and might have tried to persuade her to sing again.*

Perhaps it's stupid, but I feel this is really personal. I thought Vic would have trusted me with pretty much anything. Wrong, apparently. Does that mean she thinks I am untrustworthy? Perhaps she thinks I am just like anyone else. But that means she doesn't know me at all, doesn't it? I don't like this one bit. It's like it's sucked the truth out of the last few years. Like the rug's been pulled out from under me and I'm flat on the floor. But why? Why does it matter so much?

The book fell out of his hand, and he woke with a start. He looked at his watch: barely ten minutes had passed, and nothing had changed. He sighed. *Well, if in doubt, pray.* He closed his eyes again. *Lord, as you see, I am out of my depth. Maybe I always am, but usually I don't know it. Please help me to unravel this thing so that I know how to act.* It was very far from being his usual kind of prayer; to his mind it lacked the appropriate respect, but his own bafflement was beginning to plague him. No answer came to his prayer, no clarity. *You're on your own here, boy. Just do what you normally do when there's a problem – think it through logically, step by step. More coffee – sharpen up the brain.*

He went along the corridor to the kitchen. The clock on the wall told him it was one-fifteen. While the kettle boiled he sorted out his music for the following day, and put it into his music-case. He made coffee and sat down, blowing away the steam from the mug and staring into it as if some great truth lurked inside. No great revelation presented itself. He knew himself to be floundering, and it gave him great discomfort.

Bottom line: I feel almost betrayed. Perhaps that's too strong. I feel Vic ought to have trusted me. But if I am right, and her trust is limited, why is that hurtful? It must be because I thought we were better friends. I really did think so – I'd have put money on it. How can you be so wrong about someone? Or am I exaggerating? Should I just shrug it off as one of those things? Perhaps I should, but I don't think I can. Not yet, at least. Maybe I should wait till the morning, sleep on it, really think it through in the light of day when my mind is clearer. He got up and took his cup to the sink, and for a moment stood there, brooding. *Lord God, help me here. Not too sure what's going on.*

Don

22 January 2006

To Don's surprise, Matthew got up early and came down washed and shaved and with his bag packed. 'Thought I'd come to church with you,' he announced. 'See how it compares with the Baptists. I've packed my stuff so I can go straight back to Aunt Vic's afterwards. Thanks for having me, Don. Appreciate it.'

'You're welcome.'

Matthew consumed several pieces of toast, washed down with copious quantities of tea. 'I hope,' he said between mouthfuls, 'I haven't made anything awkward, telling you about Aunt Vic and her singing. I didn't think for a moment it was a big deal.'

'I'm sure it's no problem,' Don said quietly. 'Don't give it another thought. Look, I have to be over at the church in a few minutes, but there's no need for you to hurry. Just finish your breakfast and come when you're ready.'

Don brought his opening voluntary to an end as Frankie emerged from the vestry. There was no choir at the morning service and he had nothing to think about, for the moment, except the hymns. As Frankie greeted the congregation he glanced down the church and saw Matthew sitting between Bel and Vic. Matthew grinned and sketched a little wave. Bel and Vic looked up and they, too, smiled. Something about the way Vic looked, so different with her hair short, made Don's stomach muscles clench. The style made her look at once more vulnerable and more commonplace. He turned back abruptly to his hymn book.

Little had come of his ruminations during the night; but now, seeing Vic, his heart hardened and his mind closed. What seemed to him her dishonesty contrasted starkly with the new, younger, almost innocent look conferred by the haircut. A wave of nausea passed through him, making him sweat. If he had hoped for clarity with the morning, he was disappointed. He knew at some level that he was behaving irrationally,

182

but that was how he felt, right or wrong: disappointed and deceived.

He barely noticed what went on in the rest of the service. He played competently as usual, but mechanically, at one remove. Frankie spoke to him, but he didn't hear her, and she had to repeat herself, with a quizzical lift of her eyebrows.

After he finished the closing voluntary he went into the vestry and found her sitting at the table, filling in the service register.

'Heavy night, Don?' she asked.

'What? Oh. No, not specially. Why?'

'You seem a bit distracted, that's all.'

'Do I?'

Vic came into the vestry with the collection plate. 'Are you ready, Don?' she asked, smiling. Don thought she looked tired; then he told himself there was little reason to care. It was a wild and painful thought, but he clung to it. He could not have said why.

Then the words tumbled out, seemingly of their own cruel volition. 'I'm not coming for lunch today,' he said. He spoke in a low voice, hoping that Frankie would not hear. 'I've got some things to catch up on. Say goodbye to Matthew for me.' He could hardly look at her; he knew his face was burning. But before her face closed up, before she put on her mask of cool indifference, he saw the bafflement and the hurt. *Now we are both the same.*

'Oh, all right,' she said as if it was nothing unusual. Her voice was steady. 'If you're sure.'

He nodded, gathered up his music and left by the south door, crossed the churchyard at a great pace and let himself into his house. He stood still in the hallway for several seconds, breathing deeply. *I don't know what I've done. Except that it isn't good.*

Vic

'Everything OK, Vic?' she heard Frankie say. Then her own voice, neutral and calm. 'Yes, fine, thanks.'

'I see you have another visitor.'

'My nephew, Bel's son. Matthew.'

'Oh, so they found one another again! Good. And you have acquired a nephew.' She looked up at Vic, her eyes narrow. 'You sure you're OK? You look pale.'

'I'm fine.'

Frankie heaved herself up from her seat. 'Are they still here? I'd like to meet Matthew.'

'I imagine they are, since I'm the only one with a house key. Yes, do go and be introduced. He's heard a bit about you.'

'Has he indeed? I'd better go and make sure he hasn't got a false impression. Do you have a church key?'

'Not on me. I'll just put a few things away. I won't be long.'

'Right.' Frankie pulled off her surplice and cassock and hung them on a peg. 'See you tonight?'

'Perhaps. I'm not sure.'

She watched Frankie lumber down the church. Bel and Matthew were waiting by the west door, and she saw them greet Frankie. She put the hymn numbers in their box and closed the gaping door of the cupboard where the elements were kept. She could hear talking and laughter, but it seemed miles away.

Beneath her carapace of calm her heart was beating far too fast, and she felt sick. It was nothing to do with her ulcer, she was certain; it felt like someone had dealt her a ringing blow to the head, and the vestry floor seemed to judder under her feet. She sighed deeply. *Oh, for goodness' sake! Sort yourself out, Victoria. So Don isn't coming for lunch. Yes, it's most unusual. And he seemed very peculiar. But there must be some explanation.*

She left the vestry and closed the door. Bel, Frankie and Matthew turned their eyes towards her as she walked down to join them, and she saw that they were no longer laughing.

'What's the matter?' she said. 'You all look as though you've had bad news.'

'Look,' Frankie said, 'this is a family thing. You don't want anyone else butting in. You three go on home while I lock up. If anyone needs me you know where I am. And, Vic, I've heard you've been in hospital. I knew you didn't look right. Perhaps you shouldn't be here at all. For goodness' sake, go home and rest.'

She held the door open for them, and they went out in silence. Then she locked the door and walked slowly and painfully across the road to the Vicarage.

'What on earth's going on?' Vic said. 'Everybody is behaving most strangely. Why are you looking at me like that, Bel? Have I suddenly grown another head?'

'Let's walk, Vic. It's freezing. We'll talk indoors.'

'No, now,' Matthew said as they started up the track to the house. 'Look, Aunt Vic, it's my fault. But I didn't know.'

'What's your fault, Matthew? What didn't you know? Why are you all talking in riddles?'

'He told Don about your singing, Vic.'

'Oh. That.' Light began to dawn in her baffled brain. 'Is that why Don's charged off? Gone all cold and distant? Oh, dear.'

'I'm really sorry,' Matthew said miserably. 'I had no idea.'

Vic laughed grimly. 'I'm surprised he believed you.'

Matthew kicked a loose stone across the track. 'I told him about the tape as well.'

Vic paused and turned to him, her hand on her garden gate. 'Tape?'

Bel interrupted. 'We both had a copy of the recording, didn't we? The one that was made at the concert. I kept mine. A very long time ago, when Matt was about twelve or so, I played it to him, didn't I, Matthew? He's heard you sing, Vic.'

'It was beautiful,' Matthew said simply.

They arrived at the front door and Vic put her key in the lock. 'Well, it isn't now,' she said, her voice harsh. 'Look, this isn't your fault, Matthew. It's mine, for not being honest. Don't worry. I'll sort it out. Now, let's get some lunch. What time did you say your train was? Three something? It looks like I'll be the one driving you to the station.'

Don

22 January 2006

Don knew he was driving too fast. He knew it was against his own sense of what was right, and what anyone who knew him would have said of him, but after a few miles pounding down the motorway it took a conscious effort to slow down. Fortunately there was little traffic about on this dull, cold January day. No doubt most sensible people were in their own warm homes, awaiting their Sunday lunch.

He took the slip road and braked down to a sensible speed. As he came to the T junction at the top of the slope he realised that he was gripping the wheel with unnecessary tightness, and his head was pounding. He turned off the roundabout into a narrow lane and slowly released his fingers from the steering wheel. He took several deep breaths. *You are behaving like a lunatic. What are you trying to do, kill yourself?*

Five miles down the country road he turned into an opening with a green signboard to one side, marked 'Stoke Martin Nature Reserve.' It was one of his favourite haunts: close enough to home to spend a few hours, but miles from anywhere, and utterly peaceful. He parked the car by a wooden building that advertised itself as a coffee shop, now boarded up. He put on walking boots and a waterproof, slung a small backpack over his shoulder, locked the car and started down a gravelled track pitted with holes full of rainwater and edged by wintry trees. A few hundred yards down two people came towards him, similarly dressed against the weather in green and brown waxed jackets, binoculars slung round their necks. A short, apple-cheeked elderly man, wisps of white hair escaping from under his hat, smiled and nodded to Don as he passed, and the woman with him said, in an almost reverent whisper, 'If you go to the lake hide you might see some black-winged stilts. Oh, yes, and an egret.'

Don nodded his thanks and smiled to himself as he left them behind. He became aware as he walked that the wind was strengthening, and ominous black clouds were streaming in from the west. He quickened his pace. The first cold drops fell on his shoulders as he pulled open the wooden door of the hide and let it bang shut behind him. Inside it was dark, and he felt his way to the bench beneath the window and pulled up the flap, securing it at the top. As he sat and peered out the rain came, whipped into a frenzy by the savage gusts, stippling the surface of the shallow mere, bending the tufts of grass on the banks, and obscuring any possible view. If there were birds out there in the riot of wind and rain he could not see them.

Leaving the flap open for light he sat on a bench by the far wall, shivering even inside his quilted waterproof. He thought that at least he would be undisturbed; few people would want to spend a winter afternoon in a draughty hide in the freezing rain. He opened up his backpack and took out a silver flask and the sandwich he had put together in haste before leaving home. For a while he sat, sipping hot coffee, munching his sandwich, listening to the rain pounding on the roof of the hide, and staring gloomily out at a wet unwelcoming wilderness whose cold grey vistas so echoed the state of his mind.

After a while he recalled the Bible study, the first of the new year, held at the Vicarage the previous Thursday, resuming the study of Jeremiah, and he remembered wanting to discuss things with Vic afterwards, as he often did; but that evening Vic had been very quiet, almost preoccupied, and had hurried home afterwards with hasty goodbyes before they even made the coffee. Now, of course, he knew, or thought he knew, some of the reason why: Vic had probably even then been feeling ill. But he remembered his disappointment and discomfiture, and he admitted to himself, as he had never done so unequivocally before, that there was no one in his life like Vic – no one he could talk to quite comfortably about almost anything. As this realisation came to him he felt a flood of remorse, took too big a gulp of too-hot coffee and almost choked. What was he thinking of? How could he reasonably complain about her apparent lack of trust in him? What was he doing right now, running away without a word of explanation, if not being mistrustful? He shuddered and thrust the thought away.

Thinking back to that evening of the Bible study he saw Frankie, lolling on an ancient sofa, her bare feet drawn up under her voluminous floor-length scarlet dress, waving her hands expressively as she looked back at what they had already covered. He remembered she had linked what was happening in Jeremiah's time to the present day – priests performing meaningless tasks; rule-breaking rulers; the people perverse, frivolous, ungrateful, unteachable, blindly following the current convention that

Yahweh was one with and indistinguishable from Baal and all the other false gods. 'But if God is out of the picture,' Frankie had said, 'or even merely reduced to one power among many, then, in the end, anything goes. Nothing is forbidden, nothing is beyond the pale, every passing fad gets credence, everything is fair game. But you know,' she had added sombrely, 'God is not mocked, nor is he trifled with. His laws are not for twisting to suit our own ends.'

Someone in the group had remembered something from an earlier chapter of Jeremiah about humans having sense in other areas of life: 'I mean, if we fall down, we get up, if we can. If we're on a journey and take a wrong turning, we go back and find the right road. But in moral or spiritual matters we seem to just keep on doing the same old wrong things, even though it's been shown time and again that it doesn't work.'

Frankie nodded, her face unusually serious. 'The idea that sin and folly lead to death is true in any age.'

Don shifted on the hard bench, feeling its cold damp unforgiving surface bite into his bones. There came to his mind something else that Jeremiah had said: 'Lord, I know that no one is the master of his own destiny; no one has control over his own life.' This had given rise to animated discussion among the group on a previous evening, and Don remembered that both he and Vic had contributed their views on that occasion; but today he had no stomach for dispute. Now, in the bleak, damp hide, Jeremiah's words rang truer to him than they had ever done, and drove him to prayer. *Lord, I am like Jeremiah in this, though of course I am no prophet. My life is full of dilemmas, and foolishly I thought it was all so tidy. Please, guide me into the right way.*

He thought about the leopard and its spots, and recalled Frankie's challenge. Can people really change? Could any member of the group? Could he? Surprising himself with his own unwonted openness he prayed again. *Lord, those old people of Israel needed to change their attitudes and their ways. Teach me where I need to change, and give me the courage to do it.*

The rain thundered down less violently, and in a moment it pattered and ceased. Drops of water dripped off the edges of the hide's roof. Don moved over again to the open flap that gave on to the lake and raised his binoculars to his eyes. He scanned across the surface of the water as a weak sun broke through the washed cloud in shafts of lemon light. Something moved out on the shallows, two jerky dots that resolved themselves into the shape of a pair of black-winged stilts. He followed them through the lenses, smiling to himself.

Then something prompted him, and he let the binoculars fall, supported by their strap, and pushed up the sleeve of his jacket to look at his watch. To his burning dismay it was almost two thirty. He had promised to take Matthew to the station, and even if he set off immediately, by the time he got back it would almost certainly be too late. Believing her to be unwell and in need of rest, he had wanted to save Vic the trouble. He put his binoculars away and hastily gathered up the remains of his lunch. He shouldered the backpack, lowered the window flap and secured it, and opened the door. As he stood in the doorway there came to him in a moment of clarity something he had never before voiced even to himself, perhaps because until now he had never seen the need. Nothing in his life was as important as Vic's friendship and good opinion. Next to his service of God, her wellbeing was his priority. And yet here he was, offended over nothing, trying to escape from thoughts that he could not control or understand, abandoning her when she needed his support. He shook his head, puzzled and exasperated with himself, and set off back down the sodden path to his car.

Coming off the slip road down into Thackham Don turned right up the farm track that led to Vic's house, but when he got to her gate he could see that her car was gone. As he had feared, he was too late. He sighed and turned his car round, back into the village. Already the afternoon light was waning, with that bleached insubstantial look that often came in the dead of the year, and he shivered and thought gratefully of his own warm, if not always welcoming, home. He parked the car on the drive, went indoors, and shed his boots and coat. He put the kettle on and drew the curtains all around the ground floor, shutting out the depressing early darkness. For a moment he contemplated ringing Vic's number, then decided against it. *She won't be back yet from the station. And chances are I'll see her at the evening service.*

Bel

22 January 2006

'Well, he's gone. That's that.'

Vic looked at her sister and frowned. 'Why make it sound so final? You'll see him again, won't you? Soon enough?'

Bel smiled and took Vic's arm as they made their way out of the station and back to the car park. 'Yes, of course I'll see him. *We* will see him. But I don't know about soon. Huddersfield's not just in the next street. And he's busy with his studies.'

'But now you can talk on the phone, can't you? And didn't he say he'd come down again some time, and bring Jessica with him?'

'Yes, I know. But who knows when?' She paused by the car door as Vic fished in her pocket for the key. 'Look, Vic, I'm really sorry that Matthew told Don, you know, about your singing. I should have warned him, but it just didn't cross my mind.'

'It doesn't matter.'

They got into the car and put on seat belts.

'Well, I think it does matter,' Bel said. 'It must be the reason Don didn't come for lunch today. I expect he's feeling annoyed and hurt you didn't tell him.' She looked sideways at her sister. 'All the signs point one way, Vic.'

Vic started the engine and pulled out of the space, looking over her shoulder, unable to avoid Bel's eye. 'Could we please not discuss it?' she said stiffly. 'The fact is, none of us really knows what another person is thinking, and it's quite useless to speculate.'

'Please yourself,' Bel said. 'By all means cut your own throat. I'll try not to let it bother me.'

They were silent for the rest of the journey, until Vic swung off the motorway and onto the slip road.

'Vic, can you drop me off here?' Bel said. 'I fancy looking at the old house. If Don's right it might not be around much longer. I can walk home from here – the exercise will do me good.'

'All right.' Vic pulled in to a layby, and Bel unbuckled and got out. 'Do you think,' she said hesitantly, pausing before she closed the car door, 'this might be not too bad a time to go and see Frankie? She said I might if I wanted to discuss something.'

'I've no idea,' Vic said. 'You say I'm a dinosaur, but this would be a good moment to own a mobile phone, wouldn't it?'

'I had one,' Bel said, 'but it fell out of my pocket and down the loo. I haven't got round to replacing it. Vic, there's a car coming. You'd better go. I'll see you later.'

By the time Bel plodded down the main road to the Vicarage the street lights were coming on. She hesitated at the door. *Is this a bad idea?* Something, however, she hardly knew what, spurred her on, and she gathered herself up and rang the doorbell.

'Coming!' she heard Frankie's voice from inside. Before the door opened she heard Frankie puffing and muttering and felt a twinge of guilt that she was disturbing the scanty rest of a very pregnant vicar on a Sunday; but when Frankie opened the door she was smiling warmly. 'Sorry I took so long,' she said. 'Can't move so fast these days. But come in – don't hover in the doorway. I was expecting you.'

'Were you?' Bel was astonished. 'How come?'

Frankie shrugged. 'Not necessarily today. But soon. Time's not on our side, is it?' She patted her huge belly. 'And something's nagging away in your head, I think.'

Bel followed her into the hallway. 'I'm sorry to disturb your precious hours of privacy,' she said. 'Just tell me to go away if it's inconvenient.'

'As it happens, my son's asleep,' Frankie said, nodding her head in the direction of the upstairs rooms, 'and my husband is ensconced on the sofa, likewise unconscious, sleeping off an enormous lunch which he cooked, and all I have to do is put the polish on this evening's sermon, so come into my study away from Rob's snores and you can tell me what's on your mind. Do you want a cup of tea or anything?'

'No, thank you, I won't keep you long, and I'll brew up when I get home.' She followed Frankie into her study and sat in a cracked leather armchair that Frankie indicated. 'I've walked down from the bypass,' she said. 'I thought I'd look at our old house before it gets pulled down.'

'Is it going to be pulled down?' Frankie sat in an upright chair behind her littered desk.

'Possibly. Someone Don knows was told by someone else in the pub.'

'Ah. That sort of story.'

'Well, as I'm here, I thought I'd better take a look, in case the rumours are true.'

'And what did you see?'

'Not much. It's just as Vic said. Mouldering and crumbling after so many years. I saw a hole in the roof at one end, and what looked like a massive bird's nest in the chimney. It's a shame – it was a fine house once.'

Frankie cocked her head on one side and looked at Bel thoughtfully. 'And do you have happy memories of living there as a child?'

'Not really. Everything is overshadowed by Johnnie dying. Something like that seems to have its effect backwards as well as forwards. Even a happy past is overshadowed.' She paused. 'I used to persuade myself that things were all right until we lost Johnnie. But since I've been here, and heard Vic's take on it, I'm beginning to realise I was probably fooling myself. I guess I don't find the truth easy. Too damn' brutal.' Frankie nodded slowly, but said nothing. 'But actually that's not what I wanted to talk to you about. As long as you're sure I'm not being a complete bore and wrecking your Sunday.'

'No, no. Go ahead.'

'I'm worried about Vic,' Bel said in a rush. 'Just two days ago she was in hospital. Then Matthew came, the nephew she didn't know she had, and I'm sure the memories of her own tragic little son were all stirred up, though she didn't say anything. There wasn't room at Vic's for Matthew to stay over last night, and he could hardly go back to Huddersfield so late, so Don kindly offered to put him up. And I'm afraid Matt let the cat out of the proverbial bag.'

'Oh? About what?'

'You probably have no idea about this either. A long time ago, when we were both still at school – you knew we went to Repley, didn't you? – Vic was a terrific singer. She had an amazing voice, especially for one so young. In the sixth form, at Easter, just before her A levels, she sang in a concert at the school. It was superb. And she was going to make a career of it. After school she did several more public concerts, not here, somewhere up north, which were very well received, I believe. She married her singing teacher – did you know that?' Frankie, her eyes wide, shook her head. 'Well, not to dwell on the details, which really are Vic's private business, it all went wrong, and Vic never sang again. She's allowed everyone to believe she can't sing a note – including Don, who is her closest friend. I didn't think to warn Matt – I was too excited that he was coming. There was a recording made at the school concert, and I kept a copy for years.

Still have it. Ages ago, when Matthew was just a lad, I played it to him. So he had heard his Aunt Vic, and innocently he mentioned it to Don. And Don went off after church this morning, obviously quite upset, and I'm sure Vic is too, though she's keeping it all under her hat, and I feel terrible about it. I want to put it right, and I don't know how.'

Frankie thought for a moment, stretching her legs out under the desk, wincing at some discomfort. 'You know, it may be that you aren't the one to do it.'

'Do what?'

'Put things right. This misunderstanding may have been instigated by you and Matthew, even if unwittingly. But the issue is between Vic and Don, isn't it?'

'Of course it is. But that's just it. I'm afraid they won't sort it out, and that would be a terrible waste.'

Frankie looked at Bel with a slight smile. 'They've managed to keep friends for a long time before you came on the scene.' She spoke gently, but there was censure in her words.

Bel gripped her hands together in her lap. 'I'm just afraid that because of me, and my son, something's happened to challenge that friendship.'

'You know what, Bel? For what it's worth, I think you should back off. What comes over to me is a failure of trust all round. Perhaps you should trust them to sort it out. They're sensible, charitable, grown-up people.'

'Yes. But one of them is a very damaged person. And sometimes that trumps sense and charity.'

Frankie shook her head. 'They both have someone on their side, Bel. Someone who loves them and wills what's best for them. I'll pray for them, of course. But I'm not worried.'

Bel blew out her breath. 'It must be quite something to have that, whatever it is.'

'Faith? Of course. But you can have it too.'

'Me? I don't think so. I've been on the outside too long.'

Frankie looked at her and spoke almost casually. 'Of course you can. Look, I, and Vic, and Don, we're no different from you. No better, anyway. The only real difference of any importance is that we know we're forgiven. We know we have God's Holy Spirit within us, restraining, encouraging, guiding.' Bel said nothing; she just stared. After a while Frankie said, 'Do you feel you need to be forgiven?'

'Of course I've done some bad things,' Bel said, almost in a whisper. 'And just lately I feel as if I'm looking back and judging myself by a different standard. Different from what I used to do, I mean. I always thought, I don't know, I'm no worse than many others, I try not to do harm, all that, but somehow now it doesn't seem anywhere near enough.'

'Can I ask you a question, Bel?'

'Of course.'

'What do you think your purpose is? What's the point of Isabel Ilthwaite?'

Bel smiled faintly. 'Other than being my son's mother – too late now that he's grown up; I should have been a better mother years ago – I have no idea.'

'Do you ever feel there's something missing, somewhere inside your head or heart or soul, whatever you care to call it? And I don't mean a flashy car or a bulging bank balance.'

'Yes, I do. I think a lot of people feel that way. But I don't think religion is the answer, not for me.'

'Ha!' Frankie spat. 'Religion you can keep. Or at least the outward forms, the rituals, the conventions. I'm not talking about "religion" here, Bel. I'm talking about your unique purpose and the only person who can make it real for you.'

'OK... Go on.'

'Do you want to know what I think?'

'Of course I do. That's why I came here this afternoon.'

'Well, I'm not talking about my personal opinion. That wouldn't be worth a hill of beans, not with this subject. How do you suppose human beings went wrong?'

Bel shrugged. 'The snake chatted up Eve and persuaded her to do something that was forbidden. Then she corrupted her husband – and men are weak so he did as he was told and then blamed her.'

Frankie chuckled. 'Yes, that's a common view among women. So what was wrong with what they did? It must have been something big, because it led to them being chucked out of Eden, and to the trouble humanity's been in ever since. It led to the Cross too.'

'Disobedience?' Bel said dubiously.

'Yes, that, but I don't think it was just a case of humans being naughty, like children,' Frankie said. 'I think it was more serious than that. It was something we all, even those of us who are believers, in our unguarded moments, are prone to, and have been ever since that day in the Garden of Eden: the tendency to dethrone God and put ourselves in his place. If God made everything, including us, then we are creatures, his creation, to

194

make and unmake as he sees fit. Usurping his rightful place means denying our own. And it's only by being who we really are and where we belong that gives us the dignity of purpose.' She paused. 'Do you know, that's rather neat. I think I'll put it in a sermon.'

Bel shivered. 'So you reckon we're all the same? People I mean, all gone bad?'

'In that way, yes. Man as a species has lost something important – his unique original nature, the way he was made to be, the only way he can truly be happy. But we're also a cussed and self-destructive race. We like nothing better than shooting ourselves in the foot.'

'I suppose that's why so many people seem to believe in all sorts of weird things these days. They can feel a gap somewhere. I've certainly become more aware of my own gaps since I've been hanging around with the Thackham Christians.' She smiled wryly. 'They're a dangerous bunch.'

Frankie tore a scrap of paper from a pad on her desk and scribbled something on it. She pushed it across to Bel. 'Your sister'll tell you I like sending apparently random texts. Bible texts, I mean, not text messages. Here's one for you. Deuteronomy chapter 30, verse 19. Look it up when you get home. Talk to Vic. She'll understand.'

Bel pushed herself up out of the chair. 'All right, I will. Thanks, Frankie.' She hesitated by the door. 'I'll think about what you've said. But I can't promise anything. Old ways are hard to get rid of, even supposing you want to.'

'Thinking will do nicely,' Frankie said. 'You'd be surprised how few people are willing to attempt it.' She followed Bel into the hallway. 'Do you want to borrow a torch? There are no lights up on the track, and it's dark now.'

'Yes, thanks. I'll probably come down for the evening service.' She grinned suddenly. 'Got to hear this sermon, haven't I! I'll return it then.'

Frankie held the door open. 'Just one thing. If you do discover your unique, God-given purpose, if you get that sense of being uniquely loved, and I pray that you do, then there's no despair, no ultimate defeat, however low you may feel you're sinking at times. I'd never say it was easy, but then life isn't for most people. And at least we – me, Vic, Don, all the rest of us down the ages – we have help. We're not alone.'

Vic

Vic sat in the big armchair in her tiny living room. Solomon lay curled up at her side, purring like a rumbling volcano. He stretched out his front legs and flexed his curved black claws, catching them in Vic's cardigan. Vic unhooked them and gently tapped the errant paws. 'Scratch me not, Solly,' she murmured, 'or I shall get up and abandon you, and then you won't be quite so warm.' She saw that the fire was sinking, but she couldn't be bothered to get up and put another log on. She closed her eyes, and a tear dribbled down her face unchecked till she could taste its salt on her lips.

An hour or so earlier Bel had come in from her visit to the Vicarage pink-cheeked and flustered.

'Tea?' Vic offered.

'Yes, thanks. Vic, can I borrow your Bible?'

'Of course,' Vic said, surprised. 'Anything I can help with?'

'Maybe. I'll tell you later. Frankie's given me something to look up.'

'Oh. Yes, she does that sometimes. It's quite extraordinary how she can pick a verse or two that fits the occasion or the person, seemingly out of her head. My Bible's on the kitchen table. Help yourself.'

Bel seemed preoccupied and disinclined to talk. She took the proffered tea when Vic made it, and from the living room Vic heard her turning pages and muttering to herself. Then she heard Bel's feet on the stairs and her bedroom door closing. After a while she came down and put her head round the door. 'I'm going down to the evening service. Are you coming?'

'No, I don't think I will. Take the torch – it's on the shelf by the front door.'

'Thanks. I'll return Frankie's at the same time. You sure you won't come?'

Vic smiled wanly and shook her head, and a few moments later the front door banged shut and she heard Bel's booted feet scrunching down the front path.

Rarely in recent years had she felt so bleak. It was as if every tiny bobbing light in the darkness of her life was winking out, one by one. Her marriage had failed, and along with it her naive hopes. Her only child had barely lived before his thread was cut. Her voice, bringing with it joy to herself as well as those who heard it, was nothing now. Her memories were all corrupted. Bel's arrival back in her life had brought unlooked-for satisfactions as well as worrying disturbance; but no doubt she would be gone as soon as some work opportunity presented itself, and with Matthew back in her orbit she would have plenty enough to occupy her mind without much need for a bitter old sister.

I wasn't doing so badly. I had a job I loved. I lived quietly among good people. I had one trusted friend. But what now? My health is compromised, my job threatened, and I have lost my friend. At this moment that's the sharpest cut, and it's my own fault, just by the way I've handled it. What a fool you have been, Victoria.

Solomon squeaked in protest as Vic shifted in her chair. He got up, yawned, arched his back and jumped down. He went to the door and looked back at her with his unblinking green eyes.

Vic got to her feet and sighed. 'Well, there's still you, Solly. I suppose you think it's dinner time. Come on then. If I must be the mad old lady with the cat, then I must.' She pulled the door open and followed Solomon's black flag of a tail into the kitchen. 'And you know what, Sol,' she said. 'I'm telling myself that self-pity is useless and rather ridiculous, and trying to convince myself that no doubt at some point the good Lord will have something for me to do.' She put food in Solomon's dish and watched him devour it with delicacy and total concentration. 'It's just that, right now, the whole shooting-match seems utterly futile.' She groaned. 'Come on, woman. Get a grip.'

She noticed her Bible lying open on the table where Bel had left it, and a crumpled piece of paper beside it. She smoothed out the paper, put on her glasses, and read, in Frankie's distinctive black pen, 'Deuteronomy 30, verse 19.' Running her finger down the open page she found the verse that Frankie had given Bel. It was from Moses' final exhortation to the Israelites as they stood on the borders of the Promised Land. 'I am now giving you the choice between life and death, between God's blessing and God's curse, and I call heaven and earth to witness the choice you make. Choose life.' So Frankie was challenging Bel openly, as Vic had hardly dared to do; and Bel had gone alone to the evening service. What did it mean, if it meant anything at all? Frowning in perplexity, she filled the kettle and switched it on.

Despite her attempt at courage, there were tears behind her eyes and an unappeased ache deep in her chest. Solomon finished washing his face and paws, and without a backward glance disappeared through the cat-flap in one graceful bound, despite the fact that it was almost too small a gap for his girth. The silence of the house, usually so welcome, now lay on her spirit like suffocation, and her loneliness rose up, threatening to swamp all her puny resolve. She glanced at the clock. It was just after six. She flicked on the radio that sat on the kitchen shelf, thinking that she might catch the end of the news, and even more, to hear a voice that had nothing to do with her.

Turning away to pour boiling water into her mug, she froze with the kettle in her hand as she heard the news that the Northern Bottle-nosed whale found swimming in the Thames had died of convulsions, despite concerted efforts to save it and return it to the open sea. Her hand shook so badly that water spilled out of the kettle onto the worktop. She put it down. Gripping the back of the chair she gave vent to the howls that were building in the back of her head. *Oh, God. Oh, Lord. Even the poor bloody whale is dead.* Her sobs heaved up and spilled out, loud and irresistible, and she made no attempt to silence them.

Don

'Are you all right, Don?' The kind enquiry came from Marjorie Allen, one of the older choir members, as she took off her robe after the evening service.

'Just tired, that's all,' Don said, smiling. 'I didn't accompany the anthem very well, I know.'

'Oh, no, I didn't mean that, it was fine. You just seemed, I don't know, not quite with us.'

'Creeping old age, then,' Don said.

'Nonsense! That I don't believe.' She glanced towards the vestry door. 'Someone wanting to speak to you, I think.'

Don turned and saw Bel, hovering in the doorway, an anxious frown on her face. Looking down at the congregation earlier he had been puzzled and rather dismayed to see her there without Vic. 'Oh, hello, Bel. Was it me you wanted? I'll be with you in a minute.'

He hung up his robes and gathered his music into his briefcase. Unhooking his coat from its peg he joined Bel. 'Do you want to come over to the house for a while? Was there something you wanted to talk about?'

'No, it's OK,' Bel stammered. 'Thank you all the same. I just wanted to give you something. And to say I'm sorry that my son's accidentally caused trouble. It's the last thing we'd want, Don.'

'I understand that,' Don said gently. 'Please don't worry.'

'But I do. You remember I nearly gave the game away, didn't I, when we were coming back from Stoke that time. And afterwards I quizzed Vic about it, and she was quite short with me and told me not to rock the boat. So of course I went along with what she said, even though I didn't really understand. But I'm afraid Matthew didn't have a clue.'

'No one blames Matthew.'

Bel turned tragic eyes on Don as they walked slowly down the nave, and for a moment Don wondered if this was Bel the woman or Bel the

199

actor. He dismissed the thought as uncharitable; she seemed genuinely mortified.

'What can I say?' Bel said. 'I feel I've just messed up my sister's life.'

'That's a bit of an exaggeration, don't you think? I'm sure we'll all get over it.'

'But will you, Don? Are you two still friends?'

He shook his head. 'Don't think me rude,' he said, 'but it's between me and Vic. I'm sure you understand.'

'Yes, of course,' Bel said faintly as colour rose in her cheeks.

Frankie came up the nave towards them, her surplice billowing. 'Thanks, Don, as ever. Nice to see you in church again, Bel. Did you look up that text?'

'Yes, I did, thanks.' Bel was distracted. 'Look, Don, I can't say any more. But don't ask me not to worry.' She scrabbled in her handbag. 'I wanted you to see these.' She handed him a cassette and a thin printed leaflet.

Don frowned. 'What's this?'

'It's the tape of Vic's concert. The only recording in existence that I know of, though I suppose there might have been others, later on, when she was giving recitals with Eric. And this,' she tapped the leaflet, 'is the school newsletter for the summer of that year. There's an article in there about Vic.'

Don saw Frankie look back at them as she sailed into the vestry. He turned back to Bel. 'Does Vic know you are letting me see these?'

Bel sighed. 'No, and maybe she'd kill me if she knew. I just want to make amends. Maybe I'm going about it all the wrong way, but I don't know what else to do.'

Don took her elbow and guided her towards the church door. 'I understand your motives,' he said. 'I know you want only good for Vic. As do I. Maybe we have different ideas as to what that good is. I may read the article. But I would never listen to the tape without Vic's knowledge and permission. It seems this whole thing is a very sensitive issue. I think I'm beginning to understand why; I've been mulling it over all day. But you must let it go, Bel.'

'All right.' She made as if to say something else, then thought better of it. 'I'll say goodnight, then, Don. Please don't stay away too long.'

She hurried out of the door, and Don followed more slowly. He watched her scuttle up the church path and onto the road before turning across the graveyard to his own front door.

Sitting at his kitchen table with a cup of coffee he looked at the things Bel had given him. He would never, as he had told her, listen to the tape. It may have belonged to Bel, but it was Vic's business; and if she wanted to exclude him from it, that was her prerogative. He opened the old school newsletter and turned over the brittle pages until he came to a full-page article about Vic's recital that Easter. In one corner there was a grainy black-and-white photograph. *Vic aged eighteen.* It gave him the strangest feeling. *How old was I then? Twenty-three. I was working at Allsop's, and I hadn't even met Ellen. How odd it all is.*

He read the article. It was full of superlatives, glowing with praise. Vic's singing had clearly made a deep impression on the writer, who claimed that it had met with universal predictions of a shining future. He – or she – spoke in terms of the 'spiritual quality' of Vic's voice, her musicality, her control, and subtleties of expression rarely found in one so young. Reading it he felt a confusing mixture of pride, puzzlement, and sadness. Where was that hopeful young woman now? What was she feeling at this moment?

The phone rang, jangling fiercely in the silence. He flinched, then got up and picked up the handset.

'Don, it's Frankie. I'm not interfering, OK? I trust you. I'm not prying, I'm just praying.'

'What are you talking about, Frankie?'

'You're a good bloke, Don. But we can all make wrong choices. I just wanted to say to you, "Choose life." That's all. Goodnight, Don.' She rang off abruptly, leaving him holding the receiver, staring stupidly.

Vic

22 January 2006

At about the same time, the phone rang in Vic's house. Vic was sitting at her kitchen table, her hands wrapped round an empty mug. Hearing the shrilling from the hall she sighed wearily and went to answer it.

'Hello,' said a strange man's voice, slightly accented. 'Can I speak to Bella, please?'

'I'm afraid not,' Vic said. 'May I ask who's calling?'

'Yeah, yeah, I'm her agent, Jason Korba. You must be her sister.'

'Yes. I'm sorry, Mr Korba, Bel's not back from church yet. Shall I ask her to call you back?'

'Church, eh? That's a new one.' Vic heard him chuckle and conceived an instant and quite unreasonable dislike. 'Sure, if you could get her to call me. Soon as.'

'I'll pass on your message,' Vic said. 'Goodbye.'

Bel came in half an hour later.

'How was the service?' Vic said.

'Oh, all right.' Bel's brows were knitted together; she looked worried and baffled.

'Is something wrong?' Vic asked.

'Lots of things are wrong,' Bel said, and for a moment she wore such a mutinous expression that Vic was reminded of much younger sister.

'Well, here's something that might turn out to be right,' she said briskly. 'Your agent rang – Jason. He wants you to call him back.'

'Jason?' Now Bel's truculent mood seemed to evaporate. 'What did he want?'

'He didn't say. But I don't imagine he rang just to enquire after your health. Why don't you call him and find out? While you're doing that I'll get the kettle on and make you a sandwich.'

'Thanks,' Bel said breathlessly. 'Yes, I'll go and ring him now.'

She went into the hall and closed the door. A minute later Vic heard

202

her speak, and it seemed she had adopted another personality, that of someone breezy and confident, someone without shadows. She heard laughter and exclamations punctuated by brief silences, then a shriek, and Bel saying in a loud voice, 'No! I don't believe it! Jason, you old fraud!'

When Bel came back into the kitchen she was grinning broadly. 'You know what, I think my fortunes might be on the up.'

'Well?' Vic looked up from spreading butter on bread.

'It's not Shakespeare, and it's not, unfortunately, a Sunday evening prime-time costume drama.' She looked wistful. 'I quite fancy a heaving-bosom, bustle-rustling kind of role. But I'm too old: all I'd get would be the local gossip in a lace cap. No, nothing like that,' she said matter-of-factly, 'but at least it's money in the bank. Jason has got me some advertising voice-over, for a very well-known brand of beer. It's hard work for a few weeks, but well-paid. They wanted a recognizable voice, apparently, and someone who could do sultry. Sultry's no problem.' She beamed. 'Done that many times, in life as in art.'

'I can imagine,' Vic said. She put a plate of sandwiches in front of Bel. 'Tea coming up.'

Bel sat at the table. 'You not having any?'

'I found some soup in the freezer and warmed it up,' Vic said. 'I'm not very hungry.'

Chewing, Bel eyed her critically. 'You'll fade away.'

'Don't start. I've managed to stay alive this long. I'm probably good for a few years, God willing. Here's your tea.' She put the mug on the table and leaned back against the worktop, her arms folded.

'Thanks.' For a few minutes Bel ate and drank in silence. Then she said slowly, 'Vic, I've been thinking.'

'I can tell that, from your tortured grimaces,' Vic said wryly.

'Ha, ha. Seriously, something's been puzzling me. Ever since we first broached the whole sad subject of Johnnie. Something didn't seem quite right about that story about you and the farm boy. I mean, we'd only been home from school a week or two. How did you get to know him so quickly? And you said you were an innocent, ignorant kid. So I should hope, at thirteen. Which doesn't seem to fit with your story of a brazen little strumpet throwing herself at some red-faced local clodhopper with turnips in his pockets.'

Vic looked at her and smiled faintly. 'I should know better, shouldn't I, than to underestimate you. It was you who saw through me just a few years later, wasn't it?'

'When was that?'

'When you somehow ferreted out my real feelings for Eric. I'd told absolutely nobody.'

'Did I? I'd forgotten. But you're avoiding my question.'

'Yes, you're right to be suspicious. I admit to fantasising and fabricating.'

Bel's eyebrows arched. 'What, all of it?'

'No, not all. Joe Crompton did, does, exist. I'd met him in the High Street one afternoon. There was a bunch of kids, and I tagged along and joined in the banter and flirtation. Or tried to.'

'So where was I?'

'No idea. Not there, anyway. At first I hung around with that girl from Repley, the only other one we knew who actually lived in Stoke – what was her name? Can't remember. She was fifteen, and I think rather keen to get rid of me. I was an embarrassing hanger-on, a style-cramper. So she was only too pleased to join the other teenagers and distance herself from me. Joe was there. Six-foot-four, built like a barn, black hair, bristles on his chin, sizing up all the girls. And I mean all – he even favoured me with a lecherous wink, and I was a skinny nondescript little thing, barely out of short socks. I thought he was terrifyingly sexy.'

Bel leaned forward. 'So – was there an assignation?'

'No. Only in my fevered brain, assisted by one Macchiavellian adolescent called Cheryl, whose idea of fun was to make other people look ridiculous.' Vic sighed deeply. 'Over and over, after that, I asked myself what would have happened if I'd stayed with you that afternoon, as I should have. If I think, now, that it was irresponsible of our parents to leave us with Johnnie, it was even more irresponsible of me to leave him with a ten-year-old.'

'You were just a kid too,' Bel said softly.

'Yes. A kid desperately looking for a prop for her fragile ego, a kid looking for love in all the wrong places.'

'Is that how you see it?' Bel said, frowning.

'You know how I see it. Maybe we'll never agree. Maybe your memories are different. Maybe you're inclined to put a more charitable construction on the actions and attitudes of our parents. It does you credit. But don't forget I had the dubious pleasure of inside information, all those months I was at Angleby, looking after our very sick mother.'

'You told me: all those lost babies in the search for a son.'

'Yes, there was that.'

Bel looked up, her eyes narrowed. 'Vic, is there something you aren't

204

telling me?' Vic said nothing. Her lips were pressed tightly together, as if holding in unpalatable truth by physical force. 'If there's something I should know, then you should cut me in.'

Vic sat down opposite her, stretched out her hand and took hold of Bel's, gripping it tightly. 'Bel, I've thought and thought about this,' she said, her voice cracking. 'I'd pretty much come to the conclusion that no good would be served by spilling all the tawdry details. Especially now, tonight, when things are going better for you. You've got Matthew back. And the promise of work. I thought, I hoped, that this difficult patch was coming to an end, that you were getting your life back together. Why let something dead ruin that?'

Bel shook her head. 'But you have let something out,' she said. 'You can't just leave me dangling, wondering what the heck it's all about.'

'Please, Bel,' Vic said. 'Knowledge isn't always power. Some kinds of knowledge weaken you.'

'Tell me, Vic. I'm not a child. I can take it.'

Vic shook her head. 'There's no point, not now.'

'Yes, there is,' Bel said urgently. 'It's time to get all the bad stuff cleared away. And I'd be for ever wondering. Please, Vic. I have a right.'

'Oh, yes. You have a right, certainly. But pursuing your rights doesn't always lead to sleeping at night.'

'Well, I'm claiming my right,' Bel said, the stubborn scowl on her face reminding Vic again of her sister as a child. 'Tell me.'

'Let me make some more tea. This requires courage.' Vic pushed her chair back, filled the kettle and switched it on. 'Do you want some?'

'No, thanks.' Bel sat in silence while Vic made herself a mug of tea and sat down again. She waited, still and tense, as Vic gathered her thoughts.

'All right,' Vic said at last. 'But please note, I seriously doubt that this is a good idea. For ten months I nursed our mother. I was with her for many hours, every day, most nights. Our father tried to help, especially after he retired, but she wasn't comfortable with him tending to her, especially as her illness grew worse, and all the indignities that entailed. It was during those long nights that she talked, while I sat half-dozing by her bedside. That was when she told me about all the babies, among other things. She got steadily worse, of course. The doctor started her on morphine for the pain, and that didn't help her mental clarity. Sometimes she seemed to be rambling, but over the course of a few nights, about six weeks before she died, I began to hear something I'd never for a moment suspected.'

'Go on – I'm listening.'

205

'As I said, she rambled and mumbled and repeated herself. It wasn't easy to piece it all together, but I began to get a picture of what had happened.' She paused, breathing deeply, as if gathering herself up for some painful task. 'In all their striving for a son, she and our father had many medical appointments. She concluded she couldn't carry boys, and she felt hopelessly inadequate because of it. Both her husband and her father-in-law, of whom she was very much in awe, were so set on the whole antiquated idea of the male heir to carry on the family name. What absolutely stupid nonsense. What poison it generated.' She took a deep breath. 'On one of these medical visits, after her fourth miscarriage, I think after you were born, one of the doctors said something, or hinted something, that made her sit up and listen. It was no more than a passing comment, but the doctor seemed to be implying that the genetic fault need not be hers at all, but could be on our father's side. She couldn't give me any details, but it seemed possible that it was the combination of her and our father that was causing the problem, rather than her alone. And that set her thinking.'

Bel groaned. 'I have the feeling you are going to tell me that Johnnie is some other man's child. That she had an affair. But Mummy was such a quiet, timid person. I can't believe she'd have had the courage to embark on some hole-and-corner thing, even if she'd managed to find someone willing and discreet. And Johnnie was a Colbourne through and through. He was just like Daddy as a child. There was a photo of Daddy when he was at school, on the dresser. You must remember that.'

'Oh, yes. Johnnie was a Colbourne all right,' Vic said grimly. 'Our mother must have thought and pondered what that doctor said, and she took a drastic and rather dangerous step. I think by then she'd become infected by the whole mad obsession. Considering she was such a timid little thing, as you rightly say, so desperate to please, it was quite a risk she took.' Her voice lowered. 'She figured there was only one person, apart from her husband, who could give her a child without anyone ever suspecting that she had been unfaithful. Someone who had proven his own ability to father a son.'

Bel's eyes widened. 'I'm feeling sick at my own thoughts. God, Vic, tell me this isn't what I'm thinking.'

'Mother went to London,' Vic ploughed on. 'She went to see Judge, her own father-in-law. She spelled out her proposition. And he agreed. Why did he? He could have sent her packing. Perhaps he should have. Who knows why he went along with it? Now, after all these years, I have to admit the possibility of his doing it for his own son's sake. Twisted logic! But you see why Margaret was safe, once he'd committed himself. He would never give her secret away, because it was his secret too. And in fact even she wasn't absolutely certain whose son Johnnie was. He was blond, and Judge was blond as a child. Genes work in unfathomable ways. But after all the years of failure, suddenly, there was a healthy baby boy. Well, I know where I'd place my bets.'

Bel held her head in her hands. 'Oh, God. This is horrible.' She looked up wildly. 'It can't be true. Judge was an old man.'

'He was sixty-nine at the time. Fit and well. Not too old, I think.'

'Maybe Mother didn't know what she was saying.'

Vic shook her head. 'It was her confession, something she had to get off her chest before she died. She couldn't tell anyone outside the family because she was ashamed. But I'm certain she knew exactly what she was saying.'

'Or maybe,' Bel's voice hardened, 'maybe it's you that are the fantasist.'

'What?'

'Well, haven't you just admitted to making all that up, that story about Joe Crompton? Didn't you tell me you put moss and dirt and grass all over yourself, so that I'd think you were at it with him in the woods? How do I know you aren't making all this up? How do I know it's not some nasty product of your own diseased mind? You've always hated them – Mummy, Daddy, Judge as well! How convenient that they're all dead, and no one can contradict your disgusting lies!'

'What are you talking about?' Vic shook her head in bewilderment. 'I'm not lying, for goodness' sake! Why would I? It's what Margaret told me. Maybe she was confused. But I'm just telling you what she said, and it all fits.'

Bel stood up, and the chair legs screeched on the wooden floor. Her eyes glittered. 'It all fits, oh, yes, but only to someone with a sick, warped mind. My God, Vic, I knew you were bitter. I knew you always felt ill-treated. But I never thought you'd stoop this low. It disgusts me, the way you blame dead people, people who can't defend themselves, for your own failure.'

'I can't believe you are saying all this,' Vic said faintly. 'I warned you it wasn't a pretty tale.'

'No,' Bel said grimly. 'Not pretty, but a tale it is. A filthy, slanderous tale from your cesspit of a mind.' She backed towards the door. 'I can't stay here any more,' she said, disdain in her every word. 'I'm going back to London tonight. I don't care if I have to stay all night on the station. Anywhere's healthier than here.'

She left the room and banged the door shut. A moment later Vic heard her phoning for a taxi. Then came her footsteps on the stairs, and a slammed door.

Vic sat immobile in her chair, her cold tea before her. It felt as if someone had dealt her a hard punch in her stomach, just before the roof fell in with a crash. In all her self-questioning, her doubt about the wisdom of telling Bel her suspicions, she had never contemplated for one moment that she would not be believed; and to be disbelieved with such venomous rejection left her gasping and trembling, like, she thought with a random pang of pity, that lost whale, whose journey up the Thames had been, after all, a detour to death.

She sat, cold and shivering, hearing Bel moving about upstairs, drawers and doors opening and closing. She sat, her heart pounding, her mouth dry, listening to her sister's fury. Then a car horn sounded in the lane outside, and there were footsteps again on the stairs and in the hall, and then the front door slammed shut, a car door banged, and an engine faded into the silence.

She found she was shuddering with cold, and she got up and went into the hall, pulling her coat down from its hook and putting it on, wrapping it round herself in a desperate attempt to be warm.

The phone rang, and as she picked it up in her stiff, cold fingers she almost dropped it.

'Vic? It's Don. I just wanted to say –'

'Oh, Don, thank God it's you!' Vic hardly recognised her own croak.

'Whatever's the matter?'

'It's Bel, she's gone.'

'What do you mean? Gone where?'

'To the station. She called a taxi. She was lucky to get one on a Sunday night. She said she was going back to London.'

'But why?'

'Because I told her something about our family. I didn't want to tell her; I'd already decided not to. She insisted on knowing, she said she had a right, and of course she does, but when I told her she couldn't handle it. And then she accused me of lying, of making it up, out of hatred. Sometimes I've wondered if I've got it all wrong, but I wasn't lying, and I don't feel hatred. But Don, there's only one train this time of night, and she'll be pushed to catch it. I don't even know if she's got any money. She left in such a state.'

'What do you want me to do?'

'Please, I hate to impose on you, but would you go and see if she's there? At the station? It's freezing tonight. I think if I got my car out I'd have an accident. And I don't think she'd listen to me anyway.'

'Don't even think about getting your car out. You haven't been well. No, I'll go right away. Just let me put some shoes on.'

'Oh, thank you, Don. Thank you so much.'

'I'll come and let you know, shall I? Does it matter what time it is?'

'No, I don't care if it's late.'

'Will you be all right?'

'Yes, yes of course. Please hurry, Don.'

'I'm going now.'

Don

By the time Don got back to Thackham it was after ten, and already a fine frost was forming on the wintry fields. He parked outside Vic's fence, locked his car and trudged up her garden path, his breath coming in clouds. The lights were on in the house, and Vic opened the front door before he had a chance to knock. He saw that she had her coat on, and under the new short hair her face was pale and pinched, her eyes deeply shadowed. A wave of pity gathered his brows together and thinned his lips. He had never seen her so racked; but then, he thought with a shaft of remorseful clarity, how well had he ever taken care to know this quiet, competent, inward woman?

'Come in, Don, out of the cold,' she said. 'Never mind your boots. I've got a fire going.'

He followed her into the living room, and she turned to him. 'You didn't see her, did you?'

He shook his head. 'I'm sorry, Vic. The station was deserted, and the London train had gone. There was no one to ask. There never is anyone on the station at this time of night. Either she caught the train, or she missed it and went elsewhere. Does she know anyone in Stoke?'

'Only the old Stoke Players people, like Connie Dawson,' Vic said. 'I don't think she'd have the money for a hotel.' She laid a hand on his arm. He still had his coat on. 'But I'm really grateful to you for dropping everything for me. There's nothing we can do, is there? Bel will do as she does. I thought she would be shocked and upset, of course, but I never imagined anything like this. But then,' she added, 'I've had all these years to get used to it. It came like a bolt of lightning for Bel.'

'You forget,' Don said gently, 'that I have no idea what you're talking about.'

'Oh, Don, what an idiot I am! Of course you don't. Why don't you take your coat off, and I'll make you some tea to warm you up.'

'All right. But I won't stay long. It's late. I hope you're not thinking of going to work tomorrow.'

Vic sighed. 'No, I'll be sensible and take a couple of days off. I'll ring the school office in the morning. Perhaps, when I go in, you can take me. Then I can bring my car home. It's been there since Friday.'

'It'll be safe enough, won't it?'

'I suppose so. I'll just get the kettle on.'

Don slumped in a chair at one side of the fireplace and closed his eyes. A few minutes later Vic brought him a cup of steaming tea.

He took it from her, murmuring his thanks. 'Are you still cold? It's warm enough in here.'

She sat opposite him. 'I think my blood is getting thin. I can't seem to get any warmth in my bones tonight. Perhaps you've been right all these years – perhaps I should get central heating after all.'

Don took a sip of his tea. 'At last. So, why did Bel decamp? What was so bad that she couldn't handle?'

A moment passed before Vic answered. 'You know the story of little John, my brother, don't you?'

Don nodded, watching her. 'Yes, up to a point. He drowned in the Angle, in the woods at the end of your garden, when he was four years old. You and Bel were looking after him, so I suppose you've never forgiven yourselves, either of you.'

'I think Bel has relegated her sense of guilt to the outer darkness,' Vic said, 'just in order to survive. But yes, of course I haven't forgiven myself. But it's more than that. And while we're mentioning forgiving oneself, I want to ask your pardon, for not telling you something important about me, and letting you find out from someone else. I know it looks as if I don't trust you. But that is totally untrue. As far as humans go, I trust you above anyone I know.' She blinked away tears. 'I know if I'd asked you never to refer to it, you wouldn't have. But I guess I wanted to forget all that part of my life, because the loss of it was painful.'

'You don't need to say another word,' Don said quietly, putting his tea cup down on the small table beside his chair. 'Your past is your own business, and so is what you decide to keep to yourself. It's me that should apologise for running away like that. I should have known better. And I should have been here for you.'

'Are we friends again, Don? I don't think I could cope if we aren't.'

He leaned forward, his hands clasped tightly in his lap. 'Of course, always, as far as I'm concerned.' His pale blue eyes were kind under his sandy brows, and he seemed about to say something more, but then he coughed and leaned back. 'But you were going to tell me what upset your sister.'

211

'Yes.' She took a deep breath. 'You remember I looked after my mother in the months before she died. I found out a lot of things during that time. I think she felt guilty too, at being so under the thumb of my father, and his father, and being so uncaring to us girls. Anyway, you know something of that already. There's no point in rehashing it. What I told Bel tonight was what I pieced together from my mother's drugged ramblings in her last illness. It looks very much as if she propositioned my grandfather, the judge, to give her the son they were all so obsessed with. And he did, apparently. I can see her motivation, of course, but it's a lot tougher fathoming out his. Surely he must have known what a Pandora's box he'd be opening! My cynical half tells me he could have risked his career, his reputation, and produced another girl. Ha! Some kind of poetic justice that would have been. But Bel doesn't have quite my jaded view of the family. Or maybe she just wanted to hold on to some of her illusions. Anyway, she thought it was a pack of appalling inventions. That I was sick, foul-minded, at best deluded, at worst a wicked liar. But I understand her revulsion – I feel it too. These were respectable, church-going people, Don. My father was a churchwarden in his time. I've thought about it over and over, of course. I've asked myself whether they were more villains or victims. Whatever they were, we girls were definitely victims. There was never any obvious neglect, but we had no love. Not really. And of course, we are left with this shadow, this tainted heritage.'

Don's face was sombre. 'You can never tell, can you, what's behind an apparently normal façade,' he said softly. 'But as for your "tainted heritage," as you call it, surely it's commoner than you think. You know, or at least suspect, what your forebears got up to. And I admit it's not something I'd expect in the normal way of things. But most of us don't know much about our parents and grandparents and great-grandparents, do we? For all I know, one of my ancestors might have been an axe-murderer.'

'Granted. But this was very close to home, Don. Bel and I experienced it first-hand.'

'I understand that, and I don't underestimate it,' Don said. 'But what matters is now. Your present, and your future.'

'What matters to me at this moment is Bel,' Vic said. 'Where is she? Is she all right? And will I ever get her back?'

Don smiled slightly. 'My guess is she'll see sense. And you have Matthew to talk sense to her if she doesn't. He won't care much what his granny and his great-grandfather got up to. He seems a good-hearted young chap, if a little wayward. As far as you and Bel are concerned, I think he's a force for good.'

'I hope you're right.'

'And now,' Don said firmly, 'you should go to bed. Fill a few hot-water bottles, wrap up warm, and get some sleep.' He pushed himself to his feet, and towered over her. 'Promise me you will, or I shall be obliged to put you to bed myself.'

Vic laughed shakily. 'What a thought.' She saw him flush suddenly, a wash of embarrassment rising right up to his eyes. 'I'll do as you say, of course.' She got up out of the chair. 'Thank you for everything, Don. I really am grateful.'

She followed him out into the hall, and he put on his coat.

'One thing,' Don said, fishing in his pocket. 'You should have this back. It's Bel's, but you must have it.' He handed her the cassette that Bel had given him, and she took it, looking down at it in silence, then up at him with anguished eyes.

'Did you listen to it?' she whispered.

'Of course not. But I read this.' He handed her the school newsletter. 'Maybe we'll talk about it one day,' he said gently. 'But only if you want to. All right?' She nodded. 'I'm going now, Vic. Go straight to bed, won't you? I've got to go to work tomorrow, but I'll ring you when I get home.' He patted her shoulder. 'Goodnight now. Try not to worry.'

'Goodnight, Don.' For a moment she held on to his coat-sleeve. Then she let him go, and he opened the door and went out into the darkness.

Vic

Vic lay in bed, a dim bedside lamp her only light. A hot-water bottle warmed her back, and her arms were wrapped round another. Solomon did the same duty for her socked feet.

She felt very strange, as if something unusual, but not especially unpleasant, was taking place somewhere deep inside: whether brain or body she could not be sure. There was a lightness in her head, a faint sibilance in her ears. She closed her eyes and groaned softly. Of all the flashing pictures that occupied her mind, Bel's was the most insistent. She felt no rancour at Bel's vicious words, or her accusations. Some of them she felt were probably true; the ones that were not were understandable and forgivable. Besides, there was still something she hadn't told Bel, or indeed anyone, which brought her own guilt close to her eyes. There was no room for her to sit in judgment.

Lord, you know that I am a very flawed being. Sometimes I feel I have no right even to draw near to you and ask anything. For years I have skirted round the periphery of my faith, saying that I trust in you but never, not really, laying myself open to your gracious influence. I have been afraid for so long. But it's long enough, Lord. Perhaps today, tonight, just by letting you take all the weight, holding nothing back, I shall dare an even bigger step than the one I took when I was eighteen, when I saw St Paul in the school library. I wish I could see him again. Perhaps then I'd know I was doing the right thing. But I don't think that's likely.

I know I need to pray about many things in my disjointed life. There are good things I need to thank you for, things I hardly deserve. But tonight there's just one thing on my mind: my sister. Lord, Don said he reckoned it was your doing, bringing Bel back into my life. I don't know if it was or not, but as Frankie would say, it has your signature. It's your style. Ha! She's cheeky. Please, Lord, look after Bel. Let her anger cool. Keep her safe. Let her not throw away everything that's been gained. If I have done wrong, telling her the sordid secrets of our family, I'm sorry. Let it not be the end, please, Lord. She turned over in bed, arranging her limbs more comfortably, and Solomon growled in protest. *My eyes are heavy. Can we talk some more*

214

tomorrow? I'm so tired, Lord. I ache in every bone. Maybe in the morning I'll make more sense.

When she came to, the first thing she noticed was the cold: a chill that emanated from within, making her teeth ache. As the fog in her brain cleared, she realised that she was lying on her bedroom floor, between the bed and the wall. Her head was jammed against the skirting-board, and ached violently. All these observations took only seconds, and blurring them, crashing in with relentless force, there came a pain so savage, so intense, that she thought she would pass out again. She clutched her abdomen and wailed, drawing up her knees. *Oh, God, what now? This is unbearable.* Involuntary tears stung her eyelids as she pushed herself up into a kneeling position, rocking and keening. Then a spasm of nausea rose up into her throat, and she made herself crawl, painfully and slowly, sobbing with anguish, to the bathroom. She grabbed the side of the toilet and leaned forward, barely in time, as something like a cold merciless hand wrung her stomach as if it was a wet rag, making her retch uncontrollably. Her eyes and nose dripped, blinding her with salt tears. As the fit of vomiting passed, she reached behind her, pulled off some toilet paper and wiped her face, gulping back the foul taste. Only then did she see that the toilet was full of blood. *Oh, no.*

She reached up and flushed, then staggered to her feet, swaying. The pain clawed at her gut, making her cry out. *I have to get to the phone. But I am so cold. Dressing gown. Coat. Anything.*

Holding on to the walls she lurched back into the bedroom and unhooked her dressing gown from where it hung behind the door. Her head swam, and for a moment she stood still. She managed to get her arms into the sleeves and wrap the warm fleece around her body. Something was dribbling from the side of her mouth. She wiped it away, and saw that there was blood on the back of her hand. *Phone.*

Slowly, painfully, stopping every few steps, sucking in her breath against the vicious clawing in her stomach, she manoeuvred round the landing and down the stairs, one at a time, holding onto the rail as the hallway below approached and receded in waves like some demented sea. As she got to the bottom step she felt her knees give way, and she grabbed the phone as she fell. There was a darkness in front of her eyes. *No, no, I have to dial.* She jabbed three nines, and with a tiny wash of relief heard the phone ring in some distant call centre.

A human voice, blessed contact. 'Ambulance, please,' she croaked.

215

Somehow, in answer to the voice, she gave her name and address. 'Can you get to your front door?' the voice said. 'Make sure the paramedics can get to you?' 'Yes, I think so.' Somehow, teeth gritted, panting with pain and effort, she stretched up and opened the front door a crack, letting in cold starlight. 'All right, hang on there. They'll be with you very soon.' But these last words went unheard. The phone fell from her hand as she curled up on the carpet and the darkness rolled back over her.

Bel

Bel opened her eyes and stared at the ceiling. For a long moment she had no idea where she was. Then memory started to return, at first jerky and piecemeal, then a black torrent. She was in Connie Dawson's spare bedroom in Stoke, and her life was in a mess. She flung one arm across her eyes and groaned.

After a few minutes of trying, unsuccessfully, to erase the events of the night before from her mind, she sighed, sat up and put her feet on the rug. Her head throbbed dully, but she knew that was the result of one G and T too many. *Oh boy, have I screwed up.*

When she had flung herself into the taxi, demanding to be taken to West Stoke station, she had no clear idea of her onward path. The taxi driver, dropping her outside the station, had said hesitantly as she paid him, 'Not sure if there are any more trains tonight, love. It's Sunday.'

'Thanks,' she said shortly. 'That's a chance I'll have to take.'

Of course he was right. The station was deserted and dimly-lit, and the timetable informed her that the last train to London had gone twenty minutes before. The next was at six-forty the next morning; but it was a freezing January night – she could hardly spend the night on the station. Besides, her resolve, in the face of difficulty, was beginning to evaporate, and her righteous (*righteous?*) anger to be replaced by cold dismay.

She left the station and began to plod down Stoke's main street, her suitcase in her hand. What to do? She might have begged a bed for the night from Connie, but she had no idea where Connie lived. The taxi had taken a chunk out of her money, and what was left would be needed for her train fare, so she had little to spare for a hotel room, even if she could find anywhere. One place she couldn't go was back to Thackham, not after all the terrible things she had said to Vic. *Oh, Vic, what have I done?* Then, trudging disconsolately down the road, head down, she had an inspiration, and her pace quickened. A few turnings later she came to the Green Lion, its welcome light spilling out into the street, and there to her relief were

217

some of the old stagers of the Stoke Players, with Connie Dawson in their midst, holding court, a tall glass in her hand.

As she pushed open the swing door, gratefully feeling the warmth that came from a huge log fire, Connie looked up and saw her.

'Bella, *darling!* How lovely! Do come and join us! Budge up, Bunny, there's a dear. What brings you to our humble watering-hole? We haven't seen you since New Year.'

Bel squeezed onto a long bench, already crowded. 'Hello, Con, everyone,' she drawled. 'Been a bit busy. Also been a bit of an idiot, I'm afraid. Nothing new there.' She shrugged and smiled. 'Missed the last train to London! Forgot to check the times! What a fool!'

'Oh, Bella, are you leaving us?'

''Fraid so, Connie. My idle excuse for an agent finally got me some work. Just a bit of advertising voice-over, but at least it'll keep me from *total* penury for the time being.'

'For goodness' sake, someone, Lou, you're nearest, get the poor girl a drink,' Connie commanded. 'Gin, Bella?'

'Lovely.'

'So,' Connie pursued, 'do you need a lift back to your sister's?'

'Probably not a great idea,' Bel said, rolling her eyes. 'Had a bit of a falling-out – you know how it is. Anyway, I must get back to London asap. Don't suppose you could put me up tonight, could you, Connie?'

'*Delighted*, darling! My spare room's only tiny, and Gareth has the other, but it'll be fine for one night. And here's your drink.'

'Thanks,' Bel said, looking up at Lou, a large florid man in a frayed tweed jacket, who beamed at her as he handed her the gin. 'And thank you, Connie. You've saved my bacon.'

They'd stayed in the Green Lion till closing time, and many of the group were well-oiled by then. Bel herself, although she knew she had drunk too much, still felt depressingly sober as they split up and went their separate ways, their loud goodbyes echoing down the quiet street. Connie linked arms with her and together – Bel holding Connie up as she staggered on her ridiculous heels – they made their way to Connie's modest bungalow.

Now, with grey morning light seeping in between the curtains, Bel looked at her watch. Nine forty-five. She put on a dressing gown from her suitcase and opened the door. There was no sound. Connie, clearly, was sleeping off her lavish consumption of alcohol. Quickly Bel dashed to the bathroom, washed as quietly as she could, then returned to her bedroom, dressed and repacked her case. There was still no sign of life from Connie or her lodger. She tiptoed along the passage, shoes in hand, to the hallway. She found pen and paper on the table by the phone. 'Dear Connie,' she wrote. 'Didn't want to disturb your beauty sleep, but have to get to London. Thanks for rescuing me – you've been a real pal. I'll be sure to look you up if I'm back in these parts. Love, Bella xx. PS Don't forget to listen out for the Star lager adverts!'

She put on her shoes, carefully opened the front door, and stepped out into a foggy morning. Closing the door quietly behind her, she made her way back to the main street and the bus stop. *I have to put things right with Vic. If that's possible, after what I said. Oh, God, what a fool I am, what a big mouth! But I have to try, or I'll never forgive myself.*

Vic's car was still parked at her house as Bel approached. So it seemed she had shown sense and not gone to work. At the front door Bel put her key in the lock and paused. For a moment she stood, eyes closed, heart thudding. Then she took a deep breath and opened the door.

Almost at once she saw that things were not right. But before she had time to take in the details Solomon came hurtling through from the kitchen and wound his sleek bulk round her ankles, miaowing loudly.

'All right, all right, cat,' she muttered. 'Where's your mistress?' She looked up the stairs. 'Vic?' she called tentatively. There was no answer.

Bel crept into the kitchen, followed by Solomon, who hovered by his bowl. She frowned, perplexed: Solomon's bowl was not only empty, but unwashed. This was unheard of: Vic was most particular. Harassed and head-butted by the hungry cat, Bel picked up the bowl, washed and dried it at the sink, and put food into it. Solomon barely allowed her to set it on the floor before he began to devour it.

'Puss, I don't understand this,' Bel murmured. 'I'm going to look upstairs.'

Leaving him finishing off the last scraps, she took off her shoes and padded up the stairs. Hesitantly she put her head round Vic's open bedroom door. The bed was rumpled and unmade, but there was no sign of its occupant. She went into the bathroom, and there her heart lurched. The toilet had been flushed, but there were dull red-brown smears of blood on the seat, and spots on the floor. *Oh, my God. Vic.*

Bel's first terrifying thought, later laughed off as ridiculous but very real for a second, was that Vic had been murdered. Sweat broke out on her forehead and upper lip, and she felt momentarily faint. *No, stupid, there's got to be some other explanation. But where the heck is she?*

She went back downstairs. Breathing deeply, she looked all round the house. Vic's coat was still on its peg. Her handbag was on the hall table. But her house key was not on its hook. She shook her head. Then she noticed that Vic's address book, which she kept on the table next to the phone, was missing. She rang Directory Enquiries and dialled the number they gave her. A moment later a voice said, 'Repley College Office, can I help you?'

'Ah, yes,' Bel said, clearing her throat. 'Is it possible to speak to Miss Colbourne, please?'

'I'm afraid not. She's not here today. Who's calling?'

'I'm her sister.'

'Oh, I see. Well, then you'll know she was taken ill on Friday, so we weren't expecting her in, but she hasn't phoned.'

'Right. Well, thank you. Goodbye.'

Bel replaced the receiver. Looking down she saw, with a shrinking of her heart, something she had missed when she first came in: brownish splashes on the hall carpet.

I must do something. Someone must know where she is. She put her shoes and coat back on, and flung her bag over her shoulder. Leaving her suitcase standing in the hall, she left the house and closed the door behind her. She trudged down the garden path, then down the track to the main village street. The sun was trying to break through the fog, but the air felt cold and dank.

A few people were about, and she smiled mechanically and murmured 'Good morning,' but inside a cold fear was growing. She turned in at the Vicarage gate and rang the doorbell. Just the thought of Frankie's good sense was enough to warm her.

But when the door opened it wasn't Frankie that stood there, but a large, broad woman in her fifties, her grey longish hair untidy, her sleeves rolled up. She was drying her hands on a kitchen towel, and she smiled at Bel distractedly, politely waiting.

'I'm sorry to bother you,' Bel stammered. 'I was hoping to speak to Frankie.'

'I'm afraid you can't,' the woman said. 'She's in the hospital, in labour. Rob's with her, of course. I'm her mother, here to look after Noah.'

'Oh, I see,' Bel said faintly. 'Right, thank you.' She began to retrace her steps.

'Hold on a minute,' Frankie's mother said. 'Is there something I can help with?'

Bel turned back to her. 'I doubt it,' she said, and was surprised by the bleakness in her own voice. 'I'm looking for my sister.'

The other woman frowned. 'You're not Isabel, by any chance, are you?'

'Yes, I am,' Bel said.

'Then I've got something for you,' Frankie's mother said. 'Wait a moment, please.'

A moment later she was back. 'I've been expecting you,' she said.

'You have?' Bel gaped stupidly.

'Yes, Frances said you might call in. She left this for you.' She handed Bel a dog-eared paperback.

'Thanks. Um, she didn't say anything about my sister, did she? Only I don't know where she is.'

'Who's your sister?'

'Vic. Victoria Colbourne.'

'No, I'm afraid not. Sorry. My dear, you look frozen. Would you like a hot drink?'

'No, thanks. It's kind of you, but I have to find my sister. When you see Frankie, please thank her for the book.'

Back on the pavement Bel stood for a few moments, her mind a blank. Her options, it seemed to her, were shrinking. She trudged back to Vic's and let herself in. The house was cold. She picked up the phone, realised that without Vic's address book she had no idea of Don's number at work, and again, with a spurt of irritation at her own ignorance, had to ring Directory Enquiries. After a few moments she was given the number and dialled with shaking hands.

'Don? It's Bel. Thank God you're there.' The relief when she heard his voice was like a warm bath, and she felt foolish tears spring to her eyes.

'Bel? What's up?'

'Don, it's Vic. She's not here. She's not at work. The bed's unmade, Solomon was hungry, and there's blood in the bathroom.'

She heard him suck in his breath. 'You're there now?'

'Yes. Did she tell you what happened last night?'

'She sent me to the station to look for you, but you weren't there.'

Bel laughed shakily. 'I missed the train. Spent the night in Stoke with a friend. Came back to try and make peace. But Don, where can she be? I'm worried sick.'

'I don't know. When I left her last night she promised to go straight to bed. Look, Bel, I think she must have been taken ill. You'd better ring the hospital. It's best if you do it – they're more likely to speak to a relative. Here's the number.' He dictated it to her, and she wrote it down. Her fingers felt numb. 'Let me know what you find out.'

Fifteen minutes later, after being passed from department to department, Bel finally got an answer.

She rang Don's office again. 'Don? You were right. She's in the hospital. Whisked away by ambulance. Poor Vic! She must have rung 999 herself. Oh, Don, it sounds like she's really ill. Suspected peritonitis, they said. This is terrible. I must go and see her straight away.' Her voice broke.

'I'm going to the hospital now,' Don said. 'I'll meet you there.'

Bel finally found Don in the relatives' room, a tiny, dreary space off the Observation Ward. The armchairs were high-backed and functional, the walls severely bare except for two small and uninspiring water-colour landscapes. Don sat with his elbows on his knees, his head in his hands. He looked up when he heard Bel's footsteps; his eyes were red-rimmed.

'It's taken me ages to find you,' Bel said. 'The bus fairly whizzed along today, but this hospital – it's like a maze!' She sat down in the adjacent chair. 'How is she? Have they said?'

Don shook his head. 'They won't let me in. There's a doctor with her now, and nurses have been buzzing in and out, but they're too busy to talk to me. She's in a side-room, opposite here. You can peer in if you like, but maybe we'd better just wait for the doctor to come out.'

Bel got up and began to pace up and down the floor. 'I was so foul to Vic last night,' she said miserably. 'I can't tell you how bad I feel. And now this.' She turned to Don. Her face felt stretched, her skin scratchy. 'She will be all right, won't she?'

Don sighed. 'At least she's here, not helpless at home.' He paused. 'Vic told me some of what she told you. About your grandfather. Do you think it's true? I'm sure Vic is reporting what your mother said,' he added. 'But do you think a sick woman's memories are to be trusted?'

'We'll never know that for sure, will we?' Bel said. 'But Vic was convinced. And horrible though it is, when I really face it, it's not so hard to believe.' She walked to the door, and her legs felt unsteady. 'The doctor's coming out. Let's see if we can catch him.'

The doctor, a tall, sallow man in his fifties, with dark hair flattened to his skull, his long legs encased in grey-stripe suit trousers, was standing outside Vic's room, writing something on a clipboard as Bel and Don approached him. He pushed his glasses further up his nose. 'Ah!' he said to Don. 'Are you the husband?'

Don seemed to have lost the power of speech. He blushed, shook his head and waved vaguely in Bel's direction. The doctor turned to her, frowning.

'I'm Miss Colbourne's sister,' she said crisply, looking up at him, her chin jutting. 'Perhaps you can tell us what's going on.'

The doctor's eyebrows raised a fraction at her tone, but he made no comment. 'Come back into the relatives' room where we won't be in the way.'

Bel led, and Don followed, an expression of discomfort on his face. Bel turned to the doctor, her arms folded. Short as she was, she was on a level with the name-tag pinned to his shirt: J.E.Willoughby, Gastroenterology.

The doctor cleared his throat. 'Well, now. Miss, er, Colbourne was brought in by ambulance early this morning, I believe. Initial examination showed signs of a ruptured gastric ulcer. But she knew about this, didn't she?'

'As of Friday,' Bel said. 'She was in A and E on Friday. They sent her home with pills.'

'Yes, well, these things are not always predictable,' Willoughby murmured. 'She's poorly, of course, but fortunately she is here now, and we're giving her IV fluids and antibiotics to combat infection. What happens, you see, when an ulcer causes a split in the stomach wall, is that stomach contents can pass into the peritoneum and, if untreated, can carry infection to other organs. It's potentially a very serious situation.'

'What would have happened if my sister hadn't been able to call the ambulance herself?' Bel said. 'She lives alone.'

The doctor shrugged. 'Well, I can't say for certain, of course. But if no one had found her, and the infection had spread, which it can quite rapidly in these cases, you would probably be looking at failure of other vital organs.' He cleared his throat. 'Left untreated, that might well prove fatal.'

Bel closed her eyes momentarily. 'My God.' No one moved. 'Right, so, what now? Is she in pain now? How long will it take for the medication to work? Is she going to be all right?'

Willoughby smiled faintly. 'She's not in pain, or at least the pain is manageable. In a day or two she should be feeling much better. I should imagine we'll be able to operate next week.'

'Operate?'

'Yes. Once the infection's under control, we'll have her in theatre to repair the rupture. After that she'll be here for at least a week. If she's well enough then we'll send her home, but she'll take antibiotics for another week.' He smiled more warmly, and Bel, looking up at his face, saw how tired he looked. He laid a hand on her arm briefly. 'I'm sure she will be all right,' he said gently. 'But she'll have to take it easy for a while. Will you be around to look after her?'

'For now. But when I can't, someone will.' She glanced at Don. 'Won't they, Don? When I have to go to work?'

Don nodded; he still couldn't speak.

'She'll be monitored regularly, of course,' Willoughby said. 'And once she's been on the antibiotics for a day or two we'll have a clearer idea of whether we need to worry about the other organs. Kidneys in particular. We'll do some tests. My own feeling is that she's got away with it. She was here and being treated within a relatively short time. She was able to talk to the paramedics in the ambulance and it seems she rang for them pretty much immediately on experiencing the pain, vomiting blood and so on.'

Bel shuddered. 'Can we go and see her now?'

'Of course. She's probably asleep, which is the best thing for her. Anything else you need to know?' Bel shook her head. 'Right, then I'll be on my way.'

'Thank you,' Bel muttered. She watched him as he strode down the corridor, paused briefly at the nurses' station and then out through the swing doors. She looked up at Don. 'Let's go and see Vic.'

Quietly, tentatively, they peered round the open door. Bel went quickly to the other side of the bed and perched on its high edge. Vic was lying propped up on several pillows, her arms flat by her sides. Her eyes were closed, and her face was almost as white as the pillows she lay on. Bel took one of her inert hands in both her own. She glanced at Don. 'Do sit down, Don,' she said irritably. 'You look far too tall in this little room.' Don said nothing, but lowered himself into the armchair on the other side of the bed. His eyes were averted from Vic, as if he couldn't bear to see her in this state.

Bel stroked Vic's hand, and Vic's eyes slowly opened. She blinked several times, trying to focus on her sister's face. Her voice was a whisper. 'Bel? You came back.'

'I didn't go anywhere,' Bel said, her voice breaking. 'I missed the train. I was such an idiot, Vic. I'm so sorry. Please forgive me for all those things I said. Unkind and untrue.'

Vic closed her eyes and sighed. 'It doesn't matter. You're back. But you have to go to London soon, don't you?'

'Not till next week.'

Vic's eyes flew open again. 'Is Solomon all right?'

'For goodness' sake, don't worry about him! He's been fed, and I'll look after him while you're in here, and when I have to go to work we'll organize it, won't we, Don?'

Vic turned her head slowly and painfully, and smiled weakly at Don, as if she had only just realised he was there. Feebly she stretched out her free hand. 'Don, you're here too. Bless you.'

Don took her hand and held onto it as if it were a lifebelt in a stormy sea. He cleared his throat. 'Is there anything you need?' he said hoarsely.

'Not if you two are with me.' Vic smiled feebly. 'Oh, yes, there is one thing. When you come in again, will you bring me my Bible? They say I'll feel better in a couple of days, so maybe I can read.' She licked her lips.

'Are you in pain, Vic?' Bel asked, her brow furrowed.

'Not any more,' Vic said. Her voice was faint and slightly slurred, and they realised that she was drifting back to sleep.

'Perhaps we should go and let her rest,' Bel whispered. Don nodded, but he held on to Vic's hand for a moment longer. He seemed to want to say something, but whatever it was would not come out of his mouth.

'Come on, Don,' Bel said. 'Let's go and find a cup of coffee. You look like you need it.'

Vic

Vic awoke to a dull light diffusing through the thin white blinds. There were unfamiliar sounds coming from the corridor outside her room: voices she didn't recognise, the rumbling wheels of a trolley, the clanking of crockery. She frowned. *I am not at home. Where am I then? It's all very white in here. Even the light is white. Is this a hospital? Am I sick?*

A head appeared round the door, a dark, smiling face. 'You awake, my lovely? How you doing?'

Vic nodded, and her head felt full of wool and dead leaves. 'I'm all right, thank you.' She hesitated. 'Is this the hospital?'

The woman chuckled. 'Course it is, darling. You've been very poorly. But you'll be all right now. I'll tell Sister you're awake.'

Memory came back to her in tatters, and she shivered, remembering lying on the hall carpet with the front door open, and the deadly cold that seemed to seep out of her bones, stiffening her body like a corpse. She remembered snatches of talk between the paramedics as she drifted from life to somewhere altogether mysterious, and back again; then sirens, bright lights and garbled voices. She remembered, or thought she did, seeing Bel at her bedside. But Bel was in London, recording. Wasn't she? And hadn't Don been there too? How long had it been, anyway? She sighed.

A moment later Bel appeared in the doorway. The relief at seeing her, full of life, her face pink, her body wrapped up in coat and scarf and boots, was intense, like the first splash of a warm shower onto cold skin.

'Bel.'

'Hey, you're looking better.' Bel came across the room, bent over and kissed Vic's cheek. She smelled of soap and fresh air. 'How's it going?' She peeled the scarf from around her neck, and undid her coat. 'Boy, it's hot in here. Have you had breakfast?'

'I don't think so.' Her voice was hoarse. 'Maybe I'm not allowed any. But I don't much care.' She clutched Bel's hand. 'I'm confused, Bel. Why am I here? How long has it been?'

'Ruptured ulcer.' Bel looked at her watch. 'About thirty hours. You were at death's door,' she said prosaically. 'But someone decided your time wasn't quite up.'

'Are you exaggerating?'

'On this occasion, no,' Bel said soberly. 'A few more hours and your organs would have buckled with the infection from your stomach and you'd be wearing wings. Looks like the head angel's put your wings back in the celestial wardrobe for now, I'm happy to say.'

Vic smiled. 'You are a fool.'

'It's what I've been calling myself,' Bel said softly. 'Over and over. Do you remember Don and me being here yesterday?'

'Kind of. Did you come on the bus all this way?'

'No. Don brought me.'

Vic glanced towards the door. 'Is Don here?'

Bel grinned. 'Well, he's in the hospital. As a matter of fact he's visiting another woman. With flowers.'

'What? What woman?'

'A married woman, at that.'

'Bel, stop teasing. What are you talking about?'

Bel chuckled. 'He's gone to see Frankie, in the maternity ward.'

'Oh!'

'At around the same time as you were hurtling here with a hole in your stomach Frankie was also on her way to hospital, in labour.' Bel looked thoughtful. 'You could have shared an ambulance, couldn't you?' She caught Vic's look and relented. 'She had the baby yesterday afternoon, Vic. A girl, seven pounds something. Abigail Grace.'

'Oh, that's great, Bel. I'm so pleased for Frankie and Rob. That's where Don's gone?'

'Yes, but he'll be back. And while he's not here, you and I must talk.'

'Yes, we must.' She frowned. 'I suppose.'

'No, I don't mean about us, and our grubby past, and our suspect forebears,' Bel said. 'That can come later, when you're stronger. I mean about him.'

'You said that with a capital letter, Bel. Are you talking about God?'

Bel looked down at her hands, then up at Vic with a look of slightly alarmed defiance. 'Well, I might have to talk about him as well. Frankie's been after me. Lent me a book. But it's not him I'm talking about right now. It's the other one. Don.'

'What about him?' Vic said.

'Oh, Vic, for an intelligent woman you really are dense!'

'Now what have I done? Don't bully me, Bel. I'm fragile.'

'Yes, I know you are,' Bel said gently. 'And if I bully you it's because I may not have another opportunity. You really need to sort that poor man out, Vic. And don't tell me you don't know what I mean.'

'I know perfectly well what you mean,' Vic said stiffly. 'And if I didn't know you spoke out of concern for my well-being I'd tell you to mind your own business. But it's up to him, not just me. How can you possibly know what he's thinking?'

'Because, you utter dope, it's written all over his poor suffering face, even if it wasn't in every word he isn't saying. I'll say no more, Vic. You look as if you might expire from sheer crossness and obstinacy, and I don't want to go to jail for murdering my only sister. Just think about what I've said. For once. Don't be a martyr. Be happy.'

A martyr? Is that how she sees me? Am I? I didn't think so. But she's right about one thing: I have been ruled by fear. Fear of openness, fear of vulnerability, of rejection, of hurt. Vic lay in her hospital bed, thinking. She held her Bible, unopened, in both hands. Don, having been to visit Frankie that morning, had brought it in for her as she'd asked. He'd handed it to her with a beaming smile of sheer relief to see her looking more herself, and Vic, putting this together with Bel's knowing words, had felt a blush of embarrassed heat bloom in her cheeks.

'Thank you, Don,' she said. 'Is the baby beautiful?'

'Well, I guess you'd say so,' Don said diffidently. 'Not that I know much about babies. She's got all her tiny fingers and toes, and she's pink.'

'Pink is good,' Vic said softly. 'Very good indeed. And Frankie?'

'Frankie is…herself. Weary, I imagine. But well.'

'Thank God for Frankie. And Abigail Grace.'

Vic tore her mind away from babies. *If I have been ruled by fear, then what about Bel? I don't think she's been ruled at all, and that's also bad. I must talk to her about that. If she hasn't already thought about it for herself, with this book she's reading. What was it called? 'Christianity for the Modern Heathen' or some such title. Only Frankie could lend her a book like that.* She sighed. *Anyway, before I can offer Bel any insights on the subject of faith, there are things I have to tell her. Things about myself which do me no credit at all. They probably disqualify me from offering any opinions at all. She'd be perfectly entitled to ask what sort of a Christian I think I am. I can only answer, 'A bad one.'*

A light rap on the doorframe broke her train of thought, and she looked up.

'Oh!'

There in the doorway stood Frankie, dressed for the outside world, a small, well-wrapped bundle in her arms. Beside her stood Rob, holding a wriggling Noah.

'We're going home, Vic,' Frankie said. 'But we had to come and see you before we go.'

'Can't you come in?'

Frankie shook her head. 'No, they won't let us come any closer than the doorway. It's not for Abigail's sake – it's for yours. We might bring some germs in. So we'll have to wait for you to come out. I'll unwrap her a bit and you can see her from there.' She pulled the blankets back from the sleeping infant's face and held her out towards Vic.

'She's lovely. Congratulations, Frankie and Rob.'

'Well, she's healthy, and that's all that matters,' Frankie said. 'And that's what we want you to be too, Vic. Soon. We'll keep on praying for you, especially when you go for your surgery.'

'Thank you.'

'Just one thing, before the nurses kick us out,' Frankie said. 'You've got your Bible, haven't you?'

'Yes. I thought I'd try to keep up with Jeremiah, so I don't get left too far behind.'

'Good plan. Well, after Jeremiah comes Lamentations, and there's a lot of good stuff in there I'd recommend to you.'

'Isn't that a bit depressing for someone in hospital?' Rob interjected.

'Not a bit of it. You'll see what I mean, Vic. And then, hop back to Jeremiah. Chapter 29, verse 11. Read it over a few times and then say to yourself, "This verse is for me and about me." OK? Now we'd better go. I'll try and pop in next week, after your operation. Perhaps my mum will look after both children for an hour. See you soon.' Frankie blew Vic a kiss.

'Thanks for coming.'

'No problem.'

'I am one who knows what it is to be punished by God,' Vic read. 'He drove me deeper and deeper into darkness and beat me again and again with merciless blows. He has left my flesh open and raw, and has broken my bones. He has shut me in a prison of misery and anguish. He has forced me to live in the stagnant darkness of death. He has bound me in chains; I am a prisoner with no hope of escape.' *That's what I fear. Or perhaps what I used to fear. That if I truly faced the outworking of Johnnie's death in my life, and the deeply-flawed family relationships which it exposed, I would be flung into such grief and depression that I would never recover. And so I have built my life on self-deception and lies – on sin, not always my own. Why haven't I learned to face truth, with Christ at my side?*

None of us dealt with Johnnie's death, not one. It estranged our parents and destroyed their health and peace. Perhaps because, as well, at least one of them knew he should never have been born in the first place, if what our mother told me was true. And it affected the choices we made, Bel and I. Bel's life has been shallow, and so has my faith. She frowned. *We have to let the Holy Spirit work in both of us.*

She read on. 'The thought of my pain, my homelessness, is bitter poison; I think of it constantly and my spirit is depressed. Yet hope returns when I remember this one thing: the Lord's unfailing love and mercy still continue, fresh as the morning, as sure as the sunrise. The Lord is all I have, and so I put my hope in him.' *I should have known and understood this long ago.* 'From the bottom of the pit, O Lord, I cried out to you, and when I begged you to listen to my cry, you heard. You answered me and told me not to be afraid.' Tears rolled down Vic's face, and her vision blurred. *How have I missed this knowledge? I don't have to be afraid. The Lord is all I have, and he has answered me.* Wiping her face with her hands, she turned to Jeremiah. 'I alone know the plans I have for you, plans to bring you prosperity and not disaster, plans to bring about the future you hope for.' *But what do I hope for? Do I dare even to begin to articulate such tiny hopes as are springing up, like vulnerable shoots? Is Bel right about Don? And even if she is wrong, even if, when it comes to it, he doesn't feel any more for me than concerned friendship, shouldn't I be honest with myself at last, trusting in God for the outcome?*

Bel

'How strong are you feeling?' were Bel's first words to Vic that morning.

'Not bad. A lot better than yesterday, or the day before. I think the antibiotics are really working. Why?'

'Because I want to ask you questions. I've been reading this book Frankie lent me, and there's stuff I don't understand.'

Vic shivered. 'Frankie's much better qualified to help you than I am.'

'Maybe.' Bel grinned. 'But Frankie's got two tiny children. And you're trapped in here and can't get away.'

'Bel, Frankie's more qualified than I am in another way. Not just because she's a trained professional. We're all supposed to be able to give an account of our faith, and I should be able to as well, hard as it is. What I mean is, I'm less qualified because of all my sins.'

Bel stared. 'Isn't that true of everyone?'

'Yes. I'm not explaining this well. What I mean is that I need to confess something before I can even begin to be any kind of representative. If I don't, my witness will be tainted.'

'I've no idea what you're talking about, but here I am, listening. You sure it's me you need to be saying this to?'

'Oh yes,' Vic said firmly. 'It has to be you.'

'Go on, then.'

Vic took a deep breath. 'I told you what our mother said to me, a few weeks before she died. About herself, and Judge.'

'Yes. I don't feel good about that, the way I reacted, Vic.'

'If forgiveness is required, you're forgiven,' Vic said. 'As I hope to be, though my sin was greater. I should have known better. I did know better, but I chose to ignore my conscience and my better self.' She fell silent for a moment, and Bel waited, unmoving. 'After both our parents were dead,' Vic said sombrely, 'I went to see Judge.' Bel frowned and leaned forward. 'He didn't come to our father's funeral, as you know. He was in an old people's home by then, his mind gone, so they said. I went to see him, but

231

not for any merciful reason. I went in anger and bitter vindictiveness. For me he was the spring of all that was wrong in our family, all the poison, all the lack of love that you and I suffered and lived with, day after day. For me, he wasn't a sad old man; he was a monster.' She heaved a deep sigh. 'Well, I've had plenty of time to face it since, and I know that I was the monster, not him. Well. I went to see him. He was sitting in a chair in his room, with a blanket over his knees. By this time he was in his eighties, of course. Broken, bald, overweight, incontinent, dribbling, the whole sorry picture. I felt pity, of course I did, but that was the worst of it. I squashed that pity, I encouraged my fury, I set out to destroy.

'At first he pretended not to know me. I'm sure he did, though. I think he had periods of lucidity from time to time, and when I walked in there was something in his eyes, something like terror. Of course the staff at the home thought it was nice, that the poor old gentleman was going to have a visit from his granddaughter. How could they know?' Vic looked up, and Bel saw her flushed face, and her eyes dark with self-blame. 'I closed the door. I stood over him, and I described in detail what our mother had told me. Then I told him, in even more painful detail, about his own son's suicide. "Look what you have brought on us," I said. And, Bel, he couldn't answer me. I don't know if he could even speak, but I'm certain he understood what I was saying. He just sat there, helpless, and cried. When I think about it now, I feel so dreadful. I can never ask *his* forgiveness, can I? When I'd finished with him I just left him there, and a few months later he died. Oh, Bel. How could I have sat in judgment on him like that? How could I have known his motives? I never questioned that he was to blame, not once, even though at some level that question lurked. And afterwards, as the years went by, it became more insistent, so that now I feel I did him a great wrong. Even if everything our mother said was true, I behaved cruelly. But we can't know what was in his mind all those years ago, any more than we can know who little Johnnie's father really was.'

Bel was silent for several long moments, staring unfocused out of the window. 'You know what, Vic,' she said at last, 'I don't really care who Johnnie's father was: Daddy, or Judge, or Father Christmas. They're all dead. Yes, they went pretty far wrong, if what you were told is true. There was conniving there, and weakness, and, yes, neglect and selfishness, lies and betrayal – all that. Just like most people, though perhaps a bit more excessive. I don't know. But they're all dead. We're not, Vic. We have a chance to do better, if we'll take it. Reading this book of Frankie's' – she tapped the book in her lap – 'and thinking about things, especially just lately, when for a very bad moment I really thought I might lose you, I've realised a lot about myself, where I've gone wrong. In a different way to you, but just as wrong, if not much more so. At least you tried. And the fact that you're a sinner like me makes you perfectly qualified in my book.'

'What?' Vic whispered. 'Two battle-scarred sinners helping each other out?'

'Something like that.' Bel smiled faintly. 'What I've come to realise, not just in the last few days, or just from reading this book, but over the weeks I've been here with you, is that I've been trying to sit on the fence all my life, and it won't do. It doesn't work. I can't be neutral. There's no middle ground. I thought there was: I thought I could go my own way, causing as little harm as I could, always reserving something back for myself alone, where no one could interfere. I think a lot of people do that. But I've realised it's cowardly and dishonest.'

Vic stared at her. 'You've come a long way in a short time.'

'I needed to. It's true, though, isn't it?'

Vic smiled. 'If you refuse to let God teach you, sooner or later you'll slip into man's ways. There's no safe little spot in the centre. Any more than you can perch on a razor blade.'

'Ouch.'

'It's something you see everywhere in the Godless world man has made,' Vic said. 'People – on the whole, with noble exceptions, of course – don't like to think too deeply. Don't like to listen to anything unpalatable. Hate to be told what to do, even though their so-called own way is often aimless. They're like unruly brats, unbiddable. They worship what is false and will hurt them, eager for the next new thing, however worthless it is. And yet, Bel, if you can believe it, the best gave up everything for the worst. Like you and me. To make us see the truth.'

Bel looked at her sister, and shook her head. 'And you say *I've* come a long way.' She heaved a deep sigh. 'So what's to be done, Vic? How do we act on these things?'

'Repent, I suppose. Every day, in my case.'

'Every five minutes in mine, dear.' Bel began to laugh. 'What an extraordinary thing. Who'd have thought it? Oh, but Vic, I'm sorry, I'm wearing you out. You look exhausted suddenly.'

Vic closed her eyes. 'I'm all right. But I wouldn't mind resting a bit. The trouble with hospitals is they're always doing something for you: offering you a cup of tea, taking your blood pressure, emptying the waste bin. Resting is something you rarely get to do.'

'And then, just when you think you're going to get a bit of peace, some perishing visitor comes in and demands answers to difficult questions. I'll disappear, now, Vic, OK? I need to do a bit of shopping. But I'll be back.'

Vic's eyes remained shut, and Bel crept to the door. But as she was about to leave, Vic said, 'I'm glad you have begun at last, Bel.'

'Begun?'

'To look for love in the right place.'

'Go to sleep, for goodness' sake.'

'I will. I promise. But there's just one thing. With all this going on, I've forgotten it – my car's still at the school. It's been nearly a week. We need to get it back, Bel. I don't know how long I'll be in here. I can't leave it there indefinitely.'

'What, you think one of your kids is going to pinch the wheels?'

'Hardly. But I'd be happier if it was at home. Preferably in the garage.'

'Look, you need to be concentrating on getting well, not fretting about your wretched car, for heaven's sake. I'll get Don to sort something out. OK?'

Vic's eyes closed. 'Mm. He's good at sorting things out. Practical.'

For a few moments Bel watched her from the doorway. 'Sleep well, Vic,' she whispered.

Don

'Has she gone?'

'Hello, Vic. How are you?'

'Sorry. I'm very rude. Hello, Don. I am all right, thank you. So?'

Don subsided into the arm chair. 'Yes, I put her on the train ten minutes ago. But it was a near thing. At the last moment she said she wasn't going.'

Vic pursed her lips. 'I'm glad you persuaded her. I don't want her shipwrecked career on my conscience.'

'But I've been bombarded with instructions. I have to let her know how tomorrow goes, as soon as you are wheeled out of theatre.'

'You won't know much by then.'

'True. Nevertheless, I have to let her know you're still alive.'

'I hope she manages to forget me while she's recording tomorrow.'

Don looked at her and smiled faintly. 'She was quoting that song – how does it go? "You don't know what you've got till it's gone." Some such words.'

'Hm. Well, I haven't gone yet. Not quite. What did Bel say? Something about the chief angel putting my wings back in the cupboard.'

Don hunched forward, and looked down at the floor. 'You can make light of it, but I feel very much the same,' he said quietly. 'Only I'd say "You don't know what you've got till it might be taken from you." Maybe we're both stupid, Bel and me. Or maybe it's just people generally.' He looked up, and saw Vic staring at him, her eyes wide. 'Forget it. You obviously think I've gone mad.'

'No, not mad,' Vic said thoughtfully. 'You just don't talk like this normally, that's all.'

'Yes, well, "normal" seems to have gone out of the window just lately.' He stood up, walked to the window and gazed out. Vic's room had a view of the building opposite, a damp courtyard edged with light-starved saplings, and a wire cage full of rubbish bins.

'Has Bel said anything to you?' Vic said.

'Bel has said any number of things to me. About what, exactly?'

'What I told her, how I went to visit my grandfather.'

Don turned back to her with a frown, and saw her plucking at her sheet, her face averted. 'For heaven's sake! You're not still worrying about that!'

'Haven't you ever done something you're very ashamed of?' Vic looked up at him, biting her lip, and he saw her eyes dark and hollow with remembered pain.

He came back to her bedside and sat down, twisting round to face her. 'Of course I have,' he said gently. He took her wrist in his hand, and almost absent-mindedly rubbed her palm with his thumb. 'But I can't ever recall letting it last for thirty-odd years.'

'What if it won't go away?' Her eyes were bright with tears.

'You have to ask to be forgiven,' Don said firmly. 'And then you have to believe that you *have* been forgiven, learn from it, put it behind you and carry on.'

'I don't seem to be much good at that, do I?'

'Hand me your Bible a minute.' She passed it to him, and he felt in his jacket pocket for his glasses and put them on. He opened the Bible and turned the pages. 'Here we are.' He looked at her over the rims of his glasses. 'You listening? Right. This is from 1 John, chapter 1, verse 1. "I am writing this to you, my children, so that you will not sin; but if anyone does sin, we have someone who pleads with the Father on our behalf – Jesus Christ, the righteous one. And Christ himself is the means by which our sins are forgiven, and not ours only, but also the sins of everyone." I'm sure you've read that before, and would say you believed it.'

Vic nodded, pressing her lips together. 'There's believing and believing,' she whispered.

'Believe it for yourself, because it was written for us all, including you.' Don stood up and looked at his watch. 'It's getting late, and I have to be back for the evening service. People will be praying for you tonight, I'm sure.' He looked down at her and smiled. 'Go into that operating theatre tomorrow with a light heart and a clean conscience,' he said gently. 'And then when you're better we'll start again.'

Don

30 January 2006

He was waiting in the relatives' room when they brought Vic back from theatre. He hovered in the doorway while they manoeuvred the bed back into position.

'She won't come round properly yet awhile,' the nurse said, smiling sympathetically.

'I know,' Don said. 'I have to go soon anyway. Is she all right? Did it go as planned?'

'No problems at all,' the nurse said.

'I'll be in tomorrow morning, then,' Don said. 'If she wakes up, will you tell her that? And that I've been in touch with her sister?'

'Certainly.'

After the nurse had gone Don stayed a few minutes longer. Vic lay motionless, peaceful, somewhere he couldn't reach her. He thought of the song Bel had quoted, and berated himself savagely. *You bloody fool. Thank God she's not dead. I had my chance, and I let it slide. In my case, it's 'You don't know what you've got, or might have had, till you risk losing it.' That would make a terrible song. Oh, Lord, thank you for not letting her die. Help me to say the right thing at the right time in the right way. Sometime soon.*

Don

As he paused in the doorway, her eyes opened. 'Hello. I suppose it must be tomorrow.'

He smiled. 'No, it's today. But I know what you mean.' He came into the room and took off his jacket. 'How are you feeling?'

'Fine, I think. A bit sore. But they tell me I'll be better than I was.'

'That's good to hear.' He sat down in the armchair.

She turned her head to face him. 'Were you here yesterday?'

'Yes, for a while. I saw you taken down, and brought back up. You looked like a rather healthy corpse.'

'Thanks. What have I missed?'

'Apart from several phone calls from your anxious sister on her new mobile phone? Not much.'

'How's her recording going?'

'All right, I think. And she's heard from Matthew. He was enquiring after your health. He also has plans to come down and visit, with his young lady – Jessica, isn't it? When you're well enough. Back to normal.'

'I plan to be that as soon as they let me out of here,' Vic said.

'I've got something for you from Frankie.' He pulled a sheet of paper out of his jacket pocket and handed it to her.

Vic laughed and smoothed out the paper. 'Bible references. I should have known. She sends me texts and lends Bel a book. Did you know that? I think it's been a bit of a revelation to Bel. Frankie's a wonder. She never misses a trick.' She looked up at Don, and her smiling face and the brightness of her eyes made something tighten in his chest, almost like fear. 'Is Frankie all right? How's the baby?'

'Well, I think,' he mumbled.

'Should I read these verses now?'

'No, because I want to talk to you. About something important.' *Feet first.*

'That sounds ominous.'

'Vic –'

'What on earth's the matter? You look as though you've swallowed a brick.'

'No, but I think I might be about to spit one out.'

'What a delightful image that conjures up. All right, I'll be quiet.'

'I've been thinking, long and hard, ever since you came in here. I've come to the conclusion we need to change some things.'

'We?'

'Yes. We.' The words tumbled out like a bubbling stream. 'Neither of us is getting any younger. And seeing you so ill, and thinking you might actually have died, made me want to take better care of you. To be with you more. On the spot in case anything happened. Oh dear, I'm not doing very well.' Vic sat silent, gazing at him wide-eyed. 'Look, what I'm trying to suggest is we both sell up. My bungalow's never been much of a home. I only got it to be convenient for Ellen, and she lived in it – what? Not much more than a year. And your house is out on its own among all those fields, and it doesn't have proper heating.'

'Hold on, Don. Are you saying you want us to move in somewhere else? Together?' He nodded miserably, seeing it suddenly as preposterous. She frowned. 'I think you'd better spell it out. Maybe I'm dim, but I'm not sure I quite understand.'

He stood up abruptly and ran his hand through his hair. 'I'm doing this very badly,' he said with a grimace. 'I never was much good at saying how I really feel. Perhaps what I should have done is fall at your feet and tell you I adore you.'

She tried unsuccessfully not to laugh. 'If you'd done that I would have been quite convinced you were an impostor,' she said. 'That while you were walking along the hospital corridor, all unsuspecting, you had been abducted by aliens who had sent along a lookalike to visit me, someone who had no idea how the real Don Fincham behaved. Do sit down, Don. You look untidy, like a stork that's escaped from the zoo.'

Don subsided into the chair. 'Thanks,' he muttered.

She took his unresisting hand. 'Let me just get this straight. Are you in need of a housekeeper?'

'No!'

'Suggesting we live in sin, then?'

'Of course not. Stupid woman. I'm suggesting, no, proposing, marriage. And just to keep you from any more foolish misunderstandings, since we should start as we mean to go on, I should make it perfectly clear –' His voice died, and he gazed at her, confused and baffled.

'Don, please,' she said gently. 'We've been friends for a good many years. I think I understand what you're trying to say. I'll take the adoring bit for granted, assuming you aren't proposing a marriage of convenience.' He shook his head vehemently and opened his mouth to speak, but she waved a hand to silence him. 'God willing, now this crisis is over, we'll have a few more years. Enough time, I hope, when things are going along peacefully, for you to say how you feel once in a while. I'm not in a hurry. And just in case you're in any doubt, I've loved you for ages. There, you see,' her eyes crinkled, 'I'm finally owning up. Guilty as hell.' She failed to suppress a grin.

He grasped both her hands. 'It's a good job I don't mind being mocked,' he croaked. 'If it weren't for your stitches I'd feel like holding you so tight you couldn't breathe.'

'I shall look forward to it,' she said. She reached her arm up, pulled him down and kissed him. 'That will have to do for now.'

'I shall have to get back to the office at some point,' Don said. 'Things are backing up.' He was half-sitting, half-lying on the edge of the bed, leaning on his elbow as close to her as he could get. He looked uncomfortable, but he showed no sign of moving.

'Don't mind me.'

'That's exactly what I plan to do. For as long as I've got.'

'They'll probably turf you out soon anyway. It must be nearly lunchtime. I don't suppose I'll get anything, but they'll say I need to rest, etcetera.'

'Do you feel tired?'

'A bit.'

He heaved himself up and stretched. 'I'll go and do some work, then. Should I come back tonight?' he asked, suddenly diffident.

'I shall be lonely if you don't.'

He leaned over her and kissed her lingeringly, then pulled his face away and looked into her eyes from a distance of three inches. 'Only there's something else I want to talk about.'

She closed her eyes and sighed. 'Oh, dear. I suppose you'd better get it all off your chest in one go.'

'In this case, I'm afraid I must.'

'You sound like my headmistress.'

'Please!' He disentangled himself. 'I'll see you tonight, then. Get some rest.'

* * * *

'Did they give you any dinner?'

She shook her head. 'All I'm getting is another lot of antibiotics.' She waved a hand at the IV bag on its drip-stand. 'Another week, apparently. Once I get home you can feed me up. Did you get your work done?'

He nodded. 'Some.' He walked to the window and looked out into the winter darkness, lit only by distant street-lights made fuzzy by the drizzle.

'So what are you going to bully me about this time?'

'Did I bully you this morning?'

'Steamrollered, more like.'

'Very funny. You don't look too bad on it.'

'I'm glad you think I don't look *too bad*. I'll try not to be overwhelmed by your compliments. Go on, then. Get it over with.'

'It's this singing thing. And don't go all slit-eyed.'

'Did you listen to the recording?'

'No, of course I didn't. Didn't you ask me that before? You know I wouldn't do it without your express permission.' He turned and faced her, his arms folded.

'Well, I want you to. You might think I sound like a screech-owl. And then there'll be no more to say.'

'It's not so much to do with the recording, anyway. That was a very long time ago. You were eighteen, all promise. I dare say you improved as time went on and you practised and performed. And since then no doubt your voice has aged and lost quality, because you haven't nurtured it. But that's not really the point.'

'It's not?'

'No. What's the point of singing, in your opinion?'

'What?'

'When you sang for that audience, and other audiences, how did you feel?'

Vic shrugged. 'Pretty good. In command of my voice. A bit of triumph. Very excited.'

'How much did you need an audience at all?'

'Um, well, I suppose it gave an edge. To be appreciated was flattering. But –' Don raised his eyebrows. 'I loved to sing anyway,' she floundered. 'Whether or not anyone was listening. Or even if it was only Eric, either applauding or complaining or just making me work ridiculously hard. It was, I don't know, exhilarating.'

241

Don nodded. 'You've made my point for me.' He came over and perched on the side of the bed, and for several moments studied her, as if he was memorising every line of her face.

She frowned, perplexed. 'What is it? Have I sprouted an extra nose?'

He sighed. 'This may sound very sloppy to you, but I want you to be happy. I don't mean just ordinarily contented, bumbling along day by day. I want you to have a little bit of that glory back, all that stuff you dreamed of as a young woman, before it all went to pot. "Happy" is too weak a word for it – I want you to have the chance of joy. Seems to me it's been a bit in short supply. You don't have to worry any more about a great career as a singer. Maybe that might have happened if things had been different, but it might never have come off: then, just like now, it takes more than having a beautiful voice and working hard to succeed. It takes great drive and single-mindedness, and more than a little luck. No, I just want you to recapture some of how it felt.'

'How am I going to do that?' Vic said wonderingly.

He got up and began to walk around the room. 'When you're completely well, find someone to teach you again. Practise. Go out for walks and sing in the woods, all alone. Just try, Vic. Try and get it back, just for the joy of it. You know,' he said abruptly, stopping and looking at her, 'Marjorie Allen's been in the church choir for years, but she can't really sing at all. She wavers off the key and sings flat more often than not, but her face when she is singing radiates delight. I would give a lot to see you look like that.'

Vic was silent for several long moments. 'Well,' she said finally. 'I am speechless.' She stared at him. 'You know what we were talking about earlier? When you said you were bad at expressing how you really feel? You were wrong. I can't think of a better expression of love. To want the other person to feel joy.'

He was silent for several long moments, gazing at her, as if he didn't trust himself to speak. 'So? Will you?'

'I suppose I'll have to try. Just know I wouldn't do this for anyone else.'

'Thank you.' He smiled. 'You might just give joy to others at the same time, you know.'

'Well, for now I'll just go and sing to the trees, if you don't mind. I meant what I said earlier, though: go and listen to that tape. I just don't want to hear it myself. Or not yet. I left it on the sideboard.'

'All right. I'll keep Solomon company for a while at the same time.'

'Is he OK?'

'Sleek as ever. Wendy Green's feeding him, but you knew that. Vic, you're beginning to look tired.'

'Am I?'

'You only had the operation yesterday. You mustn't do too much.'

'I'm not *doing* anything. Just lying here and getting surprise after surprise. It's not my stomach they'll be worried about if this goes on. It'll be my heart. Literally and metaphorically,' she added slyly.

'All right, I'll go home. Some time I'll go to your home. I'll play your tape, with no one but Solomon for company.'

'He'll probably bolt. Cats don't like screeching.'

'Well, *I* won't. Bolt, that is. Not tonight, not tomorrow, not ever. And I don't believe you about the screeching.'

'Stubborn man. Come and give me a hug before you go. But mind my stitches.'

He sat on the edge of the bed and very carefully gathered her up in his arms. 'You smell nice,' he murmured into her hair. 'Please hurry up and get well. This enforced restraint is proving extremely difficult.'

Vic

1 February 2006

Vic was awakened in the night by a low moaning from someone invisible in the main ward. 'Nurse, Nurse! Please, Nurse!'

She groaned quietly and sat up in bed. There was enough light from the corridor to see her watch: it was a quarter to two. The moaner was an intermittent, far too frequent, yet pitiable curse, a confused and frightened patient, subject, perhaps, to nightmares. After a minute or two of wailing someone attended the sorry soul and the moaning abated. *Half the ward will be awake by now. Lord, let me get home. To the peace of my little house and the familiar night-sounds of owl and fox, the wind in the winter wheat, the rain on the windows.*

She pulled her dressing-gown round her shoulders, switched on the light and reached for her glasses. On the bedside table, underneath her Bible, lay the sheet of paper from Frankie that Don had brought in. She looked again at Frankie's bold scrawl: Ephesians 2, 18 to 22. She opened her Bible and found the place.

'It is through Christ that all of us, Jews and Gentiles, are able to come in the one Spirit into the presence of the Father. So then, you Gentiles are not foreigners or strangers any longer; you are now fellow-citizens with God's people and members of the family of God. You, too, are built upon the foundation laid by the apostles and prophets, the cornerstone being Christ Jesus himself. He is the one who holds the whole building together and makes it grow into a sacred temple dedicated to the Lord. In union with him you too are being built together with all the others into a place where God lives through his Spirit.'

What are you saying to me, Frankie? No – I should be asking, What are you saying to me, God? I haven't asked this question half often enough, for fear of the answer. But I must try, with God's help, to be more courageous. To trust him more. Help me, Lord, to undo the habits of a lifetime. I think I've begun. Perhaps just today I've taken a great step in the right direction, even though to my old self it still bears all the hallmarks of unease and doubt, not to say blind terror. My old self is muttering,

244

What if it all goes wrong? Then you have lost your best, your only friend. You will be doubly alone. I need a dose of my sister here, some of her robustness, her insouciance, her apparently careless optimism. Or is it, like mine and yet different, a façade?

A figure appeared in the doorway, one of the nurses, her round brown face smiling. 'You all right, my dear?' she whispered. 'Did our moaner wake you? She was very loud tonight, I'm afraid. Would you like a cup of tea?'

'Thank you. That would be lovely.'

'Right. Won't be a minute.'

A few minutes later she was back, a cup and saucer in her hand. She set it down on the bed-table. From the main ward the moaning started up again, lower now, keening and whimpering, and a smattering of voices in response called out: 'Ssshh!' 'Be quiet, you noisy old bat!' 'Nurse, can't you shut her up?'

'Oh dear,' Vic said. 'The poor soul sounds tormented.'

'She doesn't know she's doing it,' the nurse said. 'She doesn't know much at all, I'm afraid. She needs to be somewhere else really. You all right, Victoria? Not too bothered?'

'Not bothered at all, thanks,' Vic said, smiling.

'Well, at least you've got a book. I like reading too. Good book, is it?'

Vic held up her Bible. '*The* good book.'

'Oh,' the nurse said, her voice hushed. 'You must be a Christian then.'

'Yes, I am.'

'I used to go to church. Don't have the time now. But I still believe in God. Anyway, I must get on. Sounds like our moaner's quiet now. Let's hope it lasts, eh!'

'Goodnight. Thanks for the tea.'

Vic turned back to Frankie's texts. Hebrews 12, 22-24: '...you have come to Mount Zion, and to the city of the living God, the heavenly Jerusalem, with its thousands of angels. You have come to the joyful gathering of God's firstborn, whose names are written in heaven. You have come to God, who is the judge of all people, and to the spirits of good people made perfect. You have come to Jesus, who arranged the new covenant, and to the sprinkled blood which promises much better things than does the blood of Abel.'

Why did she choose these verses, I wonder? Is she trying to tell me that I am included, one of the great family of God? To remind me of the glory that is to come? That I will one day be part of that joyful gathering? There it is again, that emphasis on joy. Have Don and Frankie been colluding? It doesn't seem likely: I don't think Don would want to talk about me to anyone. Bel will have tried, but I doubt she got very far. They're right, of course: life has been short on joy and glory for a very long time. Am I brave enough to claim these promises? To risk all? But what do I think I am risking? I don't have that much to lose, do I? Oh, Lord, I am confused. What does Frankie mean? What do you mean? What does Don mean? Could it all be so much simpler than I thought? Could it be that you all want to give me something, but my hands are behind my back?

Bel

'Bel! How did you get away? I wasn't expecting you.'

Bel threw off her winter coat and came over to the armchair beside the bed where Vic was sitting, a book in her lap. 'Well, look at you. You look almost normal.' She enveloped Vic in a hug.

Vic laughed, disentangling herself. 'Thanks for the *almost*. Oh, Bel, how good to see you. You smell of fresh air and freedom.'

'I don't know about that. But I managed to squeeze a few hours away out of my tyrant of a producer. Told her my only sister was very poorly. Jumped on a train and here I am.' She sat on the edge of the bed and looked at Vic with an air of stern scrutiny. 'You look well, amazingly so,' she conceded. 'Do you feel well?'

'I feel pretty good, thanks.'

Bel folded her arms and smirked. 'Well, there you are. Ain't love grand.'

Vic winced. 'Bel, please, do give over. You really are impossible. I'm still wondering how far you are responsible.'

'Me? Responsible for what? Oh, no, I assure you. I might have nagged and hinted just a little, but believe me, the ideas are all his own.'

'I'm relieved. Though there's one idea I wish he hadn't had.'

'Which one?'

'The singing thing. He wants me to take it up again. And that's before he heard the tape. I can't see it coming off.'

'That's because you haven't quite shed your habit of feeble defeatism,' Bel said severely.

'No,' Vic said. 'I don't think it's that.' She hesitated. 'He wants me to have the joy of it back, Bel. But the joy doesn't just rest in the doing of it, but in doing it well. A long time ago I had at least the promise of doing it well. The trouble is, I know what good singing is, and the likelihood is I won't do it well enough to please myself.'

Bel shook her head. 'If it's worth doing, it's worth doing badly.'

Vic frowned. 'I bet you don't apply that to your own work.'

247

'Of course not. I do the best that's in me. But if something's important enough, you'll do it, no matter what. Of course you'll do it as well as you are able. But if your ability doesn't match up to your wishes, that's no excuse to chuck it in. Anyway, you won't be doing it just for yourself, will you?'

Vic sighed. 'No, I told Don I'd try for his sake.'

'So – no issue, then.'

'Just the issue of my own cringing ears. You must know how it feels to be praised for something you're certain you haven't done well. By kind people who don't know any better.'

'Vic, you're such a snob.'

'When it comes to music, I think I probably am.' She smiled. 'Anyway, enough of all that. How's the recording going?'

'Not too bad, but Melissa, that's the producer, is a bit of a perfectionist. No slacking. Lots of getting it minutely wrong and doing it all over. However,' she paused, grinning broadly. 'I have to take back all the rude things I've said about Jason. The dear boy's come up trumps.'

'Oh, Bel! What?'

'I've got to audition, of course. It's not in the bag yet. A nice little costume drama, Vic. Just the job, always popular with the viewing public. Filming starts in April. Not a big part, but with frequent appearances. Perfect.'

'That's wonderful, Bel. I'm really pleased for you. I shall definitely watch it, every episode.'

'You will?'

'Of course. Just as Matthew said, I shall bask in reflected glory. Have you heard from him lately?'

'Oh, yes, he rang last night. To see how you were.'

'That's kind. But Bel, where are you staying in London? Surely your old flat isn't ready yet.'

'No. I'm borrowing a sofa for the time being, from my old friend Bertie's friend Gerry. Not ideal, but this recording will be over next week, and then I shall find something more suitable once I've got some money in the bank. Don't you worry about me.'

'You can always come back to Thackham.'

'Thanks. But won't you be moving?' Bel said, one eyebrow lifted.

Vic frowned. 'Oh, so you know about that little plan.'

'I don't really know anything. It just seemed logical.'

'Well, you're right. But I don't know when.'

'In time, I hope,' Bel said, 'to acquire an enormous television on which to watch your sister strut around in a lacy mob-cap.'

Vic laughed. 'Oh, yes. Definitely in time for that.'

Bel slid off the bed and wandered over to the window. She shivered. 'At least you're nice and warm in here. The weather is quite nasty, very cold, lots of fog.' She turned to Vic, and her face was unusually serious. 'You sure you're feeling OK? Only there's something I want to talk about, and once you're back home I might not have the chance.'

'Not you as well!'

'As well?'

'Don has taken advantage of having me incarcerated in here to bend my ear and generally lecture me. And now it seems you're about to do the same.'

'No, Vic, not lecture, not harass, nothing like that. I've been thinking about what you said about Mummy, and Judge, and Johnnie. I know I reacted badly, called you some horrible things, quite uncalled-for. I'm very sorry about that. I just wanted to hear what you remember about that time. I know it's years ago.'

'What time exactly?' Vic said cautiously.

'When Johnnie was born, then later, when he died, his funeral. We were just children, and it's so long ago I don't know how far to trust my own memories.'

Vic heaved a sigh. 'I remember our father coming upstairs to tell us Johnnie had been born. We were in bed. He was, what's the word? Exultant. Triumphant. I heard him on the phone to Judge. It was as if he'd passed some sort of test. And the way he announced it to us, it was extraordinary, as though it was the best present we could ever have. Frankly, much as I came to love Johnnie, at the time I'd have much preferred a bit more loving parental attention. Do you remember that night?'

Bel shook her head slowly. 'Not really.'

'Well, you were only six. Not surprising. Do you remember Judge coming to visit afterwards?'

'Yes,' Bel said. 'I remember his pin-stripe trousers, for some reason. I think that's the time I fell in the nettles.'

'I don't remember him paying any attention to me at all. I probably hid away with a book.'

'But what about later, Vic? When Johnnie drowned? Wasn't Judge there then?'

'He was certainly invited to the party. The party that never happened, of course. I can't remember if he was there already or if he came down later.'

'We didn't go to the funeral, did we? We weren't allowed to.'

'We weren't consulted. Yet you were nearly eleven, I was nearly fourteen. I think it was their way of punishing us, Bel. For letting it happen.'

Bel chewed at her thumb-nail. 'Do you think they blamed us? I mean, really?'

'Oh, yes. We would have blamed ourselves anyway. But they did nothing to soften that, and of course we *were* partly to blame. But so were they. They were ultimately responsible. And how does it help to heap blame on your surviving children?'

Bel came back from the window and sat on the end of the bed. Her brow was furrowed, her inward eye seeking, back into the past, trying to separate fact from shadow, to strip away the layers of attendant emotion. 'Would you have wanted to go to the funeral?'

Vic shook her head. 'No. So many eyes, so many whispers. "Look, those are the girls who let their brother drown." I don't think I could have coped with all the grief. There was no one to comfort *us*, Bel.'

'No,' Bel said, her voice hollow. 'Only each other. But do you remember Judge being there?'

Vic thought, pressing her lips together. 'Yes, I think I do. I have a picture in my mind: both of us sitting on the stairs, watching everyone leave the house. I remember the black clothes, the sense of permeating gloom. Judge was the last to leave, and I'm sure he turned and saw us huddled there. His face was bleak. Of course he always seemed very old to us, but I remember how aged and crumpled and veined he looked.'

'Did you pity him then?' Bel asked softly.

'No,' Vic said sadly. 'I'm afraid I hated him, even then. What a nasty girl I was.'

Bel edged up the bed and took Vic's hand. There were tears in her eyes. 'No, Vic, you weren't nasty. You defended me and read to me and tucked me up in bed, all our lonely childhood. Where would I have been without you?'

Vic looked at her wonderingly and said nothing.

Bel wiped her eyes with her hands. 'I just wonder where the truth of it all lies,' she said slowly. 'Did Mummy really ask Judge to give her a baby? I mean, how would she have gone about it? You can't imagine the conversation, can you? And how did he react?'

'We'll never know for sure, Bel. But why would our mother say such a thing if it wasn't true? Unless her illness, or the drugs, messed up her memory, made her believe a fantasy. I don't know. I can just find it in my heart to pity Judge now, because Johnnie was either his son or his grandson, and to lose a little four-year-old must have been horrific.'

'Do you think Daddy suspected?' Bel said abruptly.

'I don't think so,' Vic said. 'He never behaved differently towards Judge, or spoke differently about him, not in my presence, anyway. No, I think our mother confessed to me because she felt the need to get it off her chest and she didn't care much what I thought.'

'Oh, Vic. When I look back now I do it through your eyes as well as my own, and I see two harmless little girls that nobody much wanted.'

'It's a long time ago, Bel. We survived. We had each other then, and by God's mercy we still do.'

'Yes. Well, I am thankful.' She took a deep breath and stood up. 'I shall have to get back, Vic. I said I'd be in the studio promptly at two.'

'It's been lovely to see you. It's seemed odd –I'd got used to having you around.'

'Well, I'll be back. Even if I get this new part, they won't start rehearsals for a while. And anyway, I plan to be at St. Mark's on as many Sundays as I can manage. The kids need me for their Easter offering. I mustn't let out too many secrets, though, must I? And also,' she said triumphantly, 'now you can ring me!' She opened her handbag and fished around among the junk she kept there. 'I've acquired a new mobile phone!' She flourished it. 'I'll write the number down for you.' After more scrabbling in her bag she produced a pen and wrote on the bottom of the sheet that Frankie had sent in. 'And I can ring you when we break for coffee. How about that?'

'That will be the next best thing. You can keep me up to date. I don't even really know what's been going on in the outside world. Being in hospital's like living in a sealed bubble.'

'Well, you can predict the big, bad world goes on much as ever,' Bel said. 'Trouble in the Middle East, as usual. Car bombs in Baghdad. Dreadful.' She shuddered. 'Oh yes, and,' her face brightened, 'an enormous jackpot in the Euromillions lottery. Someone's going to be better off by a hundred and eighty *million* euros. Not me, I hasten to add. Life's enough of a lottery without throwing your money away on one.'

'A hundred and eighty million. Good grief.'

Bel put on her coat and wound her scarf round her neck. She leaned over Vic and kissed her cheek. 'Next time I see you, you won't be in here.'

'I sure hope so. Thanks for coming, Bel.' She hesitated, as if there was something else she wanted to say, but she simply squeezed Bel's arm. 'See you at home.'

Vic

7 February 2006

When Don arrived at the hospital Vic was dressed and sitting waiting in the chair in her room, at her feet a bag containing her few belongings.

'You look keen to be gone,' he said, smiling from the doorway.

'I certainly am,' Vic said with feeling. 'It's seemed like a life sentence. Not,' she added, 'that I haven't been well treated. Everyone's been marvellous. But my little house is calling, and I miss Solomon.'

Don came into the room and picked up her bag. 'Got everything? Pills?' He seemed suddenly shy.

'Yes, and I've said my goodbyes and thank yous,' Vic said. She reached up and gripped the lapel of his jacket. 'I'm very pleased to see you, too,' she murmured.

He stifled a grin. 'I was only here yesterday.'

'Even so.'

'Come on, then.' He led the way out of the ward and down the corridor to the lift.

'You'll have to go more slowly,' Vic said. 'I'm not used to walking in shoes, poor old invalid.'

He waited by the lift doors, and though his face was grave his eyes were alight. 'How are the stitches?'

She shrugged, her lips twitching. 'We'll just have to find out, won't we?'

In the car, driving away from the hospital, Don said, 'Oh, I forgot – it turns out the rumours were true.'

'Which ones?'

'About your old house. When I passed it on the way here there was a massive yellow machine in the grounds, and from what I could see it came complete with backhoe and bulldozer. They might even have started the demolition already.'

She turned to him. 'Can we stop and look?'

'Of course, if you want to. I thought you were in a hurry to get home.'

'Oh, I am. But this isn't going to happen twice. It's rather coincidental, symbolic almost, that it should happen today.'

He looked at her, his eyebrows raised enquiringly. 'What's special about today?'

'Everything,' she said simply. 'It's the first day of the rest of my life. What a cliché that is. It's the first day of freedom, in many senses.'

He smiled. 'I'm glad you think of it that way.'

A thought struck her. 'But Bel ought to be here too! Shouldn't she see the old place come down?'

'I did think of that,' Don said. 'I rang her to tell her. But she said she can't get away. It seems to me,' he added gently, looking at Vic as he came to a halt at a red light, 'that Bel has already made her peace with the past. Perhaps she isn't quite so keen on symbolism as you.'

'Out with the old, in with the new,' Vic said. 'Heavens, I really am full of clichés today. Must be the brain-softening effects of surgery. Hadn't we better hurry?'

'I'm doing sixty already,' Don said mildly. 'I don't want to have an accident and have to go back to the hospital. If you don't mind. We'll get there soon enough.'

Fifteen minutes later he pulled in to the layby at the top of the bypass slip road. Vic climbed out of the car, blinking in the weak winter sunlight. She walked to the railing and leaned over.

Demolition had already begun. The huge yellow monster was clawing at the roof, sending tiles tumbling. The chimney lay at a drunken angle; another pass of the backhoe sent it crashing down. The ground seemed to shudder with the impact, echoed by shouts from the workmen. Clouds of dust erupted into the air, rising up almost to where Vic and Don stood.

'The place is still full of stuff,' Vic said. There was a deadness in her voice that even she could hear. 'I got rid of a few things. Sold them or dumped them. Then I lost heart and just left it. Furniture. Photographs. Old toys, Bel's and mine. Clothes in wardrobes. In the end I didn't want anything to do with any of it.'

She shivered, and Don put his arm round her shoulders. 'I very much doubt there's anything left in there,' he said gently. 'It's been empty for too many years. Bit by bit, even if you were unaware of it, it would have been stripped.'

Vic looked up at him, puzzled. 'Stripped? Who would do that?'

He shrugged. 'People are endlessly curious, endlessly acquisitive. Aren't they? Whatever was remotely salvageable would be long gone by now.'

'So it's empty?'

'There may be a few bits of rubbish, especially if it's been used as a doss. But all your things will be gone, I think. Whoever owns it now would have had to get permission to demolish, and an empty, derelict building would strengthen his case.'

'Well, I don't care.' Her voice rose, and there was a note of desperation in it. 'I'm glad to see it go. Let them raze it, cart away the bricks, fill in the holes, forget it as if it had never existed.'

Don turned to her with a frown. 'So why tears?' he murmured, wiping them away with his fingers.

'Don't ask me,' she said, trying to smile. 'Sometimes I just feel overwhelming pity for those two children, as if they were someone else, not Bel and me.'

'Well, they both came out all right eventually,' Don said. He wrapped his arms around her. 'You're cold,' he said. 'Do you really need to see it through right to the end?'

'No, I guess not. We'll leave them to get on with it. Maybe I'll come back one day and see the whole area clean and cleared. Let's go home.'

Don opened the front door with Vic's key and stood aside to let her in.

'Someone's been cleaning up,' Vic exclaimed. 'There isn't a speck of dust anywhere!'

'Bel was here for several days,' Don said. 'That's her work.'

'How very kind,' Vic said. 'She's even got rid of the blood-stains on the hall carpet.'

'She also cleared out the fridge,' Don said. 'And I've done a bit of shopping for you, and Wendy Green's made some meals and put them in the freezer. So you won't starve, and you won't have to think about cooking. Just about recovering.'

'You've all been wonderful. I'm very blessed.'

'There's been a lot of blessing about just lately,' Don said quietly. 'I'm going to light the fire. This place may be neat and tidy, but it's freezing.'

'And I'm going to look for my cat. He'll probably be asleep on my bed at this time of day.'

'If you're lucky he might open one eye and purr for about five seconds,' Don said. 'That'll be cat-speak for "Dear mistress, I have missed you terribly. They've all neglected me. Thank goodness you're back." And then he'll turn his back on you, as if he's remembered that you treacherously went off and left him.'

Vic laughed. 'Don't worry. I know what he's like. If I hug him too hard he'll be annoyed and fly out of the cat-flap. Cats don't wear their hearts on their sleeves, but they love you all the same.'

'A very praiseworthy attitude. Reassuringly British.' As Vic made to go towards the stairs he caught her wrist and planted a kiss in the palm of her hand.

She looked at him, her eyebrows raised. 'You're not getting mushy, are you?'

'Alarmingly so,' he said seriously.

'You'll probably get over it.'

'You know what,' he said softly, 'I don't think I will. I'm a lost cause. No fight left in me at all.'

'A pushover.'

'That too.'

'Makes two of us, then.'

'How convenient.'

'What was that about lighting a fire?'

The fire was roaring, and they sat on the sofa with cups of coffee.

'I should get back to work,' Don said. 'I've neglected it a bit lately.'

'That's my fault,' Vic said.

'I'm afraid it is. I can't afford to let the business crumble, or we'll have nothing to live on.'

'Especially if my job goes down the pan,' Vic said. 'I guess I'd better ring the school, remind them of my existence.'

'Someone did ring from Repley,' Don said. 'Asking after your health. It was while Bel was here. Did she mention it?'

'No, I expect she forgot in all the excitement.'

'Wondering if you were going to make it is not something I would call exciting. More like terrifying.'

She turned sideways to look at him and winced as her stitches caught. 'Maybe terror's been a good thing. If I hadn't got sick and hovered at death's door you'd have gone on as usual. We wouldn't be sitting here thinking about what we're thinking about.'

'What are we thinking about?'

'Don't ask.'

'I don't know,' he reflected. 'I might have fallen in eventually.'

'Hm. When we were well over a hundred and incapable of thinking about anything.'

'On that cheerful note, I shall leave you to settle in while I go and try to earn a crust.' He heaved himself up with a groan and flexed his shoulders.

'You will come back this evening, won't you? Help me eat one of Wendy's magnificent dinners?'

He looked down at her. 'Just try and keep me away. Remember, you've got to get used to this.'

'I'm game if you are.'

'That's hardly a resoundingly enthusiastic response.'

'All right, how about, "I can't wait?" That suit you?'

'Much better.'

'As it happens, much truer too.'

'Thank God for that.'

'Amen.'

He hesitated in the doorway.

'Don, I thought you were going to work.'

'Yes, I am. But something just occurred to me. I was listening to the radio in the car when I was driving to the hospital this morning, and the news was on. That furore over the cartoon some fool in Denmark drew of the Prophet Mohammed – you heard about that, didn't you?' Vic nodded. 'Well, it's still rumbling on. And today the Danish Embassy in Tehran was attacked. And I thought, whatever's going on in our own lives, you can be sure the world will still be going mad around us. Somehow, among it all, we have to keep hold of our sanity.'

She followed him to the front door. 'I meant to ask,' she said hesitantly. 'Did you ever listen to that old recording?'

'Oh, yes. Most certainly.' He shook his head. 'I thought, "What a waste." How life drops us in it. I can see why your ex-husband thought you could take it a long, long way, that voice of yours. But I ask myself, How could he ever have let it happen, that it was wasted like that? Seems to me he was a very selfish man.'

'You liked it, then.'

'Of course I did. It was beyond what I expected. But it makes me more determined not to waste anything. Including your singing. You may not have the voice now that you had then, but the musicality will still be there. Let's build on that.'

'Maybe.'

'I really am going now.' He leaned down and kissed her, and for a moment she felt his warmth. 'The tape's on the sideboard. With another message from Frankie.'

After he had gone, she put the tape in the player. She could feel her heart beating, almost painfully, and she took a long, steadying breath. The cat-flap clacked, and a moment later Solomon appeared and leapt up on the sofa, purring thunderously and looking up at her as if inviting her to join him.

'Oh, Solly,' she said, a shake in her voice, 'you won't like this.' She pressed 'Play' and collapsed on the sofa beside him. A few crackly seconds later she heard the piano accompaniment begin, and recognised Eric's confident touch. In a moment she was transported back to a packed school hall, the lights bright, the heating making its usual odd noises, and felt her eyes fill up. Then, through the tape's thirty-four-year-old inadequacies, came her own young voice, softly at first, perhaps a little breathless from nerves, then rising and ringing, gaining in courage, with the tone she had forgotten she had. It struck her like a physical blow, and sobs heaved up, tears spilling out and running down her face. *Oh, Lord, I really had forgotten. It's as if this isn't me at all. Maybe, in a way, it isn't. Maybe it's some other young thing, pouring out music and hope. Hopeless hope. But I think, if this really wasn't me, if someone had said to me, "Listen to this, it's something special," it would still make me cry. Or am I really crying for everything I've lost? I don't know.* The thought came to her, listening to her eighteen-year-old voice battling with some tricky passage, conquering it, rising above it, that her tears were the waters of cleansing that would wash away the rising dust and accumulated filth of Angleby House as it fell, taking her bitterness with them.

Much later, as darkness began to creep up the garden, causing her to turn on the lights and close the curtains and put more logs on the fire, she sat at the kitchen table with a mug of tea and read Frankie's latest message.

'Dear Vic,

I hope you won't think me presumptuous. I'm twenty years younger than you, and I have only the faintest inkling of what's gone on in your life. But these words keep coming to me when I think of you, and maybe it's not really me that's saying them, but God speaking through me. Whatever, I hope you will take them as they're meant: respectfully intended to be helpful, from your pastor. Ha, ha!

Vic, there's only one direction, and it's forward. All life is both loss and gain; the losses of the past shouldn't be gainsaid or underestimated, but with God's help we can deny them power over us. Of course, you know this as well as anyone. There may, there probably will, be losses as well as gains to come. But finally all losses will be swallowed up in glory for those who belong to Christ.

I know you'd be disappointed if I didn't give you a Bible text, so here it is: Matthew 10, verse 22 – and I'll even save you the bother of looking it up. "But whoever holds out to the end will be saved."

God bless you, Vic.

Your friend and fellow-pilgrim,

Frankie.'